W9-CCC-608

JUL - - 2009

Flossmoor Public Library
1000 Sterling Avenue
Flossmoor, IL 60422-1295
Phone: (708)798-3600

55

54

53

52

51

50

49

48

47

46

45

44

43

42

41

40

39

38

EVERYTHING MATTERS!
EVERYTHING MATTERS!
EVERYTHING MATTERS!
EVERYTHING MATTERS!
EVERYTHING MATTERS!
EVERYTHING MATTERS!
EVERYTHING MATTERS!

37

36

35

34

33

32

31

30

29

28

27

26

25

24

23

22

ALSO BY RON CURRIE, JR.

God Is Dead

21

20

19

18

17

16

15

14

13

12

11

10

9

8

7

EVERYTHING MATTERS!
EVERYTHING MATTERS!
EVERYTHING MATTERS!
EVERYTHING MATTERS!
EVERYTHING MATTERS!
EVERYTHING MATTERS!
EVERYTHING MATTERS!

RON CURRIE, JR.

EVERYTHING MATTERS!
EVERYTHING MATTERS!
EVERYTHING MATTERS!   VIKING
EVERYTHING MATTERS!
EVERYTHING MATTERS!
EVERYTHING MATTERS!
EVERYTHING MATTERS!
EVERYTHING MATTERS!
EVERYTHING MATTERS!
EVERYTHING MATTERS!
EVERYTHING MATTERS!
EVERYTHING MATTERS!
EVERYTHING MATTERS!
EVERYTHING MATTERS!

6

EVERYTHING MATTERS!
EVERYTHING MATTERS!

5

EVERYTHING MATTERS!
EVERYTHING MATTERS!

4

EVERYTHING MATTERS!

3

EVERYTHING MATTERS!

2 EVERYTHING MATTERS!
EVERYTHING MATTERS!
EVERYTHING MATTERS!
EVERYTHING MATTERS!

Flossmoor Public Library
1000 Sterling Avenue
Flossmoor, IL 60422-1295
Phone: (708)798-3600

VIKING
Published by the Penguin Group
Penguin Group (USA) Inc., 375 Hudson Street, New York, New York 10014, U.S.A. • Penguin Group (Canada),
90 Eglinton Avenue East, Suite 700, Toronto, Ontario, Canada M4P 2Y3 (a division of Pearson Penguin Canada
Inc.) • Penguin Books Ltd, 80 Strand, London WC2R 0RL, England • Penguin Ireland, 25 St. Stephen's Green,
Dublin 2, Ireland (a division of Penguin Books Ltd) • Penguin Books Australia Ltd, 250 Camberwell Road,
Camberwell, Victoria 3124, Australia (a division of Pearson Australia Group Pty Ltd) • Penguin Books India
Pvt Ltd, 11 Community Centre, Panchsheel Park, New Delhi – 110 017, India • Penguin Group (NZ), 67 Apollo
Drive, Rosedale, North Shore 0632, New Zealand (a division of Pearson New Zealand Ltd) • Penguin Books
(South Africa) (Pty) Ltd, 24 Sturdee Avenue, Rosebank, Johannesburg 2196, South Africa

Penguin Books Ltd, Registered Offices: 80 Strand, London WC2R 0RL, England

First published in 2009 by Viking Penguin, a member of Penguin Group (USA) Inc.

10 9 8 7 6 5 4 3 2 1

Copyright © Ron Currie, Jr., 2009
All rights reserved

Publisher's Note
This is a work of fiction. Names, characters, places, and incidents either are the product of the author's
imagination or are used fictitiously, and any resemblance to actual persons, living or dead, business
establishments, events, or locales is entirely coincidental.

LIBRARY OF CONGRESS CATALOGING-IN-PUBLICATION DATA
Currie, Ron,———.
   Everything matters! / Ron Currie, Jr.
      p.   cm.
   ISBN 978-0-670-02092-8
   1. Prophecies—Fiction. 2. Self-actualization (Psychology)—Fiction. I. Title.
   PS3603.U774E94 2009
   813'.6—dc22   2008046686

Printed in the United States of America
Designed by Carla Bolte

Without limiting the rights under copyright reserved above, no part of this publication may be reproduced,
stored in or introduced into a retrieval system, or transmitted, in any form or by any means (electronic, me-
chanical, photocopying, recording or otherwise), without the prior written permission of both the copyright
owner and the above publisher of this book.

The scanning, uploading, and distribution of this book via the Internet or via any other means without the permission of the publisher is illegal and punishable by law. Please purchase only authorized electronic editions and
do not participate in or encourage electronic piracy of copyrightable materials. Your support of the author's rights
is appreciated.

FOR MY FAMILY

What is love and what is hate
And why does it matter?

—The Flaming Lips, "In the Morning of the Magicians"

We're here because we're here because we're here because we're here.

—World War I trench song

EVERYTHING MATTERS!
EVERYTHING MATTERS!
EVERYTHING MATTERS!
EVERYTHING MATTERS!
EVERYTHING MATTERS!
EVERYTHING MATTERS!
EVERYTHING MATTERS!

PART ONE

In Utero; Infancy

97 First, enjoy this time! Never again will you bear so little responsibility for your own survival. Soon you will have to take in food and dispose of your own waste, learn the difference between night and day and acquire the skill of sleeping. You will need to strengthen the muscles necessary to sustain high-volume keening for long intervals. You will have to master the involuntary coos and facial twitches which are the foundation of infantile cuteness, to ensure that those charged with caring for you continue to provide food and clean linen. You will need to flex your arms and legs, loll your head to strengthen the neck, crawl, stagger to your feet, then walk. Soon after you must learn to run, share, swing a bat and hold a pencil, love, weep, read, tie your shoelaces, bathe, and die. There is much to learn and do, and little time; suffice it to say that you should be aware of the trials ahead so that you may appreciate the effortless liquid dream of gestation while it occurs, rather than only in hindsight. For now, all you need to do is grow.

There is one significant exception to this. You may have noticed that you share the womb with other objects. The most obvious and important of these is the fleshy tether attached to your abdomen, known as the umbilical cord. It is, quite literally, your lifeline, providing blood, nutrients, and vital antibodies, among other things. Already it has wrapped twice around your neck, and while this may not seem to you, who does not yet breathe, to be particularly dangerous or untoward, it can imperil your entry into the world. We will not lie—it could kill you. Now, be calm. You should remain as still as possible throughout the rest of your gestation. While this will do nothing about the entanglements already constricting your neck, it will go a long way toward preventing further looping or other complications—vasa previa, knots, cysts, hematoma. Any of these problems, by itself, is not particularly dangerous, but two or more occurring together can be big trouble, so you should maintain perpetual vigilance against the many temptations to move. Of course, there are some who would argue that it is unfair to ask a fetus to exercise impulse control. You, however, would do well to avoid those who complain about life's unfairness, and instead get a head start on building self-restraint.

Light and noise present the toughest challenge to your resolve to remain still. They come to you through your mother's abdomen, and you feel an impetus to move toward them, to stir the viscous bath of amniotic fluid with tiny fingers and toes in an effort to absorb the warmth of sunlight, or hear Carly Simon trill. The urge to move is natural and understandable. As will be the case throughout your life, no matter how long or brief, the choice is, in the end, yours. Simply bear in mind that most every choice will have consequences, and in this instance those consequences would likely be quite grave.

96 Your mother has one other child, your brother, who was a tornado in utero, so your lack of movement causes her alarm. We should mention that she is prone to unreasonable anxiety and nervous tension, minor disorders that have several underlying causes, not the least of which is the verbal and physical abuse she suffered as a child at the hands of her father. This is why she pokes at you and spends hours with a transistor radio pressed against her belly, trying to bait you into moving. Despite the fact that her abdomen continues to grow, she wakes one night convinced you'll be born an ashen husk, your fingers hooked forever into lifeless little claws. With this image lodged in her mind's eye she weeps, her hands laced together in a protective hugging posture under the swell of her belly. Now, a boy's aversion to upsetting his mother is among the more primal and tenacious instincts, and so you suffer an almost irresistibly powerful urge to kick and twirl, to give unmistakable evidence of your life, to turn your mother's sobs to relieved and slightly embarrassed little hiccups of laughter. Do not yield to this instinct, or you will put your life at risk. Protecting yourself now means you'll have many years ahead with which to repay her grief. Besides, you can rest assured that this is not the last time you will make your mother cry.

Eventually your father's hands, along with two unscheduled visits to the obstetrician for ultrasound and fetal monitor, soothe your mother's fears to a level she finds tolerable, and she wraps the transistor in its power cord and returns it to the closet, and stops staring for long silent hours at the television.

95 Although the biological goal of sex was achieved with conception, your father still has a hefty sexual appetite (as does your mother, though out of concern for you she will not admit it). To you his advances are terrifying. You hear him seeking entry with his tongue and other parts of his body, and your instinct is to recoil, which is perfectly normal— the perception of one's father as an omnipotent predator of great physical strength serves a vital function for most boys, and usually persists well into adulthood, though paradoxically it does not seem to preclude the desperate striving after his love and approval. You try to hold fast, but a stronger, more immediate impulse toward self-preservation takes hold, and you kick against the uterine wall, pushing away from the sniffing and growling at the entrance to your home, and as you drift slowly up the umbilical cord draws tighter around your throat, and a knot forms. Your mother, feeling you stir for the first time in two months, smiles and invites your father in, prodding him with the heels of her feet. They have sex, a rough pulsing in your warm world like the addition of a third heartbeat, and in that moment when you hear your mother moan you gain the knowledge of betrayal, what it means but also how it feels, and though it of course does not feel good you shouldn't be discouraged; we can tell you that no matter how long you live, no matter how mature or philosophical you may grow to be, almost all sudden enlightenment will feel precisely this way, like a boot in the stomach, like acid on your tongue, and the sooner you accept this the better off you'll be. In fact, you should be glad—at your age, to have understood and assimilated an abstract yet acutely painful concept such as betrayal is, in a word, prodigious. It indicates you have a better than average chance to succeed at the task for which you have been chosen.

94 Now the danger to you is quite grave. With the development of a knot, the umbilical cord will not tolerate any more tension. You must stay put. Having felt you move, from here on your mother will find every

excuse to have sex, and you will have to suffer in absolute stillness. Your life depends on it.

93 Still, when she isn't locked in sexual contortions your mother is the safest, most comfortable home you can imagine. And since the likelihood that she will be the only home you'll ever know has increased exponentially, you should make an effort, when not cowering from your father's incursions, to enjoy every moment here.

92 One small, positive development in all this burgeoning trouble is you are nearing the end of gestation, and due to a precisely timed infusion of hormones you want to move around less as you approach your birth. Slowly you roll one last time, until you are fully inverted and in position to emerge from the womb. As a bonus, your father begins to find your mother less and less sexually appealing. It's not your mother's size that repulses him, but rather her distended navel, which juts ever longer from her belly like a severed finger regenerating itself. He tries not to look at it but inevitably can't help himself, and when the wave of disgust comes over him he feels ashamed and emasculated all at once, though of course he would not admit this even if he could. Thus you are left in peace to gather your strength, every ounce of which you will need, especially since, as we'd feared, the obstetrician did not detect the knot in your umbilical cord. Had the knot been noticed, he almost certainly would have opted for a cesarean delivery, thereby reducing the danger to both you and your mother. As it stands, with a vaginal delivery planned, things are likely to be hard, protracted, and quite dangerous.

91 Soon the day comes. Your mother knows in the morning; she has slept fitfully, and as she rises and waddles to the bathroom she feels the milder contractions begin like seismic tremors in the small of her back. You know, too. You sense the swish and shift and though you can't have any idea yet what it means, you're still not sure that you like it. For one thing, your mother begins, by and by, to scream, and you're certain you don't like that, trapped as you are inside the amphitheater of

her belly. For another, the shift portion of the swish and shift causes your umbilical cord to draw even tighter, spurring your first experience with physical pain. Your mother's screams rise an octave, and the warm fluid in which you have spent your entire life flushes away, replaced by slick undulating walls equal to the fluid in warmth but hard, insistent, pressing from all sides, pushing you down, down, inexorably down and out of your home forever, and now you are certain you don't like this at all because no one likes change unless it is from something bad to something good, and besides the umbilical knot and loops have cut the flow of blood both *from* your placenta and *to* your brain, bad trouble indeed. Your heart slows, and the pinprick of consciousness grows hazy, fading from red to pink to gray. Something's wrong, your mother wails to the doctor and nurses. They ignore her; they are the experts, after all, they have done this a thousand times, and your mother is in pain and exhausted and probably not thinking right and should leave it to them. Your father tries to quiet her with a kiss, his lips and any real comfort they might offer trapped behind the minutely porous shell of a surgical mask. The delivery team goes on ignoring your mother's pleas until the image of you, stillborn, stiff and blue and twisted, returns to her, and she screams at them loud and long enough to be heard two floors down, in Oncology. At the same moment the fetal heart monitor sounds a frantic alarm, and its display of your pulse—dangerously low and still dropping—begins to flash. There is a great and sudden hustle. Hypodermic shots are administered; trays of gleaming steel instruments are deployed. By the time they pull you, purplish and limp, through the new orifice in your mother's abdomen, you are unconscious. Your expression—eyes closed but not clenched, face perfectly relaxed, tiny mouth agape—is one of perfect neutrality. This is the expression you should wear for all your life, no matter how long or brief it is, so that no one, not even you, will ever know whether you are in ecstasy or anguish.

The doctor and nurses place you on a tiny table nearby and set to work, pressing with fingertips on your chest, suctioning your nose and mouth, and eventually they succeed in reviving you. You're moved to a protective plastic box and tethered to life by tubes, wires, adhesives both high- and low-tech, hollow needles the diameter of a strand of your father's hair. Despite the harsh lights and the stinging prick of the needles, this new home is not so unlike the old one. You are swaddled in piles of soft blankets, connected and held fast by the tubes and wires. For a few days your situation is what's called "touch and go." Your parents receive a quick overview, complete with pamphlets and sympathetic embraces, of the myriad developmental problems that may crop up but are by no means, it is repeated time and again, a foregone conclusion. For now, let them worry about these things; they are the adults, your shepherds, and as adults it is their responsibility to suffer the knowledge of threats they neither understand nor can do a thing about. You have but one job, comparatively simple: surviving.

90 And it seems, eventually, that you will do just that. Your body temperature and blood pressure rise, your heart rate stabilizes, and your lungs begin to inflate on their own. Soon, to your dismay, the tubes and wires are removed, one by one, and you are taken from the incubator, forced once again to relinquish the safety of your cocoon, though you are allowed, as a small consolation, to keep the blankets. Do not be upset. These are all signs that the danger has passed, that your life has begun in earnest—you've become a person, fully formed, autonomous and self-sustaining.

89 And with this happy occasion comes the task we spoke of earlier, a life-long proposition which is likely to seem a burden to you, but which we encourage you to try to think of as a privilege, a great honor. First, though, you need to understand this truth:

Although to you we may seem quite knowledgeable, even omniscient, we in fact know only one thing for certain, which is this: thirty-six years, one hundred sixty-eight days, fourteen hours, and twenty-three seconds from now, on June 15, 2010, at 3:44 p.m. EST, a comet that has broken away from the Kuiper Belt near Neptune will impact the Earth with the explosive energy of 283,824,000 Hiroshima bombs.

That's it. We don't know anything else. For example, we have no idea if you will live long enough to witness this phenomenon. There are things we can surmise, though, one being that if you are still alive when the comet hits, neither you nor anything else on the planet will be afterward. All of which raises the question—your task, burden, privilege, call it what you like—a question which men and women, great and not-so, of every color, creed, and sexual persuasion have asked since they first had the language to do so, and probably before:

Does Anything I Do Matter?

It is our hope that, with knowledge of the epic disaster to come and the advantage of our continued assistance, you will have greater success at answering this question than those who have come before you. And we wish you much good luck.

Debbie

Ever since we brought Baby John home from the hospital I've been having this dream. The same dream night after night, only it's not just a dream since it really happened when I was a girl so that makes it more like a memory that haunts my sleep. I wake up pulling on the sheets and it feels like there's water in my lungs, and I cough and gag, trying to get the water out so I can breathe. My hands reach up and grab at my throat but by now I start to feel that there's no water, it's just air, and I'm confused for a few seconds, still gasping though now I can breathe just fine. I lay there and watch the square of orange light from the streetlamps on the little woven throw rug on the floor and scrunch the comforter up in my hands and after a few minutes my breathing calms down. There are bits of dirt at the foot of the bed and I think suddenly that I should change the sheets and it seems a funny thought to have when I'm still so scared but that's how reality comes back to me. By this point I'm wide awake and so I get up. I don't have to worry about getting out of bed quietly because there's no one there to bother, John's at the bakery working and won't be home until after eight. So I get up and go to Baby John, even though he's fast asleep in his crib and not fussing at all, because somehow this dream, in my mind, has something to do with him. Like even though in the dream I'm the one drowning it's somehow a threat to my baby and that's why I keep having it, night after night, like it's trying to tell me something.

John says I'm still just scared by how the baby almost died when he was born. That I'll stop worrying after a while, when enough time has passed that I know deep down he's okay. This is what Doctor Rengell says, too.

Baby John doesn't sleep as good as his father. Most times when I pick him up he cries and waves his arms around, opening and closing his little fingers until they find my nightgown and take hold of that. Sometimes he sucks on it, the nightgown. If he does this usually he goes right back to sleep. If he's mad about being woken up and doesn't want the fabric to suck on, he'll fuss and I'll walk around the bedroom slowly, bouncing him a bit with my arm under his bottom. I stroke his head with its soft baby hair like cotton candy. And my hands will be shaking still.

Sometimes the baby's fussing will wake Rodney. He'll come walking into the bedroom, rubbing at his eyes.

Go back to bed, I say to him.

I'm hungry, he says.

It's not time for breakfast yet, I say. Go back to bed.

I can't sleep with that baby crying.

Rodney, I won't tell you again, I say.

Usually at this point he'll realize I'm not kidding and go back to his bed, though he always drags his feet and gives me a dirty look.

I don't know what the dream is trying to tell me about Baby John. He's not actually in it. How could he be? In the dream I'm just a little girl, the same as when it happened in real life. I don't think of the baby while I'm asleep. It's only when I wake up choking. Then my first thought—even before I try to breathe—is about him. He's in trouble, I think. Something's wrong. It's that deep-gut certainty you get. Like the feeling I have sometimes while I'm standing over a pot on the stove, or else just watching *All in the Family* and out of nowhere my heart takes one big beat and suddenly it's racing and I'm trying to catch my breath even though I'm just standing there. It doesn't make any sense. But you're so certain some terrible thing has happened or is about to happen. You're so certain there's something to be afraid of.

I pay attention to these moments. Because I think this is God's way of trying to tell us things we can't otherwise know. So when I wake up afraid for Baby John, there's a reason. I've got to be careful. And I've got to pay attention.

This is how the dream goes: When I was a girl of about six my father took us all to the river. It was sunny, summer, you'd think it was the weekend because my father wasn't working but the truth is most of the time he didn't have a job so it could have been a Tuesday. Not counting my father there were nine of us, all nine kids. My mother stayed at home this time, which she must have had a good reason because normally she didn't trust my father with any of the kids except Rodney, my brother Rodney who my son Rodney is named for. At thirteen my brother Rodney was just like Dad and spent most school days shining shoes at the bars in town and could take care of himself. But my mother didn't trust my dad with me or the other younger kids, not Patti, who was probably only four or so at the time, or Drew, who was just a baby. But there we all were, walking in a line down the path to the river with Dad at the front. Behind him was Rodney, carrying the baby, and behind Rodney were Matt and Louie, carrying a big cooler. Inside the cooler was a jar of mustard and a loaf of bread but mostly it was full of Narragansett beer.

At the bottom of the path there was a grassy area along the water with enough room for the ten of us to spread out. There was a dock there, too, where people put in canoes and paddleboats. The dock was old and tilted to one side. Some of the wooden boards were cracked, and one was missing, leaving this gap in the middle of the dock like a missing tooth. The river was wide and black and ran hard toward the Scott paper mill, and past that the falls.

This is the part in the dream when I start to get scared—seeing that dirty water go past. How black it is even though the sun is big and bright in the sky. The water bugs riding on the current. I get scared. Watching my father pull open one pop-top after another, I want to get up and run. But I can't, because even though I'm me, I'm also just watching myself. And this is another way that the dream and the memory are the same—I can't change either one. I've got no control.

So I have to watch myself sit there in the grass, as far back from the water as I can get without being in the trees. I've got my back to the river because I don't want to look at it. The sun is hot in my hair and I'm playing with my Little Miss No Name doll, although playing is really the wrong word, what I'm really doing is sort of caring for Little Miss No Name and at the same time trying to make myself as small and quiet as I can while my father drinks beer and gets red around the straps of his tank top and hollers at the boys to stop throwing rocks and quit fucking around with that dead squirrel. Little Miss No Name has a pale, dirty face and a big gray tear falling from one eye, and she's wearing a burlap dress with an orange patch near the hem. The only thing that's pretty about Little Miss No Name is her hair, so blond it's almost white, and I try out different hairstyles, first putting it in pigtails, then a braid, then parting it straight down the middle.

Little Miss No Name is my one gift from the Christmas before. Since it's the only thing I have that's mine I'm selfish with it. Patti wants to play, wants to take Little Miss No Name's dress off and put it back on, and she grabs at the burlap shoulder. Patti doesn't have a toy of her own. Back around Easter she stuck her Zip the Monkey in the flame of the range top to see what would happen, and that was that. I'm sitting Indian-style and I tell Patti no and shift my weight back and forth on my butt until I'm facing away from her, my back blocking her from the doll. She gives up and starts digging in the dirt between her legs.

Time goes by, I don't know how much. Rodney and Matt and Louie and Freddie search through the rocks in the shallows for crawfish. They find a few. One finds Freddie first and pinches his finger. He runs to my father, who's lying with the baby in the shade beneath a tree, and my father takes a look at the cut and tells Freddie to walk it off. Freddie goes to walk it off and my father cuffs him on the back of the head, but this is one of those times he's just playing.

I've decided that Little Miss No Name has misbehaved somehow and so I'm punishing her. Not punishing her, but what's the word? Scolding her. I scold Little Miss No Name and that big tear keeps rolling out of her eye.

Then Dad tells Rodney, who is his right-hand man, to get the bread and mustard out and make some sandwiches. Everyone but me gathers around the cooler. They use their fingers to spread the mustard, then press the two pieces of Wonder together and eat. Their hands and mouths are covered in yellow. I am hungry but I don't join in. My father, still lying with his back against the tree and a can of Narragansett between his legs, notices I'm sitting by myself in the grass.

Debbie, he says. Eat.

I turn and look at him. I'm not hungry, I lie.

What did I say. It is not a question.

I get up and join the other kids. My knees ache from sitting Indian-style for so long. The back of my neck, the part that my hair doesn't cover, feels tight from the sun. I know it will sting later. My brothers and sisters crowd around the cooler. They push each other and laugh but when my father clears his throat they settle down and just eat.

I take one slice of Wonder and put a little mustard on it with my pointer finger and fold it over. I take small bites and it seems like I'll never be finished but every time I look up I see my father is watching me and so I eat it all. It's been a few hours and he's had enough to drink that he's got that look now. When I've put the last bit of crust in my mouth he looks away finally, across the river, and I sneak back to my spot in the grass.

When everyone's finished eating my father sits up with the baby and says to us get in the water. The baby is crying, his face all scrunched up under the bonnet, and my father bounces him on his knee but it's not helping because he's being too rough and the baby's head is jerking all over. Go on, you kids, my father says, get in the river and cool off. And this is when the fear that's been growing inside me explodes suddenly. The other kids do what they're told and get in the water and start splashing and shoving each other. I hunch over, using my fingers to comb Little Miss No Name's hair. I slow my breathing to almost nothing and keep my head down.

This is always what I do. Be quiet and still and try to sort of fade away. Sometimes it works when the others are around. Because the boys, and Freddie especially, are loud and always getting into some sort of trouble and so they attract a lot of my father's attention and make it easy for me to disappear.

But this time there's no way to hide. I'm the only one who isn't in the water, besides the baby of course.

Debbie, my father says. Get in the river, there.

I don't look up.

Girl, he says. This is his warning voice, and it scares me, but not as much as that black water. I just keep combing Little Miss No Name's hair. This is me with my head in the sand. I know it won't work, but there's nothing else I can do.

Finally he gets angry and puts the baby in the grass and stands up. The baby cries and reaches up his chubby hands as my father comes to where I'm sitting and stands over me. I'm shaking, hunched over the doll, pretending I don't notice his shadow.

Debbie, he says. I told you to do something.

I don't like the water. I can't swim.

Chrissakes everyone can swim, he says. All you do is flap your arms and legs around. Now get in there and cool off.

Except for the shaking, I don't move.

And then he's done talking and he lifts me by one arm and is carrying me that way, his hand squeezing my upper arm hard. I start to scream. The other kids stop playing and watch as my father carries me onto the dock. My feet drag along, making a sound like a drum as they thump in the spaces between the boards. My father steps over the hole where the one board is missing. When he gets to the end of the dock he turns and throws me off into the deep water, way past where the other kids are, out to where the current can grab you.

I go under, into the cold and dark. The world disappears. And I wake up and think: Baby John.

I remember to breathe, alone there in my bed, with the light coming in from the streetlamp and bits of dirt in the sheets. With my heart pounding I go to Baby John and lift him from the crib and hold him too tight against me. And pray to God to show me how to protect him, and from what.

In real life, past where the dream ends, I almost drowned. I went under and stayed under until my father realized what he'd done and came in after me. When he pulled me from the water I was half out of it but I remember a couple of the other kids crying. And I remember being on my back in the mud, my father pushing on my chest and saying Breathe, goddammit even though as far as I could tell I was breathing already. His voice was still angry but when I looked up at his face, behind the glaze of the beer buzz I could see fear in his eyes. Whether he was afraid more that I would die, or that he would be responsible if I did, I don't know. Either way it meant he cared, and that was good enough for me.

Years went by and he went from mean to just crazy, but I remembered the day he was afraid for me, and I still loved him. When he turned his hunting knife over in the light of the TV as I went up the stairs to bed and smiled at me and said Maybe tonight, I still loved him. When I got married at sixteen just to escape, I still loved him. When he died alone in his trailer two years ago, I fell down and cried for three days, because I still loved him.

This is the way, now, that I love my baby.

Father

88 Here is what you need to know about Father:

Father is a ghost, a specter, mostly absent, then appearing suddenly, in glimpses, as a huge shape under the bedcovers at twilight, a bowed silent head over newspaper and steaming coffee cup. Father is a mustache; once he shaves it and you do not recognize him and for three weeks you scream and writhe every time he appears, until it grows back. Father is nearly mute. Father was not exactly loquacious by nature, and then he went away and killed people and was almost killed himself, and when he came back a year later he decided his mouth had only three functions, and speaking was not one of them. For a while he thought his mouth's primary function was to take in liquor, and so he did that, working two jobs all the while, seeing your mother through her first pregnancy, and though he did not throw glassware or punches, did not spend money allocated for food or the electric bill on booze, did not ever wake up in a crumpled car or in jail, he nonetheless decided, after two years of drinking hard, after ballooning to 295 bloated pounds, that his mouth now had only two functions—the drinking of coffee and the smoking of cigarettes.

And though at one year old you don't yet know much about your father, you should be aware that he is the type of person who does not change his mind once he's made it up. On the one hand, this is good, since he's not likely to backslide on the drinking. He is steady, calm, a man of unremarkable but ironclad habits, who while at war learned the value of sleep, and now does not allow anything—noise, crisis, lack of time—to keep him from it. And while it is never a bad thing to have a reliable and sober man for a father, his unshakable composure can make him seem apathetic, even cold. And just as his decision not to drink is almost certainly permanent, so too is his decision to hardly speak. Know this, assimilate and accept it, so that you don't waste energy, in later years, trying in vain to elicit words like "love" and "proud" from him.

87 Unlike your mother, your father smokes in the house.

86 When he comes home from the bakery in the afternoons your father likes to lift you from the crib and hold you, but casually; he hoists you to his shoulder like a sack of rocks, holds you in place with one great forearm under your backside, and goes about his few household activities—stirring sugar into coffee, shaving his cheeks and trimming his mustache—as though you aren't even there, as though he's always had just one arm. Sometimes he forgets he is carrying you, and retires to the bedroom for an hour or two of sleep with you still clinging to him like a remora on a shark. You've learned that if you fuss a bit (but quietly, quietly, he doesn't respond well to loud noises, especially right next to his ear, and though he has never become demonstrably angry, there is, just beneath the surface of his calm, the implication of a rage so dark and violent it frightens even him, a rage he takes great care to keep under control, pausing when annoyed to breathe and flex his hands) he will remember you are there and be sure not to crush you as he settles his bulk into bed.

Because you most often cannot bear to look directly at him, you know more about how your father smells than anything else. He is a delicious combination of baker's yeast and Aqua Velva, lemon frosting and tobacco smoke, Taster's Choice crystals and warehouse dust. Some of these scents change in intensity with the time of day; in the morning the aftershave and dust are prominent; in the afternoons, the yeast and frosting. The coffee and smoke are constants, omnipresent.

85 Learn to pretend to sleep. Or else learn to wake without crying. This way, you can lie in your crib, listening to the night sounds in your parents' bedroom, and discover that your father is not entirely mute after all, only mute with everyone *except* your mother. Wait for him to return, just before dawn, from loading and unloading boxes at the warehouse. Keep your eyes closed, or else the sight of his hulking silhouette will cause you to cry, and your mother will rise and come to you and he will remain silent. Be still, and listen. Do you hear, beneath the rush and fade of the occasional car passing on the street outside, beneath the

rustle of cotton sheets and the groan of mattress springs, a sound too deep and calm to be your mother? Listen carefully; it will continue for only a minute or two; he is much too tired to talk longer than that before dropping into a profound if brief sleep. This, then, is the sound of your father's voice, the sound of absolute safety and control.

84 Having learned that your father does speak, and having heard his voice for yourself, you now want one thing more than you've desired anything else in your short life—to know *what* he's saying. Every morning, after he comes in and before he goes to sleep, when he believes no one else is listening, you hear him speak to your mother, but you can never make out the words. Sometimes she answers, a falsetto accompaniment to his baritone, and sometimes she rolls over wordlessly to greet him, to be enveloped by the comforting girth of his arms and chest. Either way, he always has words for her, words whose meaning dangles in the air above you like a mobile hung just out of reach.

And while you deprive yourself of sleep morning after morning, waiting for him to come home, straining to catch just one distinct word, we should mention that most experts in the field of pediatrics recommend children your age get at least fourteen hours of sleep every day. This, we understand, may seem an unreasonable demand, especially since adults like your father apparently require almost no sleep at all. But you should keep in mind that, first, your father is not representative of the adult population as a whole, and second, your nervous system is still fully engaged in the heavy industry of development, burning around the clock at high temperature and velocity, vacuuming up stimuli and laying synapses, and needs all the rest it can manage.

Still, you persist, refusing the sweet potatoes and rice cereal your mother offers in the evening before bed so that you'll be wakeful with hunger when your father comes home. This effort is aided by the near-constant pain of teething, which makes it impossible for you to sleep for more than an hour or so at a time anyhow, but which also, it turns out, spurs in you near-constant urges to scream, to spray drool and nonsense baby vitriol in every direction. These urges grow increasingly difficult to deny (due in part to your fatigue, for which, we should add, you have no one to blame but yourself), and several times, unable to keep silent any longer, you yield and cry out and your mother comes to you with the teething ring and your father, instead of speaking, merely sleeps. Your crankiness and refusal to eat has the predictable result of worrying her, and for several consecutive nights, when your father comes in from work, he is silent as she monopolizes the precious few minutes of conversation time, saying "I don't understand it, his appetite is just fine during the day, but for some reason after the sun goes down he won't take anything, he pushes the food away and fusses, tonight he flipped the bowl over and I ended up wearing strained peas, I think maybe I should bring him to Doctor Rengell," etc. For more than a week your father says nothing, only listens to your mother's concerns, his nightly routine of uttering a few precious if unintelligible words disrupted, and you're beginning to think that perhaps you've made a mistake, perhaps your strategy was horribly miscalculated and now that the routine has been broken it will not be reestablished, he will never speak again and you will grow up, grow old, and die never having understood a thing from or about him. Of course you don't yet possess the language to articulate this loss in such a way; all you have is the emotion, the impression of loss, which is its only authentic interpretation anyhow. Like a proper child you direct your anger over this loss at your mother and her unreasonable worry, until, one night, listening to her, your father sighs and, with an edge of irritation in his voice that renders his words just clear enough to be decipherable, says: "Take him to Rengell, then."

Your mother, after brightening briefly, saying "Yes, I think I should," begins immediately to express concern over how they will afford this unanticipated and, really, she admits, kind of unnecessary trip to the doctor; meanwhile, your father rolls on his side to sleep, and you lie triumphant and joyful in your crib, suddenly if temporarily free of the ache in your mouth, having not only heard your father's words, but understood them, in your way, *to be about you.*

83   This triumph is short-lived, because the very next afternoon you realize something horrifying about your father. He comes home from the

bakery and lifts you to his shoulder, and you notice for the first time that, unlike everyone else you know, he does not have five fingers on each hand, ten total. On his right hand the pinkie and ring finger are gone, severed just above the first knuckle and long since healed over with thick, gnarled, waxy skin. You are horrified, feeling the stumps pressed against your bare leg and knowing them to be wrong, and you cry and squirm, pushing with your little arms against his chest. Midway through his shave, when it becomes clear you mean to keep screaming and struggling, your father brings you back into the living room and puts you down on the floor with a grimace, then returns to the bathroom. Your mother, having heard the commotion, swoops in to determine what's wrong, and though you try to tell her you manage only to soak her shirt with spit and tears, and it doesn't matter anyway because you realize, young as you are, that she can do nothing about your father's monstrous deformity, except rub cream on the stumps to keep them from cracking, and help him with any tasks that require two complete hands.

Your mother believes your father lost his fingers to shrapnel from a fragmentary grenade. That was the official story from the Marine captain who filed the paperwork. But this is what actually happened: Your father was on leave in Bac My An, a military R&R base in central Vietnam known to servicemen as China Beach, when he lost his fingers. On a sweltering November evening, on the second floor of a whorehouse, in the room of a seventeen-year-old Vietnamese girl, with his wedding band on, while her infant son slept on a mat on the floor, your father committed his first and only act of adultery, and then, drunk on Pabst Blue Ribbon and tequila shooters, promptly passed out. The Vietnamese girl had no Communist sympathies, had in fact no political convictions at all, but she did have a heroin habit and a dead mother and a son whose prospects were even poorer than her own, owing to prevailing attitudes among the Vietnamese regarding children of mixed stock. And though she was losing money while your father slept, she nonetheless let him stay, even nestled close to him despite the heat, lying on her side with her legs curled and her head resting in the crook between his biceps and shoulder. Because this girl, whose name was

Tran Ly, had no solace other than fantasy, she allowed herself to imagine that your father was the father of her son, and that tomorrow, or the next day at the latest, they would be married, and soon after she and her baby would be on their way to America. She imagined clean, waterproof buildings that didn't explode without warning. She imagined her son growing tall and strong, with good teeth and perfect English. She imagined dying of old age. And then, just as she was settling into this fantasy, allowing it to distill her down through the thin mattress and into a drowsy reverie, your father flailed in his sleep, striking her in the face and breaking her nose. Tran Ly jumped from the bed, screeching in pain and confusion, and when she pulled her hands away from her face and saw the blood she was reminded of her baby's real father. Her cries turned angry. *"Cockadau! Cockadau!"* she said, meaning: *I will kill you!* She stooped and reached between the bed and the wall, grabbing the cleaver she kept there, a cleaver her mother had used, years ago, to kill and dismember chickens. By now Tran Ly's screams had brought your father around somewhat. He opened his eyes in time to see the blade over him, glinting an evil red in the light from the window. He rolled out of the way, but let his right hand trail behind, and when it and the cleaver met, his fingers leapt, twirled, fell.

In the hospital your father pleaded for, and received, discretion from the captain filing paperwork on the incident. Tran Ly was not so fortunate. Not knowing what to do with her, U.S. military police turned her over to the South Vietnamese army, who treated her as Viet Cong and shot her twice—once in the head, once in the chest—with an M-16 rifle that had been manufactured in Hartford, Connecticut. And Tran Ly's baby . . . well, it's probably best that you not know what became of him.

Rodney

So it's been a while since the baby came home and still Ma doesn't notice when I'm gone for a long time and so I go down to the trees by the ball field with Pete on our bikes and we're building a fort underground. How I know that you can build a fort underground is from Dad's books about Vietnam. The Vietnamese built all their forts underground and lived down there all the time. They even had hospitals in the ground. You have to dig around trees because the roots hold the ground together so it doesn't cave in. I learned that from the book, too.

We've been doing it a long time, like two weeks, and all we have really is this hole that's not very deep and it's a lot of work already to have nothing but this little hole. Pete says why don't we forget it and go to your house and play table hockey. Pete always wants to play table hockey because he doesn't have his own game. But I don't want to go home because I don't like the baby and Ma doesn't watch me close anymore so I can be gone all day. Once school's out I get to do pretty much whatever I want and it wouldn't be that way if we didn't have the baby. So I guess it's okay. I wouldn't have a table hockey game except that I got it from my uncle, his name is Rodney too and he's got money to buy things where Ma and Dad don't. I like Uncle Rodney but he's different from my parents. He's always eating weird stuff like goat's milk and this peanut butter that they make in the grinder at the natural food store. The peanut butter tastes weird. Uncle Rodney says that's because they don't put in refined sugar and salt and other things that are bad for you, it's just peanuts. I don't like it. But I like being at Uncle Rodney's. People come over all the time to party. Sometimes they stay and drink beer and play music and when they drink too much they walk crooked and laugh a lot and tell me jokes that I'm not supposed to repeat to anyone. Sometimes when people come over they just stay for a minute to get something from Uncle Rodney then they leave. Sometimes if I stay the night in the morning Uncle Rodney or his girlfriend Rachel will get out of bed and be naked. He says it's okay to see the human body naked and there's no shame in it. He's not weird or anything, he'll just like walk into the kitchen and pour a glass of carrot juice or blend his shake that he drinks and say hey what's up kiddo standing there naked.

Uncle Rodney is my godfather and so he has to buy me things.

Ma used to not want me staying at Uncle Rodney's too much. She would say she didn't want me around the sort of people Uncle Rodney hangs out with. But now with the baby I can pretty much go there whenever I want.

At Uncle Rodney's the people come over to party. That's what they say. Partying means drinking. It also means playing records by Lou Reed and Chicago, which I thought was a city but is also a band it turns out. Uncle Rodney explained this to me. It's a band and a city and when I'm older he'll take me to Chicago to see Chicago play, he says. A lot of times when they're partying Uncle Rodney has me run the record player. A record will end and someone will say put on that Carpenters album. Then they'll laugh and say hey just joking kid play some Peter Tosh, and because they're laughing I'll laugh too and look for the Peter Tosh record in the milk crates near the stereo and find it and slide it out of the sleeve touching only the edges so I don't leave fingerprints and put it on the turntable. I've been doing it a while and so I can drop the needle real careful right on the first song without making that scratching noise. Uncle Rodney's friends, they'd drop the needle on the middle of the record and scratch it all up and so now I run the record player, because I'm not compromised by the ravages of adult recreation, is how Uncle Rodney says it. By that he means I don't party. Once and a while I ask him for a beer and he says no way Christ your mother would kill me not to mention that beast of a father. He says if you want something to drink there's Apple and Eve in the fridge, now go play Atari and don't forget to take your vitamin C wafers. Just don't eat too many or your piss will turn nuclear yellow.

The people at Uncle Rodney's drink and smoke weed and for a while I thought that was partying but then not too long ago I learned something else. Sometimes two or three people will disappear for a while together and then come back one at a time. At first I didn't know what they were doing and didn't really think anything about it but then one day I was outside in the grass behind the house looking for cigarette butts to smoke and it was hot and the bathroom window was open and I could hear people talking and so I went up underneath the window and listened. It was Uncle Rodney and Karen and Frank, Karen's boyfriend who Uncle Rodney plays softball with. They were talking and laughing and making a sound like blowing their noses. I peeked up and saw they weren't blowing their noses. They were taking turns sucking through their noses with this thing that was like a straw except it was made of glass.

Frank scrunched up his nose and his eyes were tearing up. It's good, he said.

Of course it's good, Uncle Rodney said. How much do you want?

How much do you have? Frank said. They all laughed.

Wow this shit is killing me, Frank said. My chest is all tight. I'm out, I need a drink.

We'll talk it over, Uncle Rodney said. Just let me know.

Frank left and closed the bathroom door. Uncle Rodney and Karen were still in the bathroom together. Uncle Rodney turned toward the window so I ducked down and couldn't see them anymore. They stopped talking for a while but I could hear them moving around, making sucking sounds through their noses and laughing some more. Then they got quiet for a minute and then Karen said hey what the hell are you doing like she was mad except she was giggling.

You know I still love you, Uncle Rodney said.

Don't start with that, Rod, Karen said.

Why not? It's true, Uncle Rodney said.

No, Karen said. You love yourself, and you love your coke, and you love your mom and that's about it. Besides, you have a fiancée. And I've got Frank. Frank, the guy who was just in here? You remember him.

I'd leave Rachel now, Uncle Rodney said. Right this minute. If you'd take me back.

Get the fuck off it, Rod, Karen said. This isn't funny.

That's because I'm not joking.

Karen laughed at him. Oh crissake you're not really crying are you? You must be drunker than I thought. You actually believe the shit that's coming out of your mouth?

You don't have to be a bitch about it, Uncle Rodney said.

Oh yes I do, Karen said.

Jesus, Uncle Rodney said. Forget it.

Uh-uh. You can forget it. Let me ask you something. Do you give Rachel all the same old lines you fed me, or have you updated your material?

Uncle Rodney didn't say anything back. I heard him open the bathroom door and walk back into the kitchen.

Fucker, Karen said. I peeked up again and watched her rub her nose and fix her hair in the mirror. Then she went out.

I knew I'd heard something I wasn't suppose to. I knew Uncle Rodney would be in big-time trouble with Rachel if she heard what he was saying to Karen. I like Rachel but I wasn't going to tell her anything.

This is how I found out that cocaine is partying too, but the kind of partying you do in other rooms with just a couple people or else by yourself. It wasn't too long until I found out where Uncle Rodney keeps his cocaine. He's got so much of it he doesn't notice if I take a little bit once and a while.

The first time I tried it I didn't like it. My nose burned and there was a funny taste in the back of my throat that made me keep swallowing real fast like right before you puke. Plus the back of my throat was numb, and I didn't like that either. But then a few seconds later something happened and I got high. This is what they call it. Uncle Rodney's friends, when they're partying. Let's get high, they say. Who wants to get high?

So today me and Pete are digging the underground fort and I'm going to ask Pete if he wants to get high with me. I'm nervous because even though I've been doing it a while and I don't get nervous doing it myself anymore I'm worried because I'd be in trouble if someone found out. Uncle Rodney would be mad. Ma probably wouldn't care with the baby but Dad would be plenty mad. But Pete's my best friend and even if he didn't want to try it I don't think he'd say anything.

So I take the cocaine and the straw out of my pocket and put them on a big rock next to the pile of dirt we dug out of the hole. The cocaine is in a piece of foil from an empty cigarette pack. I saw Uncle Rodney do it once— you put the foil out flat, put the cocaine in the middle, then fold the foil over and twist up the open end so it doesn't fall out. It only works with a little bit of cocaine, but like I says I only take a little bit here and there.

Pete doesn't see me take out the cocaine and open the foil. He's looking down toward the river where a groundhog has just gone running across the floodplains where all the dead trees have fallen in the mud. He only notices when I start moving the cocaine into lines.

What are you doing? Pete says.

Cutting some bumps, I say.

Pete climbs up out of the hole and stands next to me. What's that?

Try some.

What is it?

Cocaine. You want to try it?

Pete looks around all nervous like he thinks someone might be watching. Where did you get it?

I pick up the straw and show it to him. See how I cut it? I say. You cut the end like that so it goes right up the straw.

I can tell Pete's impressed by everything.

You want to try it or not? I ask him.

I don't think so.

I think he's expecting me to razz him, say things like c'mon don't be such a pussy, but I don't. I just say okay fine and put the straw in my nose and lean down until the straw is almost touching the foil and then breathe in through my nose as I move the straw up and the bump disappears. I stand up and cough a little and squint my eyes and I can see Pete's even more impressed than before. He's staring at me like he can't believe what he saw.

That's not real, he says.

It is too, I say.

There's that gross taste at the back of my throat. I'm used to it now but it still makes me a little pukey. I swallow a couple times.

Listen Rod I gotta get going, Pete says. Our bikes are on their side in the grass and he starts to walk toward them.

Then I get high. That's how it happens, real fast.

Where are you going? I ask Pete.

Home, Pete says.

We've got a lot of work to do still, I say.

Pete watches as I fold up the foil and put it back in my pocket. He's got his bike and is standing beside it with his hands on the handlebars. I'll have to come back later and help, he says.

Pete, come on, I say, and now I'm a little scared because I've never seen him like this before and I thought he would be cool but he's not and now I'm worried he's going to say something. Let's go back to my house then. We'll play table hockey.

Pete gets on his bike. I have to go Rod. I'll see you later.

He rides down the dirt path out of the trees and up toward the road. I watch him go. Then because I'm scared I just leave everything there, the shovels and the buckets and the pick, and I get on my bike and ride hard after him but he's gone. I go by his house and see his bike out leaning against the front steps but I don't dare go and knock on the door because his mother's car is in the driveway.

I go home and for a while I read a book about Carl Yastrzemski that I got at the school book fair. Then I get high again. Later I call Pete but his mom answers and asks who it is and I tell her and she says she doesn't know why but Pete doesn't want to talk to me did we have a fight? I say no and she says well I don't know what's wrong with him but maybe you shouldn't call back for a while okay honey? I say okay and hang up and there's nothing to do. Ma is in the bathroom with the baby and Dad's at work at the warehouse. So I go outside and get on my bike and go to Uncle Rodney's.

Brother

82 Here is what you need to know about Brother:

Like you, your brother is a child, but older, more independent both in circumstance and spirit. His sovereignty and your lack thereof are inversely proportional; the more your mother dotes on you, the less time she has to care for, pay attention to, and police him. Your father, consumed by work, does not often figure into the equation except as a boogeyman—"Rodney, keep it up and I'm telling your father"—the threat of which your mother uses without much success. Rodney has therefore grown into a headstrong and willful boy whose headstrong, willful ways are likely to produce a life even more fraught with sorrow and regret than normal.

This is not the only reason why you should resist the natural impulse to emulate and imitate your brother, an impulse you've already demonstrated through your growing tendency to disobey your mother simply for disobedience's sake, and your proclivity for staging violent confrontations between stuffed animals, not to mention that one unfortunate incident with your brother's homemade nunchakus, the loss of which, following the incident, served only to inflame his resentment of you.

81 Your relationship with your brother will be, in many ways, the most complex and bewildering of all the interpersonal connections you will form. An older brother is both authority figure and peer, friend and bitter enemy, partner and rival, and will play these contradictory roles to varying degrees throughout your life. At this point the rivalry is most prominent, owing to the difference in age and the resentment your brother feels toward you monopolizing your mother's attention. Try to remember, in the face of the poor treatment you receive at his hands, that more than a pure desire to cause you harm or pain, this is an effort on his part to win back some of that attention, even if it's only through being scolded and punished.

Of course your brother makes it difficult to bear this in mind. There's the garden-variety mistreatment. The shoving and poking. The theft and withholding of toys, the gratified smirk at your subsequent howling. The sitting too close to and directly in front of the television, to obscure your view of *Sesame Street*. The one time when he holds you upside down over the gurgling vortex of a just-flushed toilet, repeatedly lowering you into the cacophony of the porcelain bowl, over and over, until your mother comes running and finds the two of you, he with your ankles in his fists, you with furious little veins pulsing at your temples and your eyes clenched shut and your hair dripping toilet water. No doubt Rodney would have subjected you to this torture again, delightful as he found it, except that several hours later the threat of your father became the actuality of your father, his bulk and fury and great swooping hand, an experience your brother has no desire to repeat any time soon.

But these minor torments are merely a warm-up, because your brother is smart, and cunning, and patient, and mischievous, the sort of person who has the ability to wait for a weakness, recognize it when it appears, and exploit it when the time is right. And he discovers and plumbs your weakness, somewhat accidentally, through the miracle of cable television.

80 The cable is installed at your mother's request. Your father doubts that they can afford it, what with the mountain of unexpected medical bills from your birth that he's still trying to scale, not to mention all the other expenses that arrive without end in thick off-white stacks, the accounts tabulated in Ohio and New Jersey even as he cuts rainbow squares at the bakery, the interest accruing as he tosses all manner of packages onto and off of trucks, the invoices printed and mailed while, in a stolen moment between shifts, he falls asleep in his ratty old easy chair with a coffee cup clenched in the fingers of his good hand. But your mother is full to bursting with compounded frustration from worrying about you—needlessly, your father believes—and dealing with your brother's insurrection, and this cable thing has become so popular and widespread that the local CBS affiliate, sixty miles away in Bangor, has

scaled back its broadcast signal to the point that she cannot get good reception of *Guiding Light*, her one afternoon solace. Thus your father concedes, and soon after a man in a hard white plastic hat and jangling tool belt comes to your apartment, and your mother gives him a cup of black coffee and directs him to the living room where, on top of the television, he places the Box. The Box is connected to the television by a thick black cable and has a row of buttons across its top which snap smartly when pressed. These buttons also control the image displayed on the screen, and since the TV is set on a low-slung coffee table, you can, standing precariously on your tiptoes with one hand gripping the back of the TV for balance, access the buttons. Make them snap. Control the image. The power is yours.

79 Since your brother cannot permit you to have any power, no matter how trivial, he tries to wrest it from you. First by force—he will find you playing with the buttons, sometimes even when the TV is off, and he will shove you away from the Box, then gloat and grin in the squall of wailing that follows, withstanding with a laughable minimum of effort your attempts to get past him and at the buttons again. But his victory is short-lived, because your mother's radar for even the faintest hint of distress from you is beyond acute, and she inevitably comes and scolds your brother and forces him to leave you be. Once, twice, three times, and on the third she tells him that this is it, do it again and she's telling your father, and the memory of the last time your father intervened is fresh enough that he desists. Instead he sits, thin arms crossed over his chest, smoldering as he watches the rapid flash of shifting images: a snippet of *Superfriends*, a millisecond of the *Creature Double Feature*, a precious half-scrambled moment of *Fat Albert*.

It goes on this way for weeks, and you notice that the more you play with the Box the less your brother is around. He retreats to the sanctuary of your Uncle Rodney's apartment across town, where he can watch TV and even play Atari for hours, unmolested, uninterrupted. On weekdays you hardly see him at all. This is fortunate, because after more than a month you're growing bored with the Box, and under the current arrangement you need only play with it for ten minutes or so when your brother comes home to change out of his one set of good school clothes, and after he leaves you're free to fool around with your Matchbox cars, or even play with your brother's Boba Fett action figure or Wiffle ball set, because he's not around to keep them from you.

78 This agreeable state of affairs comes to an end on a gray Saturday when your Uncle Rodney has left for the weekend on "business" and your brother cannot go outside to play because it's rained hard for three days, transforming the town into a massive mud pit. So the two of you play on opposite ends of the living room. Your brother would go to the bedroom to get away from you and your endless snapping, except that to save money on the electrical bill your mother will allow only one light to be turned on, in the living room, and your brother cannot bear the gray gloom of a rainy day spent inside without at least the artificial cheer of indoor lighting. Especially a Saturday, when he should be in constant frenetic kid motion from dawn to dusk, enjoying as much fun and freedom as possible in anticipation of Sunday morning and the somber proceedings of Mass and the sense that the world has been dipped in amber, not just suspended but suffocated, dead. For your brother there is only one escape from the dull hell that is Sunday: your Uncle Rodney's apartment, where Sundays are treated pretty much like any other day of the week. But of course this weekend, with your uncle out of town, that is not an option. So the two of you share the living room with a peace as fragile and uneasy as that between the Israelis and Palestinians, you with the Box, he with a stack of Topps baseball cards. He sorts the cards into multiple piles on the sofa, arranging players by team and creating separate stacks for doubles and specialty cards. Each time he opens a pack he puts the powdery stick of gum in his mouth, and at this point he's got a wad going that's large enough to choke your favorite big lizard the brontosaurus, but he keeps adding to it, stick by stick, until he has to practically unhinge his jaw to chew. You, meantime, are snapping away. The epileptic frenzy of images on the TV is like a flip book without any sort of cohesive narrative: a girl spinning on a tire swing, *snap!* a giant cartoon robot grappling with a

giant cartoon squid, *snap!* a ball of light so brilliant it turns the whole world to dust and silence.

Suddenly transfixed, you stop snapping the buttons.

This last is actually stock footage of nuclear weapons tests conducted in Nevada more than thirty years ago, incorporated into a feature on the French seer Nostradamus. Like most seers of any popularity, Nostradamus spent a lot of time predicting how the world would end, and though he was wrong, the images in the film are close enough to the truth as you know it that they frighten you almost literally to death. Still as stone except for your heart, which beats suddenly at a rate that is not at all sustainable, you watch. First, the ball of light, which expands quickly, then collapses upon itself. Houses, trees, and scary faceless people burst into flames. Languid fires lap at roofs and bodies indifferently, as tiny dust devils swirl in slow-motion on the ground. Suddenly a wall of air slams through, erasing the houses, snapping trees in half, and sending people and cars pinwheeling away into darkness. The world is gone, and in its place rises a great, fiery column of ash and smoke, and you recognize this as the Destroyer of Worlds, which until now you understood only in the abstract. Here It is made concrete, and you collapse on the ratty orange carpet before It, trembling, weeping silently, as your brother looks on with a mouth so jammed with bubble gum he can't form the words to ask you what's wrong.

It appears to him quite possible that you have croaked, and though he hates you it is with the sort of benign hatred common among juvenile siblings, and he by no means wants you dead, especially with no witnesses around to testify that he had nothing to do with it. So he is concerned, both for you and for himself, as he crosses the living room with slow, cautious steps.

"Junior," he says, standing over you, his voice garbled by fear and the wad of gum. Now he can see your minute convulsions, the small muscles in your neck and arms seized and bulging, the tears streaming from your eyes. The relief he should feel at realizing you are not dead is displaced by blossoming panic, because even though you're alive it's clear there is something very, very wrong, something which his nine short years of existence have not prepared him to confront or understand. He reaches down with one hand. "Junior?" he says again, and when he touches you and feels the fever and tension of every hysterical cell in your body he recoils as if bitten, tears welling now in his own eyes.

He then resorts to the default action of children everywhere when faced with a predicament beyond their scope of comprehension: "Maaaa!"

Your mother responds somewhat more slowly than when you are the one crying out for help. A full minute passes before she appears in the doorway between the living room and kitchen, her face held in a pinch of mild exasperation. "What is it, Rodney?" she sighs, then answers her own question as she takes in the sight of you seized and foaming on the floor.

Your mother sort of leaps to her knees beside you, giving herself second-degree rug burns. She gathers your head and supports it on her lap. "What did you do to him?" she screams at your brother. He stands mute with his hands at his sides and his eyes wide. "What did you do?" she asks again, grasping him by the front of his shirt and yanking him forward, a movement that causes the wad of gum to shoot back into his throat and lodge there.

So here is the scene: your mother on the floor, just starting to register the pain in her knees and rapidly approaching hysteria; you, your head on her lap, curled tighter than an overcooked shrimp, every muscle in your body contracting as one; your brother, reeling around the living room, eyes bulging, alternately clutching his throat and grasping at the empty air in front of him, his struggle for breath so far going unnoticed. Meanwhile, on the TV, through the miracle of cut scene the world is remade, only to be swallowed again and again by the ball of terrible light. And you, eyes fixed, continue to watch.

77 It's not until your brother collapses half-conscious against your mother's shoulder that she notices he's choking. Still under the impression that he's responsible for whatever is afflicting you, she spins him around and uses an open hand to pummel his back, much harder than is necessary. After a few sound whacks the gum hurtles from his mouth

and lands, glistening and harmless, on the floor in front of the recliner. He sputters as your mother continues to pound and curse him. The blows are remarkably consistent, all landing centered on your brother's spine between his shoulder blades, so that tomorrow he'll bear a roughly hand-shaped bruise that will, over the course of the next week, turn every nauseous color of the contusion rainbow before fading away.

Despite the fact that with each whack your mother knocks what little breath your brother has managed to catch from his lungs, he is able, in an act of pure self-preservation, to holler out: "The TV, Ma! Turn off the TV!"

Her frenzy thus broken, your mother turns her attention to the TV, then back to you. Your brother pulls a deep, ragged breath and finds he has both the need and the energy to cry for a bit.

Through her panic your mother recognizes, somehow, that she has to calm down and think clearly. With an effort of will that surprises her, she slows her breathing and wipes the scrim of tears away, then bends forward to look closely at your face. She notices how your eyes, though they appear empty and unseeing, follow the image on the screen as she lifts your head. Drawing a quick parallel between this and what your brother has said, she reaches up and slams the TV's power button with the palm of her hand.

The image blinks out, and your body goes limp as an empty pillowcase. Your eyes close. Foam runs from your mouth like an overflowing washing machine. Your mother reaches her fingers in to clear your mouth, drawing out gobs of stringy spit. She uses her other hand to gather in your brother, whose sobs have dwindled to blear-eyed sniffles.

"Rodney, honey," she says, "I need you to call your father at the warehouse. Can you do that for me, baby?" Your brother only stares at her, as if the choking spell has somehow left him deaf. "Rodney," she says again. "Honey, Mommy's sorry, she didn't mean to hit you so hard, okay, she was just scared, but right now she needs you to call Dad at the warehouse. The number's on the wall next to the phone. The third number down. Okay?"

There are several reasons why your mother has decided to have your father come and bring you all to the hospital. First, he is her protector from the world, the rock against which she hurls all her problems and sees them smashed to bits, and even when a situation clearly requires someone with an expertise your father does not possess—a doctor, say, or a CPA—he is and always will be the person she calls. Second, the only vehicle they own, a 1973 Ford Country Squire wagon, mint green with woodgrain panels and a bad starter, is with him at work. Third, even if she had the wagon she couldn't use it, because it almost always refuses to turn over, and so your father has to push it from behind to get the 5,000-pound vehicle moving, then run alongside, jump in through the open driver's-side door, and pop the clutch.

With a bit more verbal prodding and a gentle push in the direction of the kitchen, your brother does as he is told. Your mother, meantime, worries over you, smoothing your hair back with trembling hands, leaning down repeatedly to check your breathing, even though at this point there's no evidence of anything more traumatic going on than a very deep sleep.

76 Soon your father arrives from the warehouse. As always he appears calm and unfazed, though a careful observer would note some subtle signs of distress: his mustache twitching at the corner of his mouth, for example, and his carotid artery pumping furiously at the grizzled skin of his throat. He scoops you up and holds you against his chest with his bad hand, then herds your mother and brother out to the Country Squire and drives the whole sniffling, sodden-faced crew to the hospital.

75 There the nurses put dressings on your mother's knees and scope your brother's nose and throat for any further blockage. One nurse notes a drying and crusting of your brother's septum consistent with cocaine abuse. She has the doctor take a look, but given Rodney's age he dismisses it as the somewhat strange remnants of a head cold. You, on the other hand, are the real mystery case, the enigma. The young intern examines you and listens to your mother's account of what happened

and tries to sort out the bafflement and skepticism he's experiencing. It's difficult for the young intern to sort anything out this afternoon, though, because his wife, a southern woman for whom marriage to a doctor has not so far been the mildly glamorous and moneyed shopping-fest she had imagined, hinted this morning around the possibility that she maybe was thinking about considering leaving him. After less than a year of marriage. And the intern is, as a result, somewhat distracted.

"You're saying the boy's eyes were sort of *locked* on the television?" the intern asks.

"Yes," your mother says.

You're still sleeping, and the intern rolls you onto your side and listens to your lungs with a stethoscope. "And when you turned the television off," he says, "the seizure stopped? Just like that?"

"And he went to sleep," your mother adds.

"Mm-hmm." The intern places you on your back again and rubs his chin and considers. "He shows no signs of poisoning, and the tox screen was normal. It's possible that John—"

"Junior," your mother says.

"That Junior had what's called a photosensitive seizure. It can be caused by bright shifting patterns on TV screens. But you said nothing like this has ever happened before? That he's watched TV before without any problems?"

"Yes."

"Mm-hmm."

"And he's not waking up," your mother says. "Shouldn't he be awake by now?"

"It's common to see lethargy, and yes sometimes deep protracted sleep, after a seizure." This is what the intern says, but he's actually thinking that your mother is right, you really ought to be awake by now. "Listen, we're going to run a few more tests. I'm not entirely satisfied just yet."

74 But these tests disclose nothing, because no test has yet been invented that can reveal a patient is suffering from the soul-dread caused by

knowledge of the impending end of all existence. So: more pointless expenses for your father, which he will bear with the grim patience of Atlas. He also bears, with somewhat less patience, the intern's implying that your mother is batty, and he hustles the three of you out of there before he feels compelled to show this overeducated know-nothing a trick he learned in Vietnam involving two of his fingers, the intern's nostrils, and a sharp upward thrust.

73 By the time the family arrives home you've come fully awake, but you are not your usual chatty, energetic self. Quiet and glassy-eyed, you refuse the mashed carrots and Shake 'n Bake chicken breast your mother offers. While the rest of the family eats dinner you sit on the kitchen floor with your back to the cupboard and brood like an unhappy teenager, which is sort of comical in a three-year-old. But no one is laughing, least of all your mother.

Then your father excuses himself and leaves, drumstick in hand, for his shift at the bakery. You, in your Tuffskins overalls, continue to stare at the kitchen floor and play listlessly with your own hair. This goes on, in one form or another, for weeks, months, until your mother sort of forgets that you were ever an animated, happy child and stops worrying so much about it. You are now a serious child. She has met other serious children. She's not pleased about it, but after all, in most other ways you are normal, even exceptional—you've already started to read on your own and nailed potty training in less than a week. You eat and sleep normally, and there is no recurrence of your seizure episode.

72 This last is because you now fear the television like a cat fears water. And it is this fear that your brother recognizes and exploits—whenever you enter the living room he turns on the TV, and no matter what's on you turn and toddle frantically back in the direction you came. Every single time. It is a foolproof way for your brother to rid himself of you, and now when he is home he spends almost all his time in the living room, alone and unmolested, sometimes even pretending with ease that he has no brother at all.

John Sr.

At the bakery it's just me. It's a small place. Just me and the raspberry horns and the tourtiere pies and my cigarette going in the ashtray near the back sink. Every once in a while a car passes through the dark street outside the storefront windows, but that's pretty much all I see of people while I'm there, until the end of my shift at eight when Monica shows up to open the store for the day. A solid twelve hours by myself, nothing but the radio to keep me company, and I like it just fine, being alone. It's even better in the winter, during a storm, when the snow piles up outside and no cars come by at all. Inside the bakery it's warm and there's plenty to keep my hands busy. Times like that, for all I can tell I'm the only person left on earth. I could go on making pies and watching the snow pile up until the end of time, so long as there was enough coffee on hand. I don't need company like some people seem to.

Which is why I get tired of it sometimes, listening to the guys at the warehouse. They always talk about what they would've done and been if this thing or that thing had turned out different. As if the wives and babies and mortgages are all accidents that just happened to them. They talk just to hear themselves, to fill the long hours of lifting and sorting, hours that in my opinion would be better spent in silence if you don't really have anything to say. They trade stories about all the carousing and hell-raising they did as kids, and really it's pretty unremarkable stuff—mailbox base-ball, drinking their father's scotch and jumping out second-story windows into snowbanks, that sort of thing—but they tell it like they were arch-criminals, like everyone should be as impressed as they are. This is the talk that leads into the should've-could've stuff I mentioned a minute ago—look at the way we used to be, how did we become the way we are now?

Because you're grown men, I'd like to say. Act like it.

There are things I could tell them that would really blow their hair back, if I wanted to. They were all of them 4-F—flat-footed, hard of hearing, whatever excuse they could come up with—or else too young, so I'm the only one who served. I could tell them about the times I had, fun and not so fun both, if I was inclined to talk about the past. Which I am not.

But I have to listen to them talk, because I am there and they are there and none of us is leaving anytime soon. To hear them tell it they all were just one good break away from being something much more than warehouse loaders. Dan Coyne is the worst—he goes on and on about the year he spent waiting on tables in Fort Myers, how much money he made, how you can follow the season north to ritzy summer communities like the Hamptons and make enough money to have a house in both places, just keep bouncing back and forth, getting rich off rich people, and never see a lick of snow.

Sounds terrific, but the obvious question is, if it was so great, why did he stop doing it? It would be a mistake to ask this question. I know, because I did once, wanting to be polite. I had to listen to him talk about how he met a girl and she got pregnant and he brought her back here to Maine because this was home after all and they got married because that was the right thing to do but if he'd just wrapped it up he'd still be living the high life but don't get him wrong he loves his family very much, just look at what he puts up with every day in this shithole, if that's not proof he loves them then what the hell could be. He's probably right, it does prove he loves them, but to my mind it also proves he's a coward with little imagination who doesn't think before he acts. Otherwise he'd have had the good sense to realize he didn't want a family, and the discipline not to start one.

People make mistakes, of course, drink too much, say things they don't mean, spend money they don't have, start a family without planning to. I've done all these things, give or take, myself. Maybe what really bothers me is that guys like Dan never own up to their mistakes, never accept their lives as they are today, with all the accumulated blunders that brought them to this place and time. In some fundamental way they are not really *here*. They're in a past that never really existed, or a future that never will exist, even while their bodies are in the present, in this warehouse, loading real packages onto real semis, with real wives and children at home, and very real opportunities for small but meaningful pleasures all around them. Pleasures that I enjoy, in my way, and never pass up. Holding Junior, even though he's five and a little big for that now. Smoking a cigarette and watching the sky outside the bakery go from black to pink to blue every morning. Brushing Debbie's hair. Falling asleep over the morning newspaper. Taking two days off, in the fall, to split wood with Rodney. These times are not lost on me. I am here.

I'm not saying I have no regrets. Who would believe anyone who said that? When someone claims to regret nothing I just assume that he and I have different definitions for the word, and leave it at that. For my part, I've got two. I just try not to think of them much. What's the point?

They're pretty big, as far as regrets go. First thing is, I passed on being a big-league ballplayer. I was picked out of high school by the Astros in the first round of the 1968 draft. Which being drafted isn't a guarantee of playing in the big leagues—most guys never make it out of the minors—but I would have. My senior year I batted .647 with 22 home runs and 65 RBI, second-best numbers in the country. People still talk about it. I was bigger, faster, and stronger than a lot of guys already in the majors, especially at third, where players tend to give up power for average. I mean today you've got someone like George Brett, he's a big strong guy at third, has some pop and looks like he might bat .400 this year for the first time since Williams did it, but two things: I was bigger than Brett, and this is 1968 I'm talking about. Six-foot-five, 240, hit with power to all fields, could handle line drives to either side and throw to first—accurately—on the run. There wasn't anyone but me who could do all that back then.

I never gave myself a chance to prove it, though. When I got the telegram from the Astros I didn't know what to do. It wasn't a surprise; I knew I'd be drafted, but now it was real and I had to make a real decision. I sat on my bed in the room I shared with my four brothers. I read the telegram a few times to savor the moment, then put on my pea coat and marched through the rain to the military induction station before I had a chance to change my mind. I signed paperwork, gave blood, told them I wasn't queer or crazy, stripped down and spread my cheeks, took an oath, and that was that.

There were a couple of simple reasons, and I didn't agonize over them much. Every man in my family for three generations had served. My great-grandfather, a Canadian citizen, fought with the British First Battalion in the Boer War. My grandfather joined the French Foreign Legion and was killed at Verdun before the U.S. even entered WWI. And at Guadalcanal my father gained eight pounds, in the form of shrapnel, and lost a dozen friends. So there was the legacy thing. But where for rich people a legacy means you're expected to be the third generation at Harvard, around here a legacy means that if there's a war on you're expected to strap on your jungle boots and go get shot at.

Then there was my old man, the second and more compelling reason I passed on baseball. He considered it a boy's game, not a profession, and what he said went even though I was a grown man. So after graduation in June, I belonged to the Marines instead of the Astros.

And that leads direct to my other regret: it didn't have to be an either/or proposition. I could have served my four years and still been young enough to play ball. I may have had to spend a season in the Cape Cod League getting my swing back, but then it would have been like I'd never left. Except that when I got back from Vietnam a good part of my right hand was gone, and along with it any hope I had of playing baseball again.

It's not the missing fingers that I regret so much as the way I lost them, about which I'll only say that I was stupid and deserved what I got and if I can ever think of a way to confess and ask for forgiveness I will do that. And until then I will hate myself a little bit and work hard every day to be a good man. This is about all that has stuck with me from my Catholic childhood—do your job, live clean, be the best man you can—and it seems to be enough.

But it is not easy, being a good husband and father. The hard part is the worry. The work and the bills, not sleeping, those things are easy. It's the worry, and what I do with it, that gets to me sometimes.

Take Rodney, for instance, my oldest boy. There's a lot to worry about there, and Debbie doesn't seem to notice. She's preoccupied with Junior, who's had some health problems but seems to be better the last year or so. Sure, he's grown into sort of a glum kid, but it's not like he has a bad attitude or gets into trouble. He's polite and well behaved. Keeps to himself, doesn't have any friends. Reads a lot, which I guess as a parent you can't really complain about. He's really into computers, has this thing from Radio Shack that we scraped together the money to buy him for Christmas. He likes to write little programs for it. He showed me one the other day where the screen turned half-blue and half-green, like the earth and sky, and then a little bug-looking thing ran across from one side to the other. It's pretty amazing, actually, this five-year-old kid teaching himself how to program a computer. So he's smart, obviously. Which may be part of the reason why he's quiet, a loner. We went to see his teacher, Mrs. Collins, and she said that sometimes smart kids have a hard time in the lower grades because they're so far ahead of their classmates. Not to worry, she said, but Debbie worried anyway, out loud, and when Mrs. Collins said we should think about skipping Junior ahead a few grades Debbie put a stop to that idea quick enough.

At some point Debbie went to the bathroom. When she was out of earshot Mrs. Collins told me she was concerned about Junior, too. He's very morbid, she said, it's strange, I don't really know how to explain it except to say he seems preoccupied with *apocalypse*. That's how she said it, emphasizing the word. I know it sounds odd, she said. I didn't want to mention it in front of your wife for fear she would become upset. But it seems to be on his mind constantly. During art activities he draws these pictures. Just a couple of weeks ago I found Junior sitting by himself against the fence on the playground. He was staring out toward the hills on the other side of the valley. I asked him if something was wrong, and do you know what he said? He kept staring at the hills and the sky and said, It's so big, the world is so big, how can it be obliterated?

Mrs. Collins was quiet for a second, just looking at me, and then she gave this nervous laugh and said, Normally we'd be happy, not to mention a bit surprised, to hear a first-grader use a word like "obliterated" in the proper context. But surely, Mr. Thibodeau, you can see why this is troubling?

And I told her, Yes, I can.

All the trouble and tension in the world, she said. The Soviets in Afghanistan. Reagan's saber-rattling. Kids pick up on it more than we realize. They may not understand it fully, but it works its way into their subconscious.

It was at this point that I suspected we were talking less about my son and more about Mrs. Collins's politics. I could tell, from what she said and how she said it, the flower-print dress and the gentle way she moved her hands, that she'd probably been a war protester. I stopped listening to her. The point had been made, after all.

So yes I worry about Junior. I want him to be happy, goes without saying. But it's Rodney. Something is wrong. Debbie doesn't see it, and I'm not around enough to do anything. Even if I spent less time working, Rodney's twelve and isn't home a whole lot. He's either at school or at his uncle's or out with his buddies from the neighborhood, these two little hoods I don't like much, Kevin and Jesse are their names. There are a couple others whose names I haven't gotten yet, but I can tell they're trouble too. Long stringy hair, jeans ripped at the knees. Ride their BMX bikes like they think they're Harleys. They draw pictures of skulls on the back of their denim jackets with Magic Markers. Rodney did it, too. We spent thirty bucks on that jacket, because he wanted it so bad, and then he turns around a week later and writes *Iron Maiden* on the back. At first I was pissed, but I didn't say anything. It was his jacket and he could look like a clown if he wanted. I'm careful not to be too much like my old man. I don't have to control everything. Besides, once they reach an age, kids can only learn these lessons on their own.

So that's one of the more obvious signs that something's up with Rodney, the boys he hangs around with. Pete, the kid down the road on the corner, he and Rodney were best friends for years, but Pete's out of the picture at this point. Has been for a while, actually, when I think about it. Just looking at them now, Rodney and Pete, you can see the reason why. Pete's hair is still cut in the flattop he's had since he and Rodney first met. He plays basketball nonstop on the courts down the block, even in winter, and doesn't own a denim jacket that I've seen. Kids grow apart. I myself went through three or four different sets of friends from when I was a boy until I graduated from high school. Still, different as they are now, I wish the two of them could have found a way to stay close. Rodney could use a good influence.

Any event, it's not so much what Rodney's doing that bothers me. It's what he's stopped doing. No more baseball. He quit a week into the last Little League season, said he didn't want to be seen in the uniform. This is a kid who just a couple of years ago would shag fly balls for hours, until it was so dark out that it was either call it quits or take one in the face, which he did more than once. This could be a tragedy, because the kid's even better than I was at his age. A tragedy. I don't use the word lightly. And not only has he quit the game, he's stopped collecting the cards. For years we gave him an allowance of three dollars in exchange for doing any combination of the dishes or the laundry five times in a week. Until this year he always used the money to buy baseball cards. Not GI Joes, not candy cigarettes, not music tapes. Baseball cards. Always. He must have had ten thousand cards or more, all packed into cardboard boxes, collecting value in the basement. Or so I thought. Until the other day, when I took a couple hours off from the warehouse to finish putting up some paneling in Junior's room. I needed a new blade for the jigsaw, so I went down into the basement and saw all the cards were gone. They used to take up a whole corner, and now there was just this big dark stain where moisture had seeped into the broken concrete.

I'm usually not the smartest guy in the room, but even I can figure out something's wrong here. The kid goes from baseball being his world to dropping the sport almost overnight, then sells off a card collection he spent half his life putting together? There's an issue, and I wish I didn't know what it was, but I'm starting to get an idea.

I decided to ask him about it that afternoon, real casual, no big deal, hey Rodney what happened to all your baseball cards? He was on the sofa in the living room, watching TV before dinner, and his eyes got all big when I asked him. Which could be interpreted as him feeling guilty about something, except that both the boys react this way whenever I talk to them, always look like they're thinking about making a run for it. Rodney says, What do you mean, and I say, Come on, you know what I'm talking about, and he thinks for a minute, I can see him thinking up an answer, and then he tells me he sold the cards to get money for the jean jacket.

And I say, We bought you a jean jacket.

This was before, he says.

Okay, I say, what happened to the money then? I don't like talking to him like this. It reminds me of how my old man used to grill me, the way he'd poke one finger into the side of my neck and it would hurt like hell for three days afterward. But I'm not poking Rodney, and I'm not drunk. I know what's going on here, and it's my job to deal with it even if it makes me uncomfortable.

Rodney doesn't say anything.

That must have been six, seven hundred dollars' worth of cards, I say. The Yastrzemski rookie alone was worth at least fifty.

Still he doesn't speak, just sits there with the gears turning behind his eyes. His pupils are huge.

So, I say. I'm trying to keep an even tone, but the truth is I'm a little irritated at his playing dumb, because he's caught. He knows it, I know it, and I'm not one for games. Where's the money.

And I guess he can't come up with any suitable lies, because he says, It's my money. What I do with it is my business.

At first this sets me off. I feel the old anger rising in me, it's like I can hear it go *POP* in my head, and I clench my good left hand against it to give myself time to think. In a way he's right—he bought the cards with money he earned, so any money he gets from selling the cards belongs to him. No argument there. My hand relaxes some. But as far as the not being my business thing. Well.

I'm your father, kid, I tell him. Everything is my business.

And then Rodney does something that catches me off-guard. I'm expecting he'll just out with it now, he's caught and cornered and there's no way out, but instead he suddenly gets really angry and puffs himself up and starts yelling about how he's not a little boy anymore and he needs independence and privacy and how do we expect him to be trustworthy if we don't trust him. All the while as he's saying this he's walking away toward his room. And I'm so surprised that it's not until he's already slammed the door behind him that I realize: the whole thing was just a way for him to escape without having to answer my question. And it worked to a T.

But if he thinks this is the end of it, he's wrong. I know what's going on here, and I'm not about to pretend otherwise. So tomorrow, during the time between shifts when I'd normally be sleeping, I'm going to pay a visit to the boy's uncle.

Rodney left yesterday. Dad helped him pack his clothes and toothbrush and took him away. When I came home from school his bed was empty with the sheets and blankets all piled at the foot, just like he'd left them when he got up that morning. It will stay that way unless I make it. I'm not sure I want to make it, though. I look at the messy bed with the Red Sox logo on the sheets, then I try to picture it made up nice and neat, and I can't decide which is worse. Two of his dresser drawers are still open, just sitting there open and empty. That whole side of the room, all of a sudden, is haunted. I almost cried last night. But then before I went to bed, I marked an *X* on the Red Sox calendar like I do every day, and I thought about how in 29 years and 274 days everything will be gone anyway and so what does it matter that Rodney is a drug addict.

I think that way a lot. Except it's not really thinking so much as hearing someone else's voice in my head. Like last year when the baseball players went on strike and the season ended in June, I got really sad. But then the voice came in my head talking about how soon there will be no baseball at all, ever again. I know it's strange. I don't think it happens to anyone else. I went to the library and read through the *Diagnostic and Statistical Manual of Mental Disorders* (the woman at the desk looked at me funny when I asked her to take it down off the stack for me) and found that schizophrenia probably is the closest thing to what happens with me. But it's not exact. I always know what's real and what isn't. The voice doesn't tell me to do bad things. It's friendly and comforting and when I'm sad I listen to it. It doesn't really make me feel better. Just bad in a different way. But it usually keeps me from crying.

Ma and Dad don't know that I know why Rodney's gone. They think because I'm only seven I won't understand, but I do. The teachers at school want to skip me ahead to tenth grade. While the rest of the class works their times tables I'm in the corner by myself doing calculus and reading *Candide* and sort of understanding it. So yes I know what's going on with Rodney.

I knew before anyone else did.

It wasn't hard to figure out. Rodney and I share a bedroom. I noticed plenty. He was pretty careless. Maybe he thought I wouldn't rat him out, and he's right, I wouldn't. Or it's possible he just got sloppy; according to the *Diagnostic and Statistical Manual of Mental Disorders*, addicts make fewer efforts to hide drug use as their addictions worsen. Whatever the reason, he was careless around me. It was inevitable that I'd find things. He hid discarded pieces of aluminum foil in his pillowcase; when it started to look lumpy he'd empty it out. The trash can was always full of bloody tissues from his nosebleeds. I knew he'd started carrying a razor blade in his mouth because he showed it to me, and the callus that had formed between his cheek and gum. He said he kept the blade there for protection, which worried me at first, because what kind of trouble was he in that he needed to protect himself? But then I read about how razor blades are used to cut cocaine into powder and I realized he'd just been acting like a tough guy with the protection talk, trying to create an image of himself.

What I didn't know, until yesterday, is that when you're an addict that means you have to go away. It was just like any other morning. I got up and took a bath and was dressed and ready for school before Rodney even got out of bed. I was eating Kix at the kitchen table when he came in with his eyes still half-closed, rubbing the back of his head where his long hair had snarled up. He had on the same jeans he wears every day, and the same black boots, and one of four T-shirts he wears in rotation—this was the Motörhead: *Iron Fist* shirt. Rodney tore the sleeves off it a couple months ago to show off the tufts of brown hair that have sprouted under his arms. I could have teased him about showing off his pit hair, but it's not my way, besides which if I had teased him I would have gotten an Indian rug burn, or worse a Melvin, Rodney's favorite torture to inflict on me—basically a wedgie, but in the front, which hurts more than the traditional back-wedgie. And even though Ma would make him pay big for hurting me, and even though the world is going to end soon, I don't want a Melvin, and consequently I do not tease Rodney very often.

When Rodney staggered out of the bathroom with his hair pulled back in a ponytail and his jean jacket on, as far as I knew he was heading to school like me. I guess I should have known something was going on, because Dad was at home instead of at the bakery. I was surprised, when I came downstairs, to see him sitting at the table with a cup of coffee and a cigarette going in the ashtray with a long barrel of ash dangling from the end. If I'd really been paying attention I would have noticed this, the cigarette in the ashtray, because the only time Dad's cigarettes touch an ashtray is when he snuffs them out. Otherwise they're in his mouth the whole time he's smoking. He had something on his mind and had forgotten all about this cigarette, but for whatever reason I didn't notice at the time. It was only after I came home from school and Ma sat me down and told me Dad had taken Rodney away for a while and we should go to church and pray for him that I put it all together.

I go to church without complaining on Sundays because it makes Ma happy, and I participate in the process of first Communion for the same reason. But I don't know what to think of it. Is the voice in my head God? If it's the God I've been taught, the God of Christianity, then some things don't add up. Like the comet—is it Armageddon? Can't be. Not the Armageddon we read about in CCD. Because even though there is a reference in Revelation to "a great mountain, burning with fire . . . cast into the sea"— which sounds a lot like what the voice described to me—in the next chapter, after the great burning mountain, an army of 200 million men appears. According to what I've been told, there won't be any men left after the comet hits, let alone 200 million. So someone somewhere has got their facts mixed up. And so far the voice has known a lot more about what's going on in the world than Father Robideaux and Sister Bernadette and the others. All they talk about is mysterious ways, and the evidence of things unseen.

Which is not to say I don't like being at church. I do. Except for the part during Mass when we have to turn to the people around us and offer them blessings of peace. The men you shake their hands and the women you hug. If I'm unlucky enough to be sitting near one of the old French ladies with cat hair on their nylons they kiss my cheek and they usually don't smell very good. I can feel the wet lipstick mark they leave behind. That I don't like at all. But being in the church itself is pleasant, especially during weekdays when there are no services, like yesterday when I went in with Ma to pray for Rodney. It's dark and cool and quiet and always smells faintly of the spicy smoke from the censers. The rows of pews are set in a semicircle, radiating out like spokes from the hub of the chancel. One of my favorite features is the ceiling, which rises on huge wooden beams from the outer edge of the church to its highest point directly over the pulpit. I read that this sort of design improves acoustics, and the way it rises gradually from where you enter to the point above the pulpit gives the sense that the energy of the congregation, or of even just a single person praying, is being gathered and channeled right up through the ceiling and into heaven. That's what I was thinking about when I knelt in the pew next to my Ma. I thought about how I hope that Rodney will be okay, and I tried to channel those thoughts up to the high point of the ceiling and out to whoever might be listening. That's the best I can do as far as praying. I hoped, too, that I would hear the voice again soon and maybe it could tell me what's going to happen with Rodney. Whenever it tells me about the future, things always happen exactly the way they're described. That's how I know that what it says about the end of the world is true. That's how I know how Dad lost his fingers, the prostitute and her baby and how they died. That's how I knew for sure that Rodney was a drug addict. That's how I know what Dad did to Uncle Rodney when he found out my brother Rodney was a drug addict. There are so many things I know but can't say.

When I was done focusing my thoughts up toward the ceiling I just sat there enjoying the half-light and the quiet of the church. After a while I got bored staring at the big statue of Jesus on the cross that hangs over the lectern, and I stole a glance at my ma. If she'd opened her eyes and seen me looking at her instead of praying she would have been mad, but she was praying too fervently to notice me. Normally when I look at my ma I see my ma. But at that moment she could have been a stranger. She had her eyes shut tight and her hands clasped together in one big fist under her chin, the beads of her rosary strung between her fingers. Her lips moved, and I could hear the whisper of her breath going in and out, but I couldn't make out the words. She was repeating the same prayer. I concentrated on the cadence and recognized, after a couple of repetitions, that it was the Act of Contrition—"O my God, I am heartily sorry for having offended thee"—over and over, quicker each time, and her chin began to tremble and tears seeped between her eyelids and moved down her cheeks. For that moment, in my mind, she became a stranger, just a frightened, pious woman come to church on a Wednesday afternoon to beg for deliverance. It was one of those moments when you see someone you know as if for the first time. I don't know how to explain it, but it was one of the scariest moments in my life. And this time the voice offered nothing to help me feel bad in a different way, and I started to cry, too.

I tried to keep quiet but that only made it worse and I began to sob, like a baby. My mother heard me and opened her eyes. She leaned toward me until our shoulders were touching.

"Don't cry, babe," she said. "Rodney will be okay."

Of course I was crying for her, not Rodney. But I couldn't tell her that. It was just another thing I couldn't say. I put my face in the rough knit of her sweater and breathed her perfume and the bitter smell of that morning's coffee, and then she was my ma again.

We sat like that for I don't know how long, seconds or minutes or it could have even been half an hour, though it probably wasn't that long because I would have noticed a difference in the angle of the sunlight coming through the stained glass. When the crying stopped our breathing slowed. I could hear my mother's heartbeat through her ribs, and this gave me a strong sense of déjà vu that I could not place. But then suddenly she gripped me by the upper arms and shoved me back at arm's length and held me there. Her fingers pressed into my biceps and her eyes, though still full of tears, were firm on mine. I had seen her this way with Rodney many times, but never with me.

"Now you see what happens," she said, "when you act like Rodney does. He's proud, and that being proud has made us all sad. Him most of all. Do you understand, babe?"

I nodded.

"It's okay," she said. "If he lets go of his pride, Jesus will take care of him. But if not. He will be sad and sick for all of his life. There's nothing any of us can do. We can pray for him, but that's it."

"I understand, Ma."

She pulled me close again. "I know you do," she said, hugging me. "You always have."

"Yes, Ma," I tried to say, but she held my head against her chest and the words came out garbled. It felt like I was suffocating. I tried to pull my face away, to get a breath of the cool air inside the church, but she held tight and all I got, over and over, was my own hot moist recycled breath, trapped in the weave of her sweater.

Rodney

Uncle Rodney comes to the Adolescent Recovery Unit to see me today. First thing I say to him is what happened to your nose, because it's all stitched up on both sides like it had to be sewed back on his face, but he says Nevermind it doesn't matter how it happened, I deserved it and anyway it'll be fine, but really what's important is how *you're* doing, he says to me. It's my fifth day at the Adolescent Recovery Unit and I'm not doing so good. I threw up during group the second night, and the muscles in my legs feel like someone's been punching them. They hurt so bad I checked them to see if they were bruised even though I haven't run into anything. The other night I got up and went to Phil the night nurse and told him how bad my legs hurt and he said there's nothing I can do Rodney you're not to have so much as an aspirin. And the next day Rosemary my caseworker said you're old enough to hear this Rod, taking drugs is how you deal with every kind of pain and you need to learn how to accept and work through pain without the help of drugs. But having said that, she said, if it gets really unbearable we'll see what we can do. Is it unbearable? she asked, and I had to shake my head no, because it's really not and the idea here is total honesty and after five days of being locked in here and at night not sleeping because I'm so sick I just want to do whatever I have to to get out of this. The kids who are here for drinking get all the drugs they want because the counselors and nurses say alcohol withdrawal is the only kind that can kill you, so it has to be managed medically, is what they say. But the narco kids like me and Rheal Roy, the kid from Benton who's hooked on heroin and sits in group with his head down and long things of snot hanging from his nose like he's six instead of sixteen, we get nothing.

I tell Uncle Rodney all this. We're in the dayroom and he's sitting on one of the plastic chairs they keep stacked against the wall and take down twice a day for group. The chairs get really uncomfortable after like five minutes but group lasts at least an hour, longer if there's a new kid on the unit having his first group, and there usually is. Uncle Rodney doesn't seem to notice how uncomfortable the chair is, though. He's leaning forward toward me with his elbows on his knees, and while he listens he keeps touching his nose with the tips of his fingers like he's checking to make sure it's still there. It's sort of the color of an old steak, and even though it's stitched on it looks like it might just fall off onto the floor pretty much any minute now. If my nose looked like that I'd be touching it too.

I'm glad Uncle Rodney's here. I thought when he found out he'd be mad like my dad was, especially since he must have figured out that I've been pinching off his stash for years. But as I'm telling him about me spitting in the toilet at night and how Rheal's whole body shakes all the time which makes the snot hanging from his nose swing around and stick to his cheeks, my voice goes up like a girl's and it gets hard to breathe. But I try to hold it in because men don't cry and Dad said if I'm going to get through this I've got to grow up and be a man. Uncle Rodney puts his hand on my arm and rubs it and tries to smile but has a hard time smiling because of the nose thing.

Easy kiddo, he says. I know. Take it easy.

And when he takes his hand away I notice that it's shaking, and I wipe my eyes and look closer and see that both his hands are shaking and there's sweat on his forehead and he's licking his lips a lot. Also he's got a paper bracelet like the one they put on my wrist when I got here.

Uncle Rodney sees me looking at his wrist and says Yeah you got me. I'm just a few floors up, on the adult unit.

This doesn't make sense because Uncle Rodney doesn't have a problem like me. I don't know what to say.

Uncle Rodney says Yeah well I figured I was here getting my nose fixed anyway. He laughs, but I don't laugh with him because I don't know what's funny. Hey, he says, if you want me to take you to that Red Sox–Royals series you've got to get better first, and I can't rightly expect you to get better when I'm setting such a shitty example myself, right?

He smiles that tight-pain smile again. I still don't say anything. Him mentioning the game we're supposed to go to gets me thinking about the only game I went to at Fenway Park with Dad, when we sat in the right field roof box and how the stairs were so steep going down to the seats that every step felt like falling. How I'd never seen anything so big and green and the way the sun shined down over the left field wall. How the hot dog guy came by yelling Yo Hot dogs! and Dad ordered two for each of us and we ate and I shared a napkin with Junior and I dropped one of my hot dogs when some guy bumped me after Freddy Lynn hit a home run, and how Dad said to the guy Hey watch it scooter, and the guy said something back, and Dad stood up and looked at him and then the guy shut his mouth and drank his beer. It makes me want to cry, thinking about that. Everything makes me want to cry in this place.

Uncle Rodney's smile goes away. But really, he says, you know I was thinking about you and how I don't have any kids of my own and you know I think of you like my son, Rod. If I hadn't been so fucked up myself I might have seen something was wrong with you. There are other things, too, other reasons I'm here. I've hurt a lot of people and it's time for me to start behaving like an adult, finally. You've made me see that. You can take the credit.

I feel like there's something I should say but I still don't know what it is. Looking at Uncle Rodney as he's talking is sort of uncomfortable, especially when he stops talking and looks at me like there's something I should say. So I look away from him, around the dayroom. On one side is the counter and sink and the refrigerator with the sign on the door that says NO CAFFEINATED BEVERAGES ALLOWED. On the other side Gary Nale is watching TV, and Woodworth (Call Me Woody) Evans is playing checkers with the occupational therapist, whose name I can't remember. It looks like a game of checkers but what it actually is is a way for the therapist to test how Woody's brain is doing.

Shit, kid, I don't know why I'm laying all this on you, Uncle Rodney says. Telling you all about my problems when you're stuck in here. He leans back in his chair and touches his nose again. I guess we've just always been more like friends—I mean I never felt like much of an authority figure or anything. When I was your age I'd go around the bars with my old man and shine shoes, finish people's drinks, pick a pocket every once in a while. We were more like buddies than father and son. Partners in crime. I guess that's how I've always felt about you. So I need to keep reminding myself that you're a kid and there are certain things I can't just out and say.

Uncle Rodney leans forward again, and his voice gets all low. But there is something I think I should tell you, he says. I don't know if you're ready to hear it, but with everything that's going on I feel like you should know.

Across the room Woody uses a king to take the occupational therapist's last checker. He raises his arms and celebrates as she writes in a notebook. I guess he doesn't realize that they try to let you win.

It's about your ma, Uncle Rodney says. Hey, listen to me. Are you listening?

I look back at him. Yes.

She's a great woman, Uncle Rodney says. I want you to understand that. I'm not saying she's a bad person. Obviously we live different lives. I've never really been into the God thing, but that's fine, she's my sister and I love her. And she loves you very much, too, kid. But you know, she's human, and she's got a problem, and considering where you and me are we definitely can't be judging her for it, but you need to know.

Until now I've just been sitting here waiting and listening but now suddenly something clicks and I think I know what Uncle Rodney's going to say and I don't want to hear. I thought I was grown up and tough but it's only taken five days for me to know I'm not and I don't think I can handle this. But still I don't say anything.

See the thing is, Uncle Rodney says, your ma is a drunk. An alcoholic, I mean.

I look at him.

I know it's hard to believe. But think how good you were at hiding it. No one knew, right? You were using every day and no one knew. Well your ma's the same way. She drinks vodka so no one can smell it, just like our ma, your *mémère*, used to do. It's not too hard to hide it if you want to, is it kiddo?

And I want to tell Uncle Rodney, No, you're wrong, don't talk about my ma that way. I want to tell him to fuck off and get the fuck out of here and don't ever talk to me again. But he's my uncle, my godfather, and I'm not supposed to be willful because that's what got me stuck in this place to begin with. Here the adults talk and I listen. That's how it works if I want to go home. It started with Dad. He said You're going to the hospital, and I listened. Then with Rosemary, who said No more, Rodney knows everything, you work the program and you'll be fine. I listened. Claire, the day attendant, who told me no one is allowed to have forks or knives and you can eat everything with a spork that you can with a fork, and though that isn't really true I listened and didn't argue.

But this is different. It's hard not to say anything. I love Uncle Rodney and I'm really glad to see him because I'm lonely here but who does he think he is? What does he know? He doesn't live with my ma. He doesn't see her every day. Just because his family was all fucked up when he was a kid doesn't mean my family is. Even if it is true, why does he think I need to know? I can't do anything about it. It doesn't make me feel better about where I'm at.

Uncle Rodney's sitting there watching me, waiting for me to say something, and I want to stand up and say these things and punch him in his dead nose. Knock it right off his face. But I can't, if I want to get better and go home and see my friends and play ball again. If I want to go to Fenway and cut wood and hunt turkeys with my dad again, I can't.

So I don't. I don't say anything. Uncle Rodney goes on talking and I just kind of make these noises, not saying Yes you're right or No you're wrong, just little noises so he thinks I'm listening. What I'm really doing is wishing he would leave. Every minute he's still here I get more and more upset.

Uncle Rodney keeps talking but it's all blending together, the only thing that I can make out is every once and a while he says Your ma. It sounds like blah blah blah Your ma blah blah blah blah Your ma. I don't know why that's all I can hear, but I'm starting to feel weird now and all I want is to see my ma, more than I ever have in my life. My legs are hurting me real bad and I'm getting a feeling between my eyes that's not good at all. I can hear my heart beat in my ears. The light through the windows is weird, like it's bent or something. And I keep thinking I want my ma, that's all I think over and over and it's kind of embarrassing because it's not like I'm four years old, besides which it never mattered to me much before whether or not she was around. But now that's all I want, I have to admit it even though it's embarrassing because it's about honesty here, I want my ma and I don't care. Then the light starts to go away and I hear Uncle Rodney say Hey somebody help us over here and then it's nothing and when the light comes back it isn't bent anymore, it's normal like light has always been. What's different is me, my brain isn't working right somehow and nothing makes any sense. Uncle Rodney is gone and my ma is here, sitting next to me with her hand on my face, and I see that somehow I'm in a bed all of a sudden, with a tube in my arm and wires stuck on me, and there are a couple machines beeping and with things on their screens that look like the graphs we did in math class in school. For a minute I think maybe they lied to me because like I says they told me the only withdrawal that can kill you is alcohol but here I am with all these tubes and wires and machines and it looks to me like maybe I almost died. I should be scared, but I'm not. I feel really mellow and it's something to do with Ma's hand nice and cool on my face, and her voice. She's talking to God like she does, asking him to help me and I'm sure there's no way he could say no to her. For the first time since I got here I don't want any drugs at all. I listen to Ma praying and I know what Uncle Rodney said isn't true. And I know I'm going to be okay.

Love

71 At this stage in your life, just short of adolescence, the Polish army of your emotional self has fallen to the Nazi war machine of your intellect, and your relationships with most people, even your brother and parents, are cool and slight though not entirely without love. This is as you prefer it. You've developed an aversion to physical affection, and the people in your life are aware of this aversion, and respect it, even your mother, whose proclivity for PDAs is legend and has only gotten worse over the past few years, growing in direct proportion to the drinking she thinks no one knows about. Now she merely transfers your share of hugs, kisses, and clothes-fiddling to your brother, a double-duty he does not find the least bit oppressive, even though at fifteen he's reached an age when most normal boys shy away from physical affection from their parents. Rodney, of course, has not been normal for quite some time, and he bears your mother's attentions with the same dazed good humor that has been the hallmark of his personality since his "episode" in rehab. The doctors have all along referred to Rodney's brain injury as an "episode" or "incident" because, quite simply, they never could figure out exactly what went wrong. It will be a few years before scientists discover, through the use of the new ECAT 931 PET scanner, that prolonged cocaine use can cause permanent blood flow deficits to certain areas of the brain, even after the cocaine is removed. In Rodney's case these deficits were exacerbated catastrophically by a sudden spasm of several intracranial blood vessels, which damaged the portions of his brain responsible for attention, memory, concept formation, and mental flexibility. The episode, however, left him still quite functional in other ways, in particular on the ball field, and this in large part is what has the doctors puzzled. He has trouble remembering to put his pants on after his underwear, but can spray 97-mph fastballs to all fields effortlessly. His case is so unusual and baffling, in fact, that for a couple of years now your father has had

to rebuff, with increasing firmness, the overtures of research scientists determined to study Rodney.

You, meantime, are left to the solitary existence you prefer, a life beyond touch, wherein one eschews all physical contact to minimize the pain of inevitable loss. You move through your life like a ghost, semi-present, barely displacing air. When you sit at a desk in school it appears to observers that you're somehow resting not on the seat but rather just above it. Similarly, whenever you manipulate an object, such as taking an apple from the à la carte line or opening a bathroom door, the object seems to move without the benefit of any actual contact with your hand. The other kids think you're a Jedi or something. This sort of creepiness does nothing to improve your popularity, though it goes a long way toward discouraging the physical abuse that eggheads normally suffer, when early-onset puberty has enabled a small percentage of the boys to distinguish themselves with the first hints of biceps and body hair. These physically prodigious boys, for reasons only nature understands, are most often the least prodigious intellectually, and to compensate for this have a tendency to throw their weight around, so to speak. Except that in this case even the most ambitious bullies at the junior high want nothing to do with you, and venture little more than insults hurled across crowded between-period hallways.

It might surprise you to learn you're not much more popular among the teachers than the students. This becomes easier to understand when you consider that you're eight times as smart, exponentially, as the smartest among them, and moreover that they are keenly aware of this fact. Teachers are underpaid, and often do as much babysitting as teaching. They are expected to make a classroom of forty students behave, but the limits of their authority to do so are a joke, and are recognized as such by even the youngest troublemakers. The only thing they really have going for them is that they know more than their students. That's it. And when you take that away from them, whether you intend to or not, they're not going to like you very much. You have taken this away from the teachers at your school, and they do not like you very much, and they do not try very hard to pretend that they do.

70 Mrs. Harris, who in title is the Gifted and Talented teacher but who in actuality has sort of become your private tutor, is the exception. She's secure enough in her own intelligence not to be threatened by yours. And though she is not your equal in terms of raw smarts, she is sharp enough to recognize that you are still just a child. A strange, morose, prodigiously talented child, but a child nonetheless, requiring attention, encouragement, discipline. She provides all three.

It is not coincidence, then, that Mrs. Harris is and has been the object of your life's first crush. It helps that she is thin and boyish, a physical type you will find yourself drawn to your entire life. Her dark brown hair is cut in a short pageboy style she appreciates not because it is reminiscent of Audrey Hepburn, but for its practicality and ease of use. She has eyes like chocolate truffles, and is the only person you know with good teeth. She favors neutral-colored blouses that reveal almost no skin and long tweed skirts, the rough fabric of which sends little electric thrills through your body on those lucky days when it catches the fine hairs on your arm.

Trust us when we tell you that this heady, baffling cocktail of physical and emotional reactions is a crush. It is the reason you haven't yet decided to forgo school altogether. It is the reason your stomach hit the floor, as though filled with rolled coin, on the day Mr. Harris came in to drop off Mrs. Harris's lunch, forcing you to accept the actuality of his skinny, bespectacled existence. It is the reason that her image, always hers, comes to you on the nights you wait for Rodney to be asleep, so you can do to yourself that thing which you discovered by accident only a few weeks ago, when your underwear rubbed against you in a way that, if you were a cartoon character, would have produced a big shining lightbulb in the air above your head, that thing which feels so good that sometimes you're convinced you'll lose all control and pass out and wake facedown on the floor, with a sticky belly and your pajama bottoms around your ankles.

All of it—the whole sweaty sick-stomached mess—is attributable to crush.

69 The power of crush, though, daunting and impressive as it is, cannot hope to compare to that of love. You realize this, instantly and for all time, when Amy Benoit enters the G&T classroom on a Tuesday in January.

She is, at first glance, homely. Her hair has a violent natural curl exacerbated by the shortness of its cut, resulting in a dreadful rusty brown 'fro. Smatterings of pimples stand out on her cheeks and in the hollow beneath her bottom lip, the result of a premature and persistent tendency toward oily skin; for most of her early adolescence she will look as though she's taken a load of birdshot to the face. But there is something remarkable about her homeliness, or rather something remarkable *beneath* it, strong hints of genuine beauty waiting for an opportunity to emerge: her eyes, sea-glass green and simmering with intelligence; the precocious swell of her hips; her long, delicate hands, still elegant and appealing despite the fact that the nails have been gnawed to the quick. These are what you notice. These are the features that scream out to you the moment she walks through the door, a transfer from the Catholic school across town.

There's something intangible, too, one of those ineffable qualities that people who are truly in love most revere in their partners. It's the cool way her eyes take in the contents of the G&T classroom, the way she walks in without any of the self-consciousness usually displayed by someone entering a room full of people she's never met. She has a regal bearing, you think, but that's not quite right either, because there's no hint of arrogance in the way Amy comports herself. She's self-possessed, that's it. Absolutely self-possessed. She sets her bookbag on the floor and sits at the desk adjacent to yours. She looks up, and when her eyes settle on you, you feel like a bird that's just flown into a sliding glass door.

The two of you stare at each other for a long silent moment.

68 "Hi," she says finally, and like that you are done for, sunk, finished. This is love, and we don't need to explain the difference between love and crush, because you are now and forevermore fully aware of that difference, in both its vastness and its details.

67 It should be mentioned that you and Amy are not "soul mates," nor are you "meant for each other" or any other such romantic nonsense. At this moment, as you sit gawking at her, there are 4.9 billion people on the planet. One needn't be a statistician to surmise that there are tens of thousands of people with whom you could fall in love and live an equally happy life. Whom you take out a mortgage with is mostly an accident of geography and economics, and has nothing to do with destiny. Consider, for a moment, what might have happened if Amy's father hadn't recently bailed out on her mother and fled to the West Coast to drink in anonymity, thereby making private school financially impossible. The two of you could have easily lived and died in this town without ever having said hello. Not destiny. Happenstance.

66 Amy smiles, revealing teeth that came in perfectly straight without the aid of braces. "This is the part," she says, "where you say 'hi' back."

"Hi," you say, still too stunned, mercifully, to be embarrassed.

She laughs a little, not unkindly, and turns away as Mrs. Harris comes to her desk. The two of them talk quietly while you look on. When they've finished Mrs. Harris introduces Amy to the class and receives a half-dozen murmured hellos in return.

Mrs. Harris puts a hand on Amy's shoulder, smiles, and walks to the front of the classroom to resume hooking up the television. On loan from the A/V department in the library, the TV displays silent snow as Mrs. Harris struggles to attach the cable that runs in through the cinder-block wall beneath the chalkboard.

65 Normally you and Timothy Pitcairn are the only students in the G&T classroom at this time of day—the others are here just two periods a week—but today is special, which is why Mrs. Harris is setting up the television.

Amy looks to you again. You recognize the lilac scent coming off her hair, which is still damp from the shower, as White Rain shampoo, the same stuff your brother used on the long death-metal locks he sported before being transformed in rehab. White Rain is about the cheapest shampoo going, except maybe for Breck, and that is why your mother buys it.

You tense up under Amy's calm gaze, and for lack of anything else to say you tell her, "We're watching the *Challenger* launch today."

"I know. I think everyone in America is watching the *Challenger* launch today."

With a sense of relief you dive into a subject you can talk about at length. "Interest in space shuttle missions has been waning in recent years," you tell her, "just like interest in the Apollo program declined following the moon landing. So NASA created the Teacher in Space program. The end result of which is what you see here today. Or what you will see, as soon as Mrs. Harris gets that cable hooked up. The first civilian in space."

"It's exciting," Amy says. "Don't you think?"

"Somewhat," you say. "But really it's just a public relations gimmick."

Amy looks at you a moment. "You're a special one, aren't you?" she says.

"What do you mean?"

"Come on," she says. "This is exciting. The entire country has dropped what it's doing and sat down in front of the television. We're all watching the same thing at the same time. How cool."

This is not strictly true, because although NASA has arranged for live broadcast of the mission into schools, the rest of the country will be seeing the launch on slightly delayed replay. Years from now many will recall having watched live when, in point of fact, the only people to witness these events as they happen will be America's schoolchildren.

On the television an image flickers, then is replaced again by snow. Mrs. Harris, crouched behind the rolling cart, mutters to herself.

You watch as Timothy Pitcairn, who is retarded and easily bored, grows tired of waiting for the television to work and rises from his desk at the front of the class. He ambles up the aisle toward you and Amy. His face is perpetually ruddy, as though he's always just finished an especially vigorous jump rope session. His eyes bulge behind thick lenses.

Standing between you and Amy, Timothy asks her his favorite question of friends and strangers alike: would she like to see his pistol?

Amy leans around Timothy to look at you. You shake your head gravely—no, she most definitely would not like to see his pistol. She looks up and smiles and says sweetly, "No, I wouldn't. But thanks."

Still crouched behind the television, Mrs. Harris calls out: "Timothy, sit down please." Timothy laughs and makes an exaggerated sighing sound and does as he's told.

"I thought this was the Gifted and Talented class," Amy says, watching Timothy return to his desk.

"It is," you say. "But technically we're all special education. Just on opposite ends of the special spectrum. Really the thing is, Timothy's the only retarded kid in school, so they just throw him in with us. He and I are the only ones in here full-time."

"Why's that?" Amy asks.

"Because," you say, "regular classes don't work for either of us."

"I can hear the sound working," Mrs. Harris says. "Is there a picture, kids? Can you see anything?"

You can. On the screen is an image of the *Challenger*, brooding on the launch pad amidst plumes of gray steam on a cold morning in Cape Canaveral. It is 11:32 a.m., and Mrs. Harris has solved her technical difficulties just in time, as the *Challenger* will lift off in only six minutes.

The G&T students answer Mrs. Harris's question in the affirmative, and she emerges finally from behind the television cart, wiping her palms on the front of her skirt and peering at the screen. "Oh, perfect," she says. "Drew, if you could close the blinds, and I'll get the lights."

64 The room goes dark, and immediately you are more aware of Amy's presence, the scent of fabric softener on her clothes, the measure of her breath, even the heat from her body. You try to concentrate on the images on the television: a replay of the crew coming down the ramp, dressed in light-blue jumpsuits, smiling and waving to the assembled press; family and friends stiff with waiting and bundled against the cold, shielding their eyes from the sun as they gaze at the distant launch

assembly. Despite this drama and anticipation, you are unable to draw your attention fully away from Amy, and while you keep your eyes trained on the television all your other senses are fixed on her.

The sporadic murmuring in the classroom ceases as the launch countdown reaches T minus 15 and things begin to happen. Beneath the shuttle a curtain of white smoke drops to the launchpad and billows out as the public affairs officer announces T minus 10. The PAO, incidentally, was selected for this job not only because of his background in aeronautical engineering, but for his soothingly authoritative voice—no matter what he actually says, it always sounds like "Everything's just fine," especially to children.

Whoever is producing the broadcast switches cameras, and now you're looking at a close-up of the shuttle's business end, the engines and solid rocket boosters, beneath which a flood of sparks shoots out horizontally, the world's biggest pilot light. At T minus 6, fuel from the boosters hits these sparks and ignites in three distinct and massive orange fireballs. The fireballs soon narrow to white-hot cones of pure thrust, a physicist's wet dream, and you can see the shuttle strain upward against the hold-down bolts like an angry Doberman at the terminus of its leash. The PAO counts down: ". . . four, three, two, one . . ." The hold-down bolts fire and the shuttle clears the tower and rises terribly. In the classroom two or three of the students gasp loud enough to be heard over the television. "And liftoff," the PAO says, somewhat tentatively you think, and then, as the shuttle gains momentum, ". . . *lift*off," he says again, and this time you can hear the smile on his face, hear his heart swell with the courage of noble endeavor, and you, even you, find yourself moved by the spirit in his voice. Everyone claps and cheers. For a moment, as you watch the shuttle rise on a column of fire, you've forgotten about Amy.

She leans across the aisle, so close you can feel her breath in your ear. "You've got goose bumps," she whispers. "I told you this would be cool."

Your goose bumps develop goose bumps, and even though you're still staring at the screen you are now only half-seeing what's going on. As it arcs away from the launchpad the shuttle rolls 180 degrees, so that it is flying upside down. "Good roll program confirmed," the PAO says.

63 Mrs. Harris stands to the right of the first row of desks, watching along with the students. Her arms are folded across her modest chest, one slender hand grasping the opposite slender forearm, and her dark eyes shine in the light from the cathode ray tube. When she was a girl and her last name was Augden, she used to stay awake to watch the Apollo missions as they came fast and furious during 1968 and '69, one every few months, leading up to the first moon landing. Long after the public's collective attention had turned to other things, Mrs. Harris had watched and read and otherwise kept up on the program, because she'd resolved, after Apollo 8, that she was going to be the world's first female astronaut. Unfortunately for her, the America Mrs. Harris grew up in still indulgently patted the heads of little girls who said they wanted to be anything but housewives, despite the fact that by then the civil rights and women's liberation movements were in full swing. She'd applied to the Air Force Academy and been denied despite stellar grades, three varsity letters, and a recommendation from her congressman, who was a first-rate patter of little girls' heads but nonetheless willing to nominate her. Instead she'd gone to Hofstra to major in physics and minor in astronomy and had to watch as, only three years after she'd applied, the academy admitted its first female cadet. She realized, though, that even this girl wouldn't be allowed to pilot a jet, let alone go into space, and the Apollo program was over anyway, so Mrs. Harris had patted *herself* on the head and gotten her degree and her teaching certificate and married Mr. Harris.

Eight years later the Teacher in Space project was announced, and Mrs. Harris thanked God she'd put off having children and applied and chewed her fingers raw while she waited. Two months later she got a phone call asking her to come to Washington. A week after that she was asked to go to the Johnson Space Center in Texas, where they examined and interviewed her some more, and though she'd done her best, though she had just the right educational background and she'd been running six days a week even though they'd never instructed the candidates to exercise, she knew even before the decision was made that she wouldn't be the one. She predicted correctly that Sharon Christa McAuliffe would get the nod, and despite the fact that she believed Christa was chosen more for her ready smile and wholesome looks than her qualifications, Mrs. Harris wished her luck and hugged her in the cafeteria and returned home without resentment, grateful in fact to have seen the inner workings of the space program up close.

62 Still, it is hard, incredibly hard, harder than she had imagined, as she stands here watching the launch with you and the other students. In the darkness of the classroom she lets the tears come and allows herself to think words she would never say aloud, even if there weren't children around: *Goddammit that should have been me. I was so close.*

The rumble of the booster rockets fades as the shuttle hurtles away from the camera's microphone at a rate of 2,257 feet per second. The image of the shuttle moving silently through the sky takes on a surreal quality, is both peaceful and eerie all at once.

In addition to the PAO, you are able to hear exchanges between the Capsule Communicator and the shuttle commander, which consist basically of the CapCom saying something and the shuttle commander repeating it. For example, now: "*Challenger*, go at throttle up," the CapCom says, and the reply comes, "Roger, go at throttle up." The PAO says something about "Three engines now at one hundred four percent," which jolts you because the average sixth-grader knows that is a mathematical impossibility and you would hope to whatever god exists that so would the people at NASA.

Just after the throttle-up exchange the view shifts suddenly, from the distant aspect you've been watching the entire flight to a blurred, shaky close-up. This shot makes you feel like you suddenly need glasses. You can make out the shape of the shuttle, the white swoop of its tail tapering into the fuselage, and the shadows of the booster rockets on either side with novas blazing at their bases. But everything is sort of indistinct and trembling, the background sky suddenly darkened to the perpetual night of the upper atmosphere. You notice that one of the novas has gotten greedy and is flashing from the side of the booster rocket now, and you have just enough time to consider that this seems very wrong, when like some horrifying magic trick the shuttle disappears in a burst of flame and smoke.

61 This is one of those mercifully rare moments when the mind flat-out refuses to process the signals it is receiving, and so it's not that you can't believe what you're seeing, but that in a very real sense you're not actually seeing it. To add to the burgeoning sense of unreality, even as the cloud of smoke and debris that used to be the shuttle expands and begins the slow-motion descent back to Earth, the PAO continues to rattle off telemetry—distance, velocity, altitude—as if nothing has gone wrong. Finally he looks up from his computer screen and goes silent for long, long moments.

60 In actuality the shuttle has not exploded. Rather, it has been ripped apart by sudden intense aerodynamic forces far beyond its performance envelope. The booster rockets, however, are more sturdily constructed, and they fly wildly away from the initial breakup, still under their own power, tracing slow, chunky vapor trails like illiterate skywriters.

59 In the classroom nobody makes the slightest sound, or even moves, except for Mrs. Harris, whose right hand creeps slowly up through the air in front of her and comes to rest, palm-down, over her mouth.

Timothy Pitcairn is the first to break the silence. "They died!" he says. "Mrs. Harris! They died!" For a moment he is delighted at his powers of deduction, bouncing minutely in his seat and clapping his hands, but then, as suddenly as if he'd been shot, all the energy goes out of him and he sits still and stares into his lap.

That should have been me, Mrs. Harris is thinking. She is thinking about the son and daughter Christa gushed about, pictures shared over the cigarettes they'd smoked on the bench outside the space simulation lab. Virginia Slims, needle-thin cigarettes Christa had produced from her purse, laughing, saying, I don't even smoke, I don't know why I bought these things.

Sitting there watching the vapor trails spread across the sky like unraveling intestines, you all wait in desperate silence for the PAO to come back on and say something reassuring, assert some control over this mess, wrestle it down, make it behave. Why is he leaving you here in silence, you wonder. You feel Amy's palm slide down the back of your hand, and when her fingers interlace with yours and squeeze, you squeeze back. It is not nearly the thrill that it should be. It is bare comfort. And then, as the first pieces of the *Challenger* hit the water off Cape Canaveral, the PAO finally comes back on. Reluctantly, as though he's being prodded with the point of a blade, he utters what may be one of the biggest understatements of the twentieth century: "Obviously," he says, "a major malfunction."

John Sr.

Major league scouts don't wait long to start sniffing around young talent. Every once in a while I'd see one at Rodney's Legion games, but they were just snooping back then. None of them approached me, but I always knew they were there. You can spot them a mile off. Mirrored sunglasses, bald heads scorched from sitting in the sun all day, every day. Cheap dress pants, the bottoms gone shiny from rubbing against aluminum bleachers and jetliner seats. Usually they'll have something in their mouth, a toothpick or a pen cap, and be chewing the hell out of it, because most of them are old ballplayers who've been trying to kick tobacco for years. Any two of these things together is enough for me to think: *scout*. But then there's the really obvious stuff, too, like when one of them will get himself nice and comfortable in the bleachers, wolf down a hot dog from the Elks Club concession stand, wipe his hands on the front of his pants, then break out the notebooks and stopwatch and radar gun. When they make it that obvious, they want you to know they're there. Because they're getting serious at that point, and it's time to start talking business.

Rodney is not a head of cattle, but that's how most of these guys look at the boys they're scouting. To them a kid isn't a kid, but a commodity: an arm, a bat, a pair of legs. He's an equation, a set of statistics worth a certain amount of money and effort to sign. They've got it down to a science. But Rodney's game has blown their equations to hell. They fall all over themselves trying to convince me the team they represent is the best choice for him. They offer me money just to talk. No strings attached, no obligation, they say, holding out paper bags with cash inside. They ask me, What do you need? I tell them I need a lot, but I don't plan to take it from them. It's my boy you're going to pay, I say.

Sure, they say, laughing in a way that's supposed to make me feel like we're chums, sure, but the boy's only what, seventeen? As if they don't know how old he is to the very minute. What's a seventeen-year-old gonna do with the kind of money we're talking about?

We haven't talked about money, I say.

Well yeah of course but you know what I mean. Rodney's going to command a first-rate paycheck from somebody, and you know it. They wipe at their sunburned heads with handkerchiefs that are stained permanently yellow. Sometimes they clap me on the shoulder and I look at them in a way that makes clear we're not friends and they don't do it again.

I don't have anything against these guys. They've got a job to do, and based on the look of them they don't get paid very much to do it. I can relate. I try not to be an asshole but then again I don't lie awake at night worrying about whether or not they like me. I lie awake at night wondering if I do a good enough job protecting my son.

Because the truth is Rodney needs protecting, there's no two ways about it. I don't like to say anything bad about my boys, and I certainly like Rodney better now than before, but obviously since his brain injury he's not the sharpest knife in the drawer. He's so dopey that at first I thought maybe he was using again. That didn't add up, though, because he wasn't hanging with the jean-jacket crowd or cutting school. In fact he was, and still is, almost as dedicated to school as he is to church. Not that he does all that well, even in the program they've got for retarded kids, but obviously no one expects much from Rodney when it comes to the books. Besides, with his swing who cares if he struggles with simple arithmetic? He'll never be able to explain the physics of that swing, and he doesn't need to, because the results speak for themselves. From both sides of the plate, he's got the best swing since Ted Williams. And that's according to the man himself.

Williams took batting practice with Rodney's high school team this spring. I'd heard he came here a lot, liked to fish up north for brook trout and had a hunting camp around Moosehead, so he knows people in the area. Apparently Williams took a bear hunting trip with Sammy Bowdoin's father, who is a certified Maine guide. Sammy's one of the pitchers. And instead of having Williams pay for the trip, Sammy's dad asked him to take batting practice with the kids. Which Williams did. Just showed up one day and hooked his fingers through the fence and watched for about half an hour before anyone realized who he was.

So then once introductions were made and Williams signed a few bats and balls and caps and shirts, each of the kids had to stand in and take a dozen hacks with Williams behind them, watching with his arms folded across his chest. And just because Williams is old doesn't mean he's lost his eyesight or his fire. Each boy, before he got a chance to dig in, Williams asked him: What do you know about hitting? What he got in response, mostly, was wide-eyed silence. It's not a trick question, fellas, Williams said, shaking his head, after the fourth boy in a row said nothing. He wasn't here to make them feel good about themselves; he was here to teach them to hit. He got in there, yelling at the kids, using his hands to move their bodies into the position he wanted to see—hands *here,* feet *here.* Rotate your hips forward, *then* take your stride. Williams spit and threw up his hands and kicked the dirt. But he also clapped and patted backs and said Now *that's* how you do it! when they got it right. Which, according to Williams's standards, wasn't very often.

Then Rodney came to the plate, all elbows and knees and high socks, smiling that big goofy smile as if he wasn't just about to take cuts in front of the greatest hitter who ever lived. I mean, *I* was nervous—this is Ted Williams standing there, squinting in the sun with his hands on his hips. But Rodney just waltzes in like it's nothing. Bends over and picks up a handful of dirt, wipes it on his bat.

It's always just a game to him. He doesn't feel pressure. He doesn't even understand that others do. It's what makes him so good.

Williams could see this one was different—for one thing, the boy's knees weren't knocking together in terror—and he stood there a beat or two longer than he had with the other kids, sizing Rodney up and grinning. What do you know about hitting? he asked finally.

Rodney took a few lazy practice cuts, and even in these the difference between him and the other boys was obvious. I saw Williams noticed, too.

I know, Rodney said, that a level swing isn't parallel to the ground, it's in line with the trajectory of the ball.

So you've read my book, then. Williams laughed. Well, you get points for that, sure.

But Rodney shook his head. I don't read much, he said. My dad told me that. To my horror, Rodney pointed to where I was leaning against the wall of the home dugout. And then made it ten times worse by saying, He's the best hitter the state's ever seen.

Williams's eyes fixed on me. No kidding, he said, then hollered over to me, What do you say, Dad? Want to take a few hacks?

Love to, but I can't, I managed to say.

Why's that? Williams asked.

Missing part of my right hand, I said. Swing isn't what it used to be.

I'm just a big enough asshole, Williams said, to ask how you lost your hand without caring if it's rude or not.

Vietnam, I said. After a moment went by without either of us saying anything, Williams nodded and turned his attention back to Rodney. And Rodney proceeded to put on a show. He took his dozen pitches from the right side, then switched to the left when Williams didn't tell him to quit. Williams didn't tell him anything, in fact. He just stood there and watched. Pulled a toothpick from his pocket and stuck it in his mouth and gnawed on it. Didn't say a word.

Afterward he came up to me and said, That boy's got the best swing I've seen since Ted Williams. He laughed. I said, Thank you Mr. Williams. He said Call me Ted, and I said I'd really rather not, I'm not much for heroes but you are one of mine so if you don't mind too much. He clapped me on the back and said You call me whatever you like, that boy of yours is going to be a hell of a ballplayer. And it was one of the great moments of my life, walking with Ted Williams's arm around my shoulders, right up there with my boys being born.

As good as Rodney is on the field, you should see him off of it. He walks around in a fog. You have to say his name three times to get his attention, and don't bother saying anything other than his name until he's actually looking at you, because you'll be wasting your breath. He has no interest in girls, even though every other time the phone rings it's some missy from school asking for him. Whenever he sits still for more than two minutes he falls asleep, and half the time he doesn't seem to know the difference between day and night; he'll wake up at six p.m. and dress for school, and if we don't catch him before he hits the door he'll stand down at the bus stop for an hour, swinging the souvenir mini-bat he carries around, not noticing that he's the only kid there, or that it's getting dark. This has happened more than once.

So imagine letting Rodney go by himself to someplace like New York or Kansas City to play baseball. He wouldn't make it two days without wandering onto a subway track or showing up for practice at midnight. Once you get him to the park on time and in one piece, you can let him go and watch him do what he does better than just about anyone. But off the field, he needs someone to be there.

This is a problem, for obvious reasons. I already take too much time off from work so I can be at games and practices to run interference on the scouts; consequently we're robbing Peter more often than usual, and half the time Paul still doesn't get paid. Debbie can usually get the boy out of bed and make him breakfast, but beyond that she's not really worth much these days. Which I hate to say it. And I'm not blaming her; she's got a problem and isn't as good at hiding it as she once was. And yes sure when I come home from the bakery and the house is a mess and Junior's in the kitchen burning French toast because he's too busy on the phone with his little girlfriend, and Rodney's still in bed only two hours before he and I have to be at the airport, and I go into the bedroom and find a sobbing lump under the covers that's supposed to be my wife—yeah, I have to bite my tongue. Who wouldn't.

I know I am far from perfect. And it's not like I've done much to help her, even though what can you do when you ask someone over and over if you can help them with a problem and they keep saying what problem, what problem, I don't have any problem. I have no idea what to do with someone like that. So I bite my tongue and pick up the slack and hope she'll come to me when she's ready. In the meantime, I've got the boys to take care of. And now I have to hustle Rodney down to the airport in Portland and get on a plane to Chicago to talk to the Cubs GM, who wants to trade up for the first pick so he can draft my kid. Which of course means more time off work, another dent in the paycheck. But at least the Cubs are picking up the tab for the trip.

It's hot when we get off the plane at O'Hare. There's an early summer heat wave over the Midwest, and people are sweating and pissed off and won't get out of each other's way. Twice on the walk to baggage claim I have to sidestep to avoid running into someone marching in the other direction. It's a stupid reason to get mad, but I'm already on edge for reasons I can't quite put a finger on, and I decide that the next person who wants to play chicken is going to get knocked down. At baggage claim there's a black guy in a dark suit holding a sign with THIBODEAU printed on it, and he insists on taking our bags even though I tell him I've got it okay. He leads us to a Lincoln parked illegally in a fire zone. The driver opens the door for me and Rodney. Inside is soft and dark and almost cold, the AC is on so high. The driver loads the bags in the trunk and we're on our way.

I haven't been to Chicago since I flew back to the East Coast after being discharged from the Marines and spent a few days drinking my combat pay on the North Side, trying to get up the nerve to go home to Debbie and Rodney. From what I can see through the tinted windows not much has changed. I don't see a whole lot though, because the driver, whose name is Alonzo, stays off the surface streets and goes like hell, and before I know it we're in Wrigleyville. The place is packed with fans in blue jerseys and caps, herds of them coming out of the El and fouling up traffic. Alonzo picks his way slowly through the crowds, working the gas and brake like a pro. Rodney stares out the window, taking it all in with his usual slack-jawed expression. He looks fascinated and bored all at once.

Alonzo pulls up to the sidewalk in front of the players' entrance. He comes around to open the door for us, but we've already let ourselves out, so he leads us past two security guards at a riot barrier and knocks on a blue exterior door. The door has no doorknob on the outside. After a second it opens. An old man sticks his head out. Alonzo says What's shakin Lou, and Lou lets us inside. We walk past the clubhouse, which smells of disinfectant and isn't very impressive, just a long room with lockers on either side and a table in the middle, a couple of TVs hanging from the ceiling, a batting practice schedule posted on the wall. We go through the indoor batting cage, past the training room, where someone I think I recognize, maybe Jody Davis, is sitting with his leg in the Jacuzzi. We walk up a set of stairs, down a hallway with the 1945 NL pennant hanging on the wall, and into an elevator which we ride three floors to the top. When we step out it is into the air-conditioned owner's box, complete with red leather lounge chairs and a wet bar and the best view of any ballpark I've ever seen.

This is where I get off, Alonzo says.

Okay, I say to him. Thanks a lot.

The three of us stand there. Rodney's gawking at the field, where the Cubs are wrapping up their half of pregame batting practice. I keep expecting Alonzo to leave, but then I realize after a minute that he's waiting for a tip. The bartender looks away and starts wiping rocks glasses.

I don't have any money to give you, I say. It's the truth. I've got about a hundred bucks but I was hoping I wouldn't have to spend much of it, since it was set aside for a payment on Debbie's JCPenney card. I'm sorry, I say.

Alonzo just looks at me, then turns and walks away. I know he's thinking that someone who comes to Chicago on the owner's invite ought to have ten bucks to spare. I watch him go into the elevator and at first I'm embarrassed but it changes quickly to anger, like earlier at O'Hare. This is the way it's been with me lately. Every other minute I'm having to breathe deep and flex my hands. For months now, seems like.

It sounds stupid, but being angry all the time is making me angry.

Just then Dallas Green struts into the luxury box. Though we've never met in person I know it's him; he looks just like the arrogant prick I'd imagined when talking to him on the phone last week. I had a good idea then that I wouldn't like him. Now that I see him in the flesh, a peacock in a necktie, one of those big-personality types who holds his arms out wide as he approaches you, as if he's never been so happy to see anyone in his life and plans to give you the biggest hug in history pretty much the moment he gets there, I'm sure that I don't like him. I am tired, and embarrassed over Alonzo, and not in the mood. I'd rather Green just handed me a twenty to give to his driver, and me and my son would be on our way. But here we are, so when he gets close enough and sticks out his hand I shake it. To his credit, he doesn't give any sign of noticing that my hand mostly isn't there.

John, good to meet you, good to meet you. I'm Dallas Green.

Kind of figured that, I say.

And this must be our boy Rodney, he says, which I don't like, the our boy part. Not at all. He puts his hand out for Rodney to shake. Enjoying the view, son? Green asks, and I don't like that either, him calling Rodney son.

It's nice, Rodney says. Nice park. Bigger than Fenway.

Green's still got a grip on Rodney's hand, and he's pumping it so hard I think the boy's arm will come apart at the shoulder, but it doesn't seem to be bothering Rodney. Older, too, than Fenway, Green says, and while I know this isn't true, I can't tell if Green does or not. Can you picture yourself out there at shortstop? he asks Rodney. Take a good look down there, picture yourself crossing the bag, taking the throw from Ryne Sandberg, jumping over the slide, firing to first. Think of being part of the best fucking double play combination in the history of the major leagues.

Let's not get ahead of ourselves, I say to Green.

I don't think we are, Green says. He finally lets go of Rodney and turns that wooden nickel smile back to me. I'm able to guarantee that if Rodney comes to us, he will be part of the big league club next season. At shortstop. Guaranteed. And that's just one of many things I'm bringing to the table here.

Every team that's after him will have him on the major league roster next season, I say.

Maybe, Green says. Maybe. But at his position?

Most likely, I say.

Green makes his way over to the bar. Don't know about that, he says. If he goes to Cleveland they'll put him in the outfield. The Mets will want him at first base. Instead of actually asking for a drink, Green just slaps his hand on the wood countertop to get the bartender's attention. You want something? he asks me.

Thanks, no. I don't drink.

Rodney? Green says.

He doesn't either, I say. I give him a look to make sure he gets it.

Course not, Green says. He grabs his martini from the bartender's hand and walks back over to us. Rodney's a world-class athlete, after all. Body's a temple and all that. Plus of course there's the trouble he had as a younger man.

Which is no longer an issue, I say.

Green stirs his drink with the plastic pick. I don't doubt that, he says. But we still have to take it into consideration. Just like any other condition a prospective player might have. If for example we were considering a pitcher with a history of an irregular heartbeat, we would have to take that history into account. No matter how hard the kid throws, or how long it's been since his ticker skipped a beat.

I just told you, it's no longer as issue, I say. My left hand is starting to cramp up, trying to close into a fist. Rodney couldn't be any more different from how he was back then.

I'm sure he couldn't, by God, Green says. He takes a sip of the martini and motions for us to sit down. Just needed to mention it. Would be irresponsible of me not to.

Mr. Green, I say, I have to admit I'm already getting tired of this. It's been a long day and I'm missing work I can't afford to miss. So maybe you could just tell me why you asked us to come here.

Green sits in one of the leather chairs with his legs crossed at the knee. No special reason, he says. We usually ask top prospects to come and check out Wrigley, meet some of the guys, get a feel for the city. To see if they'd be a good fit.

Then I think we're wasting your time, I say. Because Rodney will not be a good fit with the Cubs.

Green smiles. C'mon, he says, you've been here ten fucking minutes and already you know he doesn't want to play here?

I knew before I got here, I say. I knew just from talking to you on the phone.

Green uncrosses his legs and sits forward in the chair. Then why in hell did you bother coming in the first place? he asks.

Because I knew you could trade up and draft Rodney anyway. So I thought I'd come and talk to you, try to convince you to pass.

So far you're doing a shitty job, Green says.

There's a challenge in his eyes that I'm more than happy to rise to. At this point I don't care much, I say.

I realize sort of distantly that both Green and I are hollering at this point. Rodney's looking at us like he's ready to dive under the sofa, and the bartender is cleaning the glasses for a third time, keeping his eyes carefully on his work.

Green puts his drink on an end table and stands up. If he had suspenders, he'd be pulling on them. I set my feet firm into the carpet.

I tell you what, Green says. How about I go ahead and draft him anyway, just to piss in your soup?

I would advise against that, I say.

Why? Green says. What the fuck can you do about it? Not a fucking thing.

Don't talk that way in front of my son.

Fuck you, Green says. You think you can come in here and intimidate me? Let me tell you something, Sasquatch—I run this team. I do what I want. Your boy goes into the draft, I trade up and take him if I want to.

Like I told you, I know that, I say. Which is why I'm asking you to pass. I don't want Rodney playing for you.

I brought you here as a courtesy, Green says. That's it. I don't consult with you, and you don't tell me how to run my organization. You can't do shit about shit.

I can break your weasel neck, I say. I can do that, I'm pretty sure.

Green steps closer. He's a head shorter and eighty pounds lighter than me, but I can see in his eyes that he's foolish enough to mean business. And I'm so angry I don't care how bad I hurt him.

You threatening me? Green says.

I don't say anything back. I'm finished talking. Instead I stand up and put my hand on Green's neck and squeeze. Something in his throat slides under my thumb, then pops and gives way. His face goes from angry red to desperate purple in just a few seconds. He windmills his arms, trying to knock my hand loose. But he's even weaker than he looks, and the blows do nothing to improve what is fast becoming a very bad situation for him.

It's Rodney who saves Green. Goofy, kindhearted Rodney. I'm not about to let go on my own. It doesn't even occur to me that I should, that Green will die if I don't. I'm just standing there feeling all the anger drain from me as Green's eyes flicker and wink out and his legs turn to pasta. A couple more seconds, another solid squeeze, and I'll be empty and at ease for the first time in months.

But lucky for everyone Rodney steps in. Dad, he says, and he puts his hand on my forearm. C'mon Dad I want to meet Harry Caray. It's enough to snap me out of it, get me to let go of Green's neck. He falls to the floor, gasping.

I don't think we're going to get to meet Harry Caray, son, I say. I'm surprised at how breathless I am.

I know, Rodney says. I just wanted you to stop choking him. I don't want you to go to jail.

Oh he's fucking going to jail, Green says. Fuck. He sits up slowly, rubbing at his throat. He's going to jail, and you're going to be wearing a Cubs uniform next year, kid.

I make a move toward Green, but Rodney steps in front of me and pushes me back, and I'm surprised that he's strong enough to move me even though by now he's an inch taller and probably ten pounds heavier. He herds me out of the room, and I see as I pass backwards through the door that the bartender is smiling at the sight of Green sitting on the carpet in front of his nice leather chairs, the bartender is smiling for the first time that I've seen, and so I must have done something right even though I'll probably end up in a cell and my boy won't get to see the game or have a Wrigley dog or meet Harry Caray.

We beat it out of there, back to the elevator, down the stairs, past the training room and batting cage and clubhouse, where now all the players are sitting around in their uniforms, listening to music, talking, playing cards, reading the newspaper. Rodney pauses in front of the open door but I grab him by the arm and pull him along. Then we're out onto the sidewalk, which is still packed with a slowly flowing stream of Cubs fans. Obviously there's no car waiting for us this time. We make our way against the current to the El stop, take the red line downtown and pick up the blue line, which takes us all the way out to O'Hare. It's a long ride, and I'm getting more and more worried that the police will be waiting for us when it finally ends, but the only cops at the airport are standing around looking bored. They obviously haven't been told to be on the lookout for anyone, let alone us.

When we get to the ticket counter, though, it's a different story. Our vouchers have been canceled. At first I'm pissed because now I'll have to spend money on bus tickets but then I figure if the worst thing that happens is Green doesn't pay for our trip home then we're getting off easy. I ask the lady at the ticket counter where the Greyhound station is, and she tells us we have to go back into the city, which is more money for the El, but eventually we find the station and I buy two tickets and spend the rest of my money on sandwiches. It take two days for us to get home, and we're hungry the whole way and I do something I've never had to do in my life, which is ask someone for a couple of bucks to get Rodney something to eat. I ask the driver and it makes my teeth hurt from embarrassment, but it's my hot temper that got us into this so I have to eat shit so my son can eat, period. I borrow five dollars and buy cheap stuff like doughnuts and I don't eat anything myself, though Rodney keeps trying to make me. Here Dad have some of my sandwich, he says. I get the driver's name and address and promise to send him the money, which I do, with interest, a couple of weeks later, when Debbie has calmed down from thinking Rodney and I were dead and everything sort of goes back to normal.

So Amy is the only person I can approach about it. I mean really full-on, you're-going-to-think-I'm-crazy-but-here's-the-thing approach about it. It's true that in the past I've made mention of it here and there, especially when I was younger. I remember drawing these horrific picture books in grade school: dead things of every variety littering the ground, a smoldering, barren earth, the remnants of skyscrapers bent and twisted against dark skies. These projects got me invited more than once to the office, where an ascending succession of school administrators—nurse, vice principal, principal, superintendent—would take a shot at figuring out what was going on in my head. Finally they called in the psychologist kept on retainer for emotionally unstable students. But no one really got anywhere with me. I was drawing pictures and making cryptic little asides not because I felt a need to communicate what I knew to anyone, but more to sort out what it meant to know these things. To figure out what this knowledge made me. Since I wasn't particularly interested in talking about it, my talks with the conga line of administrators were uniform in their pointlessness:

They: "Junior, what do these pictures mean?"

I: "M'Idunno."

And so on. These interviews were usually very brief, as conversations with the monosyllabically responsive tend to be. Sooner rather than later I was released back to my classroom of two, and the administrators were left scratching their figurative heads, relieved that I had departed and taken my strangeness with me, but probably more than a bit worried that something truly scary was going on inside my brain, something they hoped would remain dormant until I was no longer their responsibility.

To which I would now say, given the chance: You have no idea, sirs. I am not your routinely disturbed adolescent, pissed off about some generic bullying or a lack of attention from my daddy. I see visions that make Hiroshima look like a cherry bomb. Visions you would find terrifying even if you did not know, as I do, that they are true.

Of course through these administrators my parents became peripherally involved, insofar as they were asked to come in and discuss my artwork and state of mind, but they had no real insight to offer, as I shared little of myself with them. I think this is how we all prefer it. My father doesn't know how to talk to anyone, and though we feel genuine affection toward one another, the rare conversation between the two of us is even shorter-lived than my talks with the administrators, as conversations between two monosyllabically responsive people tend to be:

"Junior, put some coffee on."

"..."

Or, when I've carefully lifted the television remote from the arm of his easy chair and changed the channel, while he sits reclined and, to all outward appearances, very much asleep:

"I was watching that."

"..."

So even if I saw him more than two hours a week, my father would be a poor choice for the first person to reveal my visions to. My mother might have, at one time, been a marginally better option, but since Rodney left for Chicago she's transformed into a sad, catatonic version of herself. These days she spends most of her time sitting at the kitchen table with a plastic **Turbo Chug!** cup from the Hasty Market, complete with red plastic lid and half-inch-diameter straw, filled to varying levels with vodka and ice. Beads of condensation collect on the cup and form rings of enormous diameter on the tabletop. There are hundreds of big sixty-four-ounce stains on the part of the table that occupies the southern end of the kitchen.

This time of the year it's dark before suppertime, and my mother sits at the table and doesn't bother to turn on a light. Just sits there with her hand on the **Turbo Chug!** cup so she doesn't lose it in the dark. She holds the cup for so long that the pads of her fingers prune up from the condensation. Coming home from Amy's I'll open the front door and fumble for the light switch and turn it on and there she'll be at the table. Her pupils contract so violently I can see it from eight feet away. It's got to hurt but she never squints. She just sits there and when her eyes stop cramping and she sees me the faintest hint of a maternal smile tugs at the corners of her mouth and she says, "Hi, babe."

"Ma, you look tired," I'll say. "Maybe you should go to bed."

She'll pick up the **Turbo Chug!** cup with both hands to test its weight. She'll shake it and the ice and vodka will make a sound somewhere between sloshing and rattling. "I'll be up just a while longer," she'll say, setting the cup back down. To look at her, especially in the light from the overhead fluorescent in the kitchen, it's hard to believe she's less than forty years old.

So Dad and Ma are out, obviously, as people I could confess to. Which leaves Rodney and Amy. Even if Rodney weren't a thousand miles away, life has already bitten off more for him than he can reasonably be expected to chew—he just finished his fourth season with the Cubs, was second in National League MVP voting, and is the most popular baseball player on the North Side. He's got more money than he could spend in three lifetimes. His salary with the team is starting to look more and more like pocket change when compared to the money he's getting from Mizuno and Pepsi and even some of the smaller regional endorsements he does, like the deal he got with Portillo's because his love of hot dogs is well publicized and made him the perfect celebrity endorser for them. In return for his voice and image, he not only gets money but free hot dogs for life. As if he needs them. But there in his basement he's got a walk-in freezer full of Portillo's. Stacked floor to ceiling. This is my brother's life now. And considering that he needs a live-in attendant to get him to the buses and planes on time and to make sure he doesn't pack a suitcase full of nothing but underwear or go three days without eating, it's safe to say he's got his hands full without having to hear about my problem. Even if that problem is the rather pressing and certainly relevant knowledge of the end of all things.

So it's down to Amy. Which is a prospect well beyond daunting. I've given it plenty of thought. How to approach her, I wondered, and wonder still.

She loves me.

"I love you," she says.

So I should, in a perfect world, be able to tell her anything. On the other hand, she is not the type of girl to abide by nonsense, and I don't want her thinking I'm crazy, as her attitude toward the mentally ill is, to put it mildly, ungenerous. She concluded an essay regarding the fate of Mark David Chapman, vis-à-vis a government class debate on how best to deal with the criminally insane, thusly: "It's my opinion that Chapman got exactly what he deserved: a lifelong stay at luxurious Attica State Prison. And I don't even like the Beatles." She became a fan of Sylvia Plath's after reading *The Colossus*, printed up "The Eye-Mote" and tacked it on the wall next to her desk, and this was just another of many reasons why I love her, because who else would hang poetry up on prime pop star poster real estate? Except that "The Eye-Mote" came down the same hour Amy read about Plath's suicide. When I brought up Ted Hughes, Amy said, "He didn't shove her head in the oven. Besides, she had kids. And leaving the windows open so they wouldn't asphyxiate doesn't make her mother of the year."

This lack of sympathy for the mentally ill can be traced to Amy's mother, who is crazy, and who has pretty much made a career of beating Amy up since her father bolted a while back. Over the years Amy's family has become a cascade of domestic abuse: her father beat on her brother, who grew big and furious and beat on her mother, who had no one but Amy to vent her anger on. Based on this pattern, you'd think that if there were someone in the family after Amy, that someone would do well to take karate classes, or hit the weights. But this theoretical younger sibling would in fact have nothing to fear, because Amy seems immune to the rage that's been passed on from fist to fist. She's wry, and people who can pull off wry, put some real sting into it, rarely need to take up violence.

Her mother is not wry, and about once a month I can reliably expect to find bruises on Amy's upper arms, or scratches on her back. If she's reluctant to take off her clothes I know her mother's been smacking her around. More than once she's appeared at my window in the middle of the night, her nose bloody and her face tattooed with screaming red palm prints. Each time I fume and curse and vow revenge, or at the very least a stern talking-to with lots of overt and insinuated threats.

"You're a head taller than she is," I say. "Why do you put up with this?"

But Amy calms me, touches my face with her hands. Pressed against me on the same Cracker Jack box of a bed that I've had since I graduated from a crib, she offers no explanation. Without speaking she somehow makes clear she won't allow or tolerate retribution. The police will not be called, and I will not say or do anything. So I walk wide silent circles around her mother, and when Amy's not looking I shoot the woman hard glances, so she knows that I know.

So thanks to her mother there is the problem of Amy having no patience or sympathy for crazy people. And there is, of course, the better-than-fair chance that she will, on hearing what I have to say, think that I am crazy. But the more I ponder it, the more I realize that strange as it sounds, this is an essential part of who I am, and if I don't share it with her I'm being dishonest in some fundamental way. With the few other people in my life—Ma and Dad, Rodney—this dishonesty, and the distance it creates between us, is something I'm accustomed to and have learned to accept. But with Amy I can't tolerate it any longer. Increasingly it permeates our days, and, more often, our nights, which is always the worst time for me. Say her mother's out of town, which she often is these days, and I sleep over. When we get into bed and she curls into me and puts her head on my belly and her hair is fanned out across my chest and there's no light except from the one votive that she lets burn on the stand on my side of the bed, I am as safe and content as I've ever been in my life. I could die there. But then inevitably, in the early morning, the darkest thoughts and fears come over me, and I'll rise and put on my clothes and go out into the streets and wander around smoking and fielding questions from suspicious police officers. And when I return, usually just as the sky is starting to brighten, Amy naturally will want to know where I went, and why, and not only have I wasted a good portion of our best time together but now, on top of that, I have to lie. Bad stomach, I tell her. She asks sleepily if I feel any better, and I lie again and say yes, and she pulls me into bed and puts her back against me and wraps my arms around her and clutches my hands against her chest, but by now the whole thing's ruined and I feel almost nothing.

How to approach her, is the thing. Because obviously it's not something I can just drop casually: "Oh, you know that reminds me, did I mention that the world is going to end in nineteen years, give or take? No? Are you sure? I could have sworn I told you about that."

But after a couple of weeks of trying without luck to come up with a way to broach the subject, I realize that what I'm lacking isn't a good context in which to tell her, but simply the courage to do so. This will never be anything but the world's biggest, strangest non sequitur. And so there's nothing to it but to say it. Predictably, the courage finally comes to me at a weird, inappropriate time: while we're watching a movie in her basement after school.

"Amy," I say.

"Mm."

"There's something I need to say to you."

But then I balk.

We're lying on top of the covers on her brother's old bed. Though he went out west a couple of years after Amy's father split, the space has been only slightly modified for use as a second living room. Hence the addition of the television and VCR, perched on a loose-legged TV tray, and the subtraction of his Night Ranger and Warrant posters. Whenever Amy and I come down here to watch a movie, I always have to battle the creeping feeling that her brother's going to come home any minute and rag us out for being in his bedroom, even though I know he's in Salt Lake City.

We're lying on our sides, Amy's back to my front. She turns her head away from the television to glance at me, lizard-like, out of the corner of her eye. "Okay," she says. "Then, uh, you know. Say it."

I open my mouth again but succeed only in making a strange choking noise. I try to swallow, but I'm too dry and the walls of my throat just rasp against one another, making me wince. My heart's going like a bull getting spurred in the chute.

Now Amy pauses the movie and rolls over. She's flashing that look of amused exasperation she uses on me all the time. "Want to try that one more time, kid? Start over. Go slow."

This is just another thing I love about her—like her Dinosaur Jr. T-shirts, her purple Doc Martens, the bands she listens to that I've never heard of, and the relaxed, boyish way she carries herself—she calls me "kid." I'm four months older and outweigh her by about eighty pounds, but I'm the kid.

I hesitate. She's staring at me, calmly expectant. I could try to backtrack, claim she misheard, deny I said anything at all. But there'd be no point. She heard exactly what I said the first time I said it, and now she's waiting for me to finish the thought.

Oh, I have screwed up. Oh, this was a mistake.

"Yes?" Amy says, sliding a hand between my ribs and the mattress, tickling my back with her fingertips to prod me.

"Shit," I say, not meeting her gaze.

"Indeed," she says.

"I don't suppose I could get a takeback on that," I say.

"I'm afraid not."

I sigh. "Okay," I say, "now listen, before you get mad or jump to any conclusions, just hear me out."

The grin fades from her face, replaced by a look of burgeoning concern. She sits up. "This isn't going to be one of those 'it's not you, it's me' conversations, is it?"

"No," I say, "no, no way. God, don't worry about that."

"Okay," she says, cautious now. "Then what?"

I hold my breath for a second, eyeing her. Then I speak, quickly, before I have a chance to hesitate any more. "The world is going to end in nineteen years. Give or take."

Amy stares at me. Understandably, she doesn't know what to think. "What the hell are you talking about?"

I drop my gaze to the comforter. "Precisely what I just said."

"And did I hear you correctly?"

"I'm pretty sure you did," I say.

"And you're serious."

"Yes."

"Okay," she says, "okay, and you're going to have to forgive me here, but I guess I'm going to need a little more explanation. Like, what exactly you're talking about, Junior, when you say the world is going to end in nineteen years."

"Give or take."

She folds her arms across her chest. "I'm waiting."

Right, so. "It means," I say, "that on a day in the near future, a day we both will likely live to witness, the world—civilization, humanity, ninety-six percent of marine species and ninety-one percent of terrestrial species—will cease to be."

"And you know this how, exactly?" she asks.

Again, I didn't really plan this out, so I haven't scripted the best possible way to tell her that not only have I been hearing a voice in my head for as long as I can remember, but that I also believe everything it says. After a moment's pause, though, something comes to me. "Okay," I say, pulling myself up to sit facing her. "Okay, listen. You know how I'm always spacing out, and you get pissed off because you've just asked me a question, or else say the cashier at Wendy's is waiting for me to order, but I'm just standing there like Lot's wife, and my eye does that thing where it goes slightly cocked?"

"Yes."

"Well," I say, and stop cold. I'm performing some sort of gesticulation with my hands that I don't seem to have any control over. It goes on for a good half minute.

"What's that your hands are doing?" Amy asks.

"Not really sure," I tell her.

"Okay, enough," she says, putting her hands over mine to still them. "What are you talking about, Junior? Out with it."

I clear my throat. "Okay," I say. "So. When I go all cockeyed."

"Yes," Amy says.

"What's actually happening during those times is, I'm hearing a voice."

"In your head, you mean," Amy says. "Not, say, Wilford Brimley's voice on the TV."

"In my head."

She's pulled her hands back to rest in her lap. "And the voice says what."

"It tells me things."

"About . . ."

"The future. And the present. And the past, too, sometimes."

"And it told you that the world is going to end."

"On June 15, 2010, at 3:44 p.m. Eastern Standard Time. A comet from the Kuiper Belt will hit the Earth with the explosive energy of 283,824,000 Hiroshima bombs. Which will be unfortunate for a number of reasons, including that here in New England it will be ruining a postcard summer day."

Amy stares at me for a long moment, then leans over to grab a cigarette from the pack of Camels on the floor. She lights it, breathes deep, exhales a cloud of gray-blue smoke. "This is some sort of joke, right?" she says.

"Would that it were so."

"Like the time you thought it would be funny to let me believe, for three days, that you thought you might be gay?"

"Sadly, no."

She hands the cigarette over. "So what you're telling me, then, basically," she says, "is that you're fucking crackers."

"No." I reach for her, but she pulls her arm away and rises from the bed. "Amy. Listen to me, please. I'm not crazy. This is real."

She takes two steps toward the staircase, then turns to face me again. "I'm sure that it's very real to you. Which is the part that makes you crazy, see?"

"Everything it tells me is true. I know things I couldn't possibly have found out otherwise."

"You've got about ten seconds to convince me."

And of course I draw a blank. Everything that comes to mind is either something I know but can't prove—how my father lost his fingers, for example—or something I knew about in advance but which has already come to pass, like the revelation of Rodney's cocaine addiction. Amy's standing there, cross-armed and wet-eyed, seven seconds removed from going up the stairs, getting into her little red pickup truck, and driving away from her own house just to be shut of me, and I can't think of anything to keep her from leaving.

Then something rises. Something awful that only three people on Earth know about, including me. It is perfect, ironclad proof that what I'm saying is true, and it is too terrible to speak of.

Amy is already on her way up the steps. She brushes a lock of hair away from her face with an angry swipe of one hand, careful not to let her eyes stray in my direction. I watch her rapid ascent, weigh my two options, judge them to be bad and worse, and make my decision.

"I know something," I call out. At this she stops dead near the top of the stairs. Only her feet and ankles are visible. "Something only three people on Earth know about. Two of those three people are in this room right now. It is perfect, ironclad proof that what I'm saying is true."

But it is too terrible to speak of.

Because when Amy turns and descends the steps again, stopping half-way up, and stares at me, her eyes shimmering in the light from the bare bulb in the overhead fixture, I realize I can't say it. For all I know she's willfully forgotten, or else blocked it out, isolated it in the solitary confinement cell that comes as standard equipment in all our minds for use on just such a memory. Am I going to open the door? One look at her face and I have my answer.

"Well?" she says, still staring.

In a nutshell, sparing the easily imagined details: Camp Kennebec, on Salmon Lake. Summer 1981. Amy is seven years old. A counselor from Vermont named McDermott. Amy stayed just four days, pretended to be sick so she could go home. Actually made herself throw up several times. The next summer she played Little League baseball just so her father wouldn't send her back to Kennebec. The year after that, to her relief, he didn't mention camp at all. She never saw McDermott again, and she never told anyone.

She's glaringly expectant.

I say nothing.

She does a smart turn on her heel and climbs the steps again. "That's what I thought," she says as she disappears in increments. "You know Junior, this is really, really fucked up. Not funny at all. You should go home."

She vanishes.

"And I'm not giving you a ride, either."

Amy

I turn off the water and step out of the shower and by the time I'm halfway through combing and braiding my hair in the way Junior likes the heat is all over me again. It's only eight in the morning and already so sticky it's as though I didn't even bathe. I wipe the fog from the mirror and see, on the inside of my upper arm, the bruise, an exact imprint of my mother's hand. It's turned the sick-green color of a prison tattoo.

When he saw the bruise a few days ago, Junior as usual wanted to confront my mother, but I convinced him not to. It's way too late to fix this. When I was eight, maybe, but not now. All I want is to last the summer, because I know when I leave for college and don't come back my mother's real punishment will begin. My father long gone, my brother long gone, me gone, and she'll be trapped with herself.

I'm hoping it will destroy her.

But I worry about what it'll do to Junior. He takes everything too hard. Every time I turn around he's talking about some animal he saw broken and dying somewhere. It happens so often I'm beginning to wonder if he's making it up. Most recently it was a bat he found lying facedown in the police station parking lot. He was out wandering around, like he does at night when he can't sleep. He said at first he thought the bat was dead, but when he poked it with the toe of his shoe it picked up its head and shrieked at him. All it could do was move its head. The rest of its body wouldn't work.

"It wasn't any bigger than a mouse," Junior said, holding his thumb and finger apart to illustrate. His eyes were all teary talking about it. This was a bat, understand.

And I thought, How am I going to say goodbye to him when summer's over?

He told me he picked the bat up to move it into the grass, so it wouldn't get run over by a police cruiser, and it bit him.

"You're going to end up with rabies," I said.

He shrugged, like *What does it matter?* He's always doing that. It pisses me off. He hasn't earned the right to be so world-weary. A little light brooding is okay, even nice sometimes if it's that kind of day, if you're in the mood to listen to the gloomier tracks on *White Light/White Heat* and spend a good chunk of time feeling cool about how superior you are to the rest of the world, what with its shallowness and insincerity and Spuds MacKenzie beach towels. An occasional indulgence, fine. But with him it's nonstop, and when I ask him what's wrong he brushes it off. Nothing, he says, nothing's wrong, what makes you think there's something wrong? The fact that you look like you're ready to draw a warm bath and bust out the straight razor, I want to say. I know what the problem is, and why he won't talk about it. He doesn't want me to think he's crazy. But it's really too late for that. Things aren't getting any better. Just because he's been smart enough not to bring it up again doesn't mean I've forgotten. He still spaces out all the time. He sits around brooding about roadkill. These aren't things I can help him with.

Before the bat it was a bird he found on some old man's lawn, when we were on our way back from picking apples at the orchard in Smithfield. The bird wasn't hurt, but it was too young to fly, and Junior really went weird on that one, climbing around in the trees, looking for a nest to put the thing in. I thought the old man would have us arrested. Junior broke a branch in a willow and didn't even notice. Finally he just scooped the bird up in his T-shirt and had me drive to the vet's office.

I don't know what he expected them to do.

He acted strange that night, hardly talking at all, just pressed the whole length of his body against me like he was afraid I'd disappear. I looked back at one point and saw he had his eyes closed, wasn't watching the movie. I wasn't really watching it, either. I was thinking about the card in the bottom drawer of my dresser, the card I'd spent an hour picking out, moving slowly up and down the stacks of *Happy Birthday, Grandpa* and *On Your Anniversary* until I found just the right one.

On the front of the card is a hobo-type figure with a stick-and-handkerchief slung over his shoulder. He's stopped at a fork in the road, considering. Each way has a sign. The first reads, "Your Future." The other reads, "No Longer an Option."

I'm hoping Junior will get the message, if and when I finally get up the courage to give it to him.

There's a part of me that wants to believe everything will work out, that we'll go away to school and talk on the phone every other night and get together on breaks and come out the other side of four years not having done or said anything that can't be repaired. I love him, and there's no way around that. But there's the other part of me, the stronger, stubborn part, the part that checks the scars every day to see if they've faded, and remembers the pain of a broken nose. That part says no. That part has the patience to spend an hour in a Hallmark store.

I was ready to give him the card the day after we brought the bird to the vet's. I'd imagined the conversation to follow, rehearsed my lines, and made a deal with myself that prohibited crying. The card was in my bag, signed and sealed, with nothing left except the delivery. But that afternoon Junior asked me to take him back to the vet's, to check on the bird, and when he came out his face was dark as a thundercloud.

"They said they tried to feed it with an eyedropper," he said. "I think they're full of shit."

When I got home that night, I put the card back in the dresser.

So I'm standing here now, and every time I wipe steam from the mirror I lose a braid and have to start over. A little maddening, but it's the least I can do for Junior. I think about him for a while, and then I think about time, how it's August already, and pretty soon I'm thinking in pictures, imagining California in autumn, Fisherman's Wharf and breakers on the beach, my legs tan through Christmas, and I know this heat can't last forever and whatever I decide to do, it's got to be soon.

PART TWO

Junior

Though she's hoping to slip in and out of town without me finding out, of course I know when Amy comes back for the first time since she left for Stanford. I also know why she's here, and the why is as disappointing as it is inexplicable: she's here to visit her mother, the Joan Crawford of Temple Street, fists of stone and a heart to match. She's softened on her mother, somehow, but not on me.

I know, too, when Amy decides to meet with a few old high school friends at You Know Whose Pub. It's a calculated risk on her part. When Kerry Raymond called her earlier today Amy balked, worried she might run into me, but then she figured on a Tuesday night the chances I'd be out drinking were minimal. She doesn't realize, of course, that these days I'm out drinking every night.

Pathetic as it is, I'm glad she's thinking of me at all, even if it's only because she wants desperately to avoid me.

At first I resolve not to go. I'm not sure why. Some misplaced sense of pride, maybe. There's an element, too, of wanting to punish Amy by denying her my company, as if that's not exactly what she's hoping for. I sit in my bedroom, drinking beer from the little cube fridge and brooding and watching the Red Sox lose. I stare through the television, concentrating on Amy in spite of myself, hoping the contents of her heart will rise and I'll find a section still reserved for me, no matter how small. Nothing comes. I take the Captain Morgan from under the bed and drink straight from the bottle, making ever-angrier resolutions not to leave the house tonight, or if I leave, not to go downtown, or if I go downtown, certainly not to set foot near You Know Whose Pub.

These days, I'm finding, my powers of self-delusion are sort of epic.

I'm fully drunk by the time I walk into the place, but even so my breath catches in my throat as though I didn't expect to see Amy sitting there, drinking mojitos with Kerry and a girl I don't recognize. She's heartbreakingly beautiful, her cheeks and shoulders freckled with California sun, her hair longer by a year and straight now, an auburn fantasy falling halfway down her back. The longer hair is just one of a dozen small ways in which she's different from how I remember—new bracelet, new green tank top, fingernails elegantly manicured rather than gnawed to the quick—and the sense of having been left behind, always nagging in the back of my head, rises on a wave of fresh anger. I walk up to the table and interrupt their laughter without caring about how it makes me look. I'm going to have my say. I'm going to get some satisfaction. Except that beneath the paper-thin layer of righteous indignation, all I really want is to spend a couple of hours in her company. I'm aware, distantly, that this makes me pathetic, that I ought to have enough self-regard to turn on my heel and walk out of here. But when you're bereft of all dignity there's no sense in faking it. So instead of venting my anger, which is really just hurt dressed up for a night on the town, I ask if anyone needs a drink.

Silence from the three of them. Amy's face is a plaster mask of studied indifference, but under that there's a shimmer of surprise and fear.

I wait a few seconds for one of them to respond, then say, "What, you're approached by young men offering free drinks so often that you just can't stand it anymore?"

Kerry and the girl I don't recognize exchange an uncomfortable look, but Amy smiles a little in spite of herself. She lifts her glass, tilts it back and forth. "I'm getting a little low," she says.

Several minutes later I return to the table with three fresh mojitos and take the empty seat to Amy's right. By now she's gotten over the shock of my sudden appearance and seems almost glad I'm here. She leans close and shouts over the jukebox: "You look like shit, kid."

I look down at the tabletop, nod, say nothing. This time has been as hard on me as it's been good to her, and I know the evidence is all over my face. I've got no explanation to offer. I used to wonder why my mother and Rodney were compelled to hurt themselves, and though I understand now, it's an understanding that defies articulation. The thing I always think of is a trip we took as kids to Old Orchard Beach, where Rodney and I bodysurfed in the frigid shallows, lifted and carried along over and over by the rhythmic swells. I remember being awed and somewhat frightened by the ocean's effortless power, by how once I'd been picked up in a wave any effort to escape was futile. That's what the past year has felt like.

"Talk to me," Amy says. She leans closer still, and I catch a whiff of coconut as her hair brushes my face. I have to fight the urge to put a finger on her bare arm and play a slow, lingering game of connect-the-dots with her freckles. "How are things going?"

I lie and say, "Not bad." I tell her I'm thinking about moving to Chicago to live with Rodney. She talks about Stanford, how at first she felt overwhelmed but now couldn't be happier. The two of us laugh often and talk without pause, the easy, intuitive way we always shared returning instantly. Kerry and the other girl run out of things to say to each other and gaze absently around the room, excluded and bored. I lose track of how many times I return to the bar for fresh drinks. It seems like only half an hour has passed when suddenly the bartender whacks the bell for last call.

Outside the day's heat and stickiness have barely abated despite the late hour. Bugs swarm the light under the awning. Amy says goodbye to Kerry and the girl whose name I still haven't gotten. Then it's just her and me. I thought this was what I wanted all along, but somehow, here under the fluorescent, there's a sudden, powerful awkwardness between us. I look at my feet for a bit. She stands with her hands clasped behind her back, jingling her keys.

"You're okay to drive?" I ask finally.

"I'm fine," she says.

"You're sure."

"Junior . . ."

"Okay then."

We stand there a minute longer. I keep willing myself to say something, or else to put my arms around her. But I'm afraid to move, convinced that everything going forward hinges on this moment, that whatever we become, or fail to become, is entirely dependent on what happens in the next few seconds. And I'm paralyzed by the fear that I'll screw it up.

Then the moment is gone. Amy puts her hand on my arm briefly, says "See you," and walks away. I have all I can do not to follow her like a puppy and beg her to take me home. She gets halfway to her truck, pauses in the middle of the parking lot, and turns back, and for a moment I let myself believe she's changed her mind, that her love for me has won out and we'll be reunited in a desperate, twirling Hollywood hug right here outside the pub. But instead she reaches in her purse, rips off the corner of a page in her address book, scribbles something, and presses it into my hand.

"I'm sorry, Junior," she says. She stares at me, searching my face. Then she grasps my wrist and says, "Listen, you look terrible. You know that, right? Whatever you're doing to yourself, stop it. You should know better. You should be smarter than this."

"And you should know smart's got nothing to do with it."

I know it was a mistake the moment the words are out of my mouth. Amy holds my gaze a moment longer, then gives a resigned little nod. "Okay," she says. "Well. Call me sometime."

She lets go of my arm and walks away. And I'm left standing here, alone in the light from the awning, clutching the scrap of paper in my fist like it contains the secret to saving the world.

Chicago

58   Chicago is not the ideal place to go to when you've recently lost your mind and plan to curl up in the bottom of a bottle and wait for the feeling of having your insides ripped repeatedly from your body to subside. There are at least half a dozen North American cities better suited to such a pursuit.

Topping the list is Miami. Perfect weather and bright pastels contrast nicely with suicidal ideation, bring the misery into sharp relief. For those like you, who prefer slow suicide, this hub of the illicit drug trade offers plentiful, varied, and cheap options. Everything can be had and you needn't know anyone. If you took a stroll through the side streets of South Beach at night, you'd inevitably hear, from the shadows, unsolicited: "Pssst, meeho. You want *cocaína?* Ecstas? Trips?" Given your pharmaceutical preferences you'd most likely say no, you're not in the market for stimulants, but something on the opposite end of the spectrum would probably interest you. "I got just the thing, meeho," would be the response. "You stay here. I know a guy. He got Special K, real cheap."

But you are in Chicago, because your rich and famous brother, who is oblivious to both his riches and his fame, lives in Chicago, and because your options are dramatically limited by finances and ambition.

57   Your brother lives in the upscale Streeterville neighborhood, in a graystone on North LaSalle that is worth $4.6 million but for which he paid $5.3 just to get it over with and have a place to store his stuff. You've got the run of the house. It's late summer, and with your brother on road trips for a week or two at a stretch, most often it's just you and the Help. The Help don't care what you do. They're practiced at serving the wealthy, making themselves fade until their presence is no more noteworthy than that of the oaken banister or the ubiquitous fireplaces. A number of them have, at previous jobs, overlooked sins of tremendous violence and perversion, so having to sop up your vomit and

return your misplaced pill bottles hardly registers. If you're found lying on the floor in the master bathroom, they wait until you return to shattered-glass consciousness and stagger off to the guest room shower before they come back to scrub the basins and buff the chrome. You could, if inclined, probably literally get away with murder here, and so long as there were no interruption in pay your brother's servants wouldn't mention it to anyone or even speak about it amongst themselves.

The one potential exception to this rule is Rodney's live-in therapist/attendant, a pear-shaped, surly woman named Hilda Begin. Begin disliked you on first sight, and time has done nothing to improve this impression. She believes you are taking advantage of Rodney, which she considers all the more reprehensible given his inability to realize he's being used. In fact, she has serious doubts about whether you care for your brother at all, except as a source of income. Fortunately you have the good sense to tone down, however slightly, your drunken, erratic, and otherwise bad behavior when Rodney and Begin are in town. Still, you often catch her eyeballing you suspiciously, and she makes no effort to hide her disdain and distrust.

The reason we bring this up is to disabuse you of the notion that your early-morning phone calls are private. You are not nearly as slick or stealthy as you think. The Help hear almost everything—they just don't care. When at three a.m. you pick up and dial the campus of Stanford University, specifically room 117 of Wilbur Hall, a room shared by Anne McCutcheon, whose sleepy, irritated falsetto has greeted you several times, and Amy Benoit, who has returned for her sophomore year, the Help are listening.

56 The conversations that follow vary wildly in temperament and tempo, depending mostly on your level of intoxication and overall mood. Like most emotionally distraught people, especially those with substance abuse issues, you experience daily swings of mood that at their most dramatic resemble bipolar disorder. You can be having a drooling roofies-and-Beefeater kind of night, and do nothing but dial Amy's number and sit on the end of the line with your chin against your chest,

and for the entire forty-five minutes it takes for the telephone to slip slowly from your fingers she will sit on the other end, listening in the darkness of her dorm room to your shallow respirations, gazing out the window at the gang of black oaks lining the walkway as they wave faintly in a night breeze. Sometimes, when your breathing is particularly shallow and she's feeling sad rather than annoyed, she will put her hand up to the window and wave back. Other nights, blurry PCP-and-Wild-Turkey evenings, you'll begin talking almost before she answers the phone, and you may start off friendly and exuberant and even display a sort of teeth-grinding charm, but Amy will eventually say something fairly benign and obvious to everyone but you, e.g., "Jesus Junior, you need to stop this, look at your mother for God's sake, is that how you want to end up?" and this will be all you need to fly into a rage so quick and violent it's as though you were just waiting for an excuse, which, in fact, is the case. "What the fuck does it matter, Amy," you'll say, leaving implicit the reason it matters so little because you're afraid if you mention the Destroyer of Worlds again, you'll lose what little of her you've gained back. Short of that, though, there seems to be nothing you can say that will make her change her phone number, or not answer when you call, or just tell you to fuck off. When all the loud brawling shamelessness of the authentic drunk comes pouring forth she sits and takes it, suffers like Jesus. Enraged further by her patience, you go completely unreasonable, call her a bitch, a cunt, a spoiled child, a *fucking* bitch. You catalogue, as the pain in your chest tears and burns, every one of her shortcomings, from toenail fungus to sociopathy. With a verbal flourish you imagine is dramatic, but which in fact is merely unintelligible, you hang up on her. And you wake in the morning on top of the covers, fully clothed, the hard leather corner of your wallet poking a dent in your hip, filled with the creeping feeling of having done something for which you should be ashamed, but no solid idea what that something is.

You are pursued by this feeling all day, as if by a ghost, or a super-spy, until you return, drunk once more, from O'Toole's, and call Amy again, calm and contrite because even though we've refused to help you piece together the details of last night's call, there is some tiny, primitive part of your mind that is impervious to alcohol, the brain's black box, and it has recorded every word from the previous evening and is sending clear if nonspecific signals indicating that contrition is very much in order.

55 Though you consider the situation with Amy to be the biggest problem in your life at the moment, there are other issues you ought to be paying more attention to. We're referring, of course, to your state of mind. While we're willing to accept our portion of the responsibility for your general pessimism, we would be remiss if we didn't point out that you are also undergoing dramatic changes in brain chemistry brought on by heavy, prolonged alcohol and drug consumption. This is beyond feeling blue. This is four hours of inexplicable panic that reduced you to a mute, paralytic state similar to the episode you had as a child after watching *The Prophesies of Nostradamus*, except this time you were not a toddler but a twenty-year-old man, lying on a bench near the Dearborn Street bridge, staring straight up to where the stars would have been were they not obscured by the megawatt towers, your head resting on the lap of a young woman you'd met a few times at O'Toole's but whose name to this day you can't recall, a woman who stayed with you the full four hours, her butt numb and legs knotted with cramps, because she was genuinely afraid that you would die from fright if left alone. This is staying inside your brother's home for four days at a time, dispatching the Help for beer and burritos, and peering out from behind the shades at people on the sidewalk below like you're Quasimodo. This is butting cigarettes out on your own arms and legs and crying at diet pill commercials.

54 Again: we accept our portion of the responsibility for your despair. It's understandable you would question the relevance of human actions, moral systems, even existence itself in the context of *la fin du monde*, but honestly. Don't fool yourself into believing it's everything to do with the Destroyer of Worlds and nothing to do with the damage being wreaked on your nervous system by drugs and booze. Not to mention

suppressed fury over Amy having left you. But mostly the drugs and booze.

53   You press ahead with the getting clobbered nightly for a number of reasons, not the least of which is the centipede. You wake in late morning with your eyes popping out of their sockets and a pain in your gut like you swallowed hot coals, anxiety already scuttling about your skull as though a centipede has crawled into your ear while you slept. You limp to the bathroom, hunched over so you don't piss yourself. A cup of black coffee and the resolution that enough's enough and you will take today off, give your head and your liver a break. The centipede twitches, scurries, and suggests otherwise, because now it's not just moving around in there, it's also growing—whereas when you first awoke it was maybe an inch or so long, now it's the length of a pencil. The interior of your skull is too small for it to turn without bending itself, and you can feel it twisting its body segment by segment. One hundred needle legs prick your brain, which actually physically recoils, or such is the sensation. You attempt to distract yourself with television, or the *Tribune*, but it is difficult to concentrate on anything but what's going on in your head. Finally, foolishly, you amend your resolution to read that you will not *drink* today, leaving the implication that pills are acceptable, and you shake a handful of tablets out of your bottle, separate two of the light-green ones from the rest, and wash them down with a couple swallows of orange juice. The aftertaste of the juice is like vomit wafting up from your throat, but you fight to keep the pills down and after fifteen minutes the centipede's scurrying slows and its growth is halted altogether. Its presence in your head becomes tolerable, just so, and you even manage to smile once or twice and mean it. Soon enough, though, the frenzied laps around the circumference of your brain resume. As daylight fades, your mind, centipede-harried, spits out dozens of rationalizations for reneging on that whole not-drinking-tonight thing, the most transparent of which is the need for some sort of transition from the really heavy drinking of the night before to not drinking at all. You're just too sick to go without a few

medicinal shots, is the rationale. Again you negotiate a deal with yourself: instead of the usual twelve beers and six or seven mixed drinks,
you'll limit yourself to half that, and then *tomorrow,* always, always
tomorrow, you will stay completely dry.

Though we understand the manner in which addiction works, we're
still surprised at how easily you, of all people, can lie to yourself.

52 In any event, having made a decision you're down in the streets, negotiating sidewalk traffic like Mary Tyler Moore with a crack habit.
O'Toole's is crowded as always; the regulars know enough to get here
early and can all be found at their usual spots at the bar itself. This includes Reggie Fox, who most often is the only black person in O'Toole's,
and who is always the only person in O'Toole's, of any color, who is
missing both legs at the hip, an arm above the elbow, and most of one
ear.

Reggie reaches up to put his drink on the bar, and uses the joystick
on his wheelchair to shimmy to the side and make room for you. You
give him a perfunctory high-five and mime your desperation to Wade,
the bartender, who responds with a shot glass and a bottle of SoCo. You
pour and drink two quick shots, then hand Reggie his Crown Royal
and cola to save him the effort of reaching for it.

Reggie says something you can't make out.

"Huh?" O'Toole's hums and buzzes as one large unruly organism,
and you have to lean down to hear him.

"I said I been thinkin'," Reggie says again. "About what you and I
been discussin'."

"The banks?" you ask. A few weeks ago Reggie—who is kind and
funny but also insane—hatched this idea to turn his wheelchair into a
rolling bomb and use it to rob banks. The two of you were hitting Reggie's custom one-handed bong and discussing his ridiculously inade-
quate Social Security disability payment. The idea was your job would
be to drive the getaway wheelchair van. The one problem being that
you, of course, have no motivation to rob banks. But it's been fun to
discuss and flesh out, like any other fantasy you'd never have the balls
to try and pull off.

Reggie shushes you, as if anyone could hear what you were saying, and as if it would matter if they could. "Keep it down, now," he says, looking this way and that. "And forget the banks. The Fox got a better idea."

You straighten up and take a sip of the draft that Wade has placed on the bar for you. You wait for Reggie to continue with his big idea, but he says nothing further, just sucks his Crown and cola through a pair of those super-narrow bar straws. He's sucking so hard, in fact, that his cheeks have imploded, but if his effort produces a change in the fluid level in his glass it's not visible to the naked eye.

"You know those aren't really functional straws, right?" you say. "They're swizzle sticks. You stir with them."

Reggie narrows his eyes to slits, releasing the straws with an audible pop. "How the fuck am I supposed to swizzle anything when the only hand I got is holding the glass? And what do you know, anyway? You ain't even old enough to be in here."

"Sure I am," you say. "What are you talking about, anyway? What's this idea?"

"Ain't sayin' in here."

"Reggie, come on." You pour another drink of SoCo, and since you've already forgotten we'll remind you that this is your third and final shot of the evening, according to the terms of the agreement you made with yourself an hour ago. "*I* can't even hear you. How will anyone else?"

But Reggie shakes his head. "This is serious," he says. "You want to talk about this, you got to come with me to my place."

You consider. The bar is rowdier than you care for. A large contingent of Northwestern greeks has annexed the back third of the place, including the pool and Foosball tables, and they're beginning to exude that loose, dangerous energy peculiar to groups of college-age boys when they begin traversing the threshold between tipsy and hammered. We can tell you your concern is well founded; if you stay here much longer there will be trouble.

"Got anything to drink?" you ask Reggie.

"Whole bottle'a Wild Turkey," he says. "Plus an ounce of skunk."

"Let's go," you say, grabbing the handles on the back of his chair and wheeling him toward the cargo elevator in the back.

51 Reggie lives in a subdivision in Washington Park, south of Sixty-third. It probably goes without saying, but given your perpetually addled state we feel we should advise you never to come into this neighborhood without Reggie as an escort. Merely being in the presence of a black person does not necessarily convey safety, but being in Reggie's presence does, because he is The Fox, and because he's wheelchairbound, and because he's funny and well liked and known by everyone, including the many people who would otherwise be keenly interested in discovering what your insides look like.

Reggie's efficiency, when added up, is exactly six square feet smaller than your brother's master bathroom. The two of you sit in Reggie's living room, which is just large enough to hold his wheelchair, a Canadian rocker that doesn't really rock all that well, and a TV stand with a small black-and-white set on it.

"Pour me a shot'a that Turkey," Reggie says to you.

"Hold on a second," you say as you load the bong. "I'm busy, here. I've only got two hands, you know."

"That's one-and-one-half more than I got," he says. "So don't cry to me."

"Would you take this and shut up." You give Reggie the bong, and he uses his gnarled half-hand to light, carb, and hit a huge column of smoke.

You hear men arguing outside, an unintelligible chorus of angry voices directly below the living room window. You pour two shots and hand one to Reggie. "So what about the banks?"

"Forget the banks," Reggie says. He gets demon-red eyes from dope, and already his scleras are pinkish, as though they'd been washed accidentally with a brand-new red shirt. "This ain't about money. This is about the government treatin' disabled people better."

"So if not the banks," you say, "then what?"

"The Social Security building," he says. "Over on West Madison."

"What about it?"

Reggie downs his shot, then leans as far forward as he can and fixes you with a moist gaze. "I'm-a blow that motherfucker up," he says.

And because nothing seems to alarm you much these days, least of all the wholesale loss of human life, you have pretty much the most inappropriate response possible when someone has just threatened to commit suicide and take a thousand other people with him: you laugh and hit the bong.

"Ain't no joke," Reggie says. "I can get enough C-4 on my chair to blow that place to bits. Won't be nothing left but dust."

This isn't strictly true. The Harold Washington SSA building is twenty-two stories high, and with an average detonation velocity of 8750 m/s it would take over six hundred pounds of C-4 to level the place. Reggie's chair is heavy-duty, but it isn't a half-ton pickup. That said, it certainly could carry enough explosives to damage the building beyond repair, not to mention kill a lot of people.

"Maybe then they pay more attention to what's goin' on with cripple people. We ain't like these deadbeat motherfuckers out there." Reggie gestures toward the window, on the other side of which the men can still be heard arguing with one another. "Sittin' around all month waitin' for a check, get all the money they need, so they can cash it in for sixty cents on the dollar, spend half at the liquor store an' lose the other half in a dice game. Got two good arms and legs, every one of 'em, but ain't never thought about gettin' a job. While people like me want nothin' more than to work, 'cept we only got half a fuckin' hand."

50 Here is something you do not know about Reggie, because he never speaks of it: the reason he's hypersensitive to the plight of disabled people is because he knows firsthand how little the able-bodied care. Not so long ago Reggie was a 210-pound cement mason, his legs, arms, and ear all present and accounted for, and he'd never given a thought to the disabled beyond studiously ignoring the legless panhandler who worked the corner at his El stop. He was so perfectly functional, in fact,

that he was able to carry on a short-lived affair with a bored, moneyed white woman who had an appetite for black men, Grey Goose martinis, and Prada leather, a woman who not coincidentally was married to the owner of Fullerton Cement Company, where Reggie worked.

Their affair might have been longer-lived, if not for a coat closet quickie they indulged in at the Fullerton Christmas party in 1992. Reggie wound up with baseball-sized rug burns on both knees and a quarter-sized burn on his arm. Which is no big deal, right, rug burns hurt but so what. Except that instead of getting better, Reggie's rug burns started to hurt worse on the second day, the pain spreading up from the knees and down from the right elbow. At work they were setting the form for a foundation, which required Reggie to get on his knees repeatedly to check pitch and depth, and by the third day the pain was too much and he called out sick, which he'd never done once since he started working at age eleven.

By this point the pain had marched inexorably up into the bones in his hips. He poured sweat and puked until there was nothing left, then dry-heaved. His knees started to ooze a reddish-brown fluid that smelled exactly like the landfill at 122nd and Torrence, and that was when he finally decided to take the El to CCH, except that when he rose like an old man from his Canadian rocker he promptly passed out, and didn't wake again for eleven days.

When he did finally come to, six physicians stood in pairs around the bed he found himself in. He would have woken to just a nurse, or else no one at all, except that the incidence of necrotizing fasciitis (known commonly as flesh-eating bacteria) is about 1 in 100,000, and thus rare enough to be of great, career-making, Journal-of-the-American-Medical-Association interest to any physician lucky enough to witness a case. Because they hadn't noticed that Reggie was awake they continued with their examination, pulling the covers back from where he quite reasonably expected his legs to be, and in this especially horrifying manner he discovered a good portion of his body had been removed without his knowledge, input, or consent.

Missing limbs aside, Reggie was now staring at the business end of a three- or four-month hospital stay, and though he had health insurance through Fullerton Cement, the maximum benefit for his policy had expired with a whimper the day before he came to, leaving him with coverage as comprehensive as the average junkie's. Enter Jasper Fullerton, Harvard grad, multimillionaire, white guilt aficionado, and owner of Fullerton Cement.

Jasper came into Reggie's semiprivate room nearly at a run and held his right hand out for a full ten seconds before finally realizing that Reggie had nothing to shake it with. Loose neck-flesh bulged from the sphincter of his collar, and his eyes shone wet and anxious as he took in the sight of Reggie's wasted body. "Mr. Fox," he said, "I'm so sorry this has happened to you. I want you to know that, with as much as you have to worry about, one thing you won't need to worry about is money. I plan to continue to pay your weekly wage indefinitely, as well as any medical expenses not covered by your insurance policy."

These are things, incidentally, that Jasper would not have done for a white employee.

"That's very kind," Reggie said without much conviction. Only a few days into his career as a triple-amputee, he literally couldn't have cared less about how he would pay for his hospital bills, so Jasper's grand announcement had a less-than-electrifying effect on him.

Jasper, disappointed that his generosity hadn't aroused the sort of sputtering gratitude he'd anticipated, nevertheless pressed forward with the script in his mind, which at this point called for him to dismiss the sputtering gratitude with an aw-shucks display of humility. "Oh, it's nothing," Jasper said. "You contracted the illness at work, so it's my obligation to take care of you. It's the least I can do, really."

"I didn't get it at work," Reggie said.

"No matter," Jasper said. He placed a hand on Reggie's shoulder. "Don't speak. Just rest. I'll take care of everything." He then withdrew from the room before any more of his script could be rewritten.

From that moment forward, Reggie had nothing to worry about. He'd lost three limbs but gained a sugar daddy. He wanted for nothing and never saw a single medical bill. Jasper visited weekly during his rehab, smiling down on the results of the first-rate care his money provided. Reggie progressed briskly, and in less than three months he was released from the hospital. He rode in a top-of-the-line electric wheelchair paid for by Jasper, had a home nurse paid for by Jasper, lived in an apartment paid for by Jasper, ate food paid for by Jasper with silverware paid for by Jasper. And he hated every minute of it. Not because he felt guilt over having slept with Jasper's wife, but because having to accept charity from another man made him burn in places he didn't have anymore. Reggie worked hard and paid his own way and that's how it always had been. Obviously he would need to adjust his thinking a bit on these and other issues, but having to suffer under Jasper's paternal gaze every week for the rest of his life—no, that was something he could not adjust to.

He tried telling Jasper that, while he appreciated everything he'd done, it was probably time for him, Reggie, to figure out how to live this new life on his own, without anyone else's help. And Jasper listened and beamed sympathetically and said of course, Reggie, but how? How, with no legs and only part of one hand, would he possibly get by without anyone's help? He didn't see how Reggie had any other options at this point. Besides which, Jasper was sure there were thousands of disabled people in Chicago who prayed every day for exactly the sort of financial intervention Jasper provided, the intervention Reggie wanted to throw away, and perhaps Reggie should ruminate on that fact for a while.

For months Reggie's subsidized existence continued, until finally he realized the only way to get Jasper to stop was to tell him how he'd lost so much of his body. Jasper had stopped by to make sure the new maid service he'd hired was doing its job, and Reggie, never one to waste time or syllables, just came out with it.

"I got sick from rug burns," he told Jasper. "And I got rug burns from fucking your wife."

Jasper stared. "Why would you say something like that?"

"Sorry," Reggie said. "But there it is, man."

Jasper was quiet for a few moments, then recovered himself and gave a barking half-laugh. "That's very funny, Mr. Fox. Very funny."

"Ain't no joke," Reggie said. "We did it at the Christmas party. In the room where they put the jackets. We done it once before that, too."

Jasper's face bore the shattered expression of a man for whom long-standing suspicions are suddenly being confirmed. But he was still resistant. "Why should I believe you?" he said. "What sort of proof can you offer to support this claim?"

"Not much," Reggie said. He thought for a moment. "She got a scar on her ass. She didn't say nothin' about it. But it look to me like somebody bit her. Long time ago."

At this Jasper looked away, anger and shame sparring in his eyes. "You're telling the truth," he said, his face darkening.

"Always do."

"Well then," Jasper took up his coat and moved toward the door. "You got what you deserved, you black bastard." And he went out.

"Least you finally bein' honest," Reggie said to no one.

After that, it all disappeared fast. Jasper's assistant stopped showing up every Monday with armfuls of groceries, and Reggie found himself eating pasta and canned sauce every day, and powdered milk with his cereal. Without the maids his apartment grew filthy with shocking quickness; in just a week's time the superintendent had complaints from three of Reggie's neighbors about the smell of rotting garbage. At the end of the month he was evicted and took what little he owned back where he belonged, south of Twelfth Street, to a subdivision in Washington Park, where the reek of steel mills choked the air and he recognized the faces as his own, a subdivision where he now sits with his best white friend in the world, fucked up and sick to his soul of being legless and armless and useless.

The reason we've told you this, other than to enlighten you as to how Reggie has come to be the person you know, is to drive home a very important point: his illness and subsequent convalescence have left Reggie quite unstable, and what he's proposing is no joke.

49 "So okay," you say to Reggie, "let's pretend for a moment that I believe you're serious. How exactly are you going to get the explosives?"

"I know a guy," Reggie says.

"You know a guy."

"Pack this shit," Reggie says, handing you the bong. "Yeah, a guy.

Used to work for Fullerton, now he's with a demolitions outfit up in Oak Park."

"And you can just get him to order a few hundred pounds of C-4 for you. Have it overnighted, or whatever."

"No," Reggie says. "But I can have him order an extra five pounds here and there without anyone noticin'."

You give the loaded bong back to him. "So it'll only take, what. Four years to get together the amount you need?"

Reggie takes another of his huge rips off the bong. He holds it so long that almost no smoke comes out when he finally exhales. "That's almost exactly how long it took."

"Took," you say. "Past tense. As in."

"As in go into my bedroom closet and check out the contents of the big box that say *Lysol Basin Tub and Tile Cleaner.*"

Which you do.

"That shit ain't scrubbin' bubbles," Reggie cackles from the living room as you stand bent at the waist in his closet, trying hard to convince yourself of the reality of what you're seeing. Trust us when we tell you: this is indeed real. What you're looking at is not four hundred pounds of slate-gray Play-Doh, and Reggie is very, very serious about blowing up the Harold Washington SSA building.

And while we are glad when, after standing in the closet and thinking for a few minutes, you decide there is no way you're going to help Reggie with his plan, we have to tell you that any attempt to dissuade him is doomed to failure, and could even be dangerous. The man is too furious and sick at heart to be reasoned with.

So when you return to the living room, instead of trying to talk Reggie down, you play along. It turns out he has a very specific plan, and you have a very specific role to play. You listen and nod your head and excuse yourself at the earliest opportunity, wanting so badly to get away that you're willing to brave the streets alone. Frightened as you are, though, it still hasn't quite sunk in, so we will reiterate: Reggie is talking about blowing up a real building, and real people, with real explosives. What you do about this is, of course, up to you, but the seriousness of the situation cannot be overstated.

48 It's around four in the morning when you arrive home, too late really, but you call Amy anyway. She comes on the line after seven rings, sounding exactly as far away as she is.

"Junior," she says, and it is like Chopin, it is the most delicate and lovely of sounds, her voice saying your name.

You tell her everything—Reggie, the ghosts of his legs and arm, the explosives, his plan, how frightening it was to realize you even joked about helping him carry it off. You're about to tell her how grateful you are that she still serves as a sort of beacon to you, and who knows, if she hadn't come back into your life in even this small way you might be so sick and hopeless that Reggie's plot would have seemed like a good idea. You are about to say this, but before you have a chance she interrupts you.

"That's it," she says. "That is fucking it."

"Amy?"

"This bullshit," she says, "is going to stop. Now."

"Amy. Hey, list—"

"You call me up," she says, "at two o'clock in the morning. Hammered. On God only knows what kind of drugs. You call me up and tell me that you and your legless, armless buddy are thinking about blowing up a building by strapping four hundred pounds of explosives to his *wheelchair*. Am I getting this right, so far?"

"Yes," you say, "but listen, I told you I wasn't going to go through with—"

"Blowing up a building," she says again, "which would not be funny even if the very same thing hadn't happened in Oklahoma City just a few months ago. Would not."

"Honey, listen, you're not listening—"

"Don't call me that," she says. "Don't call me honey. In fact, don't call me at all, Junior. I've finally had it. You do whatever you want. Drink yourself to death, like your mother. Blow yourself up. Whatever. Just leave me alone. I don't want to talk to you anymore."

"Amy—"

"Do you hear me. I don't want to talk to you anymore. Are you understanding me. Is it sinking into that big brain of yours." These are statements, not questions, but you answer anyway, after a long pause.

"Yes."

The line goes dead.

You heave the telephone across the room. It hits the dresser on the far wall, leaving a jagged white scar in the finish.

47 Next morning Amy's words still cling to you like the stink of old beer. You lie there with a hand over your eyes and think about that chunk of rock and ice, the size of Rhode Island, pinwheeling through space with murderous intent, and you retrieve the phone and call Reggie and when he finally picks up you don't even bother with a greeting. "When do you want to do this?"

46 Now we have no choice but to suspend our usual stance of supportive neutrality and tell you that, from this point forward, there will be absolutely no assistance from us. You are doing something we cannot condone, though it is neither our place nor within our power to stop you.

45 It turns out that Reggie wants to do this soon. As in tomorrow, if possible. Which means you have a lot to take care of, from setting up the explosives on Reggie's wheelchair to renting a handicapped-accessible van. You do the latter first, and it takes most of the day before you find a suitable vehicle at a place in Skokie called WheelchairEscapes. Challenging as securing the van is, though, putting together Reggie's wheelchair bomb proves much worse. It doesn't require any technical expertise. Reggie has detailed printouts of how to rig up the bricks of C-4, a simple process involving fuses and detonation cable. Even so, this is the first time you've handled high explosives, and the fact that you plan to let yourself be blown up tomorrow somehow doesn't make you any more comfortable with the prospect of being blown up today.

It's our contention that this discomfort should maybe give you cause to reconsider what you're doing, and why.

"What are you sweatin' for?" Reggie asks, watching from the Canadian rocker as you work, placing the C-4 in a series of mesh pockets that have been draped over his wheelchair.

"It's August," you say. "And you live in a fifth-floor apartment with no air conditioning."

"You tellin' me," Reggie says. "That ain't why you sweatin', though."

"Actually," you say, wincing as you slide a brick into a pocket, "that is why. It's a hundred and twenty in here."

"Nah," Reggie says, "you sweatin' 'cause you afraid that C-4 is gonna explode if you so much as call it a bad name."

He's right, of course. You're convinced that the slightest jostling will set the stuff off. We could offer you some comforting facts about the relative stability of C-4, but as we said, there will be no help forthcoming from this quarter.

"I don't see why you gettin' so worked up." Reggie hits the bong, holds it until you're sure he'll pass out, then exhales and continues. "You should follow my example. Look at me: completely relaxed. Die today, die tomorrow. Makes no difference to The Fox."

"That's because you're power baked," you say. "Not to mention you've had longer to get used to the idea. I've only been on board for the last sixteen hours or so."

"Well, that's the seven-million-dollar question, though, ain't it? Is Junior really on board? And if he is, why is he sweatin' that C-4 so much?"

You pretend to ignore this, but the truth is, of course, in the clear light of day you've had a few moments when you wondered what you were doing. And riding to the rescue on the heels of this doubt came the rationalization of helping Reggie end what surely is the most miserable experience you've ever witnessed firsthand, along with your favorite refrain: the world's going to end soon so what does it matter?

We are here to tell you that this is bullshit of the first order. The real reason you've signed on to help Reggie is neither complex nor selfless: you are hurting, and you want others to feel that hurt. Simple. Common. Looked at from a certain angle in a certain light, it could even be seen as an effort to actually connect with the people you and Reggie plan to explode, to share your hurt with them, and in so sharing to create a genuine fraternity of grief: people united, however briefly, in the loss of limbs, lives, and love.

Still, there's no way to deny that Reggie is right—you're not in this all the way. We would take this as an encouraging sign that you might change your mind, except that when it comes to these types of self-destructive acts, no one ever has absolute conviction. Socrates barely topped 98% when he nipped the hemlock cocktail. Joan of Arc was about 97%. St. Peter registered a rather cowardly 89%, although this low number is due to the fact that his faith had eroded with time and persecution; if he'd been crucified with Jesus he would have registered a shade above 97%. Norman Morrison, who set himself ablaze in sight of the Pentagon to protest the Vietnam War, and Afif Ahmed Hamid, one of the Black September terrorists killed by German police in Munich, clocked an identical, Socratic 98.4%. Impressive as these numbers are, they serve only to illustrate that there is always doubt and fear, even among philosophers, fanatics, and triple-amputees with multiple addictions and relentless, agonizing memories of being whole.

44 You've finished rigging up the wheelchair bomb, and the chair's electric motor whirs dangerously as it strains to move the bulk, but move it does. By now it's dark and the heat hasn't abated in the least and you want to go out and get away from all this. Reggie wants to come along but you tell him no, and just in case he decides to go out on his own you avoid O'Toole's and instead hit The Hole You're Inn, a boarding-house/pub you keep in reserve for occasions when you find yourself booted from O'Toole's before closing.

Tonight there's a strange, good vibe in The Hole. The leather-vested biker types and thrice-divorced women who look fifty and dress twenty are a peaceful lot. None of the usual screaming catfights over a disputed man. None of the bloody, tooth-cracking scrums that often follow a bumped shoulder or perceived slight. Tonight it's all smiles and good-natured backslapping. Laughter hangs in the air like cigarette smoke. Someone has programmed the jukebox to play nothing but "Old Time

Rock & Roll," and couples sit on one another's laps, smile nose-to-nose, sway happily to the beat. It's a moment rare as a perfect game in baseball, charmed, almost magical, but though you are in the midst of the harmony, you are not a part of it in any emotionally significant sense. Put another, simpler way: you don't feel anything. You're the burned-out bulb in a string of colorful Christmas lights. You drink and drink and drink and by the time you leave, just before closing, you literally cannot talk anymore.

Which does not stop you, of course, from dialing Amy's number on returning to your brother's. The line rings at least thirty times with no answer before you finally pass out sitting up on the bed.

43 When you wake in the morning, still propped against the headboard, the phone is ringing, and though in the confusion of a crippling hangover you don't have any clear idea what to do with it, you instinctually pick up the receiver. On the other end is Reggie.

"You're late," he tells you.

"What time is it?" you ask, because you can't think of anything else to say and it seems appropriate, given what Reggie just told you.

"Time for you to get your ass over here."

"Give me a minute." You manage, after some effort, to open your eyes. "I'm just getting out of bed."

Before Reggie has a chance to chastise you further you hang up and move to the bathroom, stripping your clothes off and dropping them on the floor as you go. In the shower you listen to the hum and blare of life on the streets outside and think about how it's strange, given what you and Reggie are about to do, that you're still observing the conventions of normal behavior: answering the phone with a polite "Hello," showering and brushing your teeth.

Soon enough the centipede starts in, twisting and skittering. You try deep breathing but it's no good, so you turn off the water and towel dry with stiff, frenzied strokes, as though you're trying to wipe a battalion of angry fire ants off your body. You pick last night's clothes up off the floor and put it all back on, save the underwear, then step out.

42 By the time you reach Reggie's building you're genuinely frantic despite having swallowed three of the cool blue tablets some O'Toole's regular stole from her cat's vet. Normally these have an even greater calming effect on the centipede than the Vicodin, but this time they don't touch it. The thin integument of calm holding you together threatens to fail catastrophically and splatter the van's interior with the contents of your psyche, which would not be pretty in the least.

"Where the fuck have you been?" Reggie asks when you open the door to his apartment. His chair rolls with great whirring effort into the kitchen. He doesn't look or sound himself. You can't place your finger on what's different about him, other than to say it is not good. The net pockets swing slowly from every inch of his chair.

"Don't," you say. You slap a hand to your forehead to keep it from exploding. "Don't. Okay."

"Tell me 'don't,'" he says. "We got shit to do, here."

"Reggie," you say, eyes squeezed shut. "Just a minute ago? When I said 'Don't'? I have never before been so serious about anything. Never in my life. Now we are going to do what we planned today. But right now—for just a little bit—I need you to lay. The fuck. Off."

Miracle of miracles, Reggie actually listens. He rolls back into the living room—every time the chair moves under its burden you're certain the motor will throw some critical part and die hissing and smoking—and is silent for several minutes. You lean against the wall and press the heels of your hands into your eyes until you see brilliant, silent fireworks. You moan, long and low, for nearly half a minute. When your moaning trails off the apartment is quiet. After a while Reggie asks you in a voice you don't recognize to come into the living room and pack the bong. So you do that, not bothering to ask how he suddenly has the time for a bong hit, if he's in such a hurry. What's the point of asking questions, expecting answers? You've gone mad, and Reggie's disappeared completely and been replaced by a demon with a voice like André the Giant.

41 In what seems like no time at all you're out on the street again, guiding Reggie into the van. A few people eyeball the wheelchair, and one guy

going by in a car slows way down and rubbernecks, but to your relief no one comments or asks questions.

You slalom through surface streets for a few minutes, then turn onto the I-90 ramp and merge slowly with the midday traffic. All the while Reggie's muttering darkly in the back. His breathing grows loud and ragged and a glance in the rearview mirror reveals in his eyes an admixture of equal parts fury, grief, and pharmaceuticals. Sweat stands out on his cheeks and forehead. Whenever he stops talking to himself his mouth hangs open as though paralyzed, the lips slack and buffeted by gusts of breath. His face is transformed utterly. It is barely human, unlike anything you have seen before. He has clearly taken something other than a few bong hits. To a normal person he would be a disconcerting sight, but you've been lulled by sluggish freeway traffic back into an odd reflective state, and there is now quite a show going on inside your head, a strange retrospective of your life like a vacation slideshow put on in a neighbor's half-finished basement.

Scenes rise and fade in rough chronological order, from the earliest memory you didn't know you had—that of leaning against your father's chest with his concrete slab of a forearm propping up your diapered butt—to coming home the night Amy told you it was over. Each scene is backlit with a color that corresponds to the emotion the scene recalls: reds for anger and shame, rare yellows for joy, whites for varying degrees of apathy, and blues for sorrow. As you watch it becomes apparent that blue is the predominant shade of your life, nearly ubiquitous, appearing so frequently that it turns yellows to greens, reds to purples, etc. Your life is so blue it looks like a James Cameron movie. As the slideshow approaches the present, even the greens turn fully blue, and the purples, and then the different shades of blue themselves swirl and homogenize, until your whole life and times, birth to now, is the same color as the ocean off the coast of Easter Island, the bluest water in the world. For you, there is no anger, no joy, no indifference. There's never been anything but the sorrow of loss, paid over and over and always in advance, and your determination to go forth in the face of that sorrow. There is nothing heroic about this doggedness; there may well be, in fact, something cowardly concealed within it. Either way, you suddenly recognize—and appreciate—that more than anything else, this relentless slogging forward into life's headwind makes you truly your father's son.

40 It all goes out of you then, the blue. Disappears entirely and irrevocably. It seems important to figure out what will replace it, so you pull into the breakdown lane and put the van in park. You sit watching traffic stutter past on the left, calm as you've been since the womb, ruminating with bovine placidity over what it is you're supposed to do with the fifteen years left to you and everyone else on the planet.

We implore you to stay with this moment.

39 Reggie, meanwhile, has begun to inquire in the André the Giant voice concerning why the fuck you're stopped, but despite his tone you don't feel any particular urgency to provide an answer.

In his altered state Reggie is even less patient than normal. He waits only two seconds for you to respond, then says, "Either move this van, or I'm a blow it up."

"Reggie," you say.

"Just go ahead and keep sittin' here," he says, "if you think I'm kiddin'."

He is not kidding, we assure you.

You turn your head and see he's got the SPD detonator, which looks like a silver pen, in his half-hand. You start the van and pull forward, hoping the remaining drive will give you time to talk him out of this.

"Reggie," you say, looking over your left shoulder for an opportunity to merge, "listen, something has happened to me, here, and I don't mind telling you it has altered the way I think about pretty much everything."

"That's very interesting," Reggie says without much interest.

"Also," you say, "also, I'm starting to believe that this isn't such a great idea after all. Blowing up the SSA building. I suggest you think for a minute about what you plan to do, and then, having thought about it, call the whole thing off and go home and get high and live to watch the sun set tonight from your kitchen window."

38 Though we're beyond pleased that you've changed your mind, it's important that you understand just how dangerous Reggie is in this altered state. "I have a suggestion for you," he says, using his elbow as a lever to prop himself up. "Shut the fuck up and drive, is my suggestion."

You take the exit onto Washington Boulevard, keeping an eye on the rearview mirror as Reggie fingers the detonator and watches the city through the van's privacy glass.

At this point the Harold Washington building is only a couple of blocks away, and with Reggie still unwavering you're not sure what to do, so you pull into an alley and turn off the engine. "Okay, Reggie," you say. "This is the end of the line." A risky, risky tack. "I'm not taking you any further. You can blow us up right here, or get out and roll the rest of the way to the Social Security building. I won't stop you."

Reggie glares at you in the mirror, his eyes red and baleful. "Unstrap this shit," he says. "Let me out of here."

"We could go to O'Toole's instead," you say. "Friday night at O'Toole's, Reggie. Bacchanalia. It's what we live for. All your friends will be there."

"Friends, shit," Reggie says. "I'm not their friend. I'm their pet nigger. They like to keep The Fox around, make them feel like they good, tolerant white folks. Buy Reggie a drink like it's affirmative action night. Not today. Unstrap this thing. If you ain't goin' with me, I'll go alone. Don't make no difference."

Wisely, you do as he instructs. Soon he's down on the pavement beside the van.

"See you later, Reggie," you say.

"Probably not," he says. "I'm not mad at you, though. I understand. You just a kid. Kids don't want to die." And even though this has nothing to do with it, you see no point in correcting him.

He pushes the joystick and the chair groans toward the end of the alley. You watch until he reaches the sidewalk, then call out to him.

He spins around to face you again. "You see I'm busy here."

"Reggie," you say. "Just let the people get out first. Okay? You'll still make your point."

He waves a dismissive half-hand at you, then hits the stick and rolls south toward West Madison, disappearing from sight behind the brick wall of a walk-up taqueria.

37 You drive the van back out to Skokie. When you return to your brother's place you switch on the TV and a stab of disappointment reaches you through the lingering indifference of revelation. There are news flashes on every channel, cameras all trained on one Harold Washington Social Security Administration building, which is ringed with police cars, ambulances, and a SWAT armored personnel carrier. Emergency strobes flash in the artificial twilight produced by tall buildings. People talk anxiously behind barricades, point, hug themselves. Details are hazy, the newscasters say, but they have multiple reports that a man has entered the building with a bomb.

The scene goes on for hours, and while the only visible difference in the situation is that day has turned to night, there are updates almost every minute, speculation regarding what's going on inside. The bomber is a white man in a wheelchair, you're told. Two minutes later, correction, a black man, no wheelchair. There are unconfirmed reports that in addition to the bomb the assailant is wielding a weapon of some kind, a modified AK-47, perhaps, or maybe even they're being told it's possible a rocket-propelled grenade, but no, after hearing a description of the weapon CNN's resident tactical expert cuts in and says that based on the description it's his expert opinion that this is not an AK at all, and certainly not an RPG, but rather a FAMAS French assault rifle. Meantime, police negotiators have managed to contact the assailant through use of a throw phone, which the SWAT team tossed through the glass front door and into the lobby, but so far they've been unsuccessful at convincing the man to either give himself up or allow some or all of the six or seven hundred unconfirmed people in the building to evacuate.

Sometime during all this you notice that the strange calm you experienced earlier has faded, and you are trembling, badly. And sweating. And crying a bit, if you're not mistaken. This is not the centipede, though there are similarities; rather it is a normal, if belated, physiological reaction to having almost died.

36 Just as it's occurring to you, around ten o'clock, that you not only haven't had a drink yet, but haven't even thought about one until now, there is a sudden commotion on-screen as a mass of several hundred people rushes from the front entrance of the Washington building, running with their hands held up. They move like cattle driven by wolves, pouring through bottlenecks created by parked patrol cars and paying no heed to the officers trying to direct their escape. The television announcer says there's been no official word but it seems evident that heroic police negotiators have succeeded, and the assailant has released hundreds of hostages after a nearly eight-hour ordeal of terror.

But the ordeal isn't yet over, the announcer says, because there is still a man barricaded inside the building with a bomb and a deadly exotic French assault rifle, and no one knows his motivations or demands, and of course it is not necessary to point out the frightening parallels between this potential bombing-in-progress of a federal building and another that happened just a few months ago in Oklahoma City which united a nation in shock and mourning, and this could go on for hours or possibly even days, so we'll be right back after this break with more coverage of the *Chicago Social Security Standoff*.

You sit back and breathe deep as an advertisement comes on for a topical pain reliever with an odor so famously awful it ought to be copyrighted. Your chest hitches and shudders. You watch a commercial featuring a stubby cartoon character in a toga and laurel leaves shouting about pizza, and realize you have no idea what you wish to happen. Your legs want to move, so you go to the kitchen for a beer and return just in time for continuing coverage of the *Chicago Social Security Standoff*.

35 It has become a standoff in the traditional sense, with the police holding their ground behind walls and car doors, and absolute silence from Reggie. It's near midnight. To fill time the announcer brings in the network's crisis negotiation expert, who explains that at this stage, assuming that the subject has released everyone in the building (which is never a safe assumption when actually negotiating a crisis, the expert says, but for the purposes of discussing the current situation on

television is a fine assumption to work from), the approach to negotiating now changes; it's to be treated more as a suicide intervention rather than a hostage negotiation. Of course the alleged bomb involved makes it considerably more dangerous than your usual suicide intervention, but the basic strategy, the expert says, should be the same. In his expert opinion.

34 It's been forty-five minutes since you opened the beer, and you're only half done with it when the phone rings. Once. Twice. In the middle of the third ring you pick up. You are hoping it's Amy. You say hello, get no response. There's a faint click as whoever is on the other end hangs up. Less than a second later the Harold Washington Social Security Administration Building disappears. The image on the television wavers, goes black, and there's a quick cut to the studio anchor, who stares at the camera for a few silent seconds, then coughs and mumbles something about trying to reestablish picture on what has evidently become a worst-case scenario, and obviously everyone hopes that there really was no one else in the building other than the subject, and—yes, as he said they will try to reestablish picture and while they work on that they will discuss in-studio what's just happened. You watch for a while without really seeing anything, not certain at all how you should feel. Your hand has gone numb around the beer can. Soon the anchor tells you that they believe they've got another video feed established from the site of the *Tragedy in Chicago*, that the images you're about to see are graphic and upsetting, and soon CNN expert and crisis counselor to the stars Hank Greenlaw will be joining us to offer some tips on coping with our shared grief, but in any event this is not for the faint of heart, and you may want to have any children leave the room.

Partial transcripts from the files of Hilda Begin, M.S., Ph.D., Occupational and Mental Health Therapist, Elgin, Illinois. Client is Rodney Thibodeau. Sessions conducted between 6/98 and 9/98. Transcribed to hard copy from Dictaphone recordings.

6/15, Mon., 3:00–3:50 p.m., client's home

Even after ten years playing for the Cubs—is it ten years? Or eleven? No, it's ten, I think. I'll need to check but I think it's ten.

· · · · ·

Twelve? You're sure?

· · · · ·

Anyway it's weird coming back from a road trip because Chicago still doesn't feel like home to me. Well home's not the right word, it will never be home, really, I guess I should say it still doesn't feel like *where I live.* After twelve years. Isn't that funny? It feels like just another part of the road trip, only longer, with bigger hotel rooms.

· · · · ·

Yeah, it was easier when Junior was around, even though he was pretty messed up a lot of times and he knew how I felt about that, but I got used to having him here and now he's gone again and I feel lost. He's the brains of the operation. I just play baseball. I used to tell him that and he'd say no, brother, you've got more brains than you give yourself credit for, you're smarter than me in a lot of ways.

· · · · ·

He's gotten better but he still drinks more than he probably should. Not that I really can keep track of him anymore. I only see him once every two or three months. He'll come without letting me know but he never misses me because we're always playing at home when he comes so he must pay attention to our schedule. He just shows up here or at the clubhouse. There he'll be. My little brother.

. . . . .

New Mexico. I've never been there. The closest I've been to New Mexico is Colorado, I think. Denver. Coors Field. That's close to New Mexico, isn't it? Sort of?

. . . . .

But it's closer than San Diego? Or St. Louis?

. . . . .

So Coors Field is as close as I've ever been to New Mexico. Which is where Junior spends most of his time.

. . . . .

What does "preoccupied" mean?

. . . . .

You think I think about Junior too much?

. . . . .

Well if you're asking what I think, I don't mean to be mean or anything, and I'm not saying you're wrong Hilda but I don't think that's true at all. He's my baby brother. He explains things to me in ways I can understand, and he doesn't ever laugh like Gutierrez and Brant Alexander do, they think I can't tell they're making fun of me, and then Reynolds will holler at them and say something like Rodney's hitting .348, you fucking toolkits, what are you carrying for averages right now? .255? .260? So maybe you should shut the fuck up with your jokes.

. . . . .

I like Reynolds. He's a good guy and a good catcher.

. . . . .

Sorry so like I says, really if I'm gonna be honest all there is to say is I miss Junior. That's it. I don't see Ma and Dad much, especially during the season. I'd come back from a road trip and Junior'd be here and we'd go out to eat and see movies. Play Street Fighter III on the Dreamcast. But he's doing important work and I understand that.

. . . . .

In New Mexico, like I just says.

. . . . .

I don't know. He doesn't tell me much about it. He works with telescopes, looking at the sky at night. The way he put it is, he says I'm not there in any official capacity. He's sort of a consultant. And he doesn't get paid. I still have to send him money. Which I don't mind doing that.

. . . . .

You think he's taking advantage of me?

. . . . .

Oh. Do *I* think he's taking advantage of me. If you want to know what I think, I think no. He's doing important things, like I says. And he hardly asks for any money at all. The only time it's more than a couple hundred is when he needs a plane ticket to Boston. Which is like maybe twice a year.

. . . . .

He travels to Boston. MIT. You know what that is?

. . . . .

The school, right. I don't know what he does there, but it's part of his work, I'm sure.

. . . . .

No, I don't think he's making this up just as an excuse to ask for money.

. . . . .

Listen, I don't like you saying things like that about my brother.

. . . . .

You're not *asking* me how I feel, you're *telling* me how I *should* feel.

. . . . .

I'm not trying to be mean or make you feel bad. But like I tell Gutierrez, I'm not the smartest but I'm also not as stupid as you think. I know more about Junior's work than I'm saying. Because he told me but made me promise to keep it to myself.

. . . . .

I can't. I probably shouldn't even have said anything about the telescopes.

. . . . .

Making you believe me isn't important enough to break my promise to Junior.

. . . . .

It sure sounds like you're questioning my honesty.

. . . . .

It's time to leave for the ballpark? Really? Already?

8/13, Thurs., 1:30–2:20 p.m., Westin Hotel, San Francisco

Am I bothered by it? You mean does it make me upset? I guess the answer is yes, sort of. I'm worried. But I'm not really surprised—I've known all along what Junior was working on. Now everyone else knows too so I guess I don't have to keep the secret anymore.

. . . . .

It doesn't matter to me what they're saying. I don't read newspapers anyway.

. . . . .

See like usual I feel like you're telling me what I should think. Not asking.

. . . . .

Yes, that *is too* what you're doing. Just like everyone else you think my brother's crazy and you want me to think the same thing.

. . . . .

No, I don't believe what he's saying.

. . . . .

Because God wouldn't do that to us.

. . . . .

Maybe you're right. I don't think he's crazy, but at the same time I don't think what he's saying is true, either. So yeah I guess that doesn't really make sense. I guess it is like you say a contradiction.

. . . . .

Well, really, and please don't get mad at me for saying this like you're not smart enough to figure it out yourself, but would they be paying any attention to Junior in the newspapers and on TV if he was just another crazy person? I mean every city I go to to play ball there's at least one guy sitting on a corner somewhere wearing a parka and a winter hat in the middle of summer, talking about the end of the world. Nobody's talking to them on Fox News or writing articles about them in the *Chicago Tribute* [sic].

. . . . .

Yes, even if they're only writing the articles to *disparage* him. By *disparage* I guess you mean make fun of.

. . . . .

I still think I made a good point. Even if they are just *disparaging* him, there's something going on here because otherwise they wouldn't be talking about him at all.

. . . . .

I know the government said he doesn't work for them and they don't know who he is. Like I says before, he wasn't official. He consulted. He told me he was helping them get their telescopes to where they could see further out into space. Helping them improve the *technology*. But he wasn't an employee, and he wasn't being paid.

. . . . .

I don't know what that means. Please stop trying to confuse me.

. . . . .

But I think you are, because you know I have a hard time understanding big words and technical counselor sort of language. So when you say things like *elaborate delusional systems are*—how did you say it again?

. . . . .

Elaborate delusional systems are a hallmark of classic paranoid schizophrenia. I don't know what that means. Except I've got a feeling it's supposed to be disparaging.

. . . . .

The last time I saw him was . . . I'm not sure. You know how bad I am with time. It was maybe two or three weeks ago. We were on a home stand three weeks ago, right?

. . . . .

Right, the end of our last home stand. We played the Brewers.

. . . . .

I'm sorry, you're right, the Pirates. It was just before the thing on CNN, with the black fellow.

. . . . .

Bernard Shaw, you're right. You always know these things. I don't know why I'm always so surprised at how smart you are. Who's that black guy, I ask, and right off you say Bernard Shaw without even having to think about it, and you're right. And yet it always surprises me.

. . . . .

You're welcome. The last time I saw Junior was right before the first time he went on TV, with Bernard Shaw. Which was about three weeks ago.

. . . . .

He seemed . . . like himself. Though he did tell me that things were happening at the observatory in New Mexico and it was possible that he wouldn't be back for a while. He would be talking to people on TV and doing interviews and having meetings and he might not be able to come and see me until it was over.

. . . . .

I haven't seen him, so I guess he was right.

. . . . .

He did send a telegram asking for money a few days ago. But I didn't actually talk to him.

. . . . .

Listen I don't want to be rude. I know you're doing your job and you're very good at it and sometimes to be good at your job you have to say things that only make sense to someone as smart as you. But still I want you to be careful what you say about Junior. Because that *does* upset me.

. . . . .

And it makes me uncomfortable to have to ask you that because I don't like making conflict with anyone. At all.

. . . . .

But why is that a problem? Why is it a problem to just want to get along with everyone as much as you can? I don't understand. Honestly. I'm only asking.

. . . . .

See, there you go again. He's not taking advantage of me.

. . . . .

I know you didn't say Junior specifically, but you didn't have to. I know who you're talking about.

. . . . .

You know what, let me tell you something about what my brother did for me. It's like—do you ever read *Reader's Digest*?

. . . . .

They have a word they use to describe these little stories about things that happen to people in their lives. Like this guy who went hiking and got attacked by a grizzly bear. Or the woman who'd given up her baby for adoption and then forty years later her daughter comes to her birthday party as a surprise. There's a word for it. A *term.*

. . . . .

No, not anecdote. It starts with a "V."

. . . . .

Yes, that's it. How do you say it again?

. . . . .

Vignette. Right. In *Reader's Digest* they call them slice-of-life vignettes.

. . . . .

So if it's okay I will now tell you a slice-of-life vignette about my brother.

. . . . .

Right so you know first of all that I am a cocaine addict.

. . . . .

No, of course not. I haven't used cocaine for a long time. But the program teaches you that once you're an addict you're always an addict, even if you never touch your substance of choice for the rest of your life. Like the alcoholics say: it's alcohol-ism, not -wasm.

. . . . .

Right. So after I left rehab and came home my parents were watching me close. Dad especially. He was really mad about the whole thing. He blamed Uncle Rodney for making me a cocaine addict even though it wasn't his fault, Uncle Rodney didn't even know I knew where his cocaine stash was and he definitely wouldn't have ever given any to me. He took care of me and told me I was like his own son. This was because he never had kids of his own. He loved me and was just as sad as anybody to find out I was an addict.

But when I came home from rehab Dad said I couldn't see Uncle Rodney anymore. I couldn't go to Uncle Rodney's, which was bad enough because I pretty much lived there, and he couldn't come over to visit me, either. Nothing. So I was pretty upset. But sometimes that's the way Dad is. He's the best man I know but when he's angry he doesn't like to listen to anyone. It's just what he says goes. He even beat Uncle Rodney up, which I didn't know about then but found out later.

After a while I decided to call Uncle Rodney anyway. I called him and said why don't you come over, and he said I can't. But I told him it was okay, that my dad wasn't mad at him anymore. It was a lie. I feel bad about it even now. I just wanted to see him. And Uncle Rodney believed me and he came over. It was really good to see him. Except that Dad came home to get his toolbox because the car had broken down at the warehouse and he needed to wrench or hammer something to get it going again. And he tried to get his hands on Uncle Rodney but Uncle Rodney went running and when Dad came back in from chasing him he was so mad his face was red and his lips had spit on them. And he was mad at me.

. . . . .

No, he never really spanked us. Maybe once. I guess I don't really believe that he would have hit me. But right at that moment it was hard not to be scared.

. . . . .

But so anyway the point is that Junior saved me.

. . . . .

By telling Dad he was the one who asked Uncle Rodney to come over.

. . . . .

To understand what a big deal that is, you have to think about this: Junior and I had both seen our dad get angry like that before, and we had seen what happened to people he got mad at. Like Uncle Rodney's nose for example. Dad almost tore it right off his face. And even knowing that, Junior walked in and saw what was going on and took all the attention off me and put it on himself.

. . . . .

He didn't seem to know what to think about that. He just stared at Junior. Then he punched a hole in the kitchen wall and went down into the basement to get his toolbox.

. . . . .

I asked him that same question after. And he said he didn't think there really was a reason why, except that he saw his brother was in trouble and he thought he should do something to help.

. . . . .

That's Junior. He never gets emotional about things. But that doesn't mean you can't count on him.

[Telephone rings; client answers, speaks briefly, replaces handset.]

Did you order room service?

. . . . .

I did? When? Are you sure?

9/8, Mon., 9:15–10:00 a.m., client's home

I don't want to talk right now.

. . . . .

I don't want you here. I'm sorry to be rude.

. . . . .

Well would you want to have to sit down and talk about your dreams and what you remember from being a—what is it again? Before you're born?

. . . . .

—a *fetus,* would you want to answer questions about what you remember from being a fetus, if your brother was missing?

. . . . .

No, I don't want to talk about that, either. Talking about it won't help us figure out where Junior is. What I want is to go to the park and take batting practice.

. . . . .

I know it's an off day. But batting practice helps me relax. It's either that or play Dreamcast, and Dreamcast just reminds me of Junior.

. . . . .

I don't understand why it's important that we talk about what's going on with Junior.

. . . . .

I don't think I want to *process* anything.

. . . . .

I'm sorry. I really am. It's just I'm so worried and it's making me angry, which I'm not used to. I don't know how to be angry the right way I guess.

. . . . .

No, I'm not worried about that. I know that's what the police are saying, but they don't know Junior. They're wrong.

. . . . .

Because I'm sure, that's all.

. . . . .

I don't want to tell you what I think happened. You'll just tell me I'm wrong. Say I'm stupid.

. . . . .

Maybe you wouldn't say it that way, but that's what you would think.

. . . . .

Okay fine. I'm worried someone kidnapped him.

. . . . .

I don't know why anyone would kidnap him. But it's the only thing that makes sense. If he planned to go away he would have told me. Or Dad. But he didn't say anything.

[Client exhibiting uncharacteristic signs of agitation; tearing empty match-book into small pieces, shaking leg up and down so vigorously that the floor vibrates.]

. . . . .

Consider the possibility that *what?*

. . . . .

No. *No.*

[Long pause.]

Hilda, I want you to go.

. . . . .

No. I'm not listening to you anymore. You don't have any idea what you're talking about and so I'm not listening. Go. Don't come back.

. . . . .

Yes, my father hired you. He hired you to help me figure out the difference between clean and dirty clothes. He hired you to help me remember to blow candles out before leaving the house. He did not hire you to tell me that my brother killed himself.

. . . . .

This doesn't feel like help to me.

. . . . .

Besides, yes it's true my father hired you but I pay your salary. And I want you to leave and don't come back ever again.

. . . . .

[Client shouts something unintelligible, rising from his seat and exhibiting highly agitated and somewhat threatening behavior. Session terminated.]

Junior

Sawyer comes down the hall sometime on the afternoon of a day I am certain is not Wednesday, Thursday, or Friday. It's been roughly two months since the last time Sawyer was here. I know it's him because the wooden soles of his oxfords echo smartly through the cell block. The only other people I see during the course of my endless days are the guards, and they wear tactical boots with rubber soles that hiss and whisper on the concrete floors.

Sawyer's footfalls stop outside the door to my cell. He slides the eye-level partition aside and says, simply, "Junior."

"You again," I say. "How long has it been?"

"Long enough that I have been ordered to come to this desolate place and speak with you once more."

"No, seriously," I say. "How long has it been? I've lost track of the day of the week."

"It's Friday," Sawyer says.

I wonder how I could have been so far off. "So what brings you around, Sawyer? Things starting to resemble *The Road Warrior* out there?"

There's the static blast of a two-way radio being keyed. "Control," Sawyer says. "Open four, if you would, please." The lock buzzes, and Sawyer swings the door open, steps in with his head bowed to avoid smacking the frame, and closes the door behind him. It clicks, locking Sawyer in with me, but he has nothing to fear. Even if I presented a threat, which I do not, Sawyer is massive by most standards, not to mention a 5 dan black belt in Krav Maga. Given reason, he could and would wad me up like a typo-ridden sheet of paper.

"No," Sawyer says, "no problems. In fact it is, in spite of your best efforts, business as usual."

"No one believed me," I say.

"No one believed you," Sawyer agrees.

"Despite the evidence Ross and I put together."

"Despite all that," Sawyer says. "Good, compelling, easy-to-digest evidence. Solid science, as I've told you before."

"But no one picked up the ball after you guys disappeared us."

Sawyer sits splay-legged on the stool against the wall. The cuffs of his pantlegs ride up to reveal red, white, and blue argyle socks, a surprising dash of pizzazz for such a dry and utterly colorless man. "Well, a few . . . fringe-dwellers, I guess you'd call them," he says. "A population so large and diverse, they're always going to be out there. They present no real threat, though, because they can never settle on a conspiracy theory or whacked-out alternate religion long enough to get really organized. They're too eager to move on to the next cauldron of Kool-Aid. And of course if they did manage to organize, we have options for dealing with that."

"Waco," I say.

"E.g.," Sawyer agrees, "though that's sort of a poor example, since we usually prefer to maintain a somewhat lower profile. Also, believe it or not, we'd rather avoid wholesale killing when possible."

"Hmpf."

"After all, this is America," Sawyer says. "Well, this, where we are right now, the prison in which we find ourselves at this moment, is not, in point of fact, America. But you know what I mean."

"I'm glad you mention that," I say. "Because I've been asking but can't get an answer: Where exactly *is* here?"

"Can't tell you." Sawyer pulls a mint from his breast pocket, pops it out of its cellophane wrapper, and parks it between his cheek and gum. "I can give you a few hints, though, if you'd be willing, in exchange, to listen to a proposal."

"Okay," I say. "The hints first, though. Then I'll listen."

"Former Eastern Bloc," Sawyer says. "Savage history under Soviet rule. Harsh winters. Gorgeous young women."

"You've just described every former Eastern Bloc country."

"Well I'm not going to make it too obvious. And don't forget, sometimes Cuba and Vietnam were included in the designation 'Eastern Bloc.'"

"Great," I say. "So I know I'm not in Cuba or Vietnam. We're really getting somewhere."

"And now that I've held up my end of the bargain," Sawyer says. "If I may."

"Go ahead."

"I'm leaving tonight for Washington," Sawyer says. "I propose that you accompany me."

"For what?"

Sawyer laughs. "For what! For what," he says, entreating the cinder-block wall to share in his incredulity. "What do you think, for what?"

"I'm guessing it's not to have dinner at the White House."

"To save the world, Junior," Sawyer says. "Only that."

"From?"

He stares, bemused. "You're joking, yes?"

"You're saying you believe me?"

"Of course we do, Junior," he says. "We've always believed you. We picked up C/1998 E1 when you first started making noise and have been tracking it since. It's real. It's happening. You were right."

"So then why did you kidnap me?"

Sawyer smirks. "Because you went around *telling* people," he says. "Which in my opinion, not to mention the opinions of many other people whose opinions matter quite a lot, was a terribly irresponsible thing for you to do. Both as a person and as an American."

"What could being an American possibly have to do with this?"

"I'll get to that in a minute. First, it was irresponsible of you as a person because of minor potential side effects such as, I don't know, pulling things out of my hat here: unrest, mass panic, the resultant damage to infrastructure and economy, the collapse of all civilization. Stuff like that."

"None of which came to pass, evidently."

"True," Sawyer says. He crunches the mint between his teeth. "It was irresponsible of you as an *American*, however, because until you started running your mouth our enemies had no idea about C/1998 E1. If you'd done the patriotic thing and kept this to a handful of eyes-only Agency personnel, that would have given us months, perhaps years, to turn the situation to our advantage."

"I'm not following," I say. "How exactly do we turn a planet-killing comet to our advantage?"

"Oh, grow up, Junior." Sawyer stands and paces the cell. This is not easy, considering that the cell is only eight feet long. "We could develop systems to break up the object, then project which countries we're most likely to be in conflict with around the time of impact, and aim the shards in their direction."

"The silliest fucking thing I have ever heard."

"Not so silly," Sawyer says. "We've got a team at UVA working on it as we speak. Some of our best. They tell us it's feasible, with proper funding."

"Of course," I say. "The funding is the thing."

"Or," Sawyer continues, "or, we could have gotten a jump on extraterrestrial emigration technologies, then announced C/1998 E1 and used our head start as leverage with the world's problem children. Want a seat on the bus, Pakistan? Cease and desist with the nuclear testing. Need a ticket off the planet, Saudi Arabia? May we suggest you give Christianity another look."

"You're serious."

"As dengue fever," Sawyer says. "We're still pursuing these possibilities, but thanks to you we have no idea how much of a head start we've got on the others."

"What others?"

"There's no way to confirm this, but it's safe to assume that at least a dozen foreign entities—some friendly, some not-so—are aware of C/1998 E1 and the threat it poses."

"I thought you said no one believed me."

"No civilians. But intelligence services? Militaries? They look into these things, no matter how outrageous they may seem at first blush."

"So maybe," I say, "it's time to consider the benefits—the possible necessity—of looking at this as something other than just another geopolitical battle royale."

"Spoken like a true liberal," Sawyer says. He stops pacing, puts one foot up on the stool, and hikes up a fallen sock. "But why bother cooperating when we've got something no one else can match?"

"And that is?"

Sawyer stares. "Why, you, of course."

And it becomes clear suddenly, though it should have been earlier: the invitation to Washington is conditional upon my agreeing to help. I lace my fingers behind my head and make a show of considering. "What makes you think I care enough to help?"

Sawyer pops another mint, grins at me as he arranges it between his cheek and gum. "Your Chicken Little media tour would seem to suggest you care," he says.

"That was a long time ago. I've had—well, Sawyer, I guess only you know for sure just how long I've been in this place—but let's say I've had plenty of time to reflect. Ruminate. Come around to a different way of thinking."

"Two years," Sawyer says. "Almost two years. And I'm not buying, Junior. You wouldn't let that girlfriend of yours die. Or your brother. Or your parents."

"She's not my girlfriend," I say. "Just ask her; I'm sure she'd tell you in no uncertain terms."

Sawyer plunges his hands into his hip pockets. "Perhaps I could appeal to your self-interest?" he says. "Say yes, and this will be the last day you have to look at these walls."

"Not good enough," I say. "You'll have to do better. Consider it compensation for me doing my patriotic duty and languishing in this hole for two years."

"This isn't a negotiation, Junior," Sawyer says. "Listen: We know about your involvement in the Chicago Social Security bombing. Your brother's credit card was used for the handicapped van rental. He could be in a great deal of trouble."

"That might be an effective threat if it had even the tiniest little baby teeth. You're forgetting that Rodney has a perfect alibi, and a few hundred thousand people to corroborate: he was on a West Coast road trip with the Cubs. So you can't touch him. As for me, what are you going to do—throw me in some concrete box in the backwaters of Eastern Europe and hold me there, without due process, for years on end? Wow, would that ever be terrible. I don't think I could stand it. Whatever horrible thing you decide to do to me, please don't let it be that."

Sawyer grins. "You're good," he says. "I'm enjoying this. Would you like a mint? I've got pocketsful."

I shake my head. Wait. Watch.

"Okay," he says finally. "What's it going to take?"

"Make Amy love me again."

Sawyer crosses his arms. "How are we supposed to do that?"

"I'm sure you've got methods," I say. "Mind-control cocktails. Precision lobotomies. The particulars don't really matter."

He rubs his chin, considers. "I'll have to make some calls," he says. "Honestly, Junior, that's a tough one even for us. I'm not sure exactly how we would—"

"Sawyer, I'm having fun with you," you say. "I've got no interest in a Stepford girlfriend."

"So, what then?"

"I want my parents set up financially."

"Done," Sawyer says without hesitation.

"You can't just show up in a black Explorer and hand them a briefcase full of money, though," I say. "My father won't accept it. You can't have the bank make a clerical error. My father will march right in there and show it to them."

"What kind of idiot would turn down millions of dollars just because it didn't belong to him?"

"Careful," I say. "You want to be careful, Sawyer, because listen, life has never been any great fucking shakes in my opinion. In fact, it's always seemed a messy and heartbreaking and overall pointless affair. And it's not like I have a lot to go back to. So if you make me angry I might just say forget it, and you can leave me here to rot and figure out this problem on your own."

Sawyer holds his hands up, miming surrender. "Touchy," he says.

"The point is, you're going to have to be creative. They've got to come into the money in a manner that leaves my father no easy out."

"What about the lottery?"

"Maybe," I say. "Though I know my father has never so much as bought a scratch ticket. Which leaves my mother. Considering the state she was in the last time I saw her, that might be a bit of a stretch. I'm not even sure she leaves the house anymore."

"Right," Sawyer says. "That situation has not improved in your absence."

"So what, then?" I ask.

"For God's sake, we'll figure something," Sawyer says. "Do we have a deal? Can we please get out of here now?"

"Believe me, I'd like nothing better."

Sawyer pulls the two-way radio from the holster on his belt and raises it to his lips, then hesitates. He turns back toward me. "There is one other concern," he says. "One other small stipulation I forgot to mention."

"I'm listening."

"You can't drink. You'll be no good to us if you fall back down the rabbit hole we pulled you out of."

I wasn't expecting this. It goes without saying that the prison has served, however unintentionally, as the world's most effective detox, and after two years of forced sobriety it's been a while since I've even thought about having a drink, let alone craved one.

"Shouldn't be a problem, Sawyer," I say. "Obviously I've been dry since the day I got here."

"Noted. But I'm sure you'll agree there's a difference between staying sober in an old Soviet gulag, and staying sober in Maryland."

"As I said, it shouldn't be a problem."

"I'm going to need your word on that."

"Jesus. You've got it."

"Very good." Sawyer keys the two-way radio, and there's an electric buzzing from inside the door, then a click. "After you," he says, motioning toward the door as it swings slowly open.

John Sr.

The last thing I'd be doing, if I was you, is standing here loading these trucks, Dan Coyne says. You see earlier tonight when that fucking tree trunk came through? I kid you not, a big section of fucking *tree,* wrapped in twine like for handles. *Twine.* Must have weighed three hundred pounds. And here we're not supposed to be lifting more than seventy-five.

Guys at the warehouse go on for hours talking about what they would be doing in my position.

If I had your money I wouldn't be loading goddamn trees for anyone, Dan says. You're foolish to be putting up with this when you don't got to.

Maybe he's right. Maybe not. Either way, I'm always willing to consider the possibility that I'm a fool.

If I felt like I had to defend my decisions to Dan, I'd tell him I've cut back on hours at the bakery. Not that it was my choice—Mr. Miller hired a new guy after the Megabucks thing. When I asked him why, he said he didn't expect that with all that money I'd be sticking around much longer. I told him not to worry about that, I wasn't going anywhere, but he said maybe it was time for me to think about taking it easy.

Learn golf, he said. Buy yourself some nice collared shirts and go up to Natanis, rub elbows with the other blue bloods. He winked and patted his belly and blew smoke out of his nostrils.

Golf, I said. Even if I had two good hands, forget about it. Besides, I'm not old enough to make those pants work quite yet.

Mr. Miller pulled on his cigarette and eyeballed me. John, you've taken what, three weeks off in the past ten years? Something like that?

Something like that.

Give yourself a break, son, is what I'm saying. You don't need to bust your fucking hump anymore.

This from a man twenty years older than me, who hasn't taken a day off ever, as far as I know.

You'd think it'd be great to have a bunch of money and never work again,

Mr. Miller, I said. But try it. Give it a week, and see if you're not clawing your own eyes out trying to figure what to do with yourself.

He just puffed and winked some more. He probably thought I was talking out of my ass, because he didn't know I'd tried a week off from the warehouse. It was terrible. I came home from baking and couldn't sleep more than two or three hours—I'd be awake at noon, no alarm, ready to shower up and head to the warehouse. There was no warehouse shift to go to, so I'd just sit around drinking coffee. Read the paper twice, front to back, back to front. Actually did the crossword a couple of times, or tried to. I'm not much for TV, so that was no help. Debbie mostly watched her soaps and as usual didn't say much. The third day it snowed, thank God, and I shoveled our driveway, the Josephs' next door, the widow Mrs. Biche down the street. Shoveled paths for the oil and mailman, cleared off all the cars, spread rock salt. Everything. Took about four hours. It wasn't nearly enough; I still had six hours to fill before heading to Miller's.

This was around the same time I started having the spells. My chest goes tight and my vision gets dark and I have to grab onto something because it feels like I might go down and smash my head.

There are only a few things I've ever been afraid of. My old man. Taking a round in the throat, saw that happen to a guy and it scared me. My baby boy being dead. And these frigging spells.

Mr. Miller's new guy is named Mike, seems like a good kid, though the word from Monica is he's a drinker. But who cares as long as he's getting his work done and doesn't get an arm ripped off in the mixer or fall headfirst into the Hobart. I worked with him his first week and he's not lazy or sloppy; if he was drinking I didn't notice. Besides, it's not like he's the first baker in the history of the world to drink on a shift. Or on every shift, for that matter. Maybe a little young for that, but the sad truth is we start them young around here. I started *and* stopped young.

Part of me wishes Mike's drinking was a problem. I wish he'd burn the rolls and screw up the rainbow cakes, because he's working three of the shifts I used to have, This leaves me just four overnights, plus my shifts at the warehouse. Which means more coffee and crosswords and sitting next to Debbie on the sofa staring at *Guiding Light*.

I've thought about getting a third job. But it's hard to justify that when the paychecks from your other two jobs are all chip-clipped to the front of the fridge, waiting to be cashed. Two months' worth. It's not a whole lot of money, but in years past I used to drop my checks in the overnight deposit on the way home in the morning and pray they cleared by afternoon. Now they just sit there, worthless in a way. All that time and work is worth nothing now. Strange thing, being rich.

Still, the idea of a third job appeals. You don't realize how much time there is in a day until you've got nothing to fill it with but thought, and there's plenty to think about, starting with my missing son. My youngest boy, twenty-six years old and, judging by what he said in the newspapers and on TV, not at all right mentally. It's been three years. He could be dead. I've thought about this possibility every day of those three years. Thinking about it brings up all kind of questions that can't be answered: How? Where? Most of all, why?

This is the sort of thing that gives me trouble with the spells.

So I go to Mr. Miller.

Please, I say, it's not that I don't like this Mike guy, and I'm sure he needs the work—

He's got two little girls, Mr. Miller says, sitting behind his desk with the piles of receipts and invoices and order forms, and the big calculator and the ashtray overflowing with butts. One ten months, the other just turned two.

I'll give him money, I say. I'll give him twice what he's making here a week. If I can just get those shifts back.

Mr. Miller isn't winking or smiling. He leans back and the springs in his chair groan. He's got a cigarette between his dentures and he squints as the smoke drifts up into his eyes.

I'm sure Mike would be happy to take your money, he says. But even if he does, I'm not giving you those shifts.

It's like being slapped. Mr. Miller has never talked to me like this before. We've always been friends of a sort, even though he's quite a bit older than me and I was pretty much a kid when I started working here. Now, suddenly, he feels to me like my old man.

Mr. Miller? I say.

He looks at me for a minute, lights a new cigarette with the stub of the old one. John, we've known each other a long time.

Yes.

So I can be honest with you.

Of course. I'm actually a little pissed he feels the need to ask, but I squash it.

And I can say something about your personal life that you maybe wouldn't let someone else get away with.

Mr. Miller, I say. Pat. It's your right to make decisions about your business without asking anyone if they think it's alright. So I wouldn't ask for the shifts back otherwise. But I'm having these spells. It's like having a heart attack and a stroke all at once.

And you think working more is the cure?

Served me well in the past. He doesn't respond, so I keep talking. The spells didn't start until you gave those shifts to Mike. They're something to do with all the downtime. Too much thinking about things.

Good that you mention that, Mr. Miller says. He leans forward again and flicks his cigarette. The ash lands on top of the mountain of butts in the tray, then rolls off onto the desk. Because that's actually what I wanted to talk about. All those things you've got on your mind.

My face must darken, because Mr. Miller says: Hey, listen. Don't tear my office apart or anything. You need to hear this. Believe me, otherwise I'd be happy to keep my mouth shut, just tell you no you can't have the shifts back, and leave it at that.

I don't say anything.

John, when was the last time you and Debbie went out for dinner?

That's not really your business, Pat.

Except that it is, he says, when you've known someone for thirty years. When you've gone to birthday parties and graduations. When you've done for each other like we have. Then, you look at the state of things and realize you've got to say something.

My hands clench and unclench.

Go home, John, Mr. Miller says, and tend to your wife. Is what I'm trying to tell you.

He's right—this is not the sort of thing I'd let just anyone say. I walk out of his office before my anger gets the better of me. On my way out I stop in the kitchen and pull out my checkbook. On the stainless steel table I write a check for twenty thousand dollars and put Mike's name on it. I shake flour off the check and hand it to Mike.

Are you serious? Mike says. Is this even any good?

Yes.

I don't understand, he says. Why?

No reason at all, I say, opening the customer entrance, other than that you need it, and I don't.

I get in the Mustang and since it's only got eight hundred miles on it and the engine's still breaking in I take it onto the interstate and open it up. When I was in the service I spent most of my time thinking about a '66 Shelby GT. I sent my combat pay home to my mother to save up for a blue four-speed with four-point roll bar, steel rims, shoulder harness, the works. The closest I ever got to it was the showroom floor, because when I came home it turned out my mother had spent all the money while my old man was out of work, before he found the job at the cab stand. Now I've got the new Cobra R. They made just three hundred of them, and it only comes in red, which I'm not crazy about, but otherwise the thing's a dream. I move through the slower traffic, mid-thirties moms who hug the break-down lane and old men in Caddies with veteran's plates and handicapped stickers. I haven't gotten around to buying the tires I want, but as you'd expect the stock tires aren't half bad, and the Mustang jumps all over the road. I get it up around ninety. Not too fast—I know from a careless mo-ment a couple weeks ago that the car has another forty miles per hour in it, easy—but fast enough that I can feel the anger from Mr. Miller's talk-ing-to begin to melt away. By the time I get off at the Skowhegan exit to turn around I'm feeling calm again, and the only thing that lingers is this: whether or not it's any of Mr. Miller's business doesn't matter, because he was right.

I go home. Debbie's still at her afternoon spot on the sofa; as soon as *Oprah* is over she'll switch to the kitchen table. She looks up and smiles a little as I come in, then looks right back at the TV as the commercials end and Oprah explains that they are talking with people who have recently suffered a devastating loss and are overwhelmed with feelings of sadness and grief.

I have no idea where to start, so I just sit down next to Debbie without saying anything. It's awkward in a way I can't really explain, sitting this close to each other. Our legs are touching but we're both looking straight ahead at the TV.

Oprah is sitting on a sofa, too, with a woman whose husband was killed bungee rocketing, where apparently instead of jumping off a tall object you stand on the ground below the tall object, stretch the bungee cord out, then let go and shoot into the air. In the case of the woman's husband, whoever was responsible for doing the calculations messed up.

Oprah and the woman are sitting close together, like Debbie and me, but they aren't awkward about it at all. Their knees are pressed together, and they lean into one another as they talk. Oprah takes the woman's hand and asks her to reveal to her audience the cruel twist of irony that has made her loss so overwhelming, so difficult to process and put behind her.

At this point the woman tries to speak, but her eyes get teary and she gasps and puts her head down. Oprah pats her hand, says something too soft for the microphone to pick up. Eventually the woman gathers herself and explains that her husband had taken up high-risk hobbies like bungee rocketing and hang gliding after being diagnosed with terminal pancreatic cancer. But two months after the diagnosis—and just three days after her husband had died—the hospital called and said there'd been a mistake at the lab, that the biopsy sample had been mixed up with another and in fact the husband did not have pancreatic cancer but Von Hippel–Lindau disease, where benign tumors grow on the internal organs but usually aren't a big deal.

I look sideways at Debbie. She's sitting with her back straight and her hands in her lap. Her eyes are wet like the women in the studio. She could easily be one of them, in fact, with her short, frosted hair and her turtleneck.

But that's not the end of the story, Oprah says. She puts a hand on the woman's back and rubs little circles between her shoulder blades. Is it?

No, the woman tells her, dabbing at her eyes with a tissue. Because when she recovered a little from the shock of realizing that her husband had died because of the misdiagnosis, she realized that the person who originally had gotten her husband's lab results and had gone around the past two months thinking everything would be okay was now, possibly right at that moment, being told he had terminal cancer. And the woman decided, then and there—she still wasn't sure why, exactly—that she had to find this person, tell him what had happened, and try to make something worthwhile out of all this heartache.

Oprah looks up at her audience. Which is exactly what she did, she says. Please welcome the wife of the man who actually had cancer, Annie Leboeuf.

The crowd applauds as Annie comes out from backstage sporting frosted, permed hair and a light yellow pantsuit. She sits between Oprah and the woman and as the applause dies down the audience members wipe carefully at their eyes, using the tips of their fingers to remove tears without smudging their eyeliner.

I turn to Debbie and say, Would you like to go to the Open Hearth for dinner tonight?

Don't you have to work? she asks, without looking away from the TV. There are tears on her cheeks, but her face is blank. I'm certain this is how she looks all the time, and I wonder how I've never noticed until now.

Yes. But I can call out. I've got about three thousand hours of sick time piled up.

On *Oprah* the original guest and Annie Leboeuf are sitting practically in each other's lap, explaining how the two became best friends while Annie's husband was dying of cancer.

Why would you call out? Debbie asks. She sips from the cup on the end table, again without looking away from the TV. You never call out.

Well we never do anything together. And we've got some things to talk about, anyway.

So we do it. Debbie puts on a sweater and a big floppy hat and makes her way slowly out to the Mustang. I open the passenger-side door for her and she takes her time settling into the bucket seat. I drive across town to the Open Hearth. We don't say anything on the way over.

The restaurant is small, just seven tables, the biggest of which seats four. There's one bathroom the size of a closet with a toilet and corner sink crammed in there, and a window with a heat lamp that opens into the kitchen. The place has been around since before I was born, serving the same menu of pancakes and burgers and poutine, and I ate here a lot when I was a kid. But it's been at least ten years, if not longer, since I last saw the inside of the place.

It's seat-yourself, so I lead Debbie to the table next to the only window in the dining room. Céline Dion is playing, but there aren't any speakers in the dining room so it must be coming from the kitchen. The waitress comes and pours waters and puts two sticky menus down on the table. We both order Pepsis and the waitress walks off writing on her pad. I watch, a little bit surprised, as Debbie picks up the menu and looks it over. Just like a normal person, I think, then right away feel terrible for having the thought.

What are you going to eat? I ask her.

I'm not sure, Debbie says. I don't have much of an appetite.

Well I know, you usually don't, I say. Most of the time she just looks at food like she's not sure what to do with it. She might poke whatever's on her plate a few times, bully it around a little, and once in a while a piece will make its way into her mouth almost by accident.

We sit in silence for a few minutes. The waitress comes back and asks if we're ready.

I look at Debbie. Her eyes go from me, to the menu, to the waitress. I'll have the fried clam basket, she says.

The waitress scribbles. Baked, mashed, or fries? she asks.

Fries. With vinegar, she says, and then her eyes light up and she looks at me. John, you remember? Before the boys, when we'd go down to You Know Whose on Friday night and have a couple of beers and then right before the kitchen closed we'd order a big basket of fries to go? And we'd take it with vinegar in those little plastic cups and drive up to the airstrip with Patti and whoever her boyfriend was and sit on the tailgate and eat fries and smoke dope and watch the planes come in?

I stare at her. Yes, I say. Of course.

Debbie looks down at her lap. Those were good times, she says.

I'm so surprised that I don't even realize the waitress is waiting for me to order. And for you? she says finally.

I've got no idea what I want. I'll just have the cheeseburger, I tell her. With mashed instead of fries. I hand her the menus, and she says thanks and walks away.

We sit and wait for a while without speaking. Debbie claps her hands together and smiles that blank little smile and leans over to sniff at her Pepsi.

So there are some things, I say, stirring my drink with the straw, that we probably should have talked about a while ago.

What's that? Debbie asks, still smiling.

I look up, hoping to see our food under the heat lamps, but the window is empty. Well, I say, like how we don't spend any time together.

We are now, aren't we? Spending time together?

Yes, I say. And it's nice, isn't it?

I'm enjoying it, Debbie says. She holds her hand out over the table. But I'm shaking. Look at my hand.

Well, I say, that's probably because you haven't had anything to drink in the last couple hours. Like, you shake when you get up in the morning, right?

Yes.

Same thing, I say. You don't drink while you sleep. So in the morning your hands shake.

Huh, Debbie says. She keeps watching her hand until the food finally shows up.

The bun is soggy with blood and the potatoes are obviously out of a box, but I eat with good appetite anyway. I didn't realize how hungry I was until the waitress put the plate in front of me. Surprisingly, Debbie digs right in too, eating like she means it. She's got the squeeze bottle of vinegar and she puts a generous amount on the fries and eats them with her hands. She's kind of ignoring the clams, but it's still an impressive thing from a woman who's lived more or less on fluids for the last ten years.

Pretty good stuff, I say.

Well done, she says. Extra crispy.

I catch myself smiling around a mouthful of reconstituted potato flakes. Hey, I say. You want to do it? Go up to the airstrip after this? See if we can't spot a Cessna or two?

Debbie doesn't even pause eating. Sure, she says.

It's incredible, we leave the restaurant laughing, I don't even know what about. I drive across town again and out to the Webb Road, which runs behind the airstrip. It's full dark now. Debbie's mood takes a bit of a nosedive on the way and she asks me to stop at the store and buy a bottle of wine. I figure what the hell. The Quick Stop only has Old Duke and Wild Irish Rose, really bad stuff, but we actually used to drink Old Duke when we were kids so I buy some of that. Back in the car I hand the bottle to Debbie. The rest of the drive she tries to get the cap off the bottle without any luck, so she has to wait until I pull off into the field behind the airstrip and twist it off for her.

I give Debbie a boost onto the back of the Mustang, then jump up beside her. The day was warm for March, and that warmth has carried over into the evening. I'm comfortable even though I left my jacket at home and have on just the sweatshirt that I wear loading trucks in the winter.

We don't talk for a while. I listen to Debbie drink, the slop of the wine back and forth as she tips the bottle then brings it back to her lap. It's the only sound. No other cars come along, and there are no planes. The airstrip can go weeks without any business, especially during the winter. In the summer rich people from Boston and New York flying in to their summer homes make up most of the traffic. This time of year, it's nothing. Still, I had hoped.

Rich people. I have to keep reminding myself not to think of them the way I always have: as the opposite of me.

You know something we never talked about, I say.

Debbie's in mid-sip. What's that? she asks.

In all the craziness that came after the Megabucks, we never talked about how you actually got the ticket.

She frowns. Obviously I bought it, she says. But what's funny is I don't remember buying it.

What else is funny, I say, is that until then you hadn't bought a lottery ticket in at least five years.

But I used to buy them.

All the time, I say.

Wednesdays and Fridays, she says. It's coming back to me. Two drawings a week. I played the boys' birthdays.

But you hadn't done that for years. At least as far as I knew.

She frowns some more, staring at the half-melted snowbank in front of us, which glows bluish in the dark. I honestly don't remember, she says.

It's not a big deal. Obviously the ticket didn't appear out of nowhere. Just seemed strange that all of a sudden you decided to go and buy one. Stranger still that it ended up being a winner.

It's nice, though, she says. Having money.

I think about this a minute. I guess.

You don't like it?

I think . . . that it comes with its own set of problems.

Behind us there's a faint whirring sound, distant but drawing closer. Do you hear that? I ask her.

Hear what?

I think it's a plane. A jet, sounds like. Don't you hear it?

Debbie's face blossoms slowly into a grin. I do now, she says.

Within a few seconds a small jet comes in overhead. We look straight up to watch as it passes. Red and white lights blink on the wingtips and tail. The plane drifts slowly toward the airstrip, touches down lightly, and taxis over to the small building that passes for a terminal. Three tiny figures emerge and take luggage from the compartment in the plane's belly. Against the light from the terminal they look like shadows come to life.

I wonder what they're doing here, Debbie says.

Probably developers from Boston, I say. Gonna buy up some lake property and build condos on it.

How do you know that?

I'm just guessing, I say. They're in a jet, not a prop plane, so you know they've got money. Real money. And it's a safe bet, this time of year, that they're not on vacation.

Unless they're skiing, Debbie says.

Hadn't considered that.

We watch the figures some more as they carry stuff into the terminal, then come back out for more stuff. And wouldn't you know it, one of them pulls something long and thin from the plane, something that at this distance looks a lot like a ski case.

I turn to Debbie. So one of the things I wanted to talk about, I say. Not to ruin the mood.

What is it?

I hesitate. Well, I say, to put it plainly, it's about Junior.

Debbie has no obvious reaction. She waits for me to keep talking.

I think it's time we discussed . . . or not discussed, I guess, but more kind of *admit* to ourselves that there's a good chance he's gone.

Well of course he's gone, Debbie says. We haven't seen him for a long time now.

Three years, I say. But when I say gone, Debbie, I mean gone. As in.

Dead?

Yes. I think so.

She drinks from the bottle. I hadn't thought about that, she says. I thought he was just in Chicago or somewhere.

I shake my head. No, Debbie, he's not in Chicago. Listen, what I'm saying is I think we should do something. Some sort of ceremony or memorial.

Why?

Because I'm tired of picking up the phone and hoping to hear him on the other end. Aren't you?

No, I'm not, Debbie says. I don't do that.

I look at her. Her face is relaxed and her eyes are dry, staring up at the airfield, where the lights have been turned off again. I think of her face when she was watching *Oprah* this afternoon—tears in her eyes, her cheeks red with sadness.

I say, Maybe we should talk about the other thing first. Or instead.

What other thing? Debbie asks.

There's something I want you to do for me.

Okay.

It's pretty simple, I say. I want you to stop drinking.

She's in mid-sip, and as she brings the bottle down it crosses the moon and I see it's nearly empty. Why? she says.

Because it's killing you, Debbie. We've seen it happen enough times to know that's what it does to people.

She turns to me. Her face has changed, from the blank and friendly expression I've learned to expect, to something sharper. Did you think that maybe that's just what I'm trying to do?

Once again, I'm surprised into a few seconds of silence. Is it? I ask finally.

She looks back to the ground between her dangling feet. I don't know, she says. Some days I think so.

Why?

You want to know why, ask my father. But you can't. He's dead. So I don't know what to tell you.

I've never seen such anger in her. Not in thirty years of marriage, not even before she started in with the drinking. Somehow it makes me think things will be alright. Which is definitely no guarantee they will be; wouldn't be the first time I had a good feeling that turned out to be dead wrong. Still, it's nice to feel positive, if only during the few minutes before Debbie finishes the wine and we get back in the Mustang and I take her to the hospital and have her admitted. The way I do it is I tell them Debbie is suicidal. It's only a half-lie, but it feels strange regardless because I haven't told a lie about anything since I was in the Marines. They take her in and she goes quietly. The woman at the desk says Debbie will wear a hospital gown for the first few days but will need clothes after that, so I go outside and get in the car to drive home and pack some of her things. I've barely gotten out of the parking lot when I start in with one of the spells. My chest gets tight and my vision narrows. I can feel myself slipping all the way away this time, I'm definitely going out, but instead of slowing down and pulling over I hit the gas, I can't even say why, except that it's such a rush, it's like the couple of times I smoked opium with Jacques and his crew of artillery guys: a happiness so strong you just know you're going to pay for it one way or another.

And then, just before the world fades completely, I come back from the brink.

Work on the Alcubierre drive is coming along at a pace that surprises everyone. We've shaved about two years with the help of some tasty little morsels of extraterrestrial technology, previously kept under heavy wraps at the U.S. South Pole research station, and I'm hoping that when the prototype is tested next week and negotiations for production contracts begin with the Big Four—Boeing, McDonnell Douglas, Lockheed, and Grumman—I'll be allowed to leave for the first time since returning from Bulgaria. This was the arrangement I made with Sawyer, and though I've got nowhere to go I still intend to see that he honors it.

I'm in the lecture room off the biosphere lab, and my cell phone buzzes in my pocket. I answer and find an oddly subdued Sawyer on the other end. Absent is the usual snide tone. He makes no jokes, pokes no fun.

"We've picked up a telephone conversation that you probably ought to hear," he says.

"Can it wait?" I ask. "I'm stuck at Langley. The oxygen level in the biosphere has been dropping again."

"I would recommend you come right now. I can send a helicopter."

"Not to mention there's a problem with the flowering plants failing to produce at rates sufficient to sustain the caloric output of our guys inside. It looks like the two issues are related. Not surprisingly."

"Junior."

"Really though, whether or not the biosphere thing works out is sort of moot now that we're finally breaking through with propulsion."

"Junior, listen," Sawyer says. "You need to come back to Meade and hear this phone call. It's to do with your father."

This stops me cold. "Can't you just patch it through or something?" I ask. "You guys can do that, right? I've seen it in the movies." It's a weak attempt at levity in my sudden fear, and it comes out lame.

"Not a good idea," Sawyer says.

There's silence on the line for several moments. "This has got you rattled, huh?" I say finally.

"Yes," Sawyer says. "Oddly enough."

"Then I guess you'd better send that helicopter."

Forty-five minutes later I'm in Sawyer's subterranean office, deep below the giant obsidian cube of NSA headquarters. He has me put on a headset attached to a computer terminal.

"We picked this up a couple hours ago," he says, punching several buttons on the keyboard. There's the garbled sound of a connection being formed over a landline, then the lazy electronic purr of the ring-through. After four rings the call is answered, and I hear my brother's voice asking hello.

When my mother says hello back to him, I'm as shocked as I've ever been in my life. Imagine—my mother using the phone. And not just answering it, but dialing out, initiating a call. Clearly a lot has changed in my absence.

"Where are you, Rodney? Are you in Chicago?"

"Hi Ma, no, we're . . . hold on a minute." There's a brief, muffled conversation on Rodney's end, and then he comes back on. "Kansas City. Interleague," he says. "So we get to have a DH."

"I don't know what that means, babe," my mother says.

"It's someone who hits for the pitcher."

"Okay," my mother says, not sounding any more certain of the definition or function of a DH. "Listen, Rodney, we're going to need you to come home for a bit."

"This is the first series of the road trip," Rodney says. "I won't be in Chicago for a while." Another pause, more muffled conversation. "Almost two weeks."

"I don't mean Chicago. I mean home-home. Here. Maine."

"Jeez, I don't know, Ma. I'd have to ask Al if that's okay."

"This is important, Rodney. It's important that you come home. Do you understand?"

"I understand," Rodney says. "What's going on?"

"I'd rather not tell you on the phone, Rodney."

I could scream, right here in Sawyer's clean cool office with the generic books lining the walls and the Undercover Bear on the desk, I could scream in frustration and fear, listening to them dance around the point like this.

"Is something wrong, Ma?" Rodney asks.

This is really all it should take, because if my new mother, this woman who speaks in complete sentences and dials telephones, is anything like the old one, she has a penchant for the dramatic, not to mention a strong gossip reflex, and it shouldn't take much more than a gentle prodding to get her to out with it. And sure enough, the tears I could hear lurking in her voice spill forth. She cries for a minute, and I feel the cold tendrils of her fear reach through the phone line.

After a few moments she composes herself enough to speak. "I didn't want to tell you on the phone," she says. "Your father came home from the bakery with blood on his shirt. He was coughing up blood all night."

I don't know what I was expecting, but this was not it. The tendrils turn hard and sharp; the sensation is of being run through with icicles.

"I brought him to the hospital," my mother continues. "They took X-rays and found tumors in his lung."

Rodney is silent.

The moment does not feel like I imagine it's supposed to. There is no sadness. There is no anger. I do not cry. I am experiencing an utter lack of feeling, an emotional black hole. I worry, faintly, that this means I am a monster, but it's more likely I am just in shock and cannot reasonably be expected to feel much of anything, right at the moment. Still, it seems wrong, this absence of emotion. This is the man, after all, who raised me, paid for every morsel, toy, and transgression. This is the man who cast his long protective shadow over my existence, my one and only father. I should throw myself on the floor and wail. I should mourn extravagantly, like the Palestinian mothers I see on television, writhing atop piles of shattered mortar, oblivious to any effort to comfort them. Grief as trance, as epileptic fit. This should be me. Instead, I clamp the headset to my ear and breathe and sit very still with my free hand pressed so hard and flat against Sawyer's desktop that my fingers turn to alabaster.

"Tumors," Rodney says. "You mean cancer."

"Cancer, yes," my mother says. "Hold on, Rodney." She puts the phone down with a clunk, and I can hear her blowing her nose in the background. She comes back on, more composed now. "You still there?"

"I'm here, Ma," Rodney says, his voice reluctant and sad.

"So will you come?"

"I'll call Al," Rodney says. "He always gives me his room number when we're on the road, in case I need anything. I'll talk to him now."

"Okay. Call me back when you know."

A few moments pass when neither of them says anything.

Then Rodney finally speaks. "Jesus, Ma," he says.

"I know, babe. Call me back, okay?"

The recording ends, and I am left sitting there at Sawyer's desk, staring at the wall, staring through it, really, seeing nothing.

Sawyer has stepped out of the room to give me privacy, though I doubt very much that there is any such thing within the walls of this place. To confirm my suspicion, he returns right on cue.

"Finished?" he asks, doing a poor job of acting like he doesn't know.

"Yeah." I pull the headset off and place it on the desk.

"Hate to be the one to bring such news," he says.

"You know, I believe you mean that, Sawyer."

"I am sincere. Unfortunate that you can't be there."

"I can't?"

"No." Sawyer comes around the desk. "Not to be insensitive, but you have much more important matters to tend to. Could I have my chair back?"

I stand, and Sawyer takes his seat.

"I'm not in the mood to go round and round, so I'll save us both the trouble—I'm leaving to be with my father. You have no leverage."

"I could have you killed," Sawyer says.

I make a face. "Like I'd care. Honestly."

"Regardless, that's not my point. I'm not saying you can't be there merely because we forbid it. I'm saying you can't be there because having you materialize after eight years would add a good deal of confusion and stress to a situation that already has plenty of both. Listen to me, for once. I'm speaking as your friend here."

I raise my eyebrows.

"Trying to? Speak as your friend?" Sawyer searches my face. "Okay. Bad choice of words. Let me rephrase: I am speaking out of genuine concern and sympathy, both for you and your family."

"Still a stretch," I say.

"And as a concerned party it's my responsibility to point out that at a moment so emotionally charged, to have their son return from the grave would likely be too much for either of your parents to deal with."

"My father could deal with it," I say. "Ma, who knows. But my father can deal with anything."

"You might be surprised."

"Clearly you don't know the man," I say.

"I may know him better than you do," Sawyer says. "It's my job, after all, to dissect personalities, to figure out what makes people tick, as is said. And I made it my business to get to know your father."

"He's a bit of an enigma," I say.

"To you," Sawyer says. "Because in your eyes he's a superhero, a minor deity to be feared and worshipped in equal measure. To me he's just an unremarkable person with a notably thin file. Who do you suppose has the more factual impression of the man?"

"Factual would probably lie somewhere in the middle."

"Then you don't deny that you see him in a way that is not an accurate reflection of who he actually is, as a human being," Sawyer says. "That your perception of him is at best idealized, at worst impossible for any mortal to live up to."

"Don't know if I'd go that far."

"I would," Sawyer says. "So when without a moment's thought or hesitation you say 'My father could handle it' I have to wonder if maybe that idealized perception is interfering with your common sense. The man was diagnosed with a terminal illness less than twenty-four hours ago. No matter how tough or unflappable he is, that's probably enough to deal with, here, without his long-dead son showing up too."

"There are things you can't read in a file," I say, turning to open the door. "I'm going."

"Junior. Grow the fuck up, and realize he's not your daddy anymore. He's your father. He is in a deep, deep hole, and the last thing he needs is for you to show up with an excavator."

I stare at Sawyer, trying to remember if I've ever heard him swear before.

"I am not playing games with you on this," he says.

I let go of the doorknob and turn to face him. "Sawyer, do you know why I agreed to come here and work on the Program?"

"To impress your girlfriend?"

I ignore this. "My whole life there never was a point to anything. Oblivion was always just around the corner, so what was the use of, say, trying to make the varsity basketball team, or starting a retirement fund, or having kids, or any of the other things that normal people do? No point. To anything. Try to imagine what that would be like."

Sawyer makes no obvious effort to imagine anything.

"Needless to say, this raised some sticky philosophical questions for me. Nothing mattered at all. Things got a little loose in my head, for a while. I contemplated some fairly evil shit, I can tell you."

"Ah, yes. For example, bombing a federal building."

"No. Much worse than that. Let me put it this way: human life, as a currency, was *severely* devalued. In my view."

"And then we came along," Sawyer says.

"Eventually, yes. That's the point. When you came to me in Bulgaria, I saw an opportunity to take the world I'd always known, and change it into the world that you, and everyone else, has always enjoyed—a world where what you do and say matters. A world that has a point to it. So I took that opportunity."

"Commendable. Truly."

"And now that my father's life finally has a point, I plan to do what I can to make sure that it continues."

"Again, commendable. The sentiment, I mean. But I'm warning you, Junior . . ."

I think for a minute. "What if I approached it more creatively? What if I did something other than just showing up out of nowhere?"

"Have something in particular in mind?" Sawyer asks.

There's the barest seed of an idea, but it's nothing I can yet articulate. "Don't know. Whatever it turns out to be, though, I'm sure I'll need your help carrying it off."

Sawyer studies my face, and after a few moments seems satisfied by what he sees. "Okay," he says. "Tell me this: will the Alcubierre drive test be successful?"

"Yes."

"Even if you're not here?"

"Absolutely," I say. "The work is done. It's just a scheduling thing now. Ross can handle it. Spergel can handle it."

Sawyer picks a pen up off the desk and fiddles with it. "Understand that when I ask you if the test will be successful, and you say yes, you'd better be right. Or else it's both our hides."

"Sawyer."

He throws up his hands. "Okay," he says. "Fine. Go. I'll arrange for transportation, cash, et cetera. You realize, of course, that there's nowhere you can go I can't see you. Yes?"

"Of course."

"So that if you violate the one condition I'm setting forth—if you make direct, face-to-face contact with your family—I will know about it. And there will be consequences."

"Fair enough," I say.

Sawyer busies himself with sifting through a stack of paperwork on his desk. "Go, then," he says without looking up.

I open the door, then turn to face him again. "Sawyer."

He continues flipping pages. "Hmm?"

"It occurs to me to wonder: why do you care at all about how this turns out?"

Now he looks at me. "A minute ago," he says, "when I called your father unremarkable?"

"Yes."

"I didn't mean it." He holds my gaze a moment, then looks back at his paperwork. "Now go tend to your family."

As I leave and close the door behind me there is the briefest moment of gratitude and affection for Sawyer. It flares in my chest, then fades and is gone. I stand in the hallway outside his office, short of breath suddenly, thinking: *how very, very strange, this life.*

I go up in one of the high-speed elevators that service the subterranean portions of NSA headquarters. I clear security and step outside to find a black sedan parked at the curb and a security officer whom I do not recognize waving me over. He hands me the keys and wishes me a good trip, and just like that I am on my way home for the first time in nearly a decade.

It does not occur to me, until I pull away from the curb with a tremendous lurch and creaking of shocks, that it's been eight years since I was last behind the wheel. I've got a heavy foot and keep forgetting to use turn signals, and even blow through a red light. Though I've been in Washington for four years, for what I know of the place I might as well have been on the moon all this time. By pure luck I come across a sign for 295. I merge with painful slowness and drive another half hour before 295 connects to I-95 North, which will carry me all the way home.

I remember what Sawyer said about cash, and on a hunch I check the glove box. Instead of the usual cascading jumble of napkins and receipts and registration paperwork, there's a cell phone, a banded stack of fifty-dollar bills, and a credit card. I remove the money. The next exit bears the universal sign for food—a plate with a fork and knife on either side. Thankfully I don't have to drive all over creation and risk getting lost, because there's a McDonald's right at the bottom of the ramp.

With a full stomach and two apple pies cooling in their cardboard sleeves on the passenger seat, I hit the road again. Hour after hour of I-95's soul-numbing sameness spurs the cyclical and obsessive thinking that has become my favorite pastime over the years, and it takes a considerable effort to wrangle my thoughts away from the hopelessness of my father's sudden illness and pin them down on the more productive contemplation of how, exactly, I'm going to help him. There's very little time, and I'm disappointed with myself for not having the foresight to research this before now. Given that he smoked four packs of cigarettes a day, on top of prolonged exposure to Agent Orange in Vietnam, it didn't take a genius to figure that sooner or later he was bound to get the cancer ticket in his Wonka Bar. Yet here I am, flat-footed, fully defensive, and lost without a map.

Then, as so often happens, something is revealed to me. It is not elegant. It requires more time than we have. It is likely to fail. But it's the only chance my father's got.

When I pull into town off the interstate the apple pies are gone and the sky is just starting to pink up over the hills in the east. Nothing looks the same. The farm pastures on the outskirts have been plowed under and paved over, replaced by chain restaurant mini-malls and the neon oases of every major oil shill. There's a Wal-Mart where families used to sunbathe and splash in the fountain at Castonguay Park. The city's last elm tree, a huge, stately hardwood removed to make way for a credit card call center, has been sawed into manageable sections that wait on a sidewalk to be hauled off and forgotten. I'm so preoccupied passing by the tree's corpse that I nearly run down a stray dog with a curlicue tail and a bad case of mange. It stands in the middle of the street, mesmerized by my headlights, and I cut the wheel and end up in the parking lot of a sex shop. The dog, hackles raised in fear, skitters off into the shadows.

My heart is racing from the near-collision, and I take a few deep breaths to calm myself. A glowing red sign in the window of the sex shop makes an odd promise: PRIVATE. I switch on the radio and smoke a cigarette and take a few minutes to gather myself. I scan through the dial twice and find nothing but country and conservative talk.

When my hands stop shaking I turn the car out toward Fairfield and drive until I reach Miller's Bakery. I park on the opposite side of the street. If I can't visit my father, visiting Miller's isn't a bad substitute, since the squat gray building, plopped artlessly between two restored Victorians, is practically synonymous with him in my mind. I'm so startled when he passes by the big storefront window in his jeans and white T-shirt and apron, carrying a sheet of sticky buns, that I reflexively duck down in the seat. I watch, trembling anew, as he makes tourtière pies and fills cream horns and troubles over meringues. He works hard and dusts flour off his hands and looks just like he always has, and of course I shouldn't have been surprised that, a day removed from a terminal diagnosis, he nevertheless showed up for work. Even if everything else around here has changed, my father, certainly, remains the same.

I leave before the sun comes up, drive to the Econo Lodge on Kennedy Drive, and rent a room from a scowling girl with dirty blond hair. I'm convinced she's mute until she mutters a comment about weirdos renting rooms first thing in the morning instead of at night like normal people.

"Won't clean the room," she says, handing me the key, "if you sleep all day. Housekeepers are gone at three in the afternoon."

"That's fine." I feel wired, a little crazed, even, and so have no intention of sleeping anyway.

When I reach the room I open the blinds, crack the window to dilute the stench of aerosol disinfectant, and use the cell phone from the glove box to call Sawyer. He answers after six rings, sounding groggy and ill tempered. I tell him my plan, and what I will need from him. He surprises me by being amenable and cooperative despite the fact that I woke him from a deep sleep. He immediately agrees to provide everything I'll need, though he warns that the nearest place with the necessary equipment is the Merck lab in Boston.

"But what about the other things?" I ask. "How long?"

"I'll have a man there this afternoon."

"What time? I'm going to the library to start researching."

"I'm fairly sure," Sawyer says, "that he'll be able to let himself in."

I thank him—it feels strange to mean it—and hang up. I hold the phone for a while, turning it over in my hands, considering, then toss it on the bed before I give in to temptation. I can't call my father until Sawyer's man gets here with the voice disguiser and the other equipment. Besides, I don't yet have anything useful to tell my parents. Business, is how I need to think of this. Just another problem that needs solving.

The library won't open for another few hours, so I take a shower. I don't register the fact that I have no clean clothes until I get out and dry off. I stand naked on the bath mat for a moment, considering, then put on the dirty stuff and make a mental note to hit Penney's after I leave the library.

Though I'm not tired I lie down on the bed for a while and watch the early news. There's something comforting in how hokey and half-assed local programming has remained: the female newscaster with last decade's haircut stumbling over her lines in a studio the color of anemia; the grainy commercials with poor dubbing and folks of dubious personal hygiene hawking lumber and used cars. I grew up among these people. I understand and trust them, because they are guileless and cheerfully self-sufficient and do not put on airs. They make me realize, with some surprise, just how much I've missed home. After a while the local broadcast gives way to the national morning show, which is so intolerably dull that against all odds I sink down into the shingled stack of pillows and doze for a while.

I wake with a start at nine thirty. The library opened half an hour ago, and though it may be a bit of a stretch to say that every minute counts, it's not too far off, especially since I don't yet know the particulars of my father's diagnosis. He could have a year left, or a month. Better to assume the worst. I throw on my shoes and go, stopping at the gas station next to the motel to buy a pair of mirrored sunglasses, which with my ball cap will have to do for a disguise until Sawyer's man shows up.

At the library I sign for use of a computer terminal. I sit down and search first for clinical trials, as this is where the most advanced work is being done, work that may point me in the right direction. I scan the National Cancer Institute website to no avail, then move on to the major medical centers: Dana-Farber in Boston, Sloan-Kettering in New York, M.D. Anderson in Houston. I speed-read thousands of headers in two hours and come up with nothing. The problem is these trials are engaged with objectives far too modest for my purposes: "improved life expectancy of 1–3 months"; "slowed brain damage from spread of primary tumor"; "some survival benefit from multidrug treatment," etc. It's shameful, I think, to pursue such worthless goals so doggedly. I am not interested in discovering a better way for my father to die—I want a cure. Anything less is pattycake, a waste of everyone's time.

In any event I didn't expect much from the clinical trials, because I have a hunch that the key to curing my father lies outside the laboratory, in a farmer's field in Ohio, maybe, or growing on fallen Japanese oak trees, or circulating through the lymphatic system of an Ecuadorian frog. Or, perhaps, all of the above. I'm about to wade into the vast rollicking ocean of alternative therapies when the phone, which I've neglected to set to vibrate, rings in my pocket. There are a few grumbles from the people around me, regulars who probably have some tacit system worked out to decide who gets the newspaper first every morning, and who don't appreciate some interloper breaking the sacred studious silence.

"Hello," I say quietly.

"Clark here."

"Who?"

"Sawyer sent me. I'm at the Econo Lodge. Room 316. Waiting." He hangs up, and I'm left thinking, for not the first time, that occasionally Sawyer and his colleagues take themselves a touch too seriously.

My first impression of Clark, on entering my room and seeing him seated at the small table near the window, is he's a real Master Race–looking son of a bitch: blond brushcut, cheekbones like steel blades, and behind the sunglasses, I am certain, eyes the color of glacier ice. For all that is severe and official-looking about his physical appearance, though, he's oddly dressed: jeans and sports jacket, and beneath the jacket a T-shirt that reads: *Camping is In-Tents!*

Clark removes the sunglasses. Sure enough, cold blue. "Junior?" he asks.

"Yes."

He stands and motions to the half-dozen black cases of various sizes on the bed. "There are several changes of clothes in the closet," he says. "Let's get started. I hear you're pretty bright, so this shouldn't take long. I want to be back in Boston by dark."

He wastes no time showing me the contents of the cases, explaining the function of each object quickly and moving on to the next without asking if I understand or have questions. Voice transformer, laptop with satellite broadband, fake ID cards (including a badge that will grant me access to Merck Research Laboratories in Boston), disguise utility with simple stuff like glue-on facial hair, and the item I'm most interested in: a folder containing my father's updated medical records.

The last thing Clark hands me is a bottle of scary government-issue uppers that I've seen a few of the guys in the Program use. The drug is a lightly classified formula for G-men and spooks who need to stay awake and alert far beyond reasonable human limits. It resembles methamphetamine in its effects, but without the agitation, paranoia, or dental rot. Until now, I've avoided it like herpes.

Having fulfilled his duties, Clark shows himself the door, and when it closes behind him I feel a strange and massive sense of relief. The moment he's gone I slap the folder with my father's records on the table and spread the pages out. There are two things that will tell me all I need to know: the radiologist's report from the PET scan, and the pathology report from the biopsy. I find both.

The news is not good.

The PET scan shows a primary tumor in the left lung (bad enough) and lymph node involvement both above and below the right clavicle (even worse), as well as "highly suspicious" lesions on the liver (worse still). The pathology report fingerprints the cancer as small-cell, which if you're going to have lung cancer is pretty much the type you want to avoid.

Though I'm reluctant to know, I get on the laptop to get an idea of how long, given this information, my father can expect to live. After five minutes of research I come up with the very grim estimate of one to two months.

I knew that it would be bad, but I did not know it would be this bad. The plan I hatched on the road is far too speculative and time-consuming to have even the slightest chance of success. Unlike yesterday in Sawyer's office, when the shock of the diagnosis insulated me, I'm having no trouble feeling things now. I switch on the television and turn the volume up and cry for what seems like a long time. When I'm done I stand and pace the room, trying to ignore the sudden siren call of the bottle of pills on the nightstand.

Morning turns to afternoon. The sun begins a slow descent and glares through the west-facing windows with rude brilliance. I spend some time in bed, staring blankly at the television. I resolve a hundred times not to take any of the spook meth. Eventually I bring the bottle into the bathroom and stand poised over the toilet. I try to take the cap off and pour the tablets out and hit the flush lever, but for some reason I can't. I go back into the bedroom and sit at the table and watch the parking lot fill with cars as evening comes on, and then, because there's nothing else left to me, and because I'm afraid of the pills, and because I'm in mourning for a father who hasn't yet died, I do something I haven't done for a very long time: I pray.

The Son Becomes Father

33 You understand that we are sorry for and sympathetic to your problem. You understand, also, that our sympathy cannot extend to direct intervention on your behalf, no matter how desperate the situation. Naturally we're happy to offer what assistance we can within the limits of our long-standing policy of supportive neutrality, but even if we had the ability to make your father well, which we may or may not, it's not our place to wave our magic wand, so to speak, and make it so.

32 Having said that, we will say this: call Sawyer and have him arrange for your father to be treated at the nearest TomoTherapy center, at Brockton Hospital, south of Boston. TomoTherapy involves highly concentrated doses of radiation, and has a fair chance of buying your father enough time for your original plan, which incidentally is quite solid, to be put into action. Being a newish treatment, TomoTherapy is offered at only a dozen or so places on Earth, so you should be aware that in order to secure a spot for your father, Sawyer will have to use his influence to bump another patient whose situation is just as desperate.

We're glad this gives you pause. You wouldn't be human if it didn't. However, consider this: Do you think, when you were a boy, that your father would have been philosophical about any threat to you? Would he have weighed his options, thought on it awhile, then reluctantly come to a decision, full of ambivalence? No. Your father would kill puppies and step on old ladies' throats to protect you. For your sake he would sack and burn cities, salt the fields of all the world. Then or now. And though over the years he's set an example that any son would find hard to live up to, there will never be another time, in either of your lives, when it's so important for you to try and emulate him.

31 You call Sawyer. He answers, sounding more alert than earlier. His brusque, official tone lets you know he's at the office in his high-backed leather throne. When you tell him the situation and make your request,

however, his manner shifts again to one of sympathy and humble co-operation. While you're understandably baffled and skeptical, we can tell you it's true that your father is the reason Sawyer has suddenly become so earnest and humane. It's pretty simple, really: Sawyer considers himself a patriot, in the most basic, flag-lapel-pin way, and your father's joining the Marines during a time when just about every other young man was hiding out in the National Guard or running to Canada with his ass on fire scored big points with Sawyer. It scored bigger points still when Sawyer learned your father had turned down a professional baseball contract. But beyond all that, what really hooked Sawyer is that he wishes his own father were more like yours. Or, more accurately: he wishes that his own father—a liberal, vaguely effete, draft-dodging college professor who's perpetually drunk in that acceptable middle-class vodka rocks kind of way—had been pretty much the exact opposite of what he was, what he continues to be in a potbellied, graying form.

Sawyer readily agrees to arrange for TomoTherapy treatment. He asks if there's anything else you need.

"Not at the moment. Soon. But if you could let me know the moment it's arranged, that would be good."

"Done. I'll call you back in half an hour or so."

You sit at the table and watch the digital readout on the clock radio. Exactly twenty minutes have passed when the cell phone rings.

"Monday at two p.m. for an assessment."

"That's it?"

"That's it." There's a rustling on Sawyer's end like he's moving paperwork around his desk. "They'll put together a treatment plan and get started right away."

"Great, that's great."

"What, no concern for the fellow who got bumped?"

"Listen, just make sure I get copies of all the paperwork from his treatments, okay? Daily."

"Yes, sir."

You fold the phone and put it down on the table. All the preliminaries are out of the way. The organizing and mental networking that come so naturally to you have been exhausted for the moment, and now it's time for you to contact your father. Instead you just sit there, understandably anxious about making the call.

30 In the motel parking lot below your window a pickup truck pulls in, towing a trailer with two commercial lawnmowers. Two men get out of the truck. The driver is a man named Arthur Hopkins, Art to his friends and wife. The other man, barely out of his teens and still battling acne, is his son Cody. They talk as they put down the gate on the trailer and loosen the straps that hold the mowers in place. Art points to a grassy hill next to the motel pool. Cody points toward a strip of grass that runs alongside the road on the far side of the parking lot. They are discussing strategy, teamwork, how together they will approach and complete the job of mowing the motel's lawn. And then, the discussion concluded, they fire up the mowers and get started.

You watch the two of them work for a while. By now it's midafternoon, the hottest part of the day. The metal siding on the motel's pool house shimmers. By the time they're finished mowing and getting ready to do the trim, Art is visibly heat-fatigued. Like your father, he is a combat veteran of the Vietnam War. Two years ago he suffered a devastating myocardial infarction that destroyed 60 percent of his heart muscle, yet he insists on continuing to run his landscaping business. Cody had moved to Boston after high school, but returned to keep an eye on his father and make sure he didn't work himself into another heart attack. You watch as Art takes a bottle of water from a small lunch cooler in the bed of the truck and drinks desperately, gasping between gulps. His shirt is soaked through with sweat. He grabs a Weedwhacker and moves to resume working, but Cody stops him. He pats his father's shoulder and says a few short words, and Art reluctantly sits down on the tailgate and finishes his bottle of water while Cody trims the edges around the parking lot and pool.

29 You turn away from the window, take a deep breath, and attach the voice transformer to the cell phone with a small auxiliary cable. You're worried your father will know right away that it's you, but this

shouldn't be a concern. You'll be able to hear how different and unrecognizable your voice is through the transformer. It's set to make you sound like a woman of seventy or so; the expert NSA reasoning behind this, which is quite valid, goes that men are more inclined to listen to and heed the advice of a distinguished, intelligent older woman.

Even though there's no need to worry about how you'll sound to your father, you should take a moment to prepare for how your father will sound to you. For one thing he is extremely demoralized, and his voice will reflect this. Also, the tumor in his lung has grown into the bronchus, causing frequent, violent coughing fits that are likely to alarm and sadden you.

You put on the headset and dial your parents' number, the same number they've had for as long as you've been alive. The line rings through five, six, seven times. Part of you hopes, understandably, that no one will pick up.

"Hello," your father says, and you barely recognize his voice. Despite our warning your heart sinks at hearing him sound so low and defeated.

"John," you say, and your voice comes to you through the headset, grandmotherly and strange.

"Yes?"

"I need you to listen to me."

He coughs and clears his throat, a prolonged and liquid sound. "Who is this?"

"I know that you're sick. I want to help."

An encouraging hint of the mercurial anger you remember: "I asked you a question," your father says.

"And the answer is irrelevant," you say. The voice transformer is bringing out in you the sort of insolence you would otherwise never in all eternity consider displaying toward your father. This insolence is interesting to us, and useful to you—in order to help your father, you'll need to be able to boss him around a bit. "What is relevant, John, is whether or not you're interested in living. Because I can help you with that."

"Goodbye."

"Wait, please. Give me a minute."

"Look, I don't know what you're trying to sell. But the doctors already told me I'm done."

"That's the whole point, John. I'm going to give you more time than the doctors are offering."

Again he tries to clear his throat, two or three attempts of increasing effort, then finally a harsh, reflexive cough. "I'm listening."

It's always surprising what people are willing to sit still for when they're genuinely desperate. Your father's good sense tells him this mysterious benefactor routine is unalloyed nonsense, and under any other circumstances, being even less tolerant of nonsense than the average man, he would have ended the conversation immediately and gone back to his dinner of shepherd's pie and whole milk. But even he, the god of your childhood, can be broken down by fear. It's a sad realization, but one you must take advantage of if you're going to cure him.

"Do you have pen and paper? I need you to write something down." You wait for him to be ready, then recite the telephone number for the Brockton Hospital radiology department. "Give them your name and say you've misplaced the information for your appointment and ask could they give it to you again. Write down what they tell you. I'll call again in ten minutes."

The moment ten minutes have passed you hit redial, and your father answers immediately.

"What's TomoTherapy?" he says. "I asked the woman but she said my primary care doctor arranged the appointment, and he could explain it to me."

"It's a new treatment," you say. "Very, very promising type of radiation. Some people are even cured. But at the very least it should buy you some time, so that we can come up with something else."

"Something else?"

"What I'll be working on while you're in Brockton. I'm developing a treatment of my own."

There's a pause. "Who the hell is this?" he asks again.

"As I said," you tell your father, "who I am isn't important. All you need to know is I have your best interests firmly in mind. And I am going to make you well. Who else is offering you that?"

"No one," he says. Again, the harsh, liquid throat-sound.

"But you need to trust me."

"We'll see."

"I'll take that," you say. "So you'll go to Brockton?"

"You think it will help?"

"I do," you say, feeling a little thrill at his soliciting your advice and encouragement. "And in the meantime, as I said, I'll be working on something else. So . . . hang in there. John."

"Okay."

28   You hang up, still vaguely surprised that you got him to agree to anything. It hasn't occurred to you, though it should have by now, that this is the real reason Sawyer forbade you to have direct contact with your father—because no matter the circumstances, he would not take advice or help directly from you. From a completely anonymous elderly woman he's never laid eyes on, yes. From you, no. He is the father and you are the son, and even in this weakened and vulnerable state he is incapable of relying on you for anything, ever.

I spend the next week researching endlessly. Sleep becomes an afterthought, and in my anxiety and fatigue I have to resist the urge to take any of the government-issue meth pills. As the week goes on I talk to no one and ingest nothing but soda and vending machine snacks. During rare moments when I'm not at the library or the local hospital or in front of the laptop, I worry over whether or not my father actually went to Brockton, because I've got a promising list of potential ingredients for a cancer-killing cocktail—everything from interleukin-12 to hazelnuts, bovine cartilage to cannabis—but I need the time that TomoTherapy would provide in order to research my hunches at the Merck labs.

I also need tissue from my father's biopsy. I e-mail Sawyer, and on Friday a small box arrives at the motel with four samples packed in dry ice, along with paperwork from Brockton. This last is both a relief and a worry. The upside is that my father is following through with treatment, but the latest PET scan shows, just two weeks after the initial diagnosis, new cancer growth in his spine. It's spreading even faster than I'd feared, and I realize my hand has been forced.

I call Sawyer and give him the list of ingredients and tell him I need everything at the Merck labs within twelve hours. I drive in a buzzing stupor of protracted sleep deprivation, a semipsychosis exacerbated by grief and fear. In what seems like no time at all Boston looms up out of the night. Dazzled by the streetlamps and the lonely lighted windows high in the skyscrapers, I make four laps around Brookline and the Back Bay before finding Avenue Louis Pasteur and the Merck building more or less by accident.

I get out and pump the parking meter full of quarters before realizing that, at three in the morning, it's not necessary. The Merck labs don't open until six, so even though the clock's ticking I have no choice but to wait. I sit in the car with the radio on low, smoking cigarettes and tapping my fingers on the steering wheel.

Dawn breaks slow and gray over the city. I check my watch and see it's after five. I'm feeling a little less frenzied, but a cup of tea and some food might be in order before going to the labs. I lock the car and walk up to Brookline Avenue, then over to Longwood, where there's a Dunkin' Donuts. When I order tea and a bagel the girl behind the counter seems spooked by me. I take a seat by the window, and the doughnut girl keeps looking up and eyeing me. I start to wonder what it is about my appearance or bearing that she finds so unnerving, and hope that whatever it is, it won't be a problem when I try to clear security at Merck.

It turns out I could have probably walked into the labs naked and slathered in peanut butter, because when I go into the lobby and show my ID badge I get the VIP treatment. One of the guards checks some paperwork and smiles and insists on taking my bags as he escorts me upstairs to a private lab. It's not big, but it's got everything I need—microscopes, a good centrifuge, autoclave, incubator, pipettes, test tubes and Petri dishes, dyes and razors—and based on my reception so far it seems certain that if I require anything else it'll be provided posthaste.

Sitting on the counters are a dozen boxes, taped heavily along the seams and bearing shipping labels with return addresses as random and far-flung as if someone had thrown a dart repeatedly at a map. I open them and find everything I requested of Sawyer, from hawthorn fruit to freeze-dried anole lizards. I empty the boxes and organize these items, setting aside those that require refrigeration. I can't help marveling once more at Sawyer's commitment and reliability. God help me, I'm actually starting to feel beholden to the son of a bitch.

Despite the obvious urgency, I can't start trying out the mung bean and lapacho tree bark until I grow cultures from my father's biopsy samples. I could've had Sawyer find some mature SCLC cultures to begin testing on right away, but I'm trying to cure my father's cancer, not the cancer of some anonymous person from the Baltimore-Washington area who has probably been outlived by the cell samples he donated. One of the fundamental problems with cancer research to date is it presupposes that a single treatment can be successful against any number of cases of, say, prostate cancer, when in fact the only reliably effective treatment is one that's custom-fitted to every last nucleotide of a particular renegade cell.

It's probably just as well there's not much to do now; I'm about twenty hours of sleep and three large meals removed from thinking with the sort of power and clarity I'll need to make this work. I thaw the biopsy samples, sterilize two dozen cell growth plates, and set up cultures in the incubator. By the time I've finished it's midafternoon, and a week's worth of hunger and fatigue finally hit me all at once. It's all I can do to leave the lab and walk back over to Longwood, where I rent a room at the Best Western, take the elevator to the fifth floor, order juice and a chef's salad from room service, and pass out on the bed in a large rectangle of afternoon sunlight.

When I wake it's still daytime, but something about the light is wrong. It takes a minute for me to realize that the sun is now on the opposite, eastern side of the building—I've slept through the night. My insides feel raw and hollow. I remember ordering room service, and I go to the door and find a tray on the floor of the hallway. The juice is lukewarm, the salad wilted and topped with graying ham, but I eat and drink with the mindless greed of a starving animal. Afterward I stand in the shower for a long time with my back to the spray, head down, eyes closed. I step out and dry off and change into fresh clothes, surprised at how much better I feel.

I have every intention of heading back to the Merck labs, but when I step outside it's an unbelievably gorgeous day, and the vibrant, optimistic motion in everything—the sun and the people and the pedicabs and the trains—draws me out into the streets, so instead of going to watch cancer cells multiply and conquer like some microscopic Sherman's March, I walk up to Brookline Avenue and follow it north toward the river, not really thinking about where it will take me and not really caring, and the next thing I know I'm standing on the corner of Brookline and Landsdowne, looking up at the great green façade of Fenway Park's left-field wall. Across the street, in the window of the Cask and Flagon, a sign reads: "Bud Light Half Price Night! Come In And Watch The Sox Take On The Cubs!"

The Cubs. I remember suddenly what Rodney told my mother over the phone: a two-week road trip. Interleague play. By now my father will surely have sent Rodney back to be with the team. Which means my brother, who I haven't seen in eight years, is here, in Boston, at Fenway Park, probably sitting in the visitors' clubhouse, watching TV and waiting for batting practice to begin, just a few hundred yards from where I stand.

For obvious reasons I don't normally put stock in the notion of fate, but

I decide in an uncharacteristic moment of superstition that it is meant to be, this meeting between me and Rodney. Sawyer be damned. He didn't say anything about not having contact with my brother, after all. Just my parents, my father specifically. No doubt poor Rodney is feeling even more broken and alone than I am, and one way or another I'm going to see him.

This may prove difficult, though. The ballpark doesn't open for another three hours and in any event I don't have a ticket, so I yell out to a couple of valets standing behind a set of aluminum barricades at the players' parking garage. The taller of the two, with the reluctance of someone accustomed to being hollered at by strangers, moves toward me down the blocked-off street.

"My brother is with the Cubs," I say. "I need to talk to him."

"Right," the guys says. "If he's ya brothah, shouldn't you have his phone numbah?"

"Seriously," I say.

"Okay, I'll bite, chief. Which one's ya brothah?"

I tell him Rodney's name.

"Uh huh," he says. "Move it, buddy, outta heah." He turns and walks back to his place against the wall. A Hummer with a huge shining chrome grill and spinning rims rolls in, and the two attendants busy themselves moving the barricades aside and fawning over the driver, a tall Hispanic who gives over his keys and shakes their hands absently, then saunters into the park's interior.

So I'll have to buy a ticket. Unfortunately Red Sox tickets are rarer than yellow-tailed woolly monkeys, and harder to find. My only hope is to walk around the park in the couple of hours leading up to game time and try to find a scalper, which means I've got some time to kill.

Two hours later I emerge from a taqueria on Landsdowne, my belly full of fish tacos and iced tea. By now the streets are choked with baseball fans, and I have to pause at the bottom of the bar's outside staircase and wait for an opportunity to merge with the happy flow of foot traffic. I haven't made it half a block before a skinny guy in glasses and a greasy white shirt passes by, waving his hand in the air and asking no one in particular if they need tickets.

"Ticket," I say, and the guy stops and says, "Tickets." "Ticket," I say again. The guy straightens his glasses and says, "Look, I've got two, you want 'em both or not." I ask how much and when he tells me it's like being kicked in the groin, but I figure it's Sawyer's money anyway and hand it over.

I've been inside Fenway once, years ago, and the only difference is that the fat old men on stools tearing tickets have been replaced by uniformed guards who frisk people and rummage through bags and never, ever smile. Other than that it's the same families and young couples and roving packs of college boys, wearing the same authentic jackets and jerseys and caps, eating the same hot dogs and drinking the same beers, which are being sold at the same 800 percent markup.

It's the aroma, though—spilled Budweiser, popcorn, piss, Italian sausage burning over propane flame—that really transports me back to the first and last time I was here, walking down this same trash-strewn promenade behind the right-field bleachers, struggling to stay dry and condiment-free under a load of two hot dogs, a bag of peanuts, and a large orange soda. My father, at the time still mute around me and Rodney, led the way. I remember mounting the staircase along the park's outer wall and trying to keep pace with the old man, who always took stairs two or three at a time as a matter of course. And then that miraculous first view of the park from the infield roof seats, one of those early-life visions that's seared into your neurons the way shadows were seared into the ground at Hiroshima. The field so vast yet enclosed by walls, by far the most sprawling interior I'd ever seen. The thousands and thousands of people. The grass impossibly neat, literally hand-trimmed along the infield dirt. The players in their startling white uniforms—big men, a couple of them bigger than even my father. The jumbotron flashing and glittering. The warm, gravelly voice over the PA. Sitting shoulder-to-shoulder with my father and eating hot dogs together. All of it wonderful, indelible.

All these years later the feeling is the same when I step out of the tunnel, five-dollar orange soda in hand, and the narrow concrete walls open onto the wide, wonderful panorama of grass and sky. I remember the moment when my father leaned over and told me ballparks are America's cathedrals, and Fenway is Notre-Dame. It was the only thing he said the entire game. I pause at the top of the landing and look around, smiling stupidly, as people squeeze along the walkway between me and the railing.

There's more than an hour before the game starts, so I work my way to the infield, where the Cubs are taking batting practice. I step down to the wall and wedge myself in among the kids holding up baseballs and Sharpies and calling frantically to every player who wanders by. Rodney is playing long-toss on the opposite side of the infield, in the grass just beyond third base.

One thing about Rodney: on the field he has always been able to transcend whatever else is happening in his life, no matter how bitter or painful. In this regard, if none other, he is like most other world-class athletes—the exceptional hand-eye coordination and 400 lb. bench press are nice, but his true gift is the ability to check his head at the clubhouse door and let himself be guided by muscle memory and instinct. To become, on the field, quite literally mindless.

Which is why, when the initial warmth I feel at first seeing him subsides, I start to worry. His shoulders are drooped, his head down. He throws the ball listlessly and drops several easy passes in the grass. After one of these he picks the ball up, tosses it back, and turns away, staring up into the stands with his glove hanging at his side. The guy he's playing catch with stands looking at Rodney's back for a few seconds, perplexed, then runs deeper into left field to shag fly balls.

As Rodney descends the stairs into the visitors' dugout, emerging with a bat a few moments later, I wonder if I should approach him before or after the game. I'd planned to wait until after, but watching him—he takes a few reluctant practice swings, waiting for his turn in the cage—I think maybe it would be better to talk to him now. But I'm inexplicably anxious, and in the time it takes me to work up the nerve to go around behind home plate and call to him, the Cubs wrap up their b.p. session and disappear into the clubhouse, while the grounds crew hustles to put the screens and ball baskets back into storage and get things ready for the game.

I go back out to right field and find my seat just as the starting lineups are being announced. The place is filling up now, and I jostle with the guy on my left for control of the tiny armrest. Rodney comes to the plate in the top of the first, but he's gone before I have much of a chance to get excited, striking out on three pitches, the third one looking.

To my knowledge Rodney has never before, at any level of baseball, struck out on three pitches. In just his second year with the Cubs he set the NL record for fewest strikeouts in a season, then tied his own record the following year. He's regarded as one of the best two-strike hitters of the modern era, no small distinction when one considers the competition: Boggs, Gwynn, Carew. To go down looking he must be in even more trouble, mentally, than I feared. Already I can't wait for this to be over.

Fortunately the game ends up being a pitchers' duel, and in just over two hours it's the bottom of the ninth, Cubs up 3–1, one on, one out. I leave my seat and go through the tunnel and walk down to the third base field box, behind the visitors' dugout, in position to get Rodney's attention when he walks over from short at the end of the game. A man behind me grumbles about people who stand while the ball is in play—people, he adds, who don't even belong in this section and probably should be out in the bleachers or the right-field grandstands or whatever other shitty section they're ticketed for so those who paid $250 for their seats can have an unobstructed view. Half of a hot dog hits me in the back and lands on the concrete to mingle with the peanut shells and empty beer cups. I don't even turn around, just continue to wait for the last out to be made.

In short order the Red Sox rookie second baseman takes a slider for strike three, and the game is over. The Cubs nine gather around the pitcher's mound, trading handshakes and high-fives, then break up and begin drifting in groups of two and three toward the dugout. Rodney comes over by himself, head down, glove slapping at his thigh. I call out to him, but he doesn't hear me. His head stays down, face obscured by the bill of his cap. His right foot hits the top of the dugout stairs. He's about to disappear.

I try again, louder. This time he looks up, sees me, and smiles broadly, his joy unsullied by disbelief.

"Junior!" He walks around to the home plate side of the dugout, where the seats come right up to the field, and I meet him there. A man in a Fenway Security jacket puts a hand out to stop me, but Rodney tells him it's okay, and I swing a leg up over the low wall and step onto the field. We embrace.

"Dad," Rodney says.

"I know."

"How do you know?"

"It doesn't matter, Rod. He'll be okay. I'm taking care of it."

He looks at me a moment. "You will, won't you?" he says. "Take care of him?"

"Of course."

"Okay." Thus satisfied, he smiles again. "It's so good to see you!" he says, slapping me on the back with one large hand.

A growing mass of kids is pressed against the wall, calling to Rodney and holding out the ubiquitous Sharpies and baseballs.

"You've got business to tend to," I tell him. "Listen, Rod, let's get together for dinner tonight."

"Yeah, I'd like that!" he says. He takes a ball and signs it without looking away from me.

"There's a Bertucci's down the street in Kenmore Square."

"I like Italian," Rodney says.

"I know you do. Will you meet me there at eight?"

"I will."

"Okay," I say. "And listen, Rod. Don't tell anyone you've seen me. Especially not Dad and Ma. All right?"

"Okay." Trusting Rodney on this is a simple matter: it would never occur to him to tell me one thing and do another.

But when I get to Bertucci's at ten past eight Rodney isn't there. I wait at the bar for nearly an hour, drinking seltzer and picking at the complimentary focaccia and olive oil while the place fills up with young besuited professional types. Rodney would never blow me off, especially under these circumstances. This makes no sense at all. After a while it occurs to me to run across the street to the Store 24 and buy a paper and check the baseball schedule, and sure enough, the Cubs are playing the Dodgers at Wrigley tomorrow. Rodney forgot it was a travel day.

Maybe it's just as well, because even though I'm still waiting for the cultures to grow there's plenty of research I could be doing. I walk back to the hotel and e-mail Sawyer to ask for more money, then spend the rest of the night eating pretzels from the vending machine in the hall and reading the latest on gene-based therapies, of which there is quite a lot, most of it useless.

Sawyer responds the next morning with the assurance that I'll have all the money I need. He also says that, fortunately for me, and for him, and let's face it for all of humanity, the test of the Alcubierre drive was a success. He goes on to say that I came dangerously close to crossing the line by meeting my brother, and I had better hope that Rodney keeps his pledge not to tell my parents. But even Sawyer, with his files and reports, his satellite cameras that can see from orbit whether a penny dropped on a sidewalk landed heads or tails, even he doesn't know my brother like I do. As flighty as he can be, when it comes to keeping a secret Rodney is utterly reliable.

Over the next couple of weeks I settle into a fruitful routine that would be almost pleasant if its ultimate aim were something other than fighting off the looming specter of my father's death. The cultures mature more quickly than I'd anticipated—good on the one hand, since it enables me to begin testing; bad, of course, because there's a correlation between how quickly cells grow in a Petri dish and how quickly they grow in the body. I apply various combinations of the fruits and herbs and bovine cartilage and frozen lizards to the cultures, testing, observing, alternating combinations, tweaking proportions, retesting.

Every afternoon I take a break from the lab and walk to Boston Beer Works, stopping on my way to grab a copy of the *Globe*. This time of day the place is usually empty except for a few slow suicides seated a safe distance from one another at the bar. I drink a Coke or O'Doul's while I flip through the paper, always checking the sports section first for the baseball box scores. Even though we didn't have a chance to eat dinner together Rodney must have taken our talk to heart, because since then he's hitting a much more Rodney-like .382, with 5 home runs and 16 RBI in 19 games. He hasn't struck out once.

Everything is coming together: my father is in treatment, Rodney's happy and playing well, the Alcubierre drive works like a charm, and the cure for my father's cancer is more or less a foregone conclusion. On particularly nice days I sit on the sidewalk patio at Beer Works and order a refill on my soda and watch people going about their lives and think perhaps

I'd like one of those for myself. A life. I cast my mind ahead, to a time when my father is well and I'm free of my obligations to Sawyer, and I think maybe I'll reestablish contact with Amy and set about building something with her in the few years we've got left before everyone has to abandon ship.

Then, on a Monday afternoon when all is well and nothing can be wrong, Sawyer calls.

"What sort of progress are you making?" Classic Sawyer, right to it without even the most perfunctory greeting.

"Coming along," I say. "Why haven't I gotten the radiology reports from Brockton this week?"

"Our two questions," Sawyer says, "are related."

That chill again. The icicles, pricking, probing.

"Okay," I say, "so, the TomoTherapy isn't working well, is what you're going to tell me. I still need the details. I still need the report."

"The details are these: It's a complete failure. The tumor in your father's lung has grown considerably. Meantime, his PET scan shows new areas of high glucose uptake on the brain, in several lymph nodes and, most ominously, on the pancreas."

He gives me a moment to absorb this. I say nothing.

"He's lost twenty-five pounds in two weeks," Sawyer continues. "Even worse, on recent nights, while he lies awake and your mother pretends to sleep next to him, his thoughts have turned, however briefly, to suicide."

"Okay, Sawyer. How do you know that?"

"I wish," he says, "that I didn't."

I think about my father's life, and as I do a sudden anger washes over me, hot like fresh blood. I think about his lost baseball career, and all the years he worked for next to nothing. I think about the money he didn't have, spent on crap that didn't work: the refrigerator that died just after the warranty had expired and cost who knows how much in rotten food; the color TV, less than a year old, that blinked out during game four of the '86 World Series; the matching Desert Desperado bikes he bought for me and Rodney that started falling apart pretty much the moment we got on, and my father's repeated attempts to repair them, to no avail, never to any avail. I think of what his afterlife might hold, and I get a vision of him as Sisyphus, but instead of pushing a rock he's pushing that bastard of a car, the green Country Squire wagon with the faulty starter, over and over again he shoves it up the hill, then watches it roll back down, and I have to admit that a tiny part of me hates him for slogging along through all eternity like this, without complaint.

Race for the Prize

27 You have roughly one week to come up with a cure. Any longer than that and it will be too late. And so you've got a decision to make for yourself. Given the situation there are really only two options.

   The first is to let your father die. We're sorry to put it so harshly, but there's no reason, at this point, to employ euphemisms.

   The second is to take the chance of killing yourself in order to save him. Because make no mistake: for you to discover the correct formulation in less than a week you'll need to spend all your time at the lab, not wasting even an hour on sleep or food, and to achieve that sort of endurance you'll have no choice but to turn to the pills Clark provided you with. It goes without saying that this is a dangerous prospect for anyone, let alone a barely reformed alcoholic and drug addict who only succeeded at sobriety after being locked away in a Bulgarian gulag, so for the sake of your own preservation we implore you to remember that there are two real options available to you here, as unpleasant as the one may be.

26 You go to the bathroom and remove the bottle of spook meth from the medicine cabinet and roll it around in the palm of your hand, considering. After a few moments' hesitation you pop the bottle open, dry-swallow two pills, and head out to the labs. One of the drug's characteristic properties is the speed with which it enters the bloodstream. The effects are improbably fast and amazing, the cleanest high you've ever had. You buzz like a dynamo and move through the streets as if friction has been written off the books. By the time you've covered the distance to the Merck building you feel quite certain that you could, if the need arose, clean and jerk a Volkswagen. Though we assure you you could not.

   You set to work, and time quickly devolves into a psychedelic blur of twenty- and thirty-hour-long lab sessions, punctuated by temporary breakdowns when the meth turns on you and you curl yourself into a corner and scream and clutch at your head, or else stare out the window weeping extravagantly at the world's beauty. No food. No sleep. You start chewing the pills, though neither we nor you are really sure why. You urinate in a bottle that used to hold Gatorade of the Fierce Melon variety, and the only time you leave the lab is to empty this bottle; since it's a two-liter and you're barely taking in enough fluids to stay alive, you don't have to step out very often. The only outside communication occurs when you pull yourself together long enough to phone Sawyer and ask for more of the drug, a request with which he complies. Under other circumstances it might be worth speculating as to Sawyer's motives here, since he's aware of the fractured mental state the drug has already produced in you. But he's also aware that there is no other way for this to work, so he reluctantly has a package dispatched.

There's a delay of several agonizing hours between when you take the last pill on hand and when the courier delivers the new supply to the door of the lab. You wrest the package from him and tear at the box and crack the cap opening the bottle and only after choking down three of the pills are you calm enough to sign the courier's portable LCD screen to acknowledge receipt.

25 Despite the intensity of your efforts, cells continue to grow and multiply with lethal, mindless obstinance. Several cultures are slowed to various degrees, but delaying your father's death is, of course, not the aim. One sample is halted altogether for nearly two full days, during which you hold your figurative breath, but then on the third day the cells burst out in furious renewed growth, as if angered by the attempt to destroy them.

24 Near the end of the week you are crippled for several hours by pain in your lower back that forces you to lie on your side on the tile floor, moaning. You reach around with one hand to massage the muscles, because this feels like the worst backache in the history of humankind, but the pain is actually being caused by your kidneys, which are in the early stages of acute failure. You pass out. When you come to again the

pain has lessened to a rotting ache. You have the sudden intractable urge to urinate, and when you do it's the exact color and consistency of maple syrup, staining the liquid already in the Gatorade bottle a sickly brown.

Your kidneys are flooded with toxins and dying muscle tissue, a condition called rhabdomyolysis. Serious, serious trouble. Though it's understandably difficult for you to think clearly at the moment, you need to marshal your wits, because you're about to make the most important decision of your life to date. There is a possibility that taking any more pills will kill you, but without them there's no way you can continue working, which means your father will surely die.

23 It's not a decision we can help you with, sadly. You alone must choose, but you are not certain you have the courage. You lean against the workbench and think that surely when your father sired you it was with the hope that you would outlive him. He wouldn't want you to die to save his life.

Forgive us, but we feel compelled to point out an obvious flaw in this argument: your father has already gone through the grief of having lost you. As far as he knows you've been dead eight years. If you died again it would make no difference, because he would never know. Sawyer would see to it that your body was quietly disposed of, and Rodney would take the secret of your Fenway meeting to his own grave, just as you asked him to.

22 You try to pull your thoughts together. The final formulation dangles somewhere in the ether just beyond your reach, all the more maddening for how close it is. You're positive you've got the right combination of constituents—the proportions are what have you stumped. We're surprised, given the fact that you're very nearly dead, how strong a pang of intellectual vanity you feel at being baffled. It pisses you off. Not because your father is dying, but because you're smarter than this.

And it's this anger, rather than love, that finally gets you to your feet. You brace yourself against the table, find the bottle, and take one more pill, feeling decidedly unheroic.

21 It's our contention, however, that this entire display is the very definition of heroic. And we make this assessment having taken into account the base, overriding appetite you have as a multidisciplinary addict—this accounts for only 10 percent or so of your motivation for taking another pill. An additional 5 percent is attributable to a subconscious longing for death, and the remaining 85 percent is, simply and heroically, a desire to help your father that is so strong it causes you to ignore biological imperative #1: self-preservation. You're risking your own life for another, no matter the jumble of motivations, and though we question the wisdom of this risk it's nevertheless difficult for us to observe without feeling inspiration and admiration in equal measure. Which is why we offer you this, in appreciation of your courage and (we admit it, yes) in fear for your life:

Despite what you believe, the formulation is in fact missing one ingredient: the humble mung bean, two parts in proportion to the other components, is the magic bullet that will make your father well again.

20 So yes you were wrong about something, and we're sorry to be the ones to tell you because we know your sense of identity, if you can be said to have one, is tangled up in your intellect, in your ability to reason and deduce. Really, you've got little else, so we understand your disappointment and embarrassment. Perhaps you can take heart in the fact that given enough time there's no question you would have figured it out for yourself. We simply determined, given the circumstances, that it would benefit both you and your father to hasten along the inevitable.

19 Now, hobbled still by your kidneys' death throes but revived enough by the pill to get to work again, you set about mixing batches of the proper and correct formulation. You'll need a month's worth of ten-ounce daily

doses. Not a lot of volume, really, but it's the detail work—shaving down the various ingredients, measuring to the exact microgram—that taxes your dwindling physical and mental resources. Eventually, though, it's time for the mixing. Even this is a challenge, because many of the ingredients can't be cooked or they lose their potency, so you cannot use heat as an aid in folding everything together.

You're bloated and slow and your mouth tastes like you've been sucking on old coins. The cramping is worse now on your right side, and to compensate you list to the right like a wounded ship. It takes a full minute for you to cross the lab, another thirty seconds to open the pill bottle and shake two into your hand. Your fingers have swelled to the point where the knuckles have disappeared and consequently your hands won't flex or grasp well. You get the pills in your mouth but they refuse to go down because your tongue is swollen and dry and the taste buds are like Velcro. You sit on the floor, swallowing over and over, trying to coax the things down. They move a quarter inch or so with each swallow and then stick fast again, and it's getting more and more painful, like one long narrow floor burn on the inside of your throat, but you've got to get them down or else you'll have no energy for packaging the mixture to ship to your father, and then you realize you've got nothing to package the mixture *with*—no containers to hold individual doses, no boxes to ship them in, no bubble wrap to pad the boxes you don't have and no tape to close them up. Nothing.

18 Time passes, though in this near-death state you hardly notice. At some point you become aware that a man is standing over you. You recognize his blond brushcut and amazing cheek bones but you're not sure how exactly, or from where. He hands you a large bottle of water with the words *Poland Spring* on the label and says, "Drink. Not too fast." Even using both hands you have a hard time lifting the bottle to your lips. With a sigh of disgust the man crouches and helps you drink. "Not too fast," he says again, as you gulp and spill water on your chest.

"When's the last time you took the pills?" the man asks.

"Just now," you gasp, and the words are hardly out of your mouth when with a few quick movements the man pulls your head forward and pries open your mouth and sticks what feels like a pen down your throat. He jumps back as you vomit with the sort of violence you wouldn't have thought possible in your weakened state. When you're finished gagging and hacking you look down and see the pills on the floor between your legs, whole and glistening in a puddle of phlegmy water.

The man hands you the water again. "Drink," he says. He looks around the lab, sees the mixer with your father's medicine. He points and asks, "That finished?"

"Yes," you say, still struggling to bring the bottle to your mouth without dumping it. "But it needs. To be packaged and shipped."

"I know about that," the man says. He puts his hands under your arms and pulls you to your feet. "First I'm taking you to the hospital."

"It has to be done properly," you say. "Dry ice. Airtight containers. And right away."

"I've got my instructions," the man says. He takes you by the elbow and hustles you out of the lab to the elevator down the hall. You're about halfway down to the lobby when the world goes hazy again, then disappears altogether.

The next thing I know I'm coming to in what looks like an emergency room. There's a bank of twelve beds, all side by side in the same long ward, the last two cordoned off with curtains. The occupants of these beds are invariably worn and dirty in appearance, the kind of homeless-dirty where the grime has bonded on a molecular level with the skin and takes at least seven or eight vigorous scrubbings to get out. I'm hooked up to all kinds of tubes and wires. I don't necessarily feel much better than before, but the pain in my flanks is gone and my fingers bear somewhat less of a resemblance to Vienna sausages, which can only be good.

I don't know how long I'm lying there, hard to tell without any windows, a while, staring up at the fluorescents, wondering whether or not Clark got my father's medicine properly packaged and shipped, when Clark himself shows up and raises hell about me being placed here in the junkie bay like some street addict.

"Do you people have any idea whatsoever who this is?" Clark asks, pointing at me. "How important he is?"

They do not, judging by the perplexed and somewhat amused looks.

"Fine," Clark says. He takes a cell phone from his pocket and makes a brief call, then stands with his arms crossed at the foot of my bed, clearly expectant, glaring alternately at the doctor and nurses in the room. Within ten minutes an older doctor in a white lab coat arrives and shakes Clark's hand, apologizing. The others in the room exchange worried looks. Next thing I know I've been moved to a private room upstairs, with an expansive view of the Back Bay's stately brownstones.

The following day a note from Sawyer arrives, passed to me by an orderly: *Your father has received the medicine. Began taking it immediately. Has complained about the taste. And who could blame him.*

A week later, when I've been eating solid food for three days and feel good enough to regret missing the high summer weather I see outside: *New PET scan shows a dramatic reduction in size of primary tumor. More than a dozen lymph nodes, previously hot, no longer displaying glucose uptake.*

A week later still I'm moved to a detox center outside Washington, a place where despite repeated requests for regular street clothes they insist I wear hospital pajamas, as a "phase one" patient. It's not clear what, if anything, is required for me to graduate to "phase two." After four days here it's obvious that infantilizing addicts is the preferred method of treatment—pj's, plastic sporks, metal mirrors, mandatory a.m. calisthenics set to the *Muppet Movie* soundtrack, occupational therapy tasks that could easily be completed by a four-year-old of submoronic intelligence, etc. But then this happy bit of news arrives: *Doctors, incredulous, order second PET scan. Now shrugging their shoulders and throwing around references to God.*

Three weeks after that, on the day I'm released from the detox: *Treatment completed. Tests, including blood, CAT, and yet another PET, show no detectable malignancies. The word remission has been used. So, final tally: Fathers cured of terminal illness: 1. Oncologists converted back to the Catholicism of their youth: 1. And now if you like, you're free to visit with your family. Take a couple of weeks.*

But I decide that there's plenty of time for that now, that I'll give my father a month or two to regain his strength and put on some weight before subjecting him to the shock of seeing his long-dead son again. Instead I return by chauffeured town car to NSA headquarters that afternoon and take the elevator to my office. I meet with Spergel and Ross and the rest of the crew, and there's plenty of backslapping and congratulations all around regarding the successful test of the Alcubierre drive. I thank everyone in turn and at length, because even though they don't know why I was gone, I'm all too aware that if they hadn't been able to pull off the test, my father would be dead. They seem perplexed but pleased by the depth of my gratitude. Spergel in particular. With a smile he says, "You certainly don't seem like yourself," and I smile back and say, "Hey, even I'm entitled to get excited about saving humanity."

"I suppose you're right," he says.

I spend the next couple of days lazing around my office, pretending to organize files, fielding the occasional phone call from reps at Boeing or Lockheed, guys who kiss my ass for as long as I'll tolerate before hanging up. All I want to do, most days, is go up to ground level and be outside, to sit on my new favorite bench in the courtyard and turn my face toward the sun and quietly revel in the work I've done. It's not something I've allowed myself much of, over the years. Reveling. But now there is plenty of good reason. I am, God help me, in a state resembling happiness.

Sawyer comes into my office a few days later, looking pale and drawn and just plain *sad,* and it is shocking, and not a little bit scary, to see such emotion on his face. And I know before he even has a chance to say it, of course I know, both because I always expect the worst and because life has never, not once, taught me to expect anything different, so as he opens his mouth to speak I clutch at the sides of my head and close my eyes and ask: "How?"

"He was driving his Mustang," Sawyer says after a moment. He puts his hand on my desk gently, as though it's an extension of my body. It's clear he wants to offer some sort of physical condolence but doesn't really understand how one goes about doing that.

There's a sudden sensation of great pressure in my skull. My pulse hammers, and I hear a tremendous incongruent blaring, like I've suddenly been dropped into Times Square at noon. Vomit rushes hot and acidic to the back of my throat. The muscles of my arms and legs set to trembling. Before too long I become convinced that I, too, am about to die, because sustained physical distress like this does not seem at all compatible with continued existence.

Strangely, though, there are no tears.

"Someone hit him?" I ask.

"One-car accident. Rollover. Hit a tree flush on the driver's side."

"That doesn't make any sense," I say, still clutching my head. "He's a very careful, a very *good* driver."

"I know," Sawyer says. "We know that. Which is why we sent someone to look into it. The local police have concluded he fell asleep at the wheel. Our man agrees with them."

"*Fell asleep?*" I ask.

"Lost consciousness somehow," Sawyer says. "You know there are probably a thousand possible explanations for sudden loss of consciousness, and a lot of them can't be revealed by autopsy. Though we're, ah, still waiting for the results on that."

I wave a hand at him, indicating my desire, right at the moment, to not hear words like "autopsy."

"Sorry, Junior," Sawyer says. "But I think you should know. When the shock wears off, you'll want to know these things."

"Give me a minute," I say. The vomit-thing starts up again, and I try to hook the heel of my shoe around the wastebasket next to the desk and drag it between my legs. But the fine motor skills aren't there, and I throw up on the floor.

"Easy," Sawyer says. He's actually moved to take his hand from the desk and place it tentatively on my shoulder.

I literally shrug it off. On my feet suddenly, backing away from him and wiping at my mouth, I say, "No, I'm okay. I'm okay." I rummage around the things on my desktop as if I've lost something essential, though I have no idea what that might be.

"Not one hundred percent convinced of that," Sawyer says.

"I'm going to step out, for a while." I don't look at him, just move unsteadily around the desk, to the door, through it. Surprisingly, Sawyer says nothing more, just watches me go.

Topside it's yet another captivating summer day. Tony, the security officer I've come lately to know by name during my daily walks, offers a hello. I ignore this and say simply, "Get me a car." It is all I can manage. As simple an act as saying hi is, it seems somehow beyond my ability to conceive of, let alone perform. I am not so far gone, though, that I fail to notice the look of I-thought-we-were-friends hurt on Tony's face as he lifts a two-way radio to his mouth and calls for a vehicle.

It occurs to me that if I can't even put together a simple greeting, driving probably isn't a super idea, but I don't have far to go, as Bill's Lounge is only a mile and a half away out on Annapolis Road. I get there okay but then clip the right rear fender of a Grand Marquis sitting out in front of the place when I pull in. I park at a 30-degree angle to the curb, with the ass-end of the Town Car jutting halfway out into the lane.

Bill's has no windows at all, and the glass door has been covered with black crepe paper. Inside is dark and cool, the kind of perpetual night in which an authentic drunk can lose himself for months at a time. A Conway

Twitty song plays softly. The flattopped army PFCs and local blue-collar types eyeball me in a bad way. I sit at the bar and order a double scotch. When the bartender sets a glass in front of me and starts to pour, I put two $100 bills on the bar and tell him to save himself some time and just leave that bottle of Glenfiddich right there where I can get to it.

Because it's been so long since I've had a drink I get pretty mindless pretty quickly, and the next thing I know I've moved to a table with two of the PFCs and we're making friends, although "friends" is probably the wrong word because I'm lying through my teeth about everything and they're only sitting with me because the scotch is free and plentiful. Still, it seems like a fairly good arrangement until my mood sours suddenly and I go from laughing to suicidal in like two seconds flat.

I look at one of the PFCs and tell him to punch me in the face.

"What?" he says. He looks at his buddy like: did I just hear what I think I heard? The two of them laugh.

"Come on," I say. "Hit me."

They continue to stare at me, smiling wide, incredulous smiles, like they're uncertain but also sort of considering taking me up on it.

"Even better idea," I say, shoving my chair back and standing over them. "How about the three of us go out back, and you two beat the everloving shit out of me and take my wallet and my phone and anything else of value that I might have, and leave me there to bleed out?"

"What the fuck," one of the PFCs says, laughing.

"Ah, come *on.*" I pour three shots, spilling scotch all over the tabletop. "Listen, you know you both wanted to roll me the moment I came in here. Tell me I'm wrong."

They exchange a look, smile at each other, say nothing.

"Right, exactly. Drink up, gentlemen." I lift my glass and toss it down. "Consider for a moment that I gave the bartender two hundred dollars for a forty-dollar bottle of scotch. What does that tell you about what's still in my wallet?"

"Probably a lot," the talkative one says.

"Probably a lot," I agree.

"Mike," says the other PFC. "I don't know about this, man."

I swing an open hand, slapping him hard and square across the face. He looks up at me, wide-eyed.

"Do you know about it now?" I ask.

"Mother*fucker.*"

"Meet you outside," I say. I grab the bottle and move to the door, walking on a tilt.

When the talkative one catches me in the gut with his boot and leaves his hands down I stay on my feet and throw a wild, swooping right hook that somehow connects dead-on. His front teeth break like pieces of blackboard chalk, and the feeling is so much better than what I felt just moments before, even when they've got me down on the pavement and have broken my nose and closed an eye and stomped one of my hands to paste it feels so very, very good. And I am laughing, through the blood and busted teeth I am laughing, right up to the moment when I pass out.

Amy

I'm waiting for a cab to take me to the airport. I've got my overnight bag on the floor next to me, and ideally I'd like to be gazing out a window, but the only windows in the foyer are stained glass, and thus unsuitable for gazing. I feel more than a little dumb just staring at the door, but I don't want to turn around and face Oscar. Naturally he doesn't want me to go. He's standing there behind me, and I know without having to look that he's got his hands stuffed in the front pockets of his slacks in that stupid, ineffectual pose he strikes when we're not getting along.

It occurs to me that when the way someone *stands* starts to drive you crazy, it's probably a good sign that things are over.

"You are the lightest-packing girl," Oscar says, "that I've ever met. One bag. One *small* bag."

He wants me to think this is a casual comment, a little attempt at levity, but really he's just fishing for info. He's hoping I'll say something like "Why would I pack a whole bunch of shit when I'm only going to be gone a couple days?" Because we haven't discussed how long I'll be gone, and he's afraid it will be a long time. He's afraid it will be forever.

Maybe it's better that he doesn't have the balls to just ask me outright, because I wouldn't have an answer for him.

What's strange is we're not even fighting. There's no real bone of contention, besides the fact that I'm flying back east to attend the funeral of my dead ex-boyfriend's dead father. But that's not what this is about. What it's about is the slow drift apart that couples do sometimes, like the movement of continents, creeping and intangible. Because it's so gradual you can go on for years, sometimes, doing all the right things to convince everyone around you, and even yourself, that you are half of a healthy and viable pairing. But the whole time you know, with increasing certainty and clarity, that the relationship is sort of undead. A zombie relationship. And like a zombie it keeps tottering forward, mimicking life, but without warmth, or soul, or even a pulse.

So that's me and Oscar, right there: a collective zombie, rotting and putrid, coming apart in chunks. Stumbling forward, mindless, moaning. With our nice town house and Camus our golden retriever and our lefty friends, their progressive hearts and well-groomed opinions. Their weekend non-profit work, saving third-world kids and feeding street people. Their fucking hybrids. Most of the women consider anything other than missionary to be the pinnacle of kink, and I'd bet my life not one of the men has ever been in a fistfight. Somehow these people are the only numbers in my cell phone.

A question I ask myself a lot lately: Am I so pathetic that to avoid being alone I'll surround myself with people I loathe?

I'm not pathetic, I keep telling myself, for clinging to Oscar and our life for so long. I wanted to make something work, for once. I'm tired of failing with people all the time, tired of worrying that I'm broken. But as I stand here waiting for a cab to take me away to a plane that will take me farther away, it's starting to seem like I do have an answer for the question Oscar won't ask, and it isn't the one he wants to hear, and maybe at the end of the day it's me who's the zombie, all by myself. Maybe I am broken, and maybe there's nothing to be done about that.

A car horn sounds outside.

I turn and pick my bag up off the floor. I look at Oscar, and when I see the sorrow he's not trying too hard to hide, I'm surprised that rather than contempt, I feel genuine pity. Not that pity's any better for a relationship than contempt, really.

"Oscar, listen," I say. "It's me, okay? I'm the zombie."

"What?" He takes half a step in my direction, and for a moment I think he's going to wrap me up and try to physically prevent me from leaving. "I don't understand what that means."

I take a step back and place my hand on the doorknob. "Never mind. I'm just saying you shouldn't feel bad. It's not you."

He pushes his hands back into his pockets and tries on a righteous expression that neither of us is buying. "Which is your way of telling me you're not returning."

I sigh. "Does it seem to you," I say, "that I have any idea what I'm doing, Oscar? That I've got a solid plan, here?"

He just stares at me. Like that, the mask of righteousness gives way, revealing the sadness and fear of a child abandoned at a highway rest stop. He is so weak. Be a man, I want to tell him. But being told by a woman to be a man is not likely to work out, so I just leave, and as I close the heavy ironwood door I hear the first undignified sounds. He'll never understand that what makes me hate him is not that he's crying, but that he wants me to hear him cry. It strikes me as sad for both of us that at the end of four years the best wish for him that I can muster is that he will grow a backbone. Not that he have wealth, or love, or achieve his goal of becoming America's foremost authority on French Rococo and Neoclassicism. Just dignity. Start with dignity, Oscar, and work from there. Is the best my heart can offer you.

Next thing, I'm on a plane. When we take off it doesn't feel like I'm lifting into the sky, but rather as though Oscar and Camus and our friends and the whole of the city are falling away from me, like the San Andreas has, praise Jesus, finally split open and sucked everything down into the Pacific. I didn't just leave San Francisco, I think. San Francisco disappeared. Fourteen years of my life here, minus the two I spent with the Peace Corps. And the only thing I'll miss is the dog.

When the flight attendant asks me, in heavily accented English, if I want something to drink, I tell him yes. He says that'll be five dollars, and I tell him it's a small price to pay.

He stares at me, nonplussed.

"Just keep them coming, please."

I don't drink much or often, so by the time we've been in the air for three hours I'm pretty well lit, having convinced the flight attendant, whose name is Alfredo, not to cut me off. He even gives me a freebie. Which is odd, because I'm something like 90 percent sure he's gay. It could be because I've got a good fag hag vibe. It could be just because we've found common ground in our mutual love of the San Francisco Symphony. Regardless, what's important is that he's kept the bad Chardonnay flowing. I'm feeling better about everything, which is nice even though I know it's artificial cheer, cheer-in-a-bottle. The only problem now is I want a cigarette, bad, and it's a direct flight to Bangor, so I've got another three-plus hours to wait.

Who knows why I do it. I'm not exactly what you'd call impulsive, after all. Maybe it's the giddiness that accompanies suddenly trashing your entire life. Maybe it's the inexplicable grief I felt at hearing Junior's dad had died. Most likely it's just the wine. Whatever the reason, I unbuckle my seat belt and move to the bathroom unsteadily, whacking seat backs as I go. My mind is on the pack of Camel Lights in my hip pocket, and the lighter the TSA guys missed.

Both the bathrooms are occupied, so I step out of the aisle and into the galley to wait. We hit some light turbulence and I have to brace myself against the narrow countertop. Minutes go by, and neither of the bathrooms opens up. We're well beyond the time frame for the usual quick airplane whiz, and I start to think that maybe I won't want to go in there after all, but in addition to wanting to sneak a smoke, after all the wine I actually have to use the toilet now. So I keep waiting.

Alfredo, who's serving drinks for the third time, comes up the aisle from the far end of the coach cabin. I worry that I look guilty even though I haven't done anything yet. I press myself against the wall to give him room.

"Need a *ree*-fill," he says, smiling and holding up an empty coffeepot. I nod and smile back. He switches the empty pot out with a full one from the hot plate, then goes back down the aisle, negotiating the bumps with effortless, practiced grace.

At the same time the door to the bathroom opens and a big man in a Giants cap ducks out. Embarrassment flashes across his face when he sees me, and it only takes a few seconds for the source of his embarrassment to hit my nose. Clearly the man eats a lot of meat. I hesitate. I could wait a while to pee. But I really, really want that cigarette. And there's something exciting about the risk of it. Pathetic, I know, but it doesn't take much to thrill you when you're so used to following the rules.

Alfredo is still way down on the other end of the cabin, so I steel myself and step into the bathroom. It's not too bad until I swing the door closed and am trapped in three square feet of space with the ghost of Big Guy's innards. I figure the cigarette will kill the stink, or at least mask it, but I don't dare light up until I disable the smoke detector, and of course in order to disable it I have to find it, which is proving difficult. Obviously I didn't do a very good job of thinking this through. It occurs to me that maybe this is a sign that I should forget about it, but when you want something enough that you've committed to inhaling a stranger's rotting bowels you're pretty much in it until the end, win or lose.

By now I really have to go, so I give up the search long enough to drop trow and hover over the toilet seat. The stink is seriously bad. I try to breathe through my mouth but it's no good; I just end up tasting it, which is even worse. The plane lurches through more turbulence and I whack my head off the wall and this sobers me up for a few seconds. I curse and rub the sore spot. By now I'm half-convinced that there's no smoke detector in the first place, that I can just go ahead and have my cigarette and there'll be nothing to worry about. But then as I'm finishing I look up once more and see, plain as day, a small round vent to the left of the mirror, just below the ceiling. It's built into the wall, so the only way to access it, I'm guessing, will be by going up through the ceiling tile.

I put the toilet seat down and stand on it and give the tile an experimental push. It gives way easily, sliding up and back. I reach my hand in and feel around until I find something that seems the size and shape of a smoke detector. It's got a few wires sticking out of the back. I hesitate, but only for a second. I give the wires a firm tug and they pop out in my hand. To my relief the light stays on and I'm not electrocuted, so I think I got the right ones.

I'm starting to worry about taking too much time. I slide the ceiling tile back into place and get down off the toilet. I pull out my pack, remove one crooked cigarette, and light up. It's delicious, like all things illicit, but within two drags the bathroom fills with smoke. I panic. I think about tossing the cigarette into the toilet and cutting my losses, but I've risked too much, at this point, for just a couple of puffs.

Suddenly, an idea: the violent suction of the toilet is probably strong enough that if I simultaneously flushed and blew a lungful of smoke into the bowl it would probably suck it right out of the room. I get down on my knees, give it a try, and find to my amazement that it actually fucking works. Unbelievable.

I sit on the floor next to the toilet, place one hand on the lever, and have a proper smoke. There's a residual cloud lingering in the air over the sink, but with each flush it swirls lazily and dissipates just a little. A minute or two goes by. I hold the cigarette up and see there's maybe three drags' worth left before I'm smoking filter. I'll finish this and go back to my seat, have another little plastic cup of wine and really relax now.

There's a firm, businesslike knock at the door. "Ello?" Alfredo. Of course.

"Occupied," I say. I try to sound natural, but my heart has leapt into my throat and lodged there, and the strain is evident in my voice.

"Amy? Choo okay?" I can't tell from his tone if he's genuinely concerned or just suspicious. He knocks again. "Choo flushed de toilet like twenny tines."

"I'm all right," I say. I toss the butt in the toilet and wave my hands around. "Just one more minute, please, Alfredo."

"Hokay," he says. Then, a second later: "Choo sure? Di'choo drink too much wine?"

"No," I say. "I'm okay, really. Be right out."

My pulse is throbbing around my scalp. I listen to Alfredo's footsteps going away, and it takes me a moment to calm down and compose myself. I look in the mirror and fix my hair the best I can and wipe a fleck of toilet paper off my pantleg. I'm aware that even though the smoke has dissipated, the smell will be strong and plain to everyone else. I should get out of here now to give the bathroom a chance to air out while Alfredo's off somewhere.

This was so stupid. I don't do shit like this.

I screw up my courage and step out and say a small prayer of thanks that no one is waiting to use the bathroom. Alfredo is nowhere to be seen. He must be in the first-class cabin, on the other side of the curtain—a little blessing. I motor down the aisle and sit down and fasten my seat belt and put my seat back and tray table in their upright and locked positions. I check my posture to make sure it is that of a model passenger who observes all airline regulations and federal laws, listens to and obeys the instructions of the crew, and would never in a million years even consider committing such a serious violation as, say, disabling the bathroom smoke detector so she could have a cigarette. Never ever.

Time passes and Alfredo still doesn't return from the first-class cabin. It's been twenty minutes by now. Surely any lingering smell is gone, and if there's no smell there's no need to check the smoke detector to see if it's been tampered with. All this is true and makes sense, I tell myself. I repeat it like a mantra. All this is true and makes sense. I actually start to believe it, and by the time Alfredo finally steps through the curtain again I'm feeling pretty good, even thinking it would be nice to have another little bottle of Chardonnay.

Alfredo stops at my seat, bends at the waist to speak to me. "Choo sure choo are okay? No problems?"

"No problems. I'm fine, Alfredo, thanks," I say. "Listen, would it be possible to get just one more glass of wine?"

"Of course," he says. He pats my arm and walks back to the galley. There's a brief surge of nervousness, but I tell myself it's been long enough, the bathroom shouldn't smell of smoke anymore.

I hear Alfredo coming back with the wine and I settle into my seat and put my tray table down, warm with genuine relief now, it's really over and I got away with it and while that was kind of thrilling it'll certainly be the last time I pull anything that stupid. I'm ready to sip some wine, maybe even doze off for the rest of the flight, but for some reason Alfredo walks right past me, empty-handed, striding purposefully toward the front of the plane. It takes a second to sink in, what this means, but once it does I am very, very scared.

And oh *fuck* here he comes now with a tall man wearing black pants and a white shirt and a very severe expression. As they get closer I see how young the man is—younger than me, certainly, no older than twenty-six or twenty-seven, but he's got on pilot's wings and he looks extremely, genuinely pissed. My hands suddenly want something to do, so I set them to putting the tray table back up, but they're shaking too much and in any event it's far, far too late for the perfect passenger routine.

The man with the pilot's wings stops in front of my seat and looks down on me from what seems like a great height. Alfredo is a few steps behind him, glaring, but there's a bit of hurt in his expression, too, as though he feels betrayed. Through my fear I feel a little bit guilty for having taken advantage of his friendliness, because it's true that if I hadn't thought he and I were buddies for at least the duration of the flight, I never would have tried to get away with this. I guess my thinking was worst-case he'd give me a brisk scolding and make me promise not to try it again and maybe, if he were really mad, he wouldn't serve me any more drinks.

Worst-case has turned out to be much worse than that. Alfredo's called in the big guns, and he is so disgusted and hurt that he won't even come close enough for me to speak to him.

"Miss Benoit?" the tall young man says. It's not really a question.

"Yes," I say. I can't look at him.

"The flight attendant has informed me that he's found a cigarette butt in the toilet and that you were the last person to use the lavatory. Were you smoking, ma'am?"

Of course. In my haste to get out of the bathroom I forgot to flush the fucking toilet. Stupidity piled on stupidity. There's no sense at all trying to deny it now. "Yes," I say. "I was."

"Thank you for your honesty," the man says, though he doesn't sound at all grateful. "Now I'm going to ask you a second question, and this, so you know, is by far the more serious of the two. When we're done speaking here, I'm going to check the smoke detector in the lavatory. And I'd like to know if I will find that smoke detector has been disabled."

The other passengers fidget and look everywhere but at me. "I disconnected it," I say.

"Are you familiar with the laws that govern tampering with smoke detectors in aircraft lavatories? The federal laws?"

"Not intimately," I say. I'm surprised to find myself near tears.

"Then you aren't aware of the penalties involved."

"No." I watch as Alfredo is summoned by a passenger in the front of the cabin. He turns his back and walks away.

"Then allow me to tell you a little bit about these laws," the tall man says. "After 9/11 they were rewritten. The laws were made stronger, the penalties more severe. Do you have any idea why, ma'am?"

"I'm guessing it has something to do with terrorists?"

"For your safety," he says. "For your safety, and the safety of all the others on board. Which safety you have jeopardized, today, for the sake of a cigarette."

"I really am sorry." My eyes are brimming and my cheeks burn.

"I'm glad to hear that," the man says. "Because it seems to me that some-one who is sorry, genuinely sorry, for having done wrong will probably not do wrong again. Is that a safe assumption for me to make in this case, ma'am?"

"Yes."

"Good. Because this flight lasts another two hours and twenty minutes, and I don't want to have to spend it back here babysitting you. The author-ities will be waiting on the ground for us in Bangor, but you can mini-mize any legal trouble by behaving yourself for the balance of our time together."

"What if I agreed to pay for the damages to the smoke detector?"

"We're beyond that."

"What if I explained that I'm on my way home to attend the funeral of my ex-boyfriend's father?"

"Ma'am, you should have discussed bereavement fares with your ticket agent."

"And that I pretty much chucked my entire life in San Francisco for this? It was a good life there, too. Great job. Friends. A man who loved me. A dog who loved me more. All gone."

"Ma'am."

"So yeah," I say, suddenly deflated and resigned. "I needed a fucking cigarette."

"I'm sorry, but it makes no difference," he says.

"I know." I swipe at my eyes with my sleeve. "That's why I stopped apologizing."

He doesn't say anything more, just gives me one last admonishing look, then wheels around and returns to the front of the plane.

The rest of the flight is quite strange. I can sense the other passengers isolating themselves from me, putting me in a sort of mental quarantine. It's an odd feeling, because obviously nothing has changed physically. We're all still crammed together in this steel cylinder blazing across the strato-sphere, but there's a real and palpable distance now; if I close my eyes it feels like there's no one for miles in every direction. The one exception is a skinny kid of maybe twenty, sporting the usual hipster gear: chain wallet, ratty vintage tee, fauxhawk. He's seated directly in front of me, and he stands and leans over the seat back and whispers in a cockney accent: "I've been dying for a smoke. Now I can have one and blame it on you. Cheers, missy."

"Eat shit and die." I don't even bother opening my eyes. There is a peculiar comfort in being completely fucked, because there's nothing to worry about anymore. You're fucked, and that's it. I'm tired and sober and feeling quite philosophical about the whole thing. I don't even have the energy to worry about what sort of backroom cold war reception I'm going to get once we're on the ground.

It seems like only a few seconds later when I find myself waking up just as we're landing. My ears need very badly to be popped. There's the jolt of the wheels hitting the tarmac. The plane bounces once—leaps back into the air, actually, and I can sense it drifting slightly sideways in relation to the runway, too, which is never a good feeling—and there's a sound of mild surprise and concern in the cabin, a collective inrush of breath. Then the wheels find the ground again, and a few moments later we're taxiing lazily toward my fate.

"Ladies and gentlemen, welcome to Bangor, Maine," the captain says over the PA. Like most flatlanders he pronounces it, incorrectly, as Bangger, and I feel that old reflexive derision toward people from away, until it occurs to me that after living in California so long, "from away" is a designation I almost certainly qualify for myself. "When we arrive at the gate, law enforcement officers will be boarding to escort a passenger off of the plane. It should only be a few minutes' delay. If you'll please remain in your seats and keep the aisle clear, we'll let you know when it's okay to deboard."

Once again, the other passengers in my immediate vicinity take great pains to turn their embarrassed expressions everywhere but at me. There's a mild forward lurch as the plane comes to a stop at the gate. I decide to preclude the further humiliation of being led through the plane in handcuffs. I grab my bag from the overhead compartment and move toward the door, ignoring Alfredo's repeated order to "seet down." He scowls at me (a bitchy, impudent look, so okay he's definitely gay, I decide finally, and a bit of a queen to boot) and makes slow, exaggerated work of unlocking the hatch. Finally he gets it open, and on the other side there's another airline employee, flanked by two uniformed police officers. Something flutters in my gut as I'm reminded by their grim expressions of just how serious this is.

I'm surprised, though, that a couple of patrol cops were sent. I anticipated G-men in Oakleys and dark suits, not a couple of Keystone Kops from the Bangor PD. All the same, handcuffs are handcuffs and holding cells are holding cells, and soon I find myself literally behind bars, rubbing my chapped wrists in the fluorescent twilight.

I haven't been processed in any way. No one's taken statements or fingerprints. My belongings have not been catalogued and stored. I have not been issued a jumpsuit or leg irons. I'm just sitting here on the cot, alone among the room's three cells, and with each minute that passes without any sort of official, administrative-type activity I get a little taste of what political prisoners, POWs, and others without the benefit of due process must experience: the quite unsettling sense of having disappeared.

Eventually a G-man does in fact show up. One of the cops who met me at the airport is with him, and in a move weighted with jurisdictional animosity he edges in front of the agent, bumping shoulders, and opens the door to the cell.

"There you go, chief," the cop says to the G-man. He steps back and out of the way. "All yours."

The G-man ignores him. "Miss Benoit," he says, sweeping one arm slowly in front of him. I step out on rubbery legs. The cop pulls up the rear, utility belt jangling loudly in the stone hallway.

We climb the stairs and walk out of the police station. The G-man doesn't cuff me, or even pay me any attention, just keeps walking without looking back. Outside it's fully dark but still quite warm. Moths swarm the streetlamps in the parking lot, rising like confetti in zero gravity. When I still lived here this kind of weather was always such a treat. Maine is Maine—meaning the weather can most often be described in one of two ways: cold, or about to get cold—but every year you can count on a two- or three-week period when it will be hot as Hades, warmer even than the usual hot spots of Florida and southern California. It seems I've come home in the midst of this year's heat wave.

There is the question, though, of how much of it I'll be able to enjoy. The G-man leads me to a late-model sedan—looks like a Buick but it's hard to tell in the dark—and we get in. Neither of us speaks until we're on the interstate heading south.

"Hi Amy," he says finally, offering his hand for me to shake. His tone at the police station was businesslike, almost robotic, but now he sounds like he could be trying to pick me up at a bar. "Can I call you Amy?"

"Sure." I look at his hand a minute, then shake it kind of hesitantly. His grip is firm enough to let you know he's there, but it's not like other guys who treat handshakes like a competition and squeeze so hard that you worry about whether you've been getting enough calcium. His palms are soft and uncallused, his nails filed and buffed. I notice the scent of sandalwood on him, so faint I think it could be my imagination.

He pushes the power knob on the stereo. "Any preference?" he asks.

"No."

"C'mon, really," he says. "Don't be polite. Anything you want to listen to. Have at it."

I try to read his face, but he's looking at the road and in the dark of the car's interior it's hard to pick up on anything. "Listen," I say. "I certainly don't want to sound ungrateful, because this is much better treatment than I imagined I would get. But what exactly is this about, here?"

He laughs. "You're wondering why I haven't slapped the cuffs on you, roughed you up a little?"

"I'm wondering why I'm sitting up front instead of back there behind the bulletproof glass. I'm wondering why you're letting me run the radio and chatting me up like we're at a singles club. I'm wondering, also, since we're on the subject, where it is you're taking me."

He turns to me, flashes a Tom Cruise smile. "Well if you prefer the authentic experience, I could pull over and bounce your head off the hood a few times. But I'll skip the cuffs, since it looks like they already had you wrapped up three times too tight."

I rub at my wrists. "I complained about it. But they said they were just as tight as they needed to be."

The G-man scoffs. "Bumpkins," he says. "Listen, Amy, really? We've got a fairly long drive here, and it's not like you committed a capital crime, so

I figure why make it any less pleasant than it has to be? This is mostly formality anyway. The federal government loves its paperwork, I can tell you. But that's pretty much all this will amount to. A ride to Boston, some paperwork, sign here, fingerprint there, and you'll be on your way. No biggie."

"I've got a funeral to attend," I say.

"I'm sorry. When's that?"

"Two days."

He waves a hand. "No problem. You could make it tomorrow. It'd be tight, but you could make it."

"Just one more question, then, if that's okay."

"Of course."

"Why do we have to go all the way to Boston?"

He sighs. "Again, formality," he says. "We've got resident agencies in Bangor, Augusta, and Portland, but the nearest full-service FBI office is in Boston. So that's where we go, like it or not."

"That's . . . inconvenient."

"Stupid, is what it is," he says. He lowers his voice to a conspiratorial stage-whisper. "To be honest, I think I'm just about done with the Bureau anyway. I'm fed up with this sort of crap. Running people in for smoking cigarettes. Seems like there's got to be a better use of an agent's time. In today's world."

I don't know anything about it, so I keep quiet.

"I'm thinking I might get out and start my own consulting business."

"Consulting for what?"

"Stuffy in here. You okay if I turn on the AC?"

" 's fine."

"Thanks." He fiddles with the climate control knobs. "There. Okay, what were we talking about?"

"Your consulting business."

He snaps his exquisitely manicured fingers. "Right, right. Well, I've got a pretty extensive background in combatives, security, that sort of thing. More so than your average agent. It was a specialty. It's what I enjoy. And there are always people who need to learn how to apply an arm bar to someone twice their size, or to effectively use an Mk-19 grenade launcher against infantry assault. It's like being a barber or an undertaker. Always work to be had."

"Sounds like you've given this a lot of thought."

"I have. Like I say, I'm tired of dealing with the Bureau's crap. Plus I've got an MBA from Stanford that's been collecting dust for the better part of a decade. Why not use it?"

"You went to Stanford?" I ask.

"For graduate work, yeah."

"I spent six years there," I say, smiling in spite of myself. "Bachelor's and master's."

He flashes the grin again. "No kidding!" he says. "When?"

"I finished my master's in '98."

"Weird," he says. We laugh.

"Were you there at the same time?" I ask.

"Some of it, yeah. Took me three years to get my MBA, for reasons too boring to go into. But that was '95 to '98."

I turn in my seat to face him. "How did we never meet each other?"

"Big school. Besides, you weren't in the business program, were you?"

"No," I say. "Fine arts."

"Well there you go."

"Still," I say, "after six years I would have sworn I knew everyone on that campus."

"We must have known some of the same people," he says. "We could play a little six degrees of separation. Pass the time."

"First," I say, holding out my hand for him to shake again, "I should probably know your name."

"Hey, good point," he says. "How rude of me. Eric Fuchs."

"Pleasure to meet you."

He laughs. "Even under these circumstances?"

"So far it's been better than I expected," I titter and toss my hair a little bit before I have a chance to realize what I'm doing, which, evidently, is flirting with the FBI agent who has arrested me. This whole thing, it seems, will only get weirder.

"Still, it stinks," Eric says. "But anyhow. Stanford. People at Stanford."

"Jesus, I don't know where to begin," I say. "Like I told you, I feel like I knew everyone."

"What about organizations?"

"Which ones?"

"Greek?" he asks.

"No."

"Sorry. Should have pegged you as a GDI."

"A what?"

He smiles. "God Damn Independent."

"And I should have pegged you as a frat boy."

"Guilty as charged," he says. "Tau Gamma Rho. Though I'm not one of those guys who wears his ring everywhere and calls complete strangers brother and breaks spontaneously into the fraternity chant. So you know."

"That's a relief," I say.

"What else, though?" he says. "I don't suppose you were part of the Aikido Club."

"Nope. I did yoga."

He snaps his fingers again; apparently that's kind of his thing. "I *know* you were in at least a few political organizations."

I eye him skeptically. "Were you?"

"Sure," he says, feigning insult. "What, just because I'm an FBI man? . . ."

"That's not what I meant."

"Sure it is," he says. "It's okay. But yeah, I did Amnesty International. And the Stanford Civil Liberties Union, even though I was the only member who wasn't a law student. Which is sort of funny, when you consider how things have turned out. I can see you're impressed."

"Surprised," I say. "Closest I came to either of those was the Friends of Tibet. And the CJME."

Eric whistles low. "That's our connection right there," he says.

"Which?"

"The Coalition for Justice in the Middle East. Did you know Eisa Jabar?"

"You're joking, right?"

"What?" Eric says.

"I dated Eisa. He's how I got involved with CJME."

"You two *dated?*"

"Briefly. Is that so strange?"

"Just an odd couple," Eric says. He turns the air conditioning down a notch. "And before you say it, no, I don't mean that in an interracial kind of way. Eisa just struck me as one of those guys whose entire life is political. Like he's such an activist there's no room for a personal life. He sort of ends up being asexual, in your mind."

"Who said anything about sex?" I ask.

"You understand what I mean."

"Sure. But how did you know Eisa?"

"Indirectly," Eric says. "I saw him at a few rallies, of course. Met him, twice I think. Once through Paul Sukarnoputri, at a joint fund-raiser for CJME and the Stanford Indonesian Club."

I can't help but smile, picturing lily-white Eric at such an event. "And you were doing what, there?"

"Oh, I was just a friend of Paul's. An acquaintance really. We were both officers in SCLU, plus we happened to work out around the same time each day. We got to know each other a bit. But whatever happened to Eisa?"

"Don't really know," I say. "You mind turning the air conditioning back up? I'm dying."

He flips the dial. "You've got no idea where he went? Seemed like he just up and disappeared."

"Like I said, we only dated for a short time. I assume he got his master's and moved on."

"You mind my asking a personal question?"

"Depends."

"Why didn't it work out? Between the two of you?"

It's been so long, and it was such a footnote of a relationship, that I'm finding it hard to remember details. "His whole life was political," I say.

"Seriously," Eric says.

I think for a minute. "Okay," I say. "Seriously?"

"Indeed." His face glows spooky green in the light from the gauges.

"I got the feeling that for Eisa I was a last-temptation sort of thing. I think he was pretty sure he was done with being American, and then I showed up, and I was smart and different and had nice creamy white girl thighs, and he used me to test his convictions. Like Gandhi and his teenage virgins."

"Or Mohamed Atta and his strip clubs," Eric says.

"Exactly. That's exactly it."

"Huh. So how did that feel?"

"Didn't really feel like anything," I say. "Eisa had a fuckload more invested in it than I did."

"And then, when it was over . . . he just disappeared."

"For all I know."

"Huh." He seems to contemplate this.

For a while we just listen to the radio. It's late, and we're the only car headed south on the interstate. I'm surprised to see the sign for the Kennebunk rest area; it's two-plus hours from Bangor to Kennebunk, and the time has flown.

"You need to stop?" Eric asks. "Food? Bathroom?"

"Both," I say. "If that's okay."

"Of course. I just hope you don't mind Burger King, because that's your only option."

"Make this trip a lot?" I ask.

"You know it."

Eric pulls into the rest area. The parking lot's empty except for a couple of semis with drivers sleeping inside, so we're able to park right in front. I go into the bathroom, and not only does Eric not follow me to make sure I don't try to get away, but when I come out he's nowhere to be found. I just stand there in the lobby, waiting. The girl behind the Burger King counter stares at me with sleepy eyes. Three or four minutes go by, and finally Eric comes out of the men's room. He sees me, smiles, walks over.

"You're lucky I didn't steal your car," I say.

"You're not exactly an escape risk," he says. "What do you want? I'm buying."

We take the food to go, and we're already a mile down the road by the time I realize there's something wrong with my drink.

"This always happens," I say. "Take it to go, you get screwed."

"What is it?"

"I'm not really sure. Coke tastes funny. It's bitter, like Moxie or something."

"That's the triazolam," Eric says around a mouthful of burger.

"The what?"

He wipes the corner of his mouth with a finger. "Triazolam?" he says. "Brand name Halcion? I put it in your Coke." He shoves several French fries into his mouth and chews. "I put a lot of it in your Coke."

It takes a second for what he's said to register. It's like I want to be scared, but the fear shorts out and instead for some reason I feel like laughing. So I go ahead and laugh, but it sounds strange and tinny to my ears, as though I were inside a giant, empty beer can.

"Not very elegant, triazolam," Eric says. "Pretty low-rent, in fact. The bitter taste, for one thing, is a serious problem. But it does the job in a pinch."

I try to understand what he's saying, but it's not sinking in. The world inside the car tilts violently and every lighted object develops a strange aura. Next thing I know I'm in an empty kitchen with an old circular fluorescent blazing overhead, my wrists and ankles cuffed tight to a chair. The linoleum floor is cracked and stained. Tree branches claw at the window over the sink. My head pounds.

The front door opens and Eric comes in, trailed by a warm night breeze. He's carrying what looks like a small blanket, which he sets on the counter and unfolds to reveal several shiny metal implements, none of which looks like it was designed with good intentions. I'm having no trouble, suddenly, feeling scared.

"You've probably figured out by now," Eric says, "that I was lying about the Stanford thing."

I'm pretty transfixed by the implements, and I don't respond.

"In fact, you probably think I was lying about everything," he says. "And you're right, naturally. I lie for a living. That's my job."

"Eric," I say.

"Not my name," he says. "Sorry. Also a lie."

"I don't really know what's happening here," I say. "But please, listen—"

"I am hopeful," not-Eric interrupts, "that you maybe will forgive me all my little fibs. You know, as one liar to another. Glass houses, and all that."

"I don't understand."

"Sure you do. Because you've been lying to me about Eisa. And before you say anything in protest, listen: I am not who you think. I am not a *nice guy*. I want information that you have, and as a professional I am willing to do unpleasant things to you in order to get that information."

I have no fucking idea what he's talking about, and I say so.

"In college you were part of a student organization whose entire purpose was to support the formation of a Palestinian state," not-Eric says. He leans against the countertop, folds his arms. "An organization that put to a vote a resolution of official support for suicide bombings in the West Bank and Gaza. Is this factual, so far?"

"Yes," I say. "And I voted against the resolution."

"Regardless," not-Eric says. "During this time you were also romantically involved with the head of this organization, one Eisa Jabar. Mr. Jabar, after leaving Stanford University short of a master's degree in poitical science, formally renounced his United States citizenship, thereby becoming a citizen of only Lebanon, where he had previously enjoyed a dual citizenship. He subsequently moved to Tripoli and, according to confirmed intelligence from multiple sources, became a Hezbollah soldier."

Oh good God. "I don't know anything about that."

Not-Eric ignores this. "But here's where it gets interesting," he says. "Because here is where you seem to come back into the picture. The Hezbollah brass, realizing the talent they had in Eisa, hastily took him off the front lines and began grooming him for a leadership position. He rose quickly, working all over the Middle East in various capacities—recruiting, arms purchases, soliciting financial benefactors. He was on just such an assignment in Nicosia, Cyprus, in February of 2002."

"Oh. No. No, no, no."

"But *yes*," not-Eric says. "Because we know that you, too, were in Nicosia at that time."

"On *vacation*," I say. "I was with the Peace Corps in Botswana, Eric.

Teaching kids how to put condoms on bananas, for Christ's sake. I had no idea Eisa was in Cyprus."

"So you say. Except that less than a year later, Eisa was in Aswan, negotiating the purchase of a large amount of RDX explosives. November 2002. Do you remember where you were, Amy?"

My recollection of the Peace Corps has always been a bit of a blur, and my mind races to unearth details. "In Egypt . . ."

"On vacation?"

"Well, yes. I went to Luxor, though. Not Aswan."

"You were in Aswan. You spent the majority of your time in Luxor. But you were in Aswan at the same time as Eisa."

"Half the point of doing the Peace Corps," I tell him, "is traveling as much as you can in the region where you're working."

"It starts to seem less and less like coincidence," he says. "Moving along—because I have some questions I want to ask you—there were several other times, which I'm sure you also have no knowledge of, when you and Eisa were in close proximity to one another. The most recent being the last four years, during which time he's been living in San Francisco again, off and on, under an assumed identity."

I put my throbbing head back, close my eyes, exhale.

"And *then*," not-Eric says, "fast forward to today. You get picked up for causing trouble on a transcontinental flight. Smoking, allegedly, though when our crew goes over that plane I've no doubt they're going to find something more damning than a cigarette butt."

"I was smoking. That's it. I swear."

"You understand, I hope, the roots of our suspicion."

"The only thing I understand," I say, "is that evidently no matter what I say, you're going to think I'm a terrorist."

Not-Eric takes a pair of latex gloves from the towel-thing and slides them on, flexing his fingers to make a snug fit. "Terrorist?" he says. "No. That's not really how I think of you. Besides, the word's been drained of all its meaning anyway. Six years of 'terrorist this' and 'terrorist that.'"

He cuffs me across the face a few times in quick succession, just hard enough to sting a little and make my head bob around. Like kneading dough, or tenderizing meat. I haven't been touched this way since Mom, but the reaction is the same all these years later: fear evaporates instantly, leaving behind crystallized defiance.

Then the questions start.

Not-Eric is not getting the answers he wants. As a consequence, he hits me: with his fists and feet, a phone book, an electrical cord. At first he thinks that hitting me will produce the answers he wants. I just keep inviting him to go fuck himself. He can't figure it out. He hits me some more and I get angrier with each blow, until I'm whipping my hair around and screaming at him and spraying my own blood all over the place.

Finally he tells me to shut up and slams me in the temple, a dazzling hammer-fist shot. It works—I shut up. My vision narrows to the size of a toilet paper roll, and I can't seem to hold my head up for more than a few seconds at a time before it drops back down to my chest. I catch glimpses, though, of not-Eric going back to the countertop and lifting one of the shiny metal implements. This one looks like a miniature set of pruning shears.

My mother, mean and crazy as she is, never used anything like this on me.

I struggle against the handcuffs as not-Eric approaches again. He asks me from what seems like very far away if I'm sure I don't have anything I want to tell him. Anything at all. I try to respond but nothing comes out of my mouth except bloody drool. Not-Eric steps behind the chair. I feel him separate my pinkie from the rest of my fingers. Then I feel the cold pinch of the shears at the top knuckle.

Anything at all?

I can't talk. And even if I could.

The shears close. I hear it but don't feel it.

I must pass out, because the next thing I know the front door flies open and a blond man with cheekbones that could not possibly exist outside of a dream steps into the kitchen with a pistol in each hand. Not-Eric makes a move for his gun on the countertop, but the man shoots him twice in the chest. When not-Eric falls the man steps calmly over to him and pumps another bullet into his head. Then he stands looking down at the body, and I'm able to read the T-shirt he's got on beneath his sportscoat: I LOVE YOU LIKE A FAT KID LOVES CAKE.

All this, fucked up and unlikely as it seems, might exist somewhere on the outer edge of plausible. Given how the rest of my day has gone, I might be able to believe that even the T-shirt is actually happening. But the next moment, Junior, eight years dead, walks through the door, and that's when I know that the trauma of my day with not-Eric has scrambled my brain. Because this is definitely not happening. No way.

The detail is amazing, though: Junior's arm in a sling, his face a swollen mass of yellow and black. The warmth of his hand, the good one, on my face. The sound of his voice, unchanged by time and death, as he hollers at the man with the cheekbones to get the cuffs off my wrists and ankles. The relief, like floating in warm water, when Junior throws off his sling and lifts me with a grimace.

I let him gather me in and I put my face in his chest.

In the dream, I go to sleep.

Love, Redux

17 For obvious reasons the sex is far and away the most painful either of you has ever experienced. Of course your own sexual experience is limited, and what's more you've never before had sex while recovering from a grade 3 concussion, eight separate fractures, and external and internal contusions too extensive to quantify. Amy, on the other hand, has had a lot of sex, with many partners, and as a woman is more accustomed to associating sex with pain, but even so she's never moaned and writhed and cried like this.

Aside from the injuries themselves, part of the reason you're in so much pain is because your body, in its excitement, is hyperalert, magnifying and exaggerating every bit of stimulus. Your cerebellum is inflamed with neural chatter, signals of pain and pleasure swirling and melding until they are more or less indistinguishable. The difference between positive and negative sensations has become irrelevant; all that matters is that the sensations be copious and intense, and they are both. Every neuron, encoded with years of stifled longing, strains toward Amy—toward her hair fanned out on the pillow, toward the boyishly modest swell of her hips, lumpy with bruises though they are. In a very literal and unsentimental way your desire for her exists and functions on a molecular level. Love, in its purest form, is biology.

16 Amy's having a pretty good time, too, despite the pain. First, because it's not as though her boyfriend Oscar was really getting it done, so to speak—they did not have sex often, and Oscar is not very deft with either his hands or his tongue. Consequently it's been a long while since Amy's had an orgasm that was not administered by the cold silicone of her Fun Factory Waterproof Deluxe Dolphin shower vibe.

On one level this makes you no more or less than an extra-extra large, warm-blooded version of the Fun Factory Waterproof Deluxe Dolphin shower vibe—except you're not really waterproof, and, sadly, you do not vibrate.

Of course that's not all you are to Amy. We'll put it plainly so there is no confusion: She loves you, but not the way you love her. No molecular-level longing on her end. She doesn't experience temporary retardation in your presence, as you do in hers. She hasn't had recurring dreams of loss and pain featuring you for the past fourteen years. In fact, she goes for months at a time without thinking of you at all.

Yet she does love you. The thrill she feels as you kiss the spot where her neck meets her jaw is not merely the rush of skin on skin. Her trembling is not just trauma and lust. The tears seeping from her swollen eyelids are spurred by several emotions, and her gratitude at being here with you after all this time is not least among them.

There is love, and then there is love. Either way, as far as you're concerned, whatever it is that Amy feels for you is more than enough to make and keep you happy. This inequity of feeling couldn't matter less. There is still enough, you think, to build a life around. Of course you believe this because you need to, not necessarily because it's so.

The question, naturally, is whether or not Amy shares this conviction.

15 At the moment it's too early to say. Which, you know, try to be fair and reasonable: In the past seventy-two hours, the woman has left behind her home, her job, her dog, and her relationship of four years. She's been arrested, kidnapped, punched, kicked, and whipped with electrical cord. She's had half a finger snipped off. She's had occasion to consider the likelihood of her own painful and premature death, strapped to a chair in some stinking abandoned farmhouse. And just as she was ready to resign herself to that fate she was rescued, in a violent and shocking manner, by her long-dead high school sweetheart and his personal government assassin.

All that considered, yes, it would probably be good form to give her some time to think things over.

14 But first things first: she wants to know about the end of the world.

You're lying very still postcoitus, pressed together down the full length of your battered bodies.

"You're not crazy," she says.

"I never was," you tell her.

"But how?" she asks. "That's what I don't understand."

"Like I explained to you before," you say, wincing as you roll onto your side to face her. "It's not as though I really understand it myself."

She thinks for a minute. "Is it God?" she asks, and her matter-of-fact tone seems odd, given the scope of the question.

"I don't know," you say. "Possibly. Or maybe it's just a form of ESP that has nothing to do with the divine."

"But a *voice?*" Amy says. "That doesn't sound like ESP to me, Junior. ESP is like visions. Dreams and visions. Not a voice in your head."

"How can we know that?" you say.

She smirks at you. "You haven't changed a bit."

"What's that supposed to mean?"

"That you're still only interested in what can be known. One hundred percent, unequivocally known," she says. "You're not willing to entertain even the fairly reasonable speculation that a voice in your head is more likely God, or someone anyway, rather than ESP."

"That's not really it," you say. "I just wonder if we have the language to describe what I hear. Maybe it's not God *or* ESP. Maybe it's both of those things—what's the word for that?"

"There is none."

"Right," you say. "Believe me, I've given this plenty of thought over the past thirty-plus years. We're not going to sort it out in an evening."

"Stands to reason."

"Besides, it's what I know, not how I know, that matters."

13 Several minutes pass during which neither of you speaks, and silence, since your father's death, has been a bad and dangerous thing. Any time you have more than a few moments to think you are haunted by memories of him. Now another one rises: You are three or four years old, and it is winter. You are tottering around the public ice rink that

the city used to put up by the river every December, back when the winters were consistently cold enough to keep the rink frozen through March. You're wearing skates that once belonged to Rodney. He outgrew them, but they're still a couple sizes too large for you. You are not skating so much as taking a series of tiny, ankle-buckling steps. Older boys buzz past at impossible speeds on either side of you, sometimes close enough to brush against the nylon shell of your jacket. You're terrified of the speed and proximity of the older boys, the way they appear suddenly from behind and then hurtle ahead, only to come all the way around again in the time it takes you to move seven or eight halting steps. You try to get off the ice, but every time you move toward the edge of the rink you are cut off. You look over your shoulder and see a large boy with premature whiskers on his top lip scream around the turn behind you with frightening speed. You are certain you'll be run down and killed, and you look away from your fate, bracing yourself, but the blow doesn't come. You feel the boy's hand on your shoulder as he sidesteps and spins at the last instant, cursing as he passes, now skating backward. You've moved one lane closer to the salvation of the outer wall but your nerve is gone, so instead of trying to escape you keep tottering forward, praying, in your manner, for deliverance.

Then deliverance comes, in the form of strong familiar hands grasping you from behind, whisking you up from the surface of the ice and setting you to rest on wide shoulders. You are flying now, and it is the older boys who make way suddenly, scattering as you rush past at twice, three times their speed, so fast that as you veer into the turn you have to lean at a fairly steep angle to compensate for the intense centrifugal force, and now you have outpaced everyone and there's nothing in front of you except open ice, and you are shrieking with glee and fear, gleeful fear, and the fear is hollow anyway, because the wide shoulders you're sitting on and the strong hands that hold you firmly in place belong to your father, and even though you know little about the man, what you do know is that he is always, always in control, and so nothing can possibly go wrong.

With this memory, as with the others that have haunted you the past few days, you wonder if they're real or just imagined, and we can tell you that this one, at least, happened exactly as you remember it.

12   "What am I going to do about my family?" Amy asks.

Her voice brings you back to the present. "Arrangements can be made for all of them. If that's what you want."

"Of course it is," she says emphatically. And then, more softly, to herself almost: "Of course it is."

"Of course." You turn and nestle and kiss the top of her head.

"No one knows where my father is, though."

"He can be found," you say, pressing gently at your eyes with the heels of your hands. "Quite easily, in fact."

"But see when you say 'arrangements,' I'm not even sure what you mean."

"We haven't talked about that, have we?"

"Nope."

"Long version, or short?"

"Neither of us has to be anywhere, right?"

"You mind if I grab another beer first?"

She shakes her head even though part of her really does mind, because she knows booze and what it does to people like you in places like this, where winter lasts half the year and nine dollars an hour is considered a good wage. She is determined not to caretake anymore, not even for you, so be warned: she won't stop you, but neither will she tolerate it beyond a certain point. You make your way painfully across the hotel room to the cube fridge, remove a Bud Light bottle, and return to the bed.

11   Amy listens intently as you tell her everything: Bulgaria. Sawyer and the Program. Warp drives and biospheres and spacecraft the size of Cleveland being constructed piecemeal by a dozen different contractors all over the country, so that those doing the constructing have no real idea what they're working on. Massive hangars hollowed out beneath the red clay of the Southwest, where, in several years, those

fortunate enough to be selected in the lottery will gather. The planet Gliese 689 d, future home of these lottery winners.

"And of course," you say, "I have the influence to secure anyone you want a one-way trip. Within reason. Your mom and dad. Your brother. A few friends."

"What about Oscar?"

"Sure," you say. "If you wanted."

"I think that I would," she says.

"Done." You worry faintly that this means she's not done with him entirely, but believe us when we tell you that she is.

Amy takes the beer from you, sips, thinks for a minute. "So in two years San Francisco is gone," she says. "Mount Sinai. Paris. Victoria Falls. Have you ever been to Victoria Falls? I went swimming there once, while I was with the Peace Corps. Amazing."

"I've seen pictures."

"And you never wanted to go there yourself? Knowing it would be gone so soon?"

"Can't see it all, I guess. It's a big world."

Amy stares into the beer bottle. "You want to hear about the most beautiful thing I've ever seen?"

"Of course."

"I was making one of my cross-country drives," she says after a long pause. "Maine to California. California to Maine. There were so many it's hard to say exactly when this was. I think maybe my first year of grad school. I had decided to go the long route through the South. It ended up being like an extra day and a half of driving, as compared to my usual route. And do you know why I went so far out of my way?"

You do not. We could tell you, but listen:

"Because someone had told me about these flowers in Texas that I just had to see. Bluebonnets. This girl who I can't even remember her name now. We were friends for like five minutes, until I realized what a nouveau-hippie Earth mother kook she was. Said it would change my life. And I guess my life felt like it needed changing at the time, because I went to Texas instead of just shooting straight across the plains."

She looks at you, eyebrows raised, waiting for a response. But you're not sure yet what response she's looking for, so you just say, "Okay."

"Right," she says, "so there's no way that a stupid wildflower can make driving an extra thousand miles worthwhile, right? There was no way I would end up being anything but disappointed, and probably a little embarrassed for having spent all that money on gas. Right?"

"Probably," you say, uncertain.

"Okay, so I'm driving through the hills west of Austin, and I haven't seen a single bluebonnet anywhere. Not one. There were stands of daisies and lilacs here and there, but nothing special. Certainly nothing life-changing. And I'm beginning to get a little pissed off about having come all this way for nothing."

Here Amy pauses. She rises from the bed, and you watch as she goes naked to the cube fridge and removes a beer of her own.

"But then I'm on this ranch road, just newly blacktopped—you know how awesome it is to drive on a brand-new road like that," she says, twisting off the cap and tossing it in the corner. "So I'm taking it pretty fast, and I come around this bend and crest a hill. As I reach the top this amazing panorama opens up in front of me, and the road straightens out suddenly and stretches ahead into a valley where—and this is the weird part—it goes right down into this massive lake."

She looks at you pointedly, and there is a deep sadness in her eyes that seems out of place. She sips her beer.

"So I slow down because it's such a shock, seeing this huge lake materialize out of nowhere, in a spot where it definitely has no business being. Plus I'm just stunned by the beauty of it. This gorgeous but peculiar shade of dark, dark blue. Almost purple. I'd never seen water quite like that before. I was so mesmerized I almost stopped the car altogether."

She pauses, drinks again. "But so you know where I'm going with this, by now."

You nod, empty your own beer with a long pull. "It's not a lake at all," you say.

"Of course not. Because who the hell would build a road running right into this giant lake? No one. Still, the illusion is hard to shake. It persists, even though I realize how impossible it is. Until finally I get close enough that I can make out the individual flowers themselves. The bluebonnets. I'm talking millions, here. I drive until I'm surrounded to every horizon. Then I get out and just walk away from the car, into the meadow, with no idea where I'm going, or why."

You rise gingerly and go to the fridge again. "You want another?" you ask, and when you turn to look at her you bump your broken wrist against the fridge door.

"No, I just opened this one," Amy says. "Are you paying attention? Are you listening, here? Because this is where it gets all mystical, and you know better than most, Junior, that I'm a cash-and-carry kind of girl. I can count on one finger the number of times this sort of thing has happened to me."

"I'm paying attention," you say through clenched teeth.

"So I just walked away from the car for who knows how long, until when I looked back it was gone, the road was gone, and all I could see were bluebonnets everywhere. I should have been worried about getting lost, but I wasn't. I just walked around with my palms skimming the flowers and the sharp little tips of the grass, and when I got tired I lay down, and then it was dark, and I slept for a while. Sometime during the night it started to rain, but even that didn't drive me away. I woke up, but I stayed there and let it rain on me. I know that doesn't make any sense."

"Makes as much sense as anything else."

"It's honestly, don't laugh at me here or I'll be really hurt, it's the closest I've ever come to feeling like there's a god. The sort of deep certainty you get when you have a revelation on acid, you know—that two-by-four-upside-the-head sort of epiphany? Like everything suddenly becomes absolutely clear and you wonder how in hell it took you so long to see it in the first place?"

At this you feel, once more, the deep tenderness and affection that your heart has always reserved for only her, and you say, "Why would I laugh at you for that?"

Amy looks at you. "Because it's a dangerous thing these days, to talk like this," she says. "This sort of earnestness rarely goes unpunished."

You think about this. "It's a good point," you say. "Of course I'm burying my father tomorrow, and shortly thereafter the world is going to come to a violent end. So given that, abject earnestness is probably in order."

"Irony is a luxury the doomed can't afford."

"I'd say." You put the beer down on the nightstand and slide your good arm under her. She rolls into you, rests her battered head in the hollow where your neck meets your shoulder.

"I have to tell you," Amy says, "and please don't take this the wrong way. But I liked it better when you were crazy, and the bluebonnets were going to keep blossoming every spring until the end of time."

10   You lift a little swatch of her hair, run your fingers through, let it fall. "Fair enough," you say.

Rodney

There's one thing I never got to ask Junior about since we got back to Chicago. It's been a year, I think. Yeah about a year, because when Dad died we were in a pennant race with Milwaukee, which I ended up missing two weeks and we lost the pennant by one game and I know some of the guys blamed me for not being there but what could I do? My dad was dead. I asked Reynolds what could I do? And he said nothing Rodney, don't even fucking worry about those cocksuckers. Now we're in a pennant race again, only this time with St. Louis. Pennant races happen once a year, in September. So that means it's been a year since Dad died. And even though I seen Dad in the coffin and seen them close it up and put it in the car and take it out of the car and put it in the ground, I still wanted to ask Junior if Dad might come back. If Junior came back, maybe Dad could, too, is what I was thinking.

But I couldn't ask Junior because even though we're living together again we always miss each other. When I'm in Chicago he's always in Washington, D.C., so instead of asking him I went and asked Amy. She's smart, maybe even smarter than Junior. She's nice to me. I trusted her to give me a good answer.

Except when I asked her she didn't want to give an answer.

Well, Rodney, I don't know if I'm the person to talk to about this, she said.

I trust you Amy, I said.

Well that's awfully nice of you, she said. She took my hand in hers, the one where part of her finger is gone, which made me think of Dad. Awfully nice, Rodney. I'm glad you trust me. Will you still trust me even if I give you an answer other than the one you want to hear?

Yes, I said.

Okay, she said. Because what I think you want to hear is that it's possible your dad will come back. But the truth is he can't. Do you understand?

What about Junior? I asked.

That's different, she said.

How?

She looked away and said something real quiet that I couldn't hear. It sounded like she was angry. Then she said to me, Well the best I can explain it, Rodney, is that Junior wasn't really dead. You just thought he was. There's a difference.

I understand, I said.

Whereas your dad, she said.

He's really dead, I said.

Her eyes were big and shiny. Yeah, she said. He is.

I get it, I told her. Even though I only sort of got it. I thought for a minute and then I almost asked her to explain it better. But I looked at her eyes again and then I felt bad and I just shut up.

But it's still bothering me. Today the team's in San Diego and it's an off day so like usual once we get checked in I spend most of the day in the hotel room. We're staying at the Hilton and like all the hotels they book us in under fake names so fans and girls won't call us all day long. I use Ron Mexico, which is the name Gutierrez picked for me a while ago. I like it because I've always wanted to go to Mexico but never have. As Ron Mexico I go down to the hotel restaurant and order the sort of dinner I think someone named Ron Mexico would eat. Chimichangas and a margarita with no tequila.

I used to have a lot of fun pretending to be the fake names I use on the road. Like sitting in a hotel restaurant in Houston and pretending that the next day I had a very dangerous flight to make in my amphibious plane to some really far-off islands, but that if I went ahead and did it then my girlfriend Desdemona would never forgive me because I had promised her no more dangerous flights to far-off islands anymore.

Now like everything else it isn't as much fun as it used to be. Plus it's hard pretending I'm Ron Mexico when people keep coming up and saying Rodney could you please sign this napkin or Mr. Thibodeau would you take a picture with my son. Not that I mind doing those things.

I take the picture and go back to eating and that's when Reynolds comes over. I didn't notice him at the bar because he had his back to me. He sits down real slow, making a face because his knees bother him all the time.

What's going on kid, he says. It's funny that he calls me kid because I'm getting old for a ballplayer but he's close to forty and is more a player-manager now. He only catches on day games following night games, to give Molina a rest.

Nothing, I say. Just eating dinner.

I thought you didn't drink, Reynolds says.

I don't, I say. There's no tequila. It's just margarita mix and ice.

He laughs and smells my drink. Of course. I might have guessed, he says.

Reynolds is drunk. He always smells real strong like beer, even at games, but I can tell when he's drunk because he talks funny like Ma used to. For some reason this makes me think about how, as much as Junior drinks, he never ever talks that way. Just out of the blue I think about this.

Listen Rod I wanted to talk to you about something, Reynolds says.

What is it? I ask.

Just want to see how you're doing, Reynolds says. He waves to the waitress and points at his empty bottle.

I'm doing okay, I tell him.

Because listen, I'm drunk enough that I'll dispense with the bullshit and just say it: You're hitting like shit, kid. I've watched you play ever since you came up, and I know the only time you hit like shit is when you've got something eating you. Unless you've finally lost a step.

I haven't lost a step, I say. Nothing hurts. I see just as good as ever. I could play another fifteen years.

I know, Reynolds says. So why are you hitting so bad? For two months, give or take. Fifty-six games. Two hundred at bats. That's how long you've been stinking it up.

From someone else it would hurt my feelings, having them say that I stink. But I know Reynolds cares and it's just his way of saying so. Gruff, is the word. I heard Junior use that word once talking about Dad, and that's what Reynolds is like. He's big and quiet and no one messes with him. Gruff. I think maybe since he's asking me I could tell him what's been on my mind and I could ask him the same question I asked Amy and maybe he could explain it to me so I'd get it.

But just then the bartender says Hey everybody quiet down you're gonna want to hear this shit. This seems weird to me because we stay in nice hotels and the help are always really polite and never swear, they're always Mr. Mexico can I help you with your bags and Would you like another drink Mr. Mexico or perhaps something from the dessert menu.

The restaurant gets quiet and the bartender turns the television up high enough for everyone to hear. It's President Huckabee and I can tell right off that whatever he's saying I won't understand, so I turn away from the bar and while I'm waiting for President Huckabee to finish so everyone will go back to what they were doing I look at the pictures on the dessert menu.

This is a fucking joke, right? Reynolds says.

I hope that he's not asking me because I have no idea if it's a joke or not. But he's not looking at me. Actually he's not looking at anyone. He's still staring at the television like everyone else.

No one says anything for a long time. I'm getting pretty bored. Then President Huckabee is done talking and all of a sudden everyone's got their cell phones out and they're all making calls and the bar gets really loud with everyone talking. Reynolds is talking on his phone, too. I listen and figure out it's his wife on the other end.

I don't know *what* this is about, Brenda, Reynolds says. He tries to tell the waitress to get another beer but her shift must be over because she puts on a fleece vest and leaves. She must be in a hurry for some reason because when she gets outside she starts running down the sidewalk past the windows. It must be a fucking hoax or something, Reynolds says into the phone.

I look around the restaurant and I'm the only person who isn't talking on a phone. Even the bartender's got the phone that normally stays under the bar, and he's talking to someone and at the same time looking up at the television screen where a different man is standing on the stage where President Huckabee was. This man is talking to reporters. Even though they have chairs the reporters are all standing and waving their hands at the man. He's got on a yellow tie with black polka dots that I like. He looks like maybe he's sick to his stomach.

I don't think so, Brenda, Reynolds says to his wife. I know. I know. Listen, I know. Let's not get fucking hysterical here, is all I'm saying. We don't even know what's going on . . . I'm sure if they're going to cancel the games and send us home they'll tell us. Where are the kids?

I wonder why Reynolds' wife would think the games are going to be canceled, but I don't ask Reynolds because he's on the phone and I don't want to be rude. Now I notice other people running past the windows, or else walking really fast like people do when they're late to be somewhere. All the people outside are talking on their phones, too.

Something's going on, even I can tell that. I decide to go outside. I get up from the table and Reynolds waves his hand at me. I stand there waiting.

Hold on a sec, babe, Reynolds says to his wife. He puts his hand over the phone and says Where the fuck you going?

I was going to go for a walk, I say.

Nah, kid, no, listen, you shouldn't go anywhere right now. You need to get on the phone to your brother and your mother and whoever else. Let me wrap this up and I'll explain what's going on. Best I fucking can.

He goes back to talking to his wife. Usually I listen to Reynolds when he tells me something, but I really don't want to be in here anymore. All the people talking on their phones are making me nervous. What I want is to get outside and walk around. I tell Reynolds I'm going to the waterfront and he waves at me again, no, but I just walk out of the restaurant and into the lobby. For some reason the doorman's not there, so I open the door myself.

Normally I get lost pretty easy but we always stay at this hotel when we're in San Diego so I know how to get to the waterfront. There are so many people I can barely move on the sidewalk. Everyone's bumping into each other and pushing. Cars are stopped in the street and there's a little more room there so I step down off the sidewalk and walk beside the cars. I can see the waterfront from here but it's really slow going with all the people. Part of the reason they're bumping into each other is they're all talking on their cell phones and no one's watching where they're going. I have to keep saying excuse me. I start to think I should have waited like Reynolds said. I think about going back to the hotel restaurant but I'm already more than halfway to the waterfront and it would take even more time to go back. I just want to get away from all these people because I never liked crowds and still don't even though I play in front of big crowds every night.

I get to the corner and that's when I see that all these people are coming from the convention center. There are so many people coming out that they're starting to push all the other people on the street in the same direction, back toward the hotel, away from the waterfront. I get pushed with everyone else. A woman near me screams and falls down and I grab her arm and hold on. It's hard to pull her up because I'm still getting pushed by all the people. She's dragging on the ground on her knees and kicking her legs a little. You've got to stand up, I tell her. I dropped my phone, she says. My hand's getting tired lady, I say. She kicks her feet against the legs of the other people and climbs out from under them and stands on her own. Her knees are bloody but she won't get stepped on now so I let go of her arm.

It's a good thing she forgot about her phone because I'm about to start crying and I don't think I can take care of anyone else. I want to get away from all these people and the pushing and shouting and the scared looks on everyone's faces but there's nowhere to go. I try to move towards the waterfront again but even though I'm one of the strongest guys on the team I'm not strong enough to move all these people. I get pushed past a palm tree and the first thing I think of is to grab it. I grab the trunk and it's like that time when I was with the Boy Scouts and I got thrown out of the whitewater raft and I grabbed onto a rock and wouldn't let go even when they were telling me I'd be okay just drift down through. The water kept grabbing at me and trying to pull me off the rock but I held on, just like now with the people moving all around me and trying to pull me along. I hold on to the trunk of the palm tree and it moves back and forth but doesn't break. I jump up as high as I can and grab the trunk and hang there. I put my legs around the tree and climb up like a rope climb. When I get to the top I wrap my arms up and over and put my hands together to hold myself there. I hope that soon there won't be so many people and I'll be able to come down and go to the waterfront and watch the boats, because my arms are already getting tired. Down on the street everybody's moving but not going anywhere, and the tree is still rocking and my arms burn and it's like the fourth or fifth time today that I wish Dad was still here because he'd know just what to do.

Amy

It takes three weeks of nagging to convince Junior to make the trip with me to Sedona. Lately he doesn't want to hear anything about anything. There's no work left for him to do, so he just sits around Rodney's house all day cursing at people on the news channels: the Ostrich Society, of course. But also the old, the childless, the depressed. Agoraphobes. Conspiracy theorists. Pathological homebodies. Holy rollers whose money is still on God. Those with an abiding attachment to the mother ship that they are unable or unwilling to break.

"Idiots," he'll say, spilling his beer a little as he waves a dismissive hand at the TV. "Dangle salvation right in front of them, and they won't take it."

The thing is, I'm not sure I want to take it, either.

Of course I want to live. Though by default I fall into the "mother ship" category, I also have a deep abiding attachment to being alive. So you'd think the decision to go would be easy. But somehow it isn't.

I can't explain why. Not in a way that makes sense when weighed against certain annihilation. But I'm not alone. Because it's not like the others, the hundreds of thousands who have given up their lottery spots, explain themselves any better than I can. They're on TV all the time with microphones jammed in their faces. Why, the reporters want to know, but these people just stand there looking bewildered. They stammer a few abortive words of explanation and then walk away, receding into their own doom.

The Ostrich Society wackos are different, goes without saying. They're more than happy to explain why they kidnap people and blow up Emigration registries. They like any opportunity to break out their ski masks and assault rifles for the news cameras. The thing with them, of course, is that not only do they want to stay, but they want to make sure everyone else does, too.

Like the reporters, Junior will want to know why. He'll expect a salient explanation, but this is all I've got: this planet is my home, and I'm quite attached to it and remain unconvinced, despite the government's multibillion-dollar advertising efforts, that Gliese 689 d (which they've started calling "Elysia" to sex it up a bit) has anything to offer that can compare to Glacier Bay, or the Sinai, or Sedona. All they really know, according to Junior, is it's about the same diameter as the Earth but doesn't rotate, so half the place is always daytime and the other always night. The half that's always daytime is really hot and the other half is really cold. Neither sounds all that great to me.

It's a quality of life issue. Like a person in a vegetative state, kept going by machines. I'm afraid that's what Gliese 689 d will be: the planetary equivalent of an eggshell-white room with bad fluorescent lighting and basic cable and a faint puke/shit stink all over everything. You know, pull the fucking plug already.

My mother is going. My brother and father. Junior, his family. But I'm not sure it's for me. And I'm hoping that this trip to Sedona will help me figure that out. Or else help me figure out how I'm going to tell him.

We leave on Monday. Junior sits in the passenger seat with a pewter flask full of SoCo. The trips I took cross-country while I was in school have taught me to love the road, so I don't mind being the only driver. On the first day we don't talk much, which is unusual, but then I realize why: we're both watching the world pass by outside the window as if it's the last time we'll see it, and for most of what we see that may well be the case. Here, for the last time, is Iowa's eastern border, better known as the Mississippi River, stilled by dams and rimmed by wooded hills. Here for the last time are the emerald acres of soybeans, the phantom stink of hog farms, the golden dome. Then Nebraska, and it is flat and dead but even the brown scrub fields and broken fences are heartbreaking when you know they'll soon be gone. We stop at roadside stands and greasy diners and eat small meals in silence. The waitresses all have bad teeth and faces seamed by a lifetime of hard work and poverty. We tip well and leave half the food behind on our plates and set out again. Our hearts may have broken in Nebraska but in Colorado they split open along the fractures, crumble to pieces, blow away. The peaks and green valleys, the lakes set at the foot of mountains like offerings. Beautiful and doomed and thus terrible.

Junior tops off his flask on a bumpy road, spills a little, takes a drink directly from the bottle before capping it again. He wipes absently at the spots on his lap. Such a waste.

"Too bad," I tell him, "you couldn't figure out a way to save all this."

He says nothing.

We hang a big left in Utah and head due south. It starts to look more and more like Arizona well before we actually cross the state line: eroded rock pillars, cliff faces scarred with the ancient story of Earth's geology. The timelessness of the landscape makes it even harder to believe that all this is soon at an end. I think about this for a while, and then when we pass into Arizona I say it out loud.

"None of this is going anywhere," Junior says. "The strata in those rocks contain evidence of at least one Earth impact, and they survived to tell the story. The problem isn't that this won't be here; it's that no one will be around to appreciate it."

"That doesn't really make me feel better," I say.

"I'm sorry," he says after a pause.

We're quiet some more after that, staring out the windows at cacti and sandstone plateaus and the narrow strip of shimmering pavement that bisects it all. Flagstaff materializes out of nothing and even though it's only twenty miles or so from here to Sedona we're cramped and hungry and so we stop to stretch listlessly and eat lunch. Junior surprises me: instead of ordering half a Coke and making up the difference with SoCo, he orders a regular, full glass of soda, like a normal person. I take this as a small, good sign.

In no time we roll into Sedona proper and find a Circle K. The place is full of men with silver ponytails and ratty sandals, old hippie women in loose flowing pants grinning vacantly as they molest the produce, and I am reminded of my old neighborhood in San Francisco. We buy enough fruit and bread and jerked meat for three days, as well as a couple spare handlers of SoCo and a big bottle of cheap Chianti for me. As I'm paying I wonder at how we cling so relentlessly to the little conventions like commerce, as though they can save us. What's the point of tallying up the total expense of my avocados and twelve-grain bread, with the end just over a year away?

The point, please, of this dutiful exchange of goods and currency? People all over the world are still giving their homes a fresh coat of paint and making weekly deposits into retirement accounts. Having babies at a record pace. God help us.

We load the food into the car and get back on 179, then take a right at the southern edge of town and head toward Red Rock State Park. We've got camping gear—tent, ground mats, and such—but those are strictly contingency. I've got directions, courtesy of an old college friend, to an abandoned ranch deep in the canyon. It's well beyond the range of the average day hiker—people who come to take a quick peek at the Grand Canyon before booking it back to the motel room in time to catch *The Sopranos*—so there's a good chance we'll find it unoccupied.

That's what my friend told me, anyway. So imagine my surprise and dismay when we get there and find an old man sitting outside the cabin, in the shade of the half-collapsed awning that shelters the front door.

"Hi," the old man says, very casual, as if he's not at all surprised to see us. He resembles the popular cliché of an old-time prospector: tan, grizzled face, salt-and-pepper beard, questionable oral hygiene for which he has clearly paid a steep price. He's shirtless and shriveled and his chest and belly are covered with a snowy pelt. He's sitting in one of those folding canvas camp chairs, but this one's some sort of deluxe model, complete with a hassock and a cup holder in the left armrest.

Junior shrugs off the heavy pack he's been struggling with in the heat. "Perfect," he says, digging for the flask in the side pocket of the pack.

"Mind giving me a shwag of that?" the old man asks him.

Junior looks at him a minute, then shrugs. "Guess not," he says, handing it over.

I'm not sure how to proceed. We could act like we're just moving through, but after five hours we're both exhausted and dehydrated and in no shape for setting up a camp.

"Is this your place?" I finally ask the man.

"It's no one's place," he says. He hands the flask back to Junior. "I can't claim any right to it, though I've been staying here awhile. You can see for yourself it's not a palace. Not really worth fighting over, I guess."

"So you won't mind if we spend a couple of nights then?" Junior asks.

The old man smiles. "That depends." He points to the flask. "How much of that stuff are you carrying?"

Junior smiles back. The instant camaraderie of fellow boozers, stronger than just about any other fraternity, squashes the initial awkwardness of the situation. "That stuff," Junior says, "constitutes by far the majority of the weight of this backpack."

"Well then I guess we're all set." The old man stands and offers his hand. "I've got the beer, and you've got the booze."

Normally I don't like sharing space with people—I hated the dorms in college and have never in my life split a hotel room with anyone—but there's something about this old guy that puts me at ease. It's a mystery of human chemistry that everyone is familiar with: liking someone instantly, well before they've given any real indication of whether or not they're likable. That's how it is with the old man.

"Amy," I tell him as he shakes my hand.

"Hi sweetheart," he says, sounding just like the grandfather he probably is. "I'm Ralph."

Ralph leads us inside the cabin and I see there won't be much privacy. Most of the interior walls are gone altogether, leaving behind only the support beams to mark where the walls once stood. Several holes in the roof are patched with a stopgap of mud and grass. Ralph's few belongings—sleeping bag, rucksack, some neatly folded clothing, a few books, a kerosene lantern—sit in the northwest corner of what serves as the kitchen. He points to the opposite end of the building and says, "Take a load off, you two."

I'm suddenly very tired. I drop my bag on the floor and sit on it. Junior opens the big backpack and starts to remove and sort its contents: spare clothes, the liquor and wine, a couple gallons of water.

"We've got a well out back," Ralph says when he sees the water. "Could have spared yourself lugging those in here."

"Naturally," Junior says. He pops the cap off one of the jugs. "It's here now, so we might as well drink it."

"Wait," Ralph says. "The well's nice and cool, though, and I bet that stuff's piss warm. Come with me. We'll sink those jugs and pull up some cold water."

Ralph leads Junior out the back door. I follow them outside into a large corral with broken, rotted fencing. The two of them walk through a gap in the fence on the far end, disappearing into the agave and banana yucca. I sit down on the splintered stoop and gaze out at a lumpy orange butte lording over the valley.

After a while I go back in, pour some wine into a tin cup from the mess kit, and sit in the shade of a desert willow with my back against the crumbling building. A breeze has come up off the hills, stirring the straw grass. I spot a shape moving near the base of the butte a quarter mile away. It's grayish and low to the ground, four-legged, and as it trots closer I begin to make out the long, tapered snout, the bushy black-tipped tail: a fox. He stops every few yards to investigate a patch of dirt or creosote bush, drawing ever nearer, until he's so close that I catch my breath. I've never been so still. I must be blending in with the shadows, because the fox doesn't see me, but he's in a ready stance, and he gives the air an investigative sniff, aware of the presence of something unseen. He's more doglike than the red foxes back home—longer, with a deep chest, big paws, and small tawny patches on his legs and the backs of his ears. He's beautiful.

Suddenly the fox bolts. At first I have no idea why, and then I hear voices approaching. With an odd sense of heaviness I watch the fox retreat, casting quick glances over his shoulder. Ralph and Junior coming back through the hole in the fence, laughing and carrying the jugs of water at their sides. The two of them stop and stand over me. The jugs aren't sealed very tight and water is dripping off them regular as a metronome: drip-drip-drip, making little indentations in the dirt. I squint up at Junior and he is smiling, gazing around as if he's just now noticed how beautiful everything is. I don't know what to think of this, but it makes me glad we came.

"Hey," I say, trying to get his attention.

He looks at me like he's just been gently awakened from a pleasant dream. "We're dropping these off," he says. "And then we're going hunting. For dinner. If you want to come."

"Hunting?" I stand and dust off the ass of my pants. "Hunting what?"

"Rattlesnakes," Ralph says.

"What?"

Junior gives this little shrug.

"Well, uh, okay, but aren't there enough rabbits and other less-deadly prey running around out here? Why rattlesnakes?"

"Well, because they're dangerous," Ralph says.

I look from one to the other. "I don't understand," I say flatly.

"Delicious, too, I can tell you," Ralph says. "People say they taste like chicken, but the flavor is more delicate than that. Similar to quail. You'll love it."

Suddenly I'm not so sure about the instantly-liking-Ralph thing. "Can I talk to you a minute?" I say to Junior.

We walk around to the other side of the building. "What's this about?" I ask him.

"What do you mean?"

"What do you think I mean, Junior."

"What? Apparently Ralph does it a lot. Sounds fun."

"Sounds stupid and risky," I say. "Besides, I'm not sure you're in any condition to be hunting anything."

"I haven't had a drink for an hour. I'm fine."

"You're going to get hurt. You've never handled a gun in your life, for one thing."

"No guns."

"No guns?"

"We find the snakes and sneak up on them and use a pinner."

"Which is what?"

"A stick, basically. Is my understanding."

"Good Christ. You're going to get killed."

"What difference does it make?" Junior asks. "Die today, die a year from now."

"What does that mean?"

"It means I know you're not going to Gliese 689 d with me. And if you're not going, I'm not going. In a year we'll both be dead. So it doesn't matter if I get zapped by a rattler and die out here."

Sometimes I still forget that he knows things. My face flashes hot, and I look away.

"Of course it matters," I say quietly. "Everything matters, Junior. Why don't you get that?"

He continues to stare at me.

"Besides," I tell him, "your sources aren't entirely correct. I haven't made a decision yet about going."

"I didn't need 'my sources' to figure this out. It's written all over you."

"So you just assumed—"

"That you had come down off the fence by now," he says. "Yes."

"Well I haven't."

He seems buoyed by this. "Then come on," he says. "Let's go hunting."

"What is this sudden obsession, anyway?"

"I don't know," he says. "Other than that it feels like I want to do everything all at once."

"Why don't we just go find a nice shaded washout and get cozy?"

"We'll have plenty of chances for that," Junior says, his smile returning.

"That's what you think."

"Come on," he says. I let him lead me by the arm.

"Ralph, we're going to pass this time," Junior says as we come around the corner. I start to protest no, it's okay, but Ralph cuts me off.

"She's the boss," he says. "Listen, it's best to hunt alone anyway; more than one person and the snakes hear you coming and take off. At least that's what I've read."

"What you've read?" Junior says. "How much experience do you have with this?"

"Until three months ago I was a grandfather and semiretired lobbyist for the Federation of Payday Loan Companies in New Jersey. Which is to say, not much."

I give Junior a poke in the ribs.

"I can see you're surprised," Ralph says. "But listen: it doesn't take long in this place before you start looking like you've been here forever. A tan, a little dirt. Leave your dentures out. Presto: backcountry snake wrangler."

"Well, shit," Junior says. He looks at me with eyebrows raised, amused and bemused.

"Exactly." Ralph smiles. "So you guys go ahead and settle in, relax, whatever, and I'll go find a mess of snakes for dinner."

"We brought food, you know," I say.

Ralph lifts a pronged stick that's leaning against the side of the building. "Quit worrying," he says, walking back in the direction of the well.

After he's gone Junior and I just look at each other for a few moments. Then we both burst out laughing.

"What the *fuck*," I say, wiping at my eyes.

"You wanted to have a singular experience," Junior says. "I'd say that's exactly what we're in for."

We stand there smiling at each other, Junior's hands light on my hips, and despite what he knows about my ambivalence the whole day has this great feel to it now. We find that shaded washout, and with the ground mats and a blanket it's comfortable enough. Junior is careful, and good. After, we lie there exulting in our nakedness, laughing and sharing wine out of the mess kit cup.

This is one of our favorite games lately: I make guesses about the lives of people we see in passing at fast food restaurants, on the highway, at the coffee shop, and Junior, with his special insight, tells me how close I came. Here's what I come up with for Ralph: as a high-level executive for the Federation of Payday Loan Companies, he basically made money, and lots of it, off other people's poverty, which in turn means that he is at best a man of dubious moral fiber. But he did always feel a little uncomfortable about how he made his living. And like many people who had the capacity to become better human beings but lacked the motivation, the announcement of the end of the world sent Ralph into a paroxysm of guilt and repentance that was partly genuine and partly a hedge against the possibility that there was an afterlife where scores were being tallied and punishment doled out. So he literally cashed in his retirement fund and spent two weeks giving it away, in increments of $100, to people outside payday loan joints in Newark and Jersey City. He was mugged several times for his trouble, but managed to keep just enough to get him to Arizona, where now he hunts snakes and contemplates the universe and waits with some trepidation for the end of all things.

"How's that?" I ask.

"Pretty good," Junior says. "You had the advantage of knowing a few details already, though."

When we gather our stuff and return to the ranch house Ralph is already there, cleaning what looks like six or seven snakes of various lengths. He cuts off the heads, peels the skin off in one long piece, guts the bodies and washes the meat with liberal doses of well water. While he's working Junior and I get wood and brush together for a fire. Junior gets it going just in time, as the canyon has fallen into late-day shadows that hint at how cool the night will be.

Ralph goes into the house and returns with a small iron skillet. There's an old T-shirt wrapped around the handle that serves as an oven mitt. After the fire has died down to embers, Ralph cooks the snake meat in batches, sitting in his camp chair, leaning forward and tossing the meat every few seconds with a practiced flick of the wrist. I get out some bread and borrow Ralph's knife to cube the pineapple we got at the Circle K. Junior pours wine for me and opens warmish beers for himself and Ralph, and before too long the three of us are sharing what is without a doubt the most haphazard meal I've ever eaten. I have the only plate, which came with the mess kit; the two of them hold their bread in one hand and pick snake and pineapple directly from the bowls. The food is surprisingly good. We freshen our drinks and build the fire up again and sit around talking as night falls.

Junior confesses the Instant History scenario we concocted earlier.

"Not too far from the truth," Ralph says matter-of-factly. He put in his teeth to eat and they've taken ten years off my estimate of his age. "Except I'm not foolish enough to stand outside a check-cashing joint giving away money. You know what kind of people hang around those places?"

"People driven to desperate acts by poverty?" I say.

"Exactly," Ralph says. "Sarcasm noted and accepted, by the way. No, I made sure my family was comfortable and then gave most of what I had to a few charities. It's a funny thing, giving money away to improve a world that's just around the corner from not-being. But what else can you do?"

"What about this family?" Junior asks. He already knows the answer, of course; he's asking more for my benefit, and for conversation's sake. "What's the story there?"

"They're very angry with me. My wife and oldest daughter, in particular."

"Justifiably?"

"You want to hear the story and decide for yourself?"

Junior rests his beer in the dirt and gets to his feet. "For that we'll need something a little stronger," he says. He goes into the house, reemerges with a half-full bottle of SoCo. Ralph fills his cup and hands the bottle back. Junior offers it to me but I shake my head no, and he takes his seat again and wraps his free arm around my shoulders. He kisses me once behind the ear, and I relax into him.

"Okay, so," Ralph says. "Long version or short?"

"Whichever paints you in the kindest light," Junior says.

"That'd be the short version," Ralph says with a laugh. His dentures are freakishly straight and uniform, like two solid bands of ivory. "As you already know, I worked as a suit for the public relations outfit of payday loan companies. Only job I ever had as an adult. Married to Beverly, Bev, for forty-one years. Two kids, both girls, both grown. Natalie, the one who hates me now, is married and gave us two grandkids, Zach and Jocelyn."

Ralph kicks at the fire. The flames surge and sparks dance into the air. "Sarah, our younger daughter, who we call Newt, never had any interest in getting married. She teaches high school art and sells her paintings on the side. She was just here a couple of weeks ago, visiting."

"So Sarah . . . Newt . . . isn't angry with you?" I ask.

"Nope."

"Why?" Junior asks. This, apparently, is a detail he wasn't aware of.

"Because she understands. She's not going either."

Oh, shit. Junior takes his arm from around my shoulders and leans back in the chair, his hands behind his head. "Ah," he says, "I get it."

Ralph smiles at him over the fire. "Do you?" he asks.

"You've chosen not to Emigrate. What more is there to know?"

"The 'why' doesn't interest you?"

"The 'why' is irrelevant, because no matter how compelling it can't be reason enough to stay and die," Junior says. I wince. I can hear how drunk he really is, and long experience tells me this isn't going to go well. "You are something of an anomaly, though, I'll admit. You've got grandchildren, and most everyone with dependent children or grandchildren has elected to Emigrate. By the same token nearly everyone who has elected *not* to Emigrate is either Ostrich Society—and that doesn't seem likely in your case—or simply doesn't believe that C1998 E1 is going to collide with Earth."

"What makes you so sure I'm not Ostrich Society?"

"I find it hard to picture you blowing up an Emigration Registry."

"Fair enough," Ralph says. "So that's all you've got? Either I'm a militant crackpot, or I'm too dumb to realize this is really happening?"

"The statistics back me up," Junior says.

"Well I do hate to skew the numbers. I was a big numbers man myself, when I was still working. But no, I am neither a member of the Ostrich Society, nor do I have any doubt about the fate of the planet or anyone who decides to continue clinging to its surface."

"And yet," Junior says.

"I plan to continue clinging."

"I see why your wife is unhappy with you," Junior says.

"Unhappy isn't really the word. Unhappy means you sleep on the couch for a couple of nights."

"*I* can understand how you feel." I'm talking to Ralph, but I'm looking at Junior.

"Can you?" Ralph asks. "Because I'm not really sure I understand it myself."

"Exactly," I say.

"I mean at first glance it doesn't seem to make much sense," Ralph says.

"It doesn't make much sense at second or third glance, either," Junior says.

Ralph smiles at me. "We're both in the doghouse, I take it."

"This isn't a joke," Junior says to him.

"You're right about that, son."

"And you know, maybe that's the real problem I'm having with this," Junior says. "I ask why, and you shrug your shoulders and smile and say, 'Gosh, if I knew I'd tell you.' Not good enough."

Ralph takes another drink. "I don't mean this to sound rude," he says, "but what makes you feel like you're entitled to an explanation? It's my choice. You're free to do what you want."

"I'm sort of a special case, when it comes to this particular topic," Junior says.

"How's that?"

"You wouldn't believe me if I told you."

"Try me."

Junior looks at Ralph for a minute, then smiles. "Okay," he says. "For starters, I'm primarily responsible for the fact that you *have* a choice about whether to stay on Earth or Emigrate. If not for me, everyone's stuck here."

Ralph gives Junior a quick once-over, takes in the cutoff shorts, the week's growth of beard, the eyes rheumy with booze. "Okay, you're right," he says. "I don't believe you."

Reluctant as I am to be involved one way or the other in this conversation, I pipe up: "It's true."

Ralph looks to me, eyebrows raised, and I nod. It's hard to tell if I'm lending credence to Junior's story, or if Ralph just thinks we're both crazy now.

"But that's not the only reason this pisses me off," Junior continues. "It gets better."

"Okay," Ralph says. "I'm listening."

But Junior demurs for a moment, staring into the fire and sipping at his beer.

"Go on," I tell him. "No sense stopping now."

"I'm just realizing that you're the only person I've ever told," Junior says to me. "Not even Sawyer. He probably suspects something's up, but in this case not even he can really know. It's probably the one thing in all the world that Sawyer *doesn't* know."

"You're losing me here, kids," Ralph says. "Of course I'm a little drunk. But still."

Junior turns back to him. "I've known about the end of the world since I was born," he says. "Date, time, circumstances."

"Huh," Ralph says. He drinks more SoCo.

"But even that's not all of it," Junior says, really warming to his topic now. He stands and paces in front of the fire, beer in hand. "Don't you want to know how I came to have this knowledge?"

"I am curious, I'll admit."

"I hear a voice," Junior says. He jabs an index finger against his temple. "Always have. It tells me things. Sometimes mundane things. Sometimes terrible things. How fun is that?"

Ralph stands and moves his chair closer to the fire. "Not much, I'm guessing?"

Junior eyes him. "You're skeptical. Understandably. If you'll give me just one more minute, I'll tell you something about yourself that will erase all doubt."

I know what's coming, of course. Junior gets the faraway cockeye-look and after a few moments comes back and talks to Ralph: "In the winter of 1951, you climbed the snowpile in the municipal parking lot they used as a snow dump during your childhood in Bridgeton, New Jersey. It was late winter, March, and so the pile was quite tall, almost forty feet. The kids used it every year for king of the mountain, for sledding, but the weather had been warm the previous week and when you got to the top you sank right in to your armpits. Stuck fast."

And Ralph is stuck fast now, standing rooted to the spot, staring at Junior.

"You struggled for a while until you got tired, which didn't take long. Then you sat still and yelled for help but no one was around to hear you, it was just an old abandoned parking lot that technically wasn't even within the city limits, and as the hours passed your voice gave out. Night fell, and fortunately the weather was still unusually warm or else you would have frozen to death. By now the police were looking for you, but no one thought to check the snowpile even though everyone knew that kids frequented the place during the winter; many of the adults in town, in fact, had played there when they were young. So who knows why it didn't occur to anyone. There you were, unable to move, buried so tight you could take only half-breaths, and you cried because you believed you were going to die.

"But of course you didn't die. You were found by another group of kids the next morning, and by noon you were in a hospital bed sipping cocoa, with heated saline warming your veins. But think back, Ralph, if you will, on the feeling you had late in the night. Now imagine having that same feeling every day of your life. Imagine being born with it. And you'll have some idea of where I'm coming from."

His anger now dissipated, Junior slouches over the fire, poking at it with the toe of his boot. For a while no one says anything. Out of the corner of my eye I catch Ralph looking at me again, and I turn my head to face him. He looks absolutely stunned.

"He did the same thing to me, a couple years back," I tell Ralph. "I know how you feel. Take a few minutes."

Ralph puts the cup to his lips and drains it, then sits down again and stares into the fire. After a while I stand up and put my arms around Junior's waist and press myself into his back. He rubs my hands with his.

For me at least, the silence is starting to get a little awkward. It feels like a rift has formed and the good humor the two of them shared is history. I'm thinking of begging off to bed. The chill hinted at earlier has now settled into the canyon, and while Junior is keeping the front of me warm, my back, turned toward the night, is quite cold. Plus the wine has given me a dirty, headachy buzz that's not going to improve if I drink more.

Then Ralph finally speaks. "I'm going to need a lot more of this," he says, holding up his empty cup.

It's only mildly funny. It's not even really a joke, just a wry little aside from an old man sitting in the desert, thousands of miles from his family, waiting to die. But for some reason it sets us to laughing. It starts off slow, a couple little chuckles, then gathers momentum until we're almost paralyzed by it and soon we're not even laughing anymore at what Ralph said, this laughter exists for its own sake, it seizes us and drains us and feels so very good, and by the time we all gather ourselves again Junior has gone into the house and returned with a fresh bottle and Ralph stokes the fire and we talk and drink for what seems like a long while. We're only quiet once, when we hear coyotes howling close by, but then the sound stops and we go back to talking and at some point, happy and drunk, we turn in.

The next morning I'm awakened early by a hand shaking my arm. It's Ralph. Junior is still asleep next to me.

"What is it?" I ask, rubbing a crust of dried drool from the corner of my mouth. "Is something wrong?"

Ralph shushes me. "Everything's fine. I just want to talk to you. Alone."

It's very cold outside the sleeping bag, and very warm inside, but there's an urgency in Ralph's voice and so I crawl out. Junior rolls toward where I used to be, but he doesn't wake up. I find a sweatshirt, and Ralph hands me a cup of coffee without a word. I try a sip and despite a few tiny grounds floating around it's strong and good and, most important, warm.

I follow Ralph outside, where a new fire is burning on the remnants of last night's blaze. There's a small saucepan suspended over the flames by a scorched metal grate. Inside the saucepan is more coffee at a full boil.

"How long have you been up?" I ask, warming my hands in the steam.

"Not sure," Ralph says. "I don't really keep track of time out here. Haven't seen the need."

"Did you sleep at all?"

"A little."

My hands start to sting, but when I pull them away the moisture from the steam cools instantly, and I get a chill. "What's the plan, here, Ralph?" I ask.

"We will ostensibly be gathering saguaro fruit for breakfast," he says, lifting a small metal pail. "We will in actuality be talking about my past, and your future."

"Oh. Okay," I say. "But no rattlesnakes."

"No rattlesnakes."

"Let's go, then. I guess."

We head to the far end of the corral, Ralph in the lead, and step out through the gap in the fence. We walk a few hundred yards down a gravelly slope. Despite Ralph's promise of no snakes I keep my eyes trained to the ground, ready to bolt, imagining there's one under every rock and bush. The sun begins to emerge from behind the buttes just as we reach a stand of saguaro, and within a few minutes it's high enough to warm us as we work.

We gather fruit for a long time without a word, and at pretty much the moment that I begin to wonder if we're ever going to have this talk, Ralph says, "You know I was lying to you kids, right? About my wife?"

"No," I say. "She doesn't hate you?"

He laughs. "Oh, she hates me. I was lying about why."

"Okay."

"Let me put it this way: She doesn't hate me because I'm not going. I'm not going, because she hates me."

"Why would you lie about that? What difference would it make to us?"

"Well I was trying to throw my lot in with yours, in a way," Ralph says. "Back you up. I felt like I'd be weakening your case if I stuck strictly to the truth: that as a result of my wife's deep, abiding hatred, I've decided to commit suicide by comet."

I stop harvesting fruit and stand up straight. "So you don't feel the way I do after all," I say. "Like there's some bond you have to Earth that you can't bring yourself to break."

"Oh, I do," Ralph says. "That's why I came to Sedona. But that wouldn't be enough to keep me here on its own. Especially if I had something else to leave for."

"Ah, I see now. Defend me in front of Junior, then try to convince me in private to go along with him."

"After seeing the two of you last night, sure. Not that it's really any of my business."

"No."

"But if you'd let me explain what I'm thinking."

"Does your wife hate you because you're a meddler?" I ask. "Is that it?"

Ralph tosses a fruit in the bucket and stands up with a hand on his lower back. "No." He laughs. "'Hate' is probably the wrong word. I know I used it myself. Bev is disdainful. She looks down her nose at me. Which is worse than being hated. Hate at least implies an intensity of feeling. I am not important enough to my wife for her to hate me. I doubt that I ever have been, not even early on."

"Sounds wretched," I say.

"It could be at times. But when you love someone like I love her, you can go for years like that. We made it more than forty ourselves. Imagine." He looks around the canyon. "Bev came from a family with money, and she grew up doing the things that monied people do. I tend to be a lot simpler than that. Boring. I would work and come home and read the evening paper, back when there still was such a thing, and have a couple glasses of whatever and maybe a couple glasses more. Listen to the game. Fish on the weekends. Bought a cabin on the lake and thought she would like that, wrong again. She couldn't abide by the quiet. Complained the smell of campfire wouldn't wash out of her clothes."

"She sounds like a bitch, frankly."

"She's not," he says. "Not really. She tried, early on. The first few years she went ice fishing at least as many times as I went to the symphony. There are pictures of us on a snowmobile, of her pulling pickerel out through a hole in the ice with her bare hands. She's smiling. She looks happy, in those pictures. But at some point—after Newt was born, I think—she realized that was all there would ever be. And she couldn't picture herself riding the back of a snowmobile every weekend for the rest of her life. Who could blame her."

"I'm sorry."

"Eh." He waves a hand. "I'm not telling you this to make you feel bad. We were a mismatch. She should have married someone who was comfortable in a tie, who could debate the merits of Russian versus Iranian caviar. That wasn't me. But I loved her. And she felt affection for me, I know, at least for a while after we got married. But we never looked like the two of you do. Not once. Not even in those early years."

He pauses for a minute, lets this sink in.

"Plus—and I'll be honest with you—what really spurred me to talk to you this morning was the look I kept seeing on his face last night."

"What do you mean?"

Ralph sets his face in a sort of *come now* expression. "I think you know."

"I don't, actually."

"Let's just say when he looks at you he reminds me of myself." He lifts the bucket of fruit from the dirt. "Listen, I'm going to run these up to camp and get them cleaned. Maybe you should take your time coming back. Enjoy all this beauty you're so attached to. Just watch out for rattlesnakes."

Before I have a chance to say anything else he's turned and gone, moving briskly back up the gravel incline toward the ranch. I'm alone, and he had to mention the fucking snakes, didn't he, because just like that the certainty that they're lurking everywhere returns, and I have no desire to hang around and enjoy the spectacle of early morning in the desert, to take a leisurely walk through the waking canyon. None whatsoever. What I want is to be back at the ranch, warm inside the sleeping bag with Junior's arm slung over my waist, his hand softly cupping my breast as he sleeps. I do not want to be alone in all this beauty. But I am, suddenly, too frightened to move.

I don't understand this sudden paralysis. There've certainly been other, more tangible dangers before that never scared me this much: the varied and numerous acts of insanity committed by members of my family; the serial Peeping Tom my junior year at Stanford who stalked the dorms watching girls take showers; and of course more recently, the evening when I nearly died at the hands of a crazed government agent in an abandoned farmhouse somewhere in Massachusetts. Somehow the theoretical snakes, theoretically lurking everywhere on this most beautiful of mornings, trump them all.

But what does being an adult teach you, daily, if not how to function in the face of fear? Move your feet, I tell myself, and I manage one slow step, then another. I scan all around for snakes, and somehow seeing none makes it worse. I keep moving, concentrate only on that, and going up the hill is slow but somehow I reach the corral fence, and I step through the gap and find Junior still asleep inside the ranch. I kneel on the floor next to him and put a hand on his forehead, smooth his hair back. He wakes slowly. He must have been dreaming because it takes him a minute to realize where he is, but when he finally does he looks up and recognizes me and it's then that I see the look Ralph was talking about. How is it possible that I never noticed it before? And he was right, there is a young Ralph in that look, too, adoring his new wife even as the seeds of her disdain for him are taking root.

I lean close and whisper in Junior's ear. "Ralph wasn't telling us the truth about his wife," I say. "About why she hates him."

Junior clears the sleep from his throat. "I know," he says. His lips brush my earlobe.

"Of course you do. But do you know what I'm going to say next?"

"No."

"Good."

A pause. "Well?"

"I think we should cut our vacation short," I say. "Drive to Phoenix, drop off the rental, and fly back to Chicago. So I can go sign up at the Emigration Registry."

There is a long moment's pause, and then he reaches up and pulls me close to him and I can actually feel his gratitude as a physical thing, and I know then that I have finally, finally stopped failing with people.

After that we're like kids at Christmas. Junior gets up and we hurriedly pack a few things, leaving most of our supplies behind for Ralph. He watches us for a while, smiling, then goes outside to build the fire up again and cook breakfast. He implores us to sit and eat but we are too excited. I see a hint of sadness in his eyes and I realize how lonely he must have been before we came. Junior shakes Ralph's hand. I hug him goodbye and he says "Thank you," and I know exactly what he means. Then we put on our bags and walk. At the point where Ralph is about to disappear forever we turn and wave, and he waves back, a tiny figure down in the dust of the canyon below, alone in all that beauty. The hike out doesn't take nearly as long as it seemed to coming in, and the car is right where we left it. Junior drives and I read the atlas and give directions. Soon we're in Phoenix, and then we're on a plane, asleep with our heads pressed together over the armrest. On the ground in Chicago we take a cab in from Midway. Rodney is there when we arrive. He's surprised and, of course, happy to see us. Junior hugs him tight, almost violently, and ruffles his hair, playing the part of big brother as usual even though he's the baby, and the two of them stand there looking at me with their arms around each other's shoulders, out of breath, their hair mussed, grinning ear-to-ear.

Rodney's chef Alice makes this incredible dinner—hanger steak with bordelaise, bok choy and roasted red potatoes—and we eat and talk with Dave Brubeck jazzing in the background. Junior drinks only two beers and they're like an afterthought. The next morning I wake up very early and shower and get dressed, and as I move around the room, Junior watches me from the bed. He's smiling at me in the half-light. When I'm finished putting myself together I lean over him and kiss his forehead, his lips.

He moves to throw the covers off and get up. "Wait a few minutes," he says, "and I'll go down with you."

I push him back against the pillow. "Just sleep in," I say. "I'll only be a couple hours. When I get back we can walk down to the Biscuit Basket for an early lunch."

He's asleep again before I leave the bedroom. I step out and make sure the door's locked behind me and go down to North State and pick up the red line. I ride downtown. At Grand I get off and cross the street to the Emigration Registry. Unsmiling soldiers in riot gear frisk me and check the contents of my purse. When I clear security I step inside and find, to my surprise, a fairly long line. So I queue up.

Directly in front of me is a woman with a baby held against her shoulder. It's staring at me google-eyed, as babies do. I make what I imagine is a funny face.

Outside there's a sudden commotion: shouting, followed by the sound of automatic gunfire. The line inside the registry fractures as people duck down and search frantically for cover, clutching at each other in groups of two and three. A man dressed head-to-toe in black runs through the entrance, setting off the metal detector. He's hollering unintelligibly, and something bulky and ominous-looking is strapped to his chest.

I don't have time to be scared. Out of nowhere there's a pop and a dazzling flash, as though someone has taken my picture with the world's largest camera, and I am lifted and thrown by what feels like a giant hand. There's an instant of heat and terrible pain, and I can hear people screaming, but the sound recedes quickly and then there is something else altogether, and it's not bad like everyone thinks it'll be when they're alive. It's neither bad nor good. It's nothing. And I will miss you, Mom and Dad and yes Oscar and my friends, especially Andrea, and of course Junior, sweetheart, poor, poor thing, I will miss you the most and I wish to God there were some way you could not be sad. I wish I could tell you there's nothing sad at all in death, but I can't. I can't. Because I'm nothing.

PART THREE

The Multiverse, and Everything in It

9 As you sit here now in the waning moments of your existence, alone at the summit of Maine's tallest mountain, waiting along with billions of others for the Destroyer of Worlds, we suppose it's as good a time as any for us to reveal to you the true nature of everything. Then you will be given the reward you were promised years ago, which is really a choice, but it is a choice you will have to make quickly, because within a few hours the skies will turn from blue to red and the Earth will become like a giant broiler oven and everything even remotely combustible will burst spontaneously into flames, you included, and no further choices will be available to you. So, forthwith:

8 As you have suspected in the past, everything exists in a multidomain universe, or multiverse. Which to put it very, very simply means that an infinite number of variations on this world exist concurrently, complete with an infinite number of variations on you. Right now, for example, at a distance of 26^{344}m from where you sit, there is another you, only it is the you of five seconds ago, staring at the sky and waiting for it to burn. 12^{597}m away from that you is yet another, only this you has been turned to blowing ash by heat so intense even your bones are incinerated. Another you is fast asleep on board an Emigration transport bound for Gliese 689 d; another, younger you is vomiting on a Chicago sidewalk early on a Tuesday afternoon; still another is locked in the bathroom of your childhood home, masturbating to the mental image of Mrs. Harris. And so on, literally ad infinitum.

7 So your reward is a simple choice, one that has never been granted to anybody else, ever. Despite all you've endured, we hope you'll agree that to be offered this opportunity—one that no one else has enjoyed in all of infinity—makes everything that you've suffered to this point worthwhile, in retrospect.

What we're offering—which you've probably already guessed at, but we'll articulate it anyway—is simply this: pick a self. Any self. We're allowing you to choose, and then become, any you that you want. It can be a you that you've already been, any you along the timeline of the life already lived. You can start over as a zygote, if you like. Or you can be any of the endless possible yous that never happened, though of course given the nature of the multiverse they really *did* happen, and continue to happen and will happen again. An example: You could choose to be the you that would have resulted if you hadn't stepped on that bumblebee with your bare foot in your aunt's backyard when you were four. You would be reasonable to think that stepping on a bumblebee wouldn't make much of a difference in the trajectory of a person's life. And you would be wrong. Because if you hadn't stepped on the bee it would have lived and gone on to begin pollination of the field behind the abandoned fire station on the north end of town, transforming this field from nothing but dull straw grass to a bright pastiche of oxeye daisies and heather, and Harry Boyd, an elderly millionaire who'd made his fortune with a regional chain of shoe stores and had become, in retirement, the greatest philanthropist the state of Maine had ever seen, would have been so struck by the beauty of these wildflowers that the recreation center for poor children he'd been planning to build in a community twenty miles south would instead go up where that abandoned firehouse stood, changing the lives of thousands of kids in myriad ways over the ensuing years. The changed life most relevant to our discussion would be that of one Marc Lavway. Instead of following in the footsteps of his several older brothers, all of whom had hit the streets as bullies and delinquents at young ages and had graduated by now to actual criminal activity of varying seriousness, Marc would spend just about every moment outside school at the recreation center, playing basketball and floor hockey and even taking a couple of classes, learning to make pottery and speak a bit of Canadian French. And because Boyd would have endowed the recreation center with money for an annual college scholarship to be awarded to the center's best all-around citizen, Marc Lavway would be given an opportunity that none of his older brothers, two of whom were by now into long stretches at the state prison, could have dreamed of. At college, freed from the awful home that he'd spent so much time at the recreation center to avoid, Marc would truly excel, earning his own way with an avalanche of merit-based scholarships and grants. Next would come medical school, following which Marc would complete his internship and residency at Beth Israel Deaconess in Boston. And though with his talent and chosen specialty in emergency medicine he could probably have done more net good at an urban trauma center, Marc would elect instead to return home, working in the quiet emergency room at Inland Hospital, where he would spend his days handing out antibiotics and treating old ladies for shortness of breath. Eventually he would treat your father, who would arrive at the ER on Friday, December 6, 2002, with his biannual bout of pneumonia, exacerbated of course by heavy cigarette smoking. Lavway would perform the standard examination, make the obvious diagnosis, and prepare to write a script for erythromycin and send your father on his way. But then, for reasons unclear even to him, Lavway would on a hunch order a CT scan. Your father would question the expense, but Lavway would tell him that emergency physicians learn to rely on their instincts more so than other doctors, and in this case his instincts were screaming for him to get a CT scan of your father's chest. Your father, liking what he perceived as Lavway's straightforward, honest approach, would acquiesce, and in this manner his cancer would be discovered four years sooner, and it would be cured simply by removing the affected lung. Though neither Lavway nor your father would have any way of knowing this, Lavway's instincts would have saved your father's life, not by curing him of cancer (which of course you would have taken care of), but by altering the timeline going forward so that your father would be in an easy chair, rather than behind the wheel of his Mustang, when he passed out on the night of March 28, 2006.

And of course all of this did actually happen, 8^{518}m from here, where a version of you saw the bumblebee just before his foot came down and spared himself a painful sting.

We realize this is a lot to absorb all at once, especially when you've already resigned yourself to dying here. We understand your frustration and sadness at having lost what little you loved, despite a lifetime spent trying to save it. We understand your skepticism regarding the chances that another go-round would result in anything other than more of the heartache and despair you're now enduring. So we'll give you some time, here. Just keep in mind, as you ponder, that there's not a whole lot of time left one way or the other.

6 One other thing, and we promise after this we really will leave you alone for a bit: Please don't allow your sorrow to blind you to the scope of possibilities on offer. You know as well as we do that with infinite choices comes the potential for infinite happiness. If we may be allowed to speak frankly, for the fourth-smartest person in the history of the world you can be quite stupid at times. In fact it seems true, at least in this case, that great intellectual capacity can sometimes be a handicap, because we're pretty certain that someone of average intelligence would have this one figured out fairly quickly, would in fact probably already have made a choice and be well on their way to (re)living a happy life.

So, yes, there is a correct choice here, is what we're saying.

Seriously, just think about it. We'll wait.

5 A hint: It didn't have to turn out this way. Despite what you may think it was not our intention to set you up for heartache. Whether you believe it or not, whether you intended it or not, you at least indirectly chose the death of all that you love. Now we're giving you the chance to choose again.

4 Interesting. Not what we expected, certainly, but it just might work. Of course you understand that this is just the beginning—whether or not you enjoy a happier life this time around depends entirely on what you do from this moment on. Nothing is guaranteed. You understand also that the choice, once made, cannot be reversed. You can't decide later that you'd rather be the you who made his fortune counting cards at blackjack tables in Vegas, Atlantic City, and Monaco, living a life of sexual and material indulgence that would have made Don Juan blanch.

Of course that's hardly your style. Still, we figured we'd at least give you the option, before it is too late. We mean, honestly: yachts in St.-Tropez? suites at the Hôtel de Paris? thousands of women, a new one every night, moths to the flame of burning money, each of whom has an exotically alluring way of pronouncing your name?

3 No? Last chance?

2 Okay. Quickly, then, before it's too late:

55 Here you are, sixteen again, in Amy's brother's bedroom, lying together with her and watching a movie on VHS. It'll take a moment's getting used to. Your vision is suddenly undamaged by years of reading in bad light, and your knees and lower back don't hurt at all. Take a look in the mirror behind the television and see your hair is all there again, every follicle precisely the same, cut in a jet-black flattop that you rarely bother to put up. You may notice, too, that you have no craving whatsoever for a drink. You are relaxed and calm and free suddenly of the frayed, raw sensation that always accompanied your sober hours as an adult, the feeling of having been rubbed all over with fine-grit sandpaper.

54 Most important, of course, you are with Amy again, delighted by the warmth of her, by the nearly forgotten scent of the sandalwood oil she favored in high school, by the soft weight of her ass pressed against your thigh.

53 You'll notice too that, as promised, everything is in its right place. Amy's hair, curly and full of flyaway static, tickling your face and nose. To the left of the TV an embarrassing family heirloom: a blackface bellhop in red suit and hat, offering up an ashtray with outstretched hands. The ashtray itself crammed with Amy's Camel Lights and her mother's lipstick-stained Virginia Slims. A Red Sox calendar, two months behind, hanging on the wall opposite the bed.

52 Pay attention, because now is when things could become different. This was the precise moment, the first time around, when you finally screwed up the courage to tell Amy about the Destroyer of Worlds, and as you know things went more or less completely to hell after that. In fact, a direct line could be drawn between this moment and you sitting alone on the summit of Mount Katahdin, waiting to be broiled alive, convinced that even your best, most loving and generous and big-hearted choices had been wrong, wrong, wrong.

Now all that never was. You are a boy of sixteen again, still too young to have done anything irreparable, anything beyond forgiveness, and Amy's love for you is intact. It is also delicate and immature, and requires nurturing in order to grow into the sort of love with the strength to endure a lifetime. The first step in that nurturing process is as simple as it is obvious: keep your mouth shut.

You find this easy enough. Instead of talking, you use your mouth to kiss the back of Amy's neck. At first she barely responds, absorbed as she is in the movie. You pop the two top buttons of her Levis, tickling the fine blond hairs below her belly button, then heading south, grasping, seeking, and realizing now that you mean business she rolls to face you. You kiss her desperately, and she pulls back and puts a hand to her mouth and gazes at you, questioning. But what she sees in your face must provide a satisfactory answer, because after a moment she folds herself into you again, meets your desperation with her own, and as good as it always was this is somehow better, fuller, so good that for the first time since infancy you are separated, however temporarily, from your awareness of the end of all things. Afterward you lie naked on the carpet, limbs entangled, rug burns stinging with sweat. You light a cigarette from her pack and pass it back and forth. The smoke rises and billows lazily, forming endless fractals in the slanting sunlight.

51 When that sunlight is gone completely you kiss Amy goodbye and walk the mile or so to your parents' home. You let yourself in and find your mother sitting in the dark with her **Turbo Chug!** cup boring a hole in the dining room table with the implacable slowness of erosion. You turn on every light in the house. You kiss your mother on the cheek

and she continues to stare straight ahead. You ask if she would like to play a game of cribbage and she continues to stare straight ahead. You cook a small simple meal of pork chops and baked potatoes and canned green beans, and you fix a plate for yourself and set another in front of her and she continues to stare straight ahead. She takes a drink from the **Turbo Chug!** cup and sets it down squarely on her pork chop, at which point you suggest to her that maybe she should go to bed, and she lets you lead her to the bathroom, where you make her brush her teeth, and then to the bedroom, where you watch as she turns back the covers and gets in all by herself.

You cover the plates of food with plastic wrap and stack them in the microwave and wait somewhat anxiously for your father to get home from the warehouse. You'll be waiting awhile, as his shift doesn't end until after midnight. When he finally comes in, hair and mustache coated with dust, boots clunking on the kitchen floor, not just alive again but *young,* so young, you greet him with a hug from which he noticeably recoils. You heat the plates of food and set them back on the dining room table. The two of you sit opposite one another and eat in silence. He keeps a cigarette going in the ashtray and takes a drag after every third or fourth bite. When he's done eating you wash the plates and forks while he makes himself a cup of instant coffee. The two of you go into the living room and watch the late news without speaking. Once or twice during commercials you catch him looking in your direction, and you don't need us to explain why: he's wondering what on earth has gotten into you.

50 Two years later, when because of the way that you have altered her timeline Amy leaves for Harvard instead of Stanford, you go with her. You move into a beautiful but outrageously overpriced loft in Union Square, and while Amy starts her freshman year you take an internship at Oxfam's headquarters across the Charles River in Boston. You've been at the job only two weeks when you formulate a framework for solving problems with aid distribution in China, where a flood has devastated the Jiangsu province. You offer this framework unsolicited to your immediate boss, Helen, who is special adviser to Oxfam's

vice president. Two days later you find yourself at Clio, trying to figure out which utensils go with which course while the vice president grills you about your background. The vice president does not have much of a poker face, and his bewilderment grows visibly with each answer you give. Over a dessert of chicory crème caramel he tells you that if Oxfam is successful in negotiating with the other agencies to implement your ideas then you can take the bulk of the credit for saving tens of thousands of Chinese villagers from starvation. He follows this by asking if you'd be interested in taking a paid position, and you tell him yes you would be very interested and thanks very much.

Afterward you stand waiting for a bus in the bracing air of early fall, hands in pockets, smiling sort of dopily as the traffic rolls past, and you are feeling good about your life, because you are about to return to your small beautiful home with the soaring ceilings and stone fireplace and find Amy there in the warm light of the dining room, and because you will pull her away from her books and papers and make love, maybe in bed, more likely on the kitchen counter, and because you will tell her what's happened and she will smile with pride, and above all because you feel like it matters that thousands of people have been saved from starvation.

You could not be more correct. It does matter. All of it.

49 Occasionally you wake to find Amy thrashing the covers and warding off phantom blows in her sleep. Sometimes she continues to tremble and weep even after you've reached your hands out in the dark to calm her fear and rage, and you have to turn on the lights and walk her to the bathroom and show her in the mirror her pale, unmarked skin, the absence of blood. On these mornings you stay awake with her and talk and share cigarettes, the ashtray resting in the comforter-valley between you. Together you watch the day begin slowly outside the windows, and for her the sun coming up is like being rescued.

48 You often take breaks during the summer to see Rodney play baseball, because it is important to him, and because what's important to him matters. Usually you go to a short home series, three games over a

weekend, and when he's not playing or lifting weights or sitting in an ice bath the two of you do the things Rodney enjoys: hot dog lunches, movies, and single-A baseball games. Despite the fact that he already spends 90 percent of his waking moments engaged in baseball in one way or another, for reasons that are mysterious even to us he likes to spend his downtime watching the Kane County Cougars, who play out of Geneva. The first time you go with him to a game at Elfstrom Stadium someone recognizes him and the next thing you know even the players are coming out with pens and baseballs, asking for autographs. Rodney handles this attention with the sort of grace and humility that have always put him way over the head of you or anyone else who could smoke him on an IQ test.

47 By the time Amy has earned her B.A. you've risen to senior agriculture director at Oxfam, and as she begins the law program at Boston University you find yourself very much interested in water. Obsessed with it, in fact: its properties, its functions, how to produce it, and how to get it where people need it to be.

It's this last conundrum—how to get water where people need it to be—that is on your mind when you take a trip to South Africa to test a small, manually operated pump you've developed that can draw water from as deep as sixty feet and irrigate almost three acres. Most experts believe a pump that doesn't run on expensive fuel or electricity can't go any deeper than thirty feet, and when they discover how young you are, they're even more skeptical. You've brought one hundred of these pumps with you to test with maize farmers in the KwaZulu-Natal midlands, hoping to prove the experts wrong. If this thing works—which it will—you'll be looking at a conservative estimate of half a million poor farmers made suddenly viable by a single piece of equipment that sells for twenty bucks and costs nothing to operate.

You planned the trip to coincide with Amy's Christmas break so she could come along, and she is more than eager, accompanying you on the long rough rides overland from Howick to the maize fields. She walks the rows and gets down in the dirt, and after watching you do your routine a few times, she starts helping teach Zulu farmers the fairly simple workings of the pump. You're happy for her company, as always, but after a week she takes sick and spends the next few days alternately in bed or in the bathroom. At first you stay with her at the hostel, but she eventually insists that she's fine, you should be out doing the work you came here for, and we have to admit we're surprised that as well as you know Amy you seem unaware that she wants you out of there not just because she's concerned about your work, but because she hates to be doted on, especially when she's sick and craves only darkness, silence, and solitude. Listen: she simply wants you to leave her alone. And so, vaguely hurt, you do, returning to the farms by day, but you are preoccupied with your concern for Amy, her refusal to see a doctor and your fear that she's contracted something serious. And this distraction causes problems, e.g., one afternoon you're trying with your very limited Afrikaans to convince a Zulu granny to allow you onto her son's farmland, and through the entire clumsy negotiation you can think of nothing but Amy lying alone in the darkness of the hostel room, unable to eat now for five days, and the granny hollers and gesticulates wildly and finally chases you back to the Range Rover with a broom.

By the end of your second week there, however, Amy's condition improves to the point that she expresses renewed interest in a hiking trip you'd planned to Howick Falls. Ecstatic that she is well again, you immediately schedule a couple of off days, and you hire a Jeep to take you to the falls trailhead, where you disembark.

46 The two of you hike the gorge trail, about one leisurely hour down through the forest to the base of the falls, where the Umgeni River plummets three hundred feet to form a wide pool of olive-green water ringed with rocks. Compared with how it will flow in February, at the end of the rainy season, the falls is a trickle right now, but still hitting the pool with enough force to send up a misty miniature rainbow. To either side of the falls the small trees and shrubs are beginning to green up with the return of the rains.

You find a large rock with a more or less flat top and take your lunch out of a small backpack: smoked fish, chicken pie, lots of bottled water, malva pudding for Amy's still-queasy stomach. You spread a towel on the rock and set out the food and eat in silence, watching two figures climb slowly up the rock face to the left of the falls. The figures are far enough up the face that you can't tell if they're men or women. What you can see for certain is that they're free climbing, no ropes. This realization gives you a bit of a jolt, and you look at Amy, about to ask her to confirm what you're seeing, when you catch her rubbing at her belly and grimacing, the half-eaten cup of pudding resting on the rock in front of her.

"Hey," you say, putting down your piece of chicken pie. "You okay?"

"Fine," Amy says, though it's clear she's anything but.

"Okay, this is going to stop. You're seeing a doctor."

She leans over the side of the rock and spits, breathing hard with her eyes closed tight. "Junior, not right now."

"No more discussion," you say. "When we get back to town you're going to the clinic."

"I don't need to go to the clinic," Amy says. The nausea abates a bit, and she sits back up and leans forward with her head in her hand. "There's nothing wrong with me."

"How can you sit there like you are and say there's nothing wrong?"

She lifts her head and looks at you. "You're going to make me say it, aren't you?"

"Say what?"

"I wanted to wait until we got home. I didn't want you to be distracted. Although now you're distracted anyway, so I guess I might as well spill."

"I have no idea what you're talking about."

She manages to smile at you, not unkindly. "Why doesn't that surprise me?" she says. "For such a smart guy, sometimes you can be pretty dumb." You raise your eyebrows, impatient, expectant, and she takes a breath and says, "I'm pregnant, kid."

45 Anyone else would have seen this coming, but you are the very picture of surprise. You could not be more shocked if Amy suddenly sloughed off her human disguise and revealed herself to be a six-limbed insectoid extraterrestrial. And it's not as though you're dealing with only the usual misgivings and fear one experiences upon discovering he's about to become a father for the first time. Because there is, of course, the Destroyer of Worlds to consider. You thought you were finished with It, but in reality It was just offstage, waiting for this moment to make a surprise reappearance, like the evil matriarch on a soap opera who keeps dying and coming back under ever more improbable circumstances. Now suddenly It wants to shake you down again, threaten your unborn child and leave you doubting all that you've built up in your new life.

People say it all the time: "I could never bring a child into this world." From your perspective, of course, they know not in the least of what they speak. Compared to the stark terror you're suddenly experiencing, generic concerns about war, environmental degradation, and the decline of empire would be positively welcome.

Naturally we understand how you feel, but you must be careful how much of this you allow to show on your face. Amy is watching you closely, and we recommend that you gather your wits and give her a response, immediately and in the affirmative.

"That's amazing," you say, not at all convincingly.

"Wow. Weak," Amy says, and you should not allow this sarcasm to blind you to her hurt.

44 When you return to town you've recovered enough from your shock to check out of the hostel you've been staying in and rent the best room you can find. You lead Amy up the stairs and invite her to shower with you. She declines, citing her upset stomach, but you should know the real reason is she wants nothing to do with you after your tepid response to her announcement. You go into the bathroom alone, turn the shower on and let it run a few minutes while you undress. You pass your hand through the stream to make sure the temperature's good

and then you get in. You soap and rinse. There are terrycloth robes in the bathroom closet, embroidered with the first letter of the hotel's name, and you put one on. You find Amy already in bed, turned on her side with her back to you. You get in and try to put your hand on her waist, but she pushes it off and flips you a backwards bird.

It is important that you say something, not just for the future of your relationship with Amy, but because common decency dictates it. You're not the only one with mixed feelings here. Amy is lying close enough to touch you but feeling very much alone, frightened suddenly by the child growing in her belly, and angered by your reaction to it.

"I guess we should probably start discussing names," you say. Not perfect, but it's a start. "Because you know, if history is any indication it'll probably take a while for us to reach an agreement."

After a long pause, Amy responds without turning around. "We don't know what it is yet."

"Simple," you say. "Two lists. Boy names, girl names. If and when we decide to discover our fate, we chuck one list and revise the other."

Another long pause, but this time she rolls onto her back. She still refuses to look at you. "Do you think we ought to try to make this kid legitimate?" she asks the air above the bed.

"Probably." You venture to gently tuck a strand of hair behind her ear, and she allows you to do so.

Suddenly she laughs, but it sounds more like a sigh. "I'm sorry," she says, patting her still-flat belly. "This thing is making me crazy. No joke. It's true, what they say. I am cuckoo for Cocoa Puffs, right at the moment."

"Well I think you get a free pass on that, considering."

Finally she turns to you and puts her head on your shoulder. "Yeah, huh. We'll see if you're singing the same tune a few months from now, buster."

You lie together like this for hours, and though it doesn't take long for her breathing to become slow and regular, for you sleep does not come quite so easily. You stare at the ceiling until the day ends and the room grows dim, and then you stare into the darkness.

43 When you return to Boston the first thing you do, other than unpack your things and fill the refrigerator with fresh groceries, is get married. Because of the haste, and because as a rule neither of you cares much for fuss or ritual, the wedding is a small and secular matter, presided over by a notary whose day job is dispatching for the Boston police, witnessed only by your parents and Rodney and Amy's brother, who since his days of smacking around their mother has quit the drugs and is now selling real estate in San Francisco. In lieu of a reception you have dinner at the Olive Garden, where you explain quietly to Rodney why you weren't married in the church. Your father and Amy's brother, meeting for the first time, actually seem to hit it off. You've never seen the old man talk so much.

42 A few months later you and Amy thumb-wrestle to resolve a long-standing debate over whether to learn the baby's sex, and you inexplicably lose a best of three, so the two of you go to the OB/GYN where the tech smears Amy's belly with gel, runs the hand unit over the burgeoning swell, and says, "It's a girl." These three words hit you with the sort of force you haven't experienced since we first told you of the Destroyer of Worlds. You're not sure if your reaction would be different if you were having a boy, but the uneasy peace you've made with the idea of bringing a child into a doomed world is suddenly shattered. You leave the exam room with Amy still on the table, and for the first time in this or any other life you go, as an adult, into a church. The storefront chapel down the block from the clinic is the size of a rich person's living room, with a narrow aisle flanked by three small pews on either side, and some perfunctory stained glass. It's a far cry from the yawning majesty of the church of your youth. You don't know what you're hoping to gain by coming here—enlightenment, or guidance, or courage, maybe all three—but none of those things are on offer today, at least not in the McChurch. After an hour you have no better idea than you had going in whether or not you are doing the right thing.

But ask yourself: at this point, twenty-five weeks into gestation, what does it matter? Short of a gruesome, dangerous, and morally suspect procedure onboard a specially modified former fishing boat in international waters, this thing is happening. And so your energies would probably be better spent on refining that list of girls' names, which thanks to Amy includes such horrors as Ruby and Imogen.

41 Ruby Imogen Thibodeau is born by cesarean section on a rainy June morning in a birthing suite at Beth Israel. You are the fourth person to hold her, after the doctor, a nurse, and Amy, but you hold her the longest of them all. She is either the grandest thing you've ever done, or the cruelest.

Our contention, for the record, is that it's possible she may be both.

40 Before you know it Amy and Ruby have been discharged and suddenly you are at home with fifty disposable diapers, no-tears shampoo, a handful of feeding bottles, and a seven-pound nine-ounce lump of utterly helpless flesh that relies on you practically minute to minute for its survival. No doctors. No nurses. Just you.

You feel like a fugitive. You're convinced that every time you put your hands on Ruby you're about to screw up irreparably. Whenever she cries, which is often, you feel to blame. When she spits up it's because you're feeding her wrong, and when she develops a rash it's because you don't change her diaper often enough. Of course, every new parent goes through this, but for you the sense of being a complete and even dangerous failure persists far longer than is normal.

39 For her part, Ruby does very little to help you out. Whenever she's left with you she kicks and punches at the air, screaming until she chokes. What's particularly vexing is that she's a model citizen for everyone else: Amy, her girlfriends from school, even Rodney, in whose huge arms Ruby is as placid as a tranquilized turtle.

Ruby's distaste for you is especially unfortunate because you've agreed to put your work with Oxfam on hold for the next year and stay at home while Amy tries to cram the rest of her graduate work into two semesters. At the end of a week you're hoping against hope that Amy can somehow cram it into one. Out of desperation you call

Rodney, whose offseason is just beginning, and ask if he'd like to come visit for a week, maybe two, a month even, or perhaps until spring training begins. He agrees, of course, because he gets lonely easily and is always looking for an excuse to come stay with you and Amy.

Still, it's more a reprieve than a permanent solution, for any number of reasons, not the least of which is that you'd like to be able to care for your daughter with your own hands. Instead you feel like you've been slapped with a restraining order as you watch her luxuriating in your brother's arms, smiling that weird toothless baby smile.

You should consider the possibility that there is something wrong with you, something fundamental and hidden, detectable only by small children. What other explanation could there be? Ruby is an absolute kitten with everyone else, even complete strangers. One of Amy's professors comes to dinner and holds Ruby up high in the air and sings songs and makes little farting noises with her lips against Ruby's bare belly, and Ruby cackles with joy throughout. She's so happy she drools everywhere. The professor laughs and says, "Sorry, I get carried away with the little ones," and when she moves to hand Ruby off you recoil as if the child were a black mamba. The professor sits there holding Ruby at arm's length for a few beats, looking ever more mortified, until Amy throws her napkin on her plate and rushes around the table to take the baby.

"You *are* the father, right?" the professor cracks.

"We never did a blood test," you answer, annoyed. The professor stares at you in incredulous horror.

"You are such a jackass," Amy says, but because she can never not appreciate a solid zinger she's got all she can do to suppress a smile.

After a couple more months of screeching and flailing, of spilled formula and flung puree, you are filled to bursting with heartache and confusion. You begin to resent Amy, which you know is unfair without us having to tell you. At night sometimes you get up and go to Ruby's room and watch her sleep, marvel at how calm and still and tiny she is, and you dig your nails into the palms of your hands and wonder just what the fuck is wrong with you, what you are doing wrong. To which we say: at least you are finally asking the right questions, which is a start.

38 Then, just as you're prepared to raise the white flag, Ruby establishes a sort of cease-fire. Suddenly, in your arms she no longer cries out or bludgeons the air with little fists. She accepts the bottle and spoon, albeit begrudgingly, and stops fighting during diaper changes. But there is no joy between you. When your hands are on her she is stiff and silent, her eyes always avoiding yours. Worse than this, though, is the way she returns instantly to life when Amy comes home or Rodney takes her. The message could not be clearer: she tolerates you, but nothing more.

37 When Ruby's first birthday rolls around the celebration is twofold, as it's also a graduation party for Amy. Six months earlier you would have been ecstatic, but now all you feel is a sad sort of relief to be freed from Ruby's newfound indifference to you. You dutifully snap pictures with the digital camera as Amy helps Ruby blow out the candles, and you think now at least you'll be able to go back to work for people who are appreciative. Immediately—and, we might add, appropriately—you feel like shit for thinking such things as you watch your daughter smear cream cheese frosting on your wife's nose.

You have no idea what to do about any of it, so you leave things as they are and go back to Oxfam. Your old position couldn't be left vacant, so you're working now under the purposely vague title of senior field consultant, a position created by the vice president with your unique and varied abilities in mind. The "field" in senior field consultant means, of course, that you're required to be out of the country a lot: Africa, mostly, but also shorter stints in drought-stricken Uzbekistan, and Honduras following Hurricane Mitch.

36 Water is still your thing. The contradiction between the simple math— 70 percent of the planet covered in the stuff, some 326 million trillion gallons—and the frequent impossibility of getting it where it's needed

in a form that won't kill people makes you furious. Unlike the situation with Ruby, though, this is a problem you can work with. When a dysentery outbreak kills two hundred in Kampala, you hop a red-eye to Uganda and arrive at Kampala's city hall unannounced. You force your way into the office of the mayor, Henry Muliira, and inquire after the thirty million UN dollars that were supposed to be spent on a modern water supply network. Naturally Henry is evasive, because when his government received the grant two years ago it was promptly laundered through the Finance Ministry, then deposited in the Cayman Island accounts of half a dozen city and national officials—including him. Of course Henry doesn't know that you know this.

Getting no answers and little satisfaction, you drive with your team to the Kamwanyi slum, the worst hit of the districts, and while the medical workers hang IV bags and issue antibiotics, you hand out bottles with built-in biological filters and explain to anyone who will listen about the importance of boiling the water from Lake Victoria before using it for drinking or bathing.

35   After a week, exhausted and demoralized, you call Amy. You tell her about the babies bathed in their own bloody feces, their skin shriveled from dehydration. You tell her about Henry and how you wanted to reach over the desk and dig your thumbs into his eyes, and she says, "Jesus, Junior, come home before you get yourself killed."

34   The next morning you hop a scary turboprop plane to London. The earliest flight out of Gatwick with an available seat is going to Portland, so you fly there instead of Boston. By the time you touch down you've got six messages in your voice mail from Oxfam's vice president, each one successively more shrill, wanting to know just what in the fuck you're doing threatening foreign officials. You rent a car and head south on narrow, dirty Route 1, a gauntlet of filling stations, motels, Elks lodges and shuttered strip clubs. After a while you get queasy from the blowing trash and dirty half-melted snowbanks and begin to wish you'd taken I-95, but then the Boston skyline looms up gray and an-

gular and you take the Tobin Bridge to Storrow Drive, which runs clean and brisk along the Charles, and soon you're home.

Amy meets you at the door. She's smiling but looks weary around the eyes. She's got Ruby, who sports a full and lengthening head of her mother's tight brown curls, slung over one hip. Amy wraps her free arm around your neck and hugs you hard. You lean in toward your daughter, but she turns away and you end up kissing the back of her head. She smells like A&D lotion, and under that, vanilla.

Amy invites you out for dinner to celebrate your homecoming, and you agree even though the queasiness dogging you on the drive in has blossomed, and you feel like you've swallowed a couple pounds of wet paper towel. She looks around for the babysitter's phone number but you want to bring Ruby along.

"It's getting late," Amy says. "And she hasn't had a nap."

"We'll make it quick," you say. "I haven't seen *her* for a month either, you know."

33 The three of you go to the Houlihan's at the galleria mall. It's nothing special, but it is quick and quiet on a weekday night. Amy orders the chicken enchiladas and a beer. Though you have no intention of eating you order the bruschetta appetizer, for form's sake. You're more interested in feeding Ruby, who sits strapped into a high chair at the end of the booth, slapping the tabletop with the palms of her hands. She knows when it's time to eat.

Her excitement is diminished, though, when it becomes clear that you're the one who will be feeding her. You ask the waitress for a small bowl, whip together a combination of apple and pear purees, and offer it up. At first Ruby refuses. To the young couple in the booth adjacent to yours, it looks a lot like any other parent negotiating at dinnertime with a fussy baby, but of course both you and Amy know the subtext here. You coax, waving the spoon around, making moronic noises. Amy sips her beer and watches and resists the urge to relieve her own mild heartache by taking the bowl and spoon and feeding Ruby herself.

Eventually Ruby's hunger wins out, and she yields with the same resentful slowness with which she accepts anything from you, from baths to bottles to Earl the plush elephant. Amy tries several times to start a conversation. She asks about Mongolia, where you were recently testing a new drip irrigation design. She tells you the nerve problem your mother was having in her shoulder has gotten worse, and the only thing the doctors can think to do is exploratory surgery. But nearly all your attention is focused on Ruby, and you barely respond, so Amy stops trying to engage you and instead gazes aimlessly around the dining room. She's hoping that the food will show up soon so she'll have something to occupy herself with and she won't have to keep sitting here pretending not to notice how much Ruby loathes you, because even though life has equipped her with some fairly solid psychic armor, this has never shielded her from the rude and sorrowful shock of the fact that her daughter hates her husband. It hurts her, every time, especially when she sees how doggedly you still carry out all the simple duties of fatherhood, never wavering in your dedication to Ruby even as the kid repeatedly stomps your heart.

32 So this is the scene: you're in this generic chain restaurant, waiting for a meal you don't want, alone among the two people you love most in the world, your wife watching football highlights—football!—on the television over the bar, and your daughter displaying toward you the sort of disdain you would never before have imagined a fourteen-month-old could be capable of, when with a few loud and ominous gurgles the nauseous weight in your stomach drops violently, and you very nearly shit your pants right there at the table.

You scramble to the bathroom and fumble with your belt and finally get your pants down at the last possible instant. You writhe and moan and press your head against the cool tile wall behind the toilet. During a glorious if brief lull in the action, as you grasp your knees and brace yourself for the second round, the cause of your sudden distress comes to you, as clear as it is obvious: you've got dysentery.

More disturbing still, and forgive us for pointing this out but it's important that you know: You've got a strain of dysentery that in the current Ugandan outbreak is holding steady at a frightening 20 percent mortality rate. In a related item, you just finished feeding your daughter her dinner. With your bare hands.

Your head feels hot and loose on your shoulders, as though it's about to pop off and float away, and you lean back against the wall again and try to collect yourself and think. Your brain wants to spend this crucial time chastising itself for not being more careful while you were in Kampala. Also for not taking the basic and essential precaution of waiting a few days in London to make sure you weren't sick before coming home to your wife and baby from an outbreak zone. For God's sake you couldn't even find a flight to Boston; it was like someone was trying to tell you to stay away, and perhaps, we would suggest, someone was.

In any event, we understand your frustration, but you need to stop worrying about what's done and start worrying about the current set of circumstances. The instant you do this you remember the phone in your pants pocket.

It takes Amy five rings to pick up. "Why are you calling me from the bathroom?" she asks, and then, after a pause: "You are still in the bathroom, right?"

"Yes. Listen, you need to take Ruby and go to the hospital."

"What? I just got my enchiladas," she says. At the mention of this you picture a plate mounded with refried beans and smeared with melted queso, and your stomach bypasses the backflip and instead performs an entire parallel bar routine. "What are you doing?"

"Listen to me. I'm calling from the bathroom because I can't leave the toilet," you say. "I can't put it any more plainly than that. I've got dysentery and I just fed Ruby her dinner. Are you following me?"

"Oh," Amy says. "Oh, *shit*, Junior."

"Very funny. Plus I've kissed you several times. We held hands, et cetera. So you need to get your things together and go—" You stop short, paralyzed by a cramp like God Himself reaching in and squeezing your guts.

"Junior?"

"I'm here," you say. "Go to the hospital and tell them what's happening. They need to start you both on antibiotics."

"What about you?"

"This can't go on forever," you say. "At least I hope not. Sooner or later it's got to let up some, and when it does I'll catch a cab and follow you there. Go to Mass General. They've got the best infectious disease people."

"Junior, stop being ridiculous," she says. You hear the sound of silverware on porcelain as she stands up from the table. "I'm coming in there. We'll wait for this to pass and get you cleaned up. Then we'll all go together."

And though you didn't want to, you now have to explain to her about the unusually high mortality rate, and how it is due in part to the fact that this strain of shigella is drug-resistant. You also have to remind her that, as with most diseases, the burden of mortality is borne in large part by two demographics: the very old, and the very young. You do not need to explain to her the significance of this last fact, as it pertains to your situation.

Amy agrees to go without you, but before leaving she says she's going to tell the restaurant manager what's going on, in case you need help. She hangs up before you have a chance to protest this, which is fortunate, because ten minutes later you pass out from dehydration and electrolyte imbalance, and if not for the manager reluctantly coming in to check on you who knows how long you would have sat slumped against the side of the stall.

31 The manager calls an ambulance and you end up not at Mass General, but Mount Auburn. The ER doctors want to ask you questions, but you're delirious from fever and dehydration, so they hang a bag of saline and wait for you to come around. When you're able to tell them what's happening they decide to take a fecal culture, which afterward you wish they'd gone ahead and done *before* bringing you back to lucidity. While they're waiting for the results of the culture they start you on the standard treatment for dysentery, which is ampicillin, and which you tell them is not going to work. But like most doctors they are (a) passionately in love with their protocols, and (b) deaf to most of what comes out of their patients' mouths, so ampicillin it is.

30 During the nearly twenty-four hours it takes for the test results to come back your temperature spikes to over 105 degrees, dangerously close to fatal, and the nurses pack your bed with ice and open up two saline drips, one in each arm, yet still can't keep you hydrated. Amy hunts you down and arrives at Mount Auburn to tell you that she's on oral antibiotics as a precaution but Mass General is holding Ruby for observation for a couple of days even though so far she's shown no signs of being ill. You're distantly aware of and grateful for Amy's presence, but none of what she's telling you really registers, because you are trapped in a fever world your mind has created, and in that world this is what's happening:

29 You are at Ruby's bedside in a very large, featureless hospital room with an overhead fluorescent and a large bare window looking out on Beacon Hill. There is nothing at all wrong with you, but Ruby is so sick that her crying produces no tears. She's turned pink with fever. Doctors and nurses come in, observe, listen, palpate, notate, and leave again. Day and night trade places several times outside the window, but little else changes. Ruby continues to cry, her skin the color of a steamed lobster. The same doctors and nurses come in, perform their listless duties, leave again. Occasionally you rise from your seat and go to the window and look out on the city. You're up so high that you have to press your face against the glass to see down to the street. People move in clusters on the sidewalks, go into and out of shops and restaurants, play Ultimate Frisbee in the park. Every day for a week the sun shines cheerfully, and people who from this height seem never to have experienced sadness go about their important and happy lives. Eventually it is too much and you turn away and sit again by Ruby's side. At night you leave the fluorescent on to mute the cheerful twinkling of the city lights through the window, and find yourself wishing often that there were curtains you could draw to block them out completely.

28 In the dream Ruby continues to cry without end. The large empty room overflows with her keening. It's a sound not of pain, nor of sorrow, but of fear. And the fear is not hers, you come to realize, but yours.

Finally the sound ends when Ruby dies. It happens early on the morning of the eighth day, while you are dozing in the chair, and at first the sudden silence is the only indication that anything has changed. You open your eyes and see she's still bright pink, her limbs still stiff and angry, tiny fists clenched against her chest—the same posture she's displayed since the ordeal began. Slowly, though, her body begins to relax. The pink runs out of her like watercolor rinsing away, and her legs and arms settle to the mattress. Her face softens and goes slack, the little mouth slightly agape and white with dryness, and for a moment you are reminded, horribly, of old roadkill lying on its back in a gutter. You lift Ruby from the bed—it's the first time you've touched her—and as you hold her to your chest you can feel the warmth leaving her body already, a cruel irony given that she was killed by fever.

It's another cruel irony that this is the only time she's ever been still in your arms.

You rock her for a while. The sun rises fully over the city outside, and the doctors and nurses come in. Now that Ruby's dead they try to offer you comfort and reassure you they did all they could, even though you were here the whole time and saw for yourself how very little was done. But even if you felt their condolences were sincere you wouldn't be inclined to accept them. You find, strangely, that you feel no need to be comforted, that you are in fact somehow buttressed by your sorrow, and all you really want is to take your daughter and leave this place.

So that's what you do.

You grab a blanket from the bed and wrap it around her, then walk out of the room and down the hall to the elevator banks. The doctors and nurses stand around you in a semicircle, saying you can't do this, there are procedures that need to be followed, paperwork that needs filling out and filing, but you ignore this, and when you're tired of listening you push through them and take the stairs. The doctors and nurses follow. Sixteen floors to ground level, with their protests echoing down through the stairwell. You come out into the lobby, which is cavernous, with marble floors and balconies and skylights, more like an imperial palace than a hospital. As you approach the revolving doors that lead out into the world the doctors and nurses call for security, and two uniformed guards step in front of you, blocking your way. You can't do anything to fight them with both your hands on Ruby. So instead you lean close to one of the guards and whisper to him. You say, "We made a mistake. We spent too much time trying to hide from the inevitable. I thought I was done with that, but I wasn't. Now I want my daughter to feel the sun on her. While she's still not too far from here. Do you understand?"

But the guard does not. He's staunch, unmoved in every sense.

"It was my mistake," you say. You hold Ruby's body out to the guard, as an appeal, and as evidence of your guilt, and he takes a step back. At first he looks at Ruby as if she's a bag of rotten garbage you've asked him to dispose of, but then, after a few seconds, something in his face shifts, softens, and he steps aside and lets you through.

27 You wake in a quarantine room at Mount Auburn and see Amy and Ruby on the other side of the glass, and you are bathed in relief. Amy notices you are awake and she lifts Ruby's arm and waggles it at you, a pantomime of a wave: *Hi, Daddy.*

26 Five days later, when the CDC doctor gives the okay, you are released from the hospital. The first thing you do is kiss Amy on the cheek, and the second thing you do is take Ruby from her. You hold Ruby precisely as you had in the dream, and she nestles against you and goggles at the world as you leave the hospital, staring up at the rooftops, grasping at strangers' lapels and mustaches and takeout lunches. For anyone else it would be a mundane thing, having a happy baby on their shoulder, but you have never experienced a moment quite like it. Your joy is matched only by Amy's shock; she walks beside you and stares in disbelief, even crashing into the end of a bench and skinning her knee. The three of you stop and sit on the bench while Amy fumes and swears and blows on the scrape to cool it. When she's finished she turns to you again and asks, "What the heck is going on here, with you two? I want answers."

You smile at her. "I don't think I could explain it if I tried."

"Try," Amy says. She makes a funny face at Ruby, who grins and squeals and turns away, playing hide.

"Okay. When I was sick, I had this dream. And I figured something out. That help?"

"Nope."

"I told you."

Ruby, of course, just takes it all in stride. So to speak.

25   But as the years pass this does not remain true. Not surprisingly, she turns out to be fairly precocious, and by the time she's four she's reading at a ninth-grade level and devours any text she can get her hands on, from Shakespeare to shampoo bottles. This is not a problem, of course, until a stormy day in January when her preschool is canceled due to snow and so instead you walk hand-in-mittened-hand with her to the public library on Broadway. You spend the afternoon sitting at a table near the window and flipping through back issues of *Rolling Stone* and the *Economist*, while Ruby reads Choose Your Own Adventure books almost as quickly as they can be pulled and reshelved.

For some reason, on one of Ruby's return trips to the stacks, the CYOA series loses her interest and she fixates, instead, on a book titled *And Then There Was One: The Mysteries of Extinction*. Twenty minutes later you look up from a brief about sham elections in Congo to find her crying quietly across the table.

"Baby?" you say. You put your magazine down and move around the table to sit next to her. "Hey."

And at the sound of your voice she stops trying to control her weeping and yields to it. It's the sort of pure, inconsolable grief that only children are capable of, and as you try in vain to comfort her and field glances from other library patrons ranging from concern to annoyance to suspicion, in the back of your mind you are reminded of a day from your own childhood involving prophesies, stock footage of nuclear weapons tests, and your own overwhelming grief.

Of course Ruby is not grieving for all of creation, merely the savaged environment and the animals that call it home. Still, as you were transformed back then, so now is she transformed. She quickly develops an encompassing interest in environmental causes. She begins carrying a tattered, heavily annotated copy of *Silent Spring* pretty much everywhere she goes, partly because she likes to have it at hand, and partly because she's found that people are curious about a little girl carrying around such heavy reading, which provides her with just the opening she needs to push her agenda. When she isn't busy with schoolwork she spends most of her time engaged in sober research or writing letters to politicians. At night, in bed, Amy worries out loud about her. You try to reassure her, and this reassurance is genuine, because there is an important difference between who you became when you first saw the Destroyer of Worlds, and who Ruby has become now: she is still happy, still quick to laugh, and that, more than anything, is what matters.

24 A few years later, when your father is diagnosed with cancer, you do not try to cure him. Instead you let the doctors do what little they can, and leave the loft in Cambridge with Amy and Ruby and move back to Maine to tend to him while he dies.

At first, though, he doesn't require any care. Most people would have difficulty reconciling the still-muscular, hulking man with the fact of his death sentence, but you are not at all surprised when you arrive home and find him pulling fence posts in the front yard without aid of tools or machinery. He is your father, after all, John Senior, a figure nearly as powerful as the Destroyer of Worlds itself; how else would you find him? He doesn't notice you and for a while you stand there watching as he works the posts loose with his bare hands, though really his hands can't properly be referred to as bare, because years of ceaseless work in all manner of weather have toughened the skin to the point where gloves would be redundant. When the posts are loosened sufficiently he squats sumo-style and yanks them free with an upward jerk so powerful that dirt flies up as if cherry bombs were going off in the post holes. Eventually you make your presence known and he shakes your hand and the two of you stand there on the lawn for a moment, looking everywhere but at each other. You feign interest in the fence posts lying on the ground, in the flags flying from the pole overhead—the stars and stripes, as well as a black POW banner—and then you ask if he wants some help and he says Sure, there are gloves in the garage if you need them.

This is as close as you will ever come to discussing his illness. You find the gloves, and put them on, and get to work.

23   For months after, this is how things are. Your father remains your father, and he does everything he's always done, and you relax in his shadow, tiny and grateful and safe. For a while you even believe it's possible he will beat this on his own, that he is simply too strong to be killed by something as mindless and piddling as mutated cells. But then one evening in November you go to dinner at the Olive Garden and when the meal is finished he cannot stand up from his seat, and suddenly you notice how the sweatshirt hangs limp from his shoulders, how he's run out of holes on his belt, and you wonder where did that portable oxygen tank come from and why is he so gray and Jesus what on earth is happening to my dad?

He needs a hand up from his seat, but because he's proud he tries to signal you to just hold down the table, keep it from tipping over while he uses it for leverage. You can see that's not going to work, so you stand and move behind him and put your hands under his armpits, and he looks like he'll weigh no more than a bucket of ash so you are surprised to find he's quite heavy even now, and as you help him rise you can feel his muscles working, weak but defiant, refusing to wither away altogether no matter what biology tells them. You give him a little extra, too, kind of lifting him off his feet for a moment, because you want him to feel your strength and know that he did a good job, that he created and raised a man in his own image.

But you fall short, inevitably, inevitably. Because whereas in your situation your father would do whatever was required of him without hesitation or exception—without really even thinking—there are times, now that he actually requires care, when you balk and fail. One such occasion: Until recently he was able to take off his own clothes and get himself up on the table for his weekly massage, but now he is too frail, and the job falls to you and Karen the massage therapist. Until this moment you have not seen him naked, but you have seen how angular he is under his clothes, the hint of his wasted body, and you are afraid. You help him up from the couch and guide him to the table. Even with his oxygen cranked to five liters the walk of ten feet and two stairs has him gasping. You keep him standing long enough for you to get his pants unfastened and down, and then he collapses to the table. His legs are pixie sticks, candy cigarettes. You could easily wrap your hand all the way around his thigh. He tries to swing his legs onto the table but he can't get them up all the way, and you hesitate, not wanting to take from him even the smallest thing, but then he says "I can't," and you lift his legs for him one at a time with grief rising in you like a throatful of vomit.

He lies down, exhausted, before you realize that he still has his T-shirt on. You ask him to sit up again, which is almost too much even though you and Karen help him. You wrangle the shirt over his head, hurrying because you don't want to touch his wasted body. You twist his arms behind him and pull and stretch the shirt, revealing the bruised chest, the belly fat with tumors, the wispy black hairs. You lay him back down, trying to avoid touching his bones, but that's all he is now, bones and skin. You light the fireplace, burning with shame at your cowardice, as Karen sets to work.

22 Then comes the night before your father dies, a cold Wednesday in December. You've just tucked Ruby in underneath her Captain Planet comforter when the phone rings. From the other end your mother tells you that she needs help; she was able to get your father to the toilet but now can't get him off. It takes you twenty minutes to drive to their house over dark country roads glazed with black ice, twenty minutes during which you cannot stop thinking about your father sitting with his pajama pants around his ankles and his bare feet on the cold linoleum, the best and proudest man you will ever know in this or any other version of your life, waiting in shame to be lifted off the toilet while his knees clack together with the chill.

You cannot drive fast enough.

You let yourself in the front door, hoping though you know better that in the time it's taken you to drive here your father has somehow found the strength to get himself up. No one's in the living room, so you walk down the hall and into the bathroom, where you find your parents exactly as you'd feared: your father on the toilet, head down, your mother crouched on the floor in front of him, her hand over his.

"Okay," you say, trying to sound decisive, proactive, up to the task. You move past your mother and squeeze into the narrow space between the wall and the toilet. "Okay."

You crouch in front of your father and look into his eyes and what you see there very nearly breaks you. "Dad," you say. "I'm going to pick you up, all right?" He drops his gaze and nods. You slide your hands under his arms and try gingerly to find the best purchase, though there is no gentle way to lift a grown man. Your mother's still on her haunches to the left side of the toilet, ready to pull your father's pants up once he's on his feet. She swipes at her eyes with the back of her hand.

"Here we go, Dad," you say. You straighten your back, as if observing proper form for lifting a heavy package, and you push with your thighs and your father gasps and then you are both up. His legs are completely dead and you're supporting all his weight, which is difficult while you have him at arm's length, so you wrap him in a bear hug and clasp your hands behind his back. This close you're forced to press your head against his chest and so you're looking straight down and you see things that will visit you every day from now until the world ends: his legs trembling so violently that in any other context it would be comical; your mother cursing as she tries to pull the pajama bottoms out from under his feet; the toilet bowl, glimpsed between his knees, full of blood.

Even after your mother succeeds in getting his pants up and fastened there is still the question of how to move him from here to the bed. He gestures toward the walker—because of a tumor pressing against his vocal cords he's lost his voice almost completely, and gesturing is pretty much all he can do now—but you know that's not going to happen, because whatever strength he had to get himself in here has abandoned him completely. Listen: you know without having to be told that there's only one choice, and every second you stand here trying to pretend there's some alternative is a season in hell for your father.

"Dad, I'm going to carry you, okay?" you say. He shakes his head and waves his hand again at the walker, wheezing in frustration, but you've made your decision and you tell your mother to get out of the way. She moves back toward the bedroom as you bend at the waist. With your right arm under his shoulders and your left behind his knees you lift, and as he rises so does a memory, at once incongruous and plainly fitting: you as a boy of seven or eight, asleep on the sofa after convincing your mother to let you stay up late to watch the *Creature Double Feature* on WLVI, waking to the smell of warehouse dust and the feel of his huge hands under you as he carried you to bed.

Suddenly your father finds his voice. He moans and cries and writhes in slow-motion in your arms, and you stand there stupidly, looking down at him, instead of moving toward the bed. He's crying because he's in pain, of course—monstrous pain, brought by you to a mind-erasing crescendo. Pain he's been denying for the last three months whenever you or your mother asked him if he had any discomfort. Pain so terrible that by the time you actually get your feet moving he has, mercifully, passed out and gone limp in your arms.

You place him in the bed, thinking: *gentle. Gentle. Gentle.*

21 Because you are a coward, rather than spend the night you leave your mother alone with him and head back into town. You drive around the empty streets, smoking cigarettes. The first time you pass You Know Whose Pub is genuine happenstance. The second you wonder what sort of subterfuge your reptile brain is up to. The third time you pull over into the dirty slush by the curb and sit, engine idling, trying to figure out what it is you're doing, exactly. You stare at the bar's tired façade: greasy glass door smeared with a thousand fingerprints, neon sign atop the awning, draped with old cobwebs even in winter. From the single window a jaundiced light emanates, giving the bar's interior the look of an aquarium filled with urine. The muffled baseline of "You Give Love a Bad Name" thumps through the brick exterior.

You light a cigarette and crack the window and sit there for a few minutes longer, thinking. Then you get out of the car, flick your cigarette into the gutter, and step in out of the cold. Over the blare of Bon Jovi you ask for a double of anything. What you end up with is supposed to be bourbon, near as you can tell.

As the liquor slides down and begins to warm you, the one thought you've been avoiding through your father's illness rises up and flits about your brain like an angry wasp: You could have stopped this from happening. You could have prevented this. You could have kept it from being so. You had the foreknowledge and you had the means.

You did nothing.

20 If we may interject here for a moment? Because already you're ten fingers deep into the bourbon, and in real danger of ruining the life you've spent two lifetimes working for. It's our contention that in this version of things you have in fact done plenty. Plenty. You want to talk about could have? How about this: We gave you infinite options, and you could have easily chosen to live in a world free of both comets and cancer. You could have sidestepped those heartaches, and certainly we would not have blamed you. You chose instead to suffer every same calamity and anguish a second time—chose, in fact, to risk suffering still others—and changed nothing but yourself.

Listen:

Everything ends, and Everything matters.

Everything matters not in spite of the end of you and all that you love, but *because* of it. Everything is all you've got—your wife's lips, your daughter's eyes, your brother's heart, your father's bones and your own grief—and after Everything is nothing. So you were wise to welcome Everything, the good and the bad alike, and cling to it all. Gather it in. Seek the meaning in sorrow and don't ever ever turn away, not once, from here until the end. Because it is all the same, it is all unfathomable, and it is all infinitely preferable to the one dreadful alternative.

You get up a little wobbly from your stool and place a twenty on the bar and walk back out into the early morning. You smoke a cigarette on the sidewalk. The cold clears your head enough that you feel okay to drive, which you do carefully, like a teen in driver's ed, hands at ten and two, eyes scanning the dark road, foot hovering over the brake pedal. You pull into the driveway slowly, killing the lights to avoid waking Ruby. When you go inside Amy is seated at the kitchen table with her hands around a mug and a pot of tea still steaming on the range top.

You sit across from her. She catches a whiff of your breath, grimaces, then stands and pours another cup of tea and sets it in front of you.

"This is your one get-out-of-jail-free card," she says, and at this moment you are more grateful for her than you ever have been in either of your lifetimes.

19 The next day you and Rodney and your mother and Amy and Ruby are with your father at the moment he dies. When he stops breathing you put your hand on his chest and feel his heart ebb and fail. Your mother climbs into the bed and holds your father and talks to him even though he can't hear her anymore. She tells him to breathe. She tells him to wake up. You call the funeral director and while you wait for him to arrive you set about preparing your father's body. You take off his oxygen and button his pajama top, which had come twisted and undone as he struggled through those last hours. His mouth wants to hang open and for a while you hold it shut, gently, so that when he stiffens it will stay closed. Rodney wants to know what he can do, and you tell him to wrap your father carefully in the bed sheet. By the time he's finished with this the funeral director has arrived. His name is Bill. He's younger than you expected and he keeps it dignified but loose. He recognizes Rodney and says, "Boy, I bet your father was proud of you." Then he asks if you want to help him remove the body. "Some people do," he says, "and some people don't. So I always ask."

You take Rodney aside and ask him if he feels up for this.

"Whatever you think is right, Junior," he tells you. "That's what I want to do."

So you tell Bill that you and your brother will do it by yourselves. Bill nods, goes out to the hearse, returns with the stretcher, and steps aside. You slide your hands under your father's shoulders and almost recoil when you feel heat lingering in the mattress. Then you and Rodney lift the body onto the stretcher and secure the straps, and together you bear your father out of his home.

Afterward you sit with Ruby by the fireplace and listen to her talk about what she saw and how she feels. She asks if smoking killed your father, and you tell her yes. Then she wants to know why you're still smoking, and you have no good answer for her. Even if you were able to tell her about the Destroyer of Worlds, she would not consider this a solid reason for continuing to smoke. And frankly, she would be right.

18 For weeks and months afterward, your father's absence, and the sad and painful manner in which he died, hangs over your family.

17 When the fallout of your father's death has settled, Ruby resumes her one-girl campaign for the environment. She sends an e-mail to Maine senator Olympia Snowe about a bill to allow oil drilling in Alaska's Arctic National Wildlife Refuge. Snowe plans to support the bill, but is impressed with such a sober and informed letter from a ten-year-old, and grants Ruby an audience. Amy's begun work at a local law firm, so you fly to Washington with Ruby. The two of you ride in a black limousine to the Russell Senate Office Building and are escorted through security and into a large office. There's a pair of sofas facing each other on the blue carpeting, and you sit on the one facing the picture window. Ruby puts her hand in yours and squeezes.

"Nervous, babe?" you ask.

"No," she says. "Not really. The flying made me nervous. But I'm okay now."

You expect to wait a long time, but after just a few minutes Snowe comes in, beaming a broad, practiced politico smile. She offers you her hand, says hello. Then she bends at the waist to greet Ruby. You feel an irresistible swell of pride at your daughter's composure. She's all business, unsmiling as she shakes Snowe's hand and looks her directly in the eye.

Snowe sits facing you on the opposite sofa.

"Senator Snowe," Ruby says. "I guess you know why I'm here."

"Yes," Snowe says. "I was very impressed with your letter."

"Thank you. So you must be ready to explain why you've decided to support the provision for oil drilling in next year's budget resolution."

You don't know what Snowe was expecting, but it certainly wasn't this. She looks at you, eyebrows raised. Maybe she thought someone else helped Ruby write the letter, that Ruby was the heart and someone else the brains. Would have been a reasonable assumption, but all the same she was mistaken, and she's just now starting to realize that.

"Senator?" Ruby says.

Thus begins a debate that lasts nearly two hours. Snowe talks about creating jobs; Ruby counters with statistics linking increased alcoholism and diabetes to drilling in the North Slope. Snowe cites reduced dependence on foreign oil; Ruby calls this a panacea to distract from the real issue of alternative energy. When Snowe talks about reducing gas prices, Ruby chides her for deliberately ignoring the fact that even if drilling began today it would take fifteen years for the oil to reach market.

An aide enters and tells Snowe she has a meeting in five minutes. Snowe looks up, thinks a moment, and tells her to cancel.

Instead she invites you and Ruby on a tour of the Capitol complex. You see the House and Senate chambers, the Supreme Court building, and the U.S. Botanic Garden, where Ruby fawns over the Baja Fairy Duster, a flower that looks like a crimson starburst.

Over a lunch of Ruby's favorites—tater tots and BLTs with Miracle Whip—she asks Snowe if her opinion on the drilling provision has changed.

"I'll need to think on it," Snowe tells her. "But when I decide, I promise to let you know personally."

16 But she doesn't need to, because the following evening, just hours after you arrive home from the airport, you see Snowe on CNN announcing that she will not support the provision. This is momentous not just because the vote is very tight, but because it means Snowe has broken party lines and defied the White House. When asked by a reporter why she's suddenly changed stances, Snowe tells of meeting with a remarkable, passionate ten-year-old who knew more about the issue than most any expert she's talked to. You grab Ruby from her bedroom, where she's still unpacking, and return to the television in time to hear Snowe refer to her by name.

It's only half an hour or so before the phone starts ringing off the hook. First the local papers want a comment, and the CBS affiliate in Bangor asks for an interview. The next day producers for *The Daily Show*, *Larry King*, and *NBC Nightly News* call. You say you'll get back to them, and together you and Amy sit down with Ruby to talk it over.

"I want to do it, Dad," she tells you. "People are finally ready to listen. I've been working for this my whole life." You have to suppress a smile, because no matter how smart or serious, Ruby is still just a ten-year-old, and to hear her say she's been working for something her whole life, like she's Nelson Mandela or something, is, let's face it, pretty funny.

You send Ruby to bed and you and Amy go back and forth for a couple of hours.

"I don't think it's a good idea," Amy says.

"You know how important this is to her," you say.

"Of course I know . . . you think I don't know that?" Amy says. "Lots of things that she needs to be protected from are *important* to her, Junior. Jai alai. Excessive chocolate consumption. If she wanted to climb into one of those redwoods and sit there for a year to keep it from being cut down, would you let her?"

"Going on *The Daily Show*," you tell her, "is not sitting in a tree for a year."

"It just feels like something we should be shielding her from, you know? First this, and the next thing we turn around and she's dancing on tables and doing coke out of serving bowls like the second coming of Drew Barrymore."

"Amy," you say.

"I know, I know."

15 The following week you are all three in New York. You tape five shows in two days, and the composure Ruby had with Senator Snowe is on full display—as you watch her you're reminded powerfully of how confident and self-possessed Amy was when you first laid eyes on her in the Gifted and Talented classroom twenty-odd years ago. She keeps pace with Jon Stewart, joking about the reproductive habits of polar bears—a crack about only having sex once every three years, which elicits raised eyebrows from Stewart and a cackle from Amy, standing with you just offstage—and tolerates Larry King's banality with a gentle indulgence unusual in someone of any age, let alone a child.

You return home to Maine, thinking that will be that, but when the shows air the whole thing starts to snowball. Next thing you know Ruby's on the cover of *People* and receives an invitation to speak before Congress next month in the week leading up to the vote. Talking heads compare your daughter to Samantha Smith, saying that what Smith did for geopolitical relations, Ruby is now doing for environmental causes, and polls show public support for ANWR drilling down to an all-time low of 11 percent, from a high of 46 percent just two months ago.

14 In the midst of all this Rodney's Chicago Cubs have made it to the World Series, and you and Ruby take a break from her media blitz to fly to Cleveland for the first two games against the Indians. You're just getting situated in your seats behind home plate, Ruby struggling happily under the weight of full fan gear and tofu dogs and cocoa, when a reporter from the *Plain Dealer* recognizes her and introduces himself.

"I didn't know you were a baseball fan," he says to her. "Where do you find time to follow baseball, with everything else you're doing?"

"My uncle plays for the Cubs," she tells him matter-of-factly, biting the bare tip off her tofu dog.

Crap, you think as the reporter warms to this new subject.

There aren't many dignified news outlets left, but even those few that remain are unable to resist such spectacular fluff, especially after the Cubs win the Series: America's newest darling just happens to be the niece of one of baseball's greatest living players? Oh, *do tell*.

13 Of course Rodney's happy to hit the talk show circuit with Ruby when the Series ends. He's always been bad at interviews, but where he stumbles Ruby picks him up, and their natural dynamic—friendly ribbing, Stooges-style antics, and the occasional spontaneous thumb-wrestling match—plays well on television. Whenever Letterman or Kimmel ask too many consecutive questions about the trick to turning a perfect double play, Rodney says simply, "What Ruby's doing is a lot more important than baseball. Maybe we should talk about that."

You know well that he's wrong. What he's doing matters just as much.

12 Ruby's efforts come to a head in December, when the Senate votes 78–22 to strip the ANWR drilling provision from the congressional budget resolution. The vote takes only half an hour, and afterward Ruby stands bundled against the cold on the steps of the Capitol, hand-in-hand with Snowe, and the two of them take turns heralding the victory for the assembled press.

11 Two days later NASA announces the discovery of the Destroyer of Worlds, and everyone forgets all about Ruby, and the Cubs' triumph, and the Arctic National Wildlife Refuge.

10 It matters, now, that you gather your family in. You're correct in assuming that the U.S. government (and possibly others) have known about C/1998 E1 for longer than they're admitting, and in an effort to minimize panic and attendant bad behavior they're now lying about how much time is left—they say over a year, when you know it's more like two months. But you're glad for this lie, because it means the trans-

portation infrastructure continues to function and so Rodney is able to fly in from New York and join you and Amy and Ruby and your mother at the house you grew up in. It also means, happily, that the Remington 870 12-gauge you buy at Dick's remains loaded but unused, racked on the wall in the mudroom. The mood in your small part of the world, far from the murderous anarchy you expected, is one more of muted grief and togetherness, like Christmas right after someone has died. People linger in large, quiet groups in restaurants. Couples who haven't enjoyed one another for years walk around holding hands as if they're soldered together. National Guard troops kick the dirt on street corners and play cribbage at checkpoints, rifles forgotten inside their Humvees. Store shelves do go barren in spots, and there's the occasional shortage of gasoline, but beyond this life is more or less normal, if full of advance grief.

9 It matters, too, that your foreknowledge of the end of all things offers no insulation from this grief. You had thought that it would, but no. And it hits you at odd times. E.g. here you are at a diner, the final Dad-and-Ruby date, staring across the table at your daughter's sad countenance, her brown hair pulled back in a tight ponytail, her skin pale and perfect like skim milk, and oh God yes your grief is full and violent, worse than you could ever have imagined, bad enough to make you dig the tines of a fork into your thigh under the table.

8 You seek every day to offer Ruby some guidance or consolation. But there is none of either to be had, and her understanding of this fact is evident in her growing silence, in the sorrow draped over her features like a shroud. What makes it worse is that her sorrow, it's plain to see, is for you, not for herself.

7 And knowing that the only alternative to your grief is the nothingness that's fast approaching, you try to embrace your own sorrow, to be open and empty and let it all pass through you. This is the key, you have learned—to relinquish control, to relinquish the desire for control.

Even in this late drama, to try and control is to go mad. And so you do your best to let it all go.

Except that there's one last thing, and to say that it's important is a gross understatement. You would be an abject failure as a son, brother, father, and husband if you just let this one go without at least thinking it through. So you spend every night of the last week thinking, and you can't decide, can't decide, it's impossible either way, so you take your dilemma to the one person you've turned to, in this and every other life, since the day the *Challenger* exploded.

Broaching the subject of the government's false timeline with Amy is not an issue, because by now the jig is up—fireballs have been raining down on São Paulo and Wichita for four days, and the comet itself, visible even in daylight since the announcement, looms ever larger in the eastern sky, like some giant murderous Q-Tip. So the topic of discussion, as you sit together on the last night, is whether or not to kill Ruby before the Earth bursts into flames.

"No," Amy says flatly, gripping your hand in a way that reminds you of your father. "No. No. No way." She's got her eyes closed against the mere thought, shaking her head back and forth.

"We need to consider this. It's going to be really bad."

"No shit," she says. "No shit it's going to be bad." Her sudden anger subsides just as quickly as it flared, and she puts her head on your shoulder. "Sorry. Jesus."

"That's okay."

"It's actually kind of pretty," she says. "Like the northern lights. I can't believe I just said that."

"Why not? It is pretty."

"Nothing this terrible can be pretty."

"That's where you're wrong. One thing I've learned, it's always to heed the evidence of your senses."

You're quiet for a few minutes. Then Amy says, "How would we do it?"

"Pills, I guess."

"And who gets to give them to her?"

"I would," you say. "If you wanted me to."

"I don't," she says.

"Me neither," you say. "I can't bear the thought of taking her life. And I can't bear the thought of letting her live."

"Junior, no," Amy says. "We're not doing this. Debate over."

"Were we debating?"

"I guess not. Not really."

"Because I was really only looking for you to tell me what I already knew," you say.

"That we're not doing this?"

"Exactly."

Amy reaches up and takes your face between her hands and kisses you. "Junior," she says, "why is this happening?"

Because you have the answer but could not explain it to her in five lifetimes, you sidestep. "Let's go to bed," you tell her.

6 And you do. You make love like the frightened teenagers you once were; quietly, carefully, all fingertips and ragged breaths. After, you lie awake. Sleep would not be possible even if the sky outside the window weren't lit up like Times Square.

5 And then a strange and wonderful thing happens: one by one the others join you. They come without words, like sleepwalkers, like dying animals seeking their den. First is Ruby. She stands at the foot of the bed, backlit by the comet's glow, her silhouette thin as God's alibi. She's carrying Tiki the global warming penguin, which is odd because Tiki's been relegated to the back of Ruby's closet since she was six. You sit forward and lift her into the bed. She nestles between the two of you and alternates resting her head on Amy's chest, then on yours. She does not fidget or cry.

4 Next comes your mother, padding across the hardwood floor in slippered feet, smelling of Nana perfume. She gets into bed on your side and drapes her right arm over you.

3   Finally, just before the sun rises, bright and redundant, Rodney lurches
    into the room. His blue sleeping cap sits cocked back on his head, the
    soft fleece cone collapsed and off to one side. Like Ruby he favors
    the space between you and Amy, and somehow manages to wedge his
    huge frame in there. Ruby offers him part ownership in Tiki, which he
    accepts.

2   You lie huddled together, silent and relaxed and fully awake, a warm
    package of humanity. All of you feel everything. The sun clears the
    hills on the far side of the valley and you think to close the shade be-
    cause the light is almost unbearably brilliant, but there is no way now
    that you're leaving the embrace of your family. After a while—you've
    no idea how long—the Earth begins to tremble and grow warm. Out-
    side you can hear the first sounds of panic. Shoes slap the pavement,
    running in every direction. There's the squeal of tires, followed by the
    nauseous crunch of metal on metal, shattering glass, and the brief,
    strange pocket of silence that always follows a car accident. From a dis-
    tance comes what sounds like gunfire. There is screaming, a collective
    scream. You listen and feel pity for these people. You wish they under-
    stood, as you do, that there is no escape and never was, that from the
    moment two cells combined to become one they were doomed. You
    wish they understood that there is joy in this fact, greater joy and love
    in just this one last moment than they experienced in the entirety of
    their lives. You wish they would stop running and screaming and shoot-
    ing each other long enough, and then they might see for themselves.
    Because even in this last moment there is still Everything, whole gal-
    axies and eons, the sum total of every experience across time, shrunk
    to the head of a pin, theirs for the asking, right here, right now. And so
    anything, anything, anything is possible.

1

Acknowledgments

First last and always, many thanks to my agent, Simon Lipskar—a dedicated, no-bullshit advocate to whom I owe just about everything.

Thanks to my editor, Molly Stern, who took a chance that I hope she feels paid off. Also to Liz Van Hoose for her keen eye, tirelessness, and patience, and of course Laura Tisdel, for all the varied things she does throughout the year to make my life easier/make me feel good about myself.

Big thanks to Monsignor Gary Socquet, partner in many, many crimes, who offered great insight into the editing of this book, but who more importantly was always willing to listen and reassure when the reflexive loathing of my own work kicked in, or whenever anything else was weighing on my mind.

Thanks to my friends and colleagues at Zoetrope, a talented and generous bunch who have been immeasurable help both artistically and personally. In particular I'd like to thank Jessica Lipnack, Jim Ruland, Stephan Clark, Roy Kesey, Dave Fromm, Don Capone, Anne Elliott, Pamela Erens, Mary Akers, Jim Tomlinson, Cecilia Baader, Myfanwy Collins, Avital Gad-Cykman, Bev Jackson, Richard Lewis, Alicia Gifford, Ellen Meister, and Cliff Garstang.

Thanks to my friends and family: you know who you are, and perhaps more importantly, who you aren't.

To my father, gone a year now as of this writing:

> *And I scarce know which part may greater be—*
> *What I keep of you, or you rob from me.*